FREED FROM GRAVITY

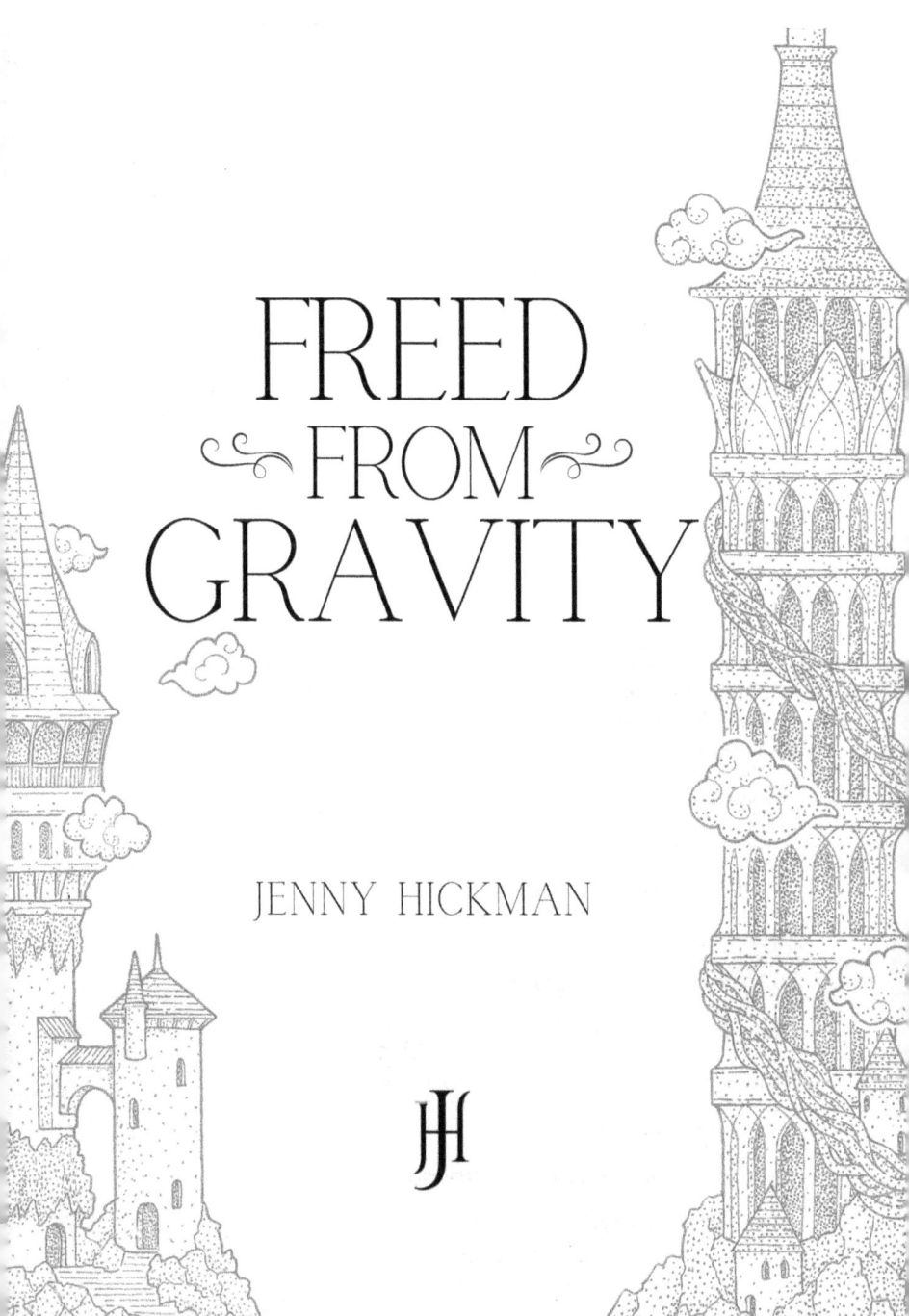

JENNY HICKMAN

Copyright © 2025 by Jennifer Fyfe

All rights reserved.

No part of this book may be reproduced in any form or by any electronic or mechanical means, including information storage and retrieval systems, without written permission from the author, except for the use of brief quotations in a book review.

No AI Training: Without in any way limiting the author's [and publisher's] exclusive rights under copyright, any use of this publication to "train" generative artificial intelligence (AI) technologies to generate text is expressly prohibited. The author reserves all rights to license uses of this work for generative AI training and development of machine learning language models.

Publisher's Note: This is a work of fiction. Names, characters, places, and incidents are a product of the author's imagination. Locales and public names are sometimes used for atmospheric purposes. Any resemblances to actual people, living or dead, or to businesses, companies, events, institutions, or locales is completely coincidental.

Published by Jennifer Fyfe

www.jennyhickman.com

Freed from Gravity / Jenny Hickman - 1st ed.

Paperback ISBN: 978-1-962278-14-0

Hardcover ISBN: 978-1-962278-15-7

Cover Design by Saint Jupiter

Illustrated Maps by Andrés Aguirre Jurado @aaguirreart

Interior Artwork by Andrés Aguirre Jurado @aaguirreart

Character Art by Anamaria Sandru @gioviia

Hardcover Case Design by Kiley Freshwater @kileyfreshwater

*For those of us who believe
true love conquers all*

Content Warning

This story contains sexually explicit content and darker themes, including: substance abuse, thoughts of suicide, grief, and death of a loved one.

I have done my best to handle these situations with care; however, if you think they might be triggering for you, please take note.

NIMBISS
SHAE
KUMULUS C
ARA
PLEIADES
ALLTO
CORVA
THE PIT
NETHER
FOREST
HAINN RIVER
COILL
SIRRIS
THE KINGD

Gallus
Faar River
Stratiss
Direc River
Straite River
The Burrows
River Solace
Aurora
River Solace
Barnacle Bay
Noctua
The Folly Sea
Kumulus

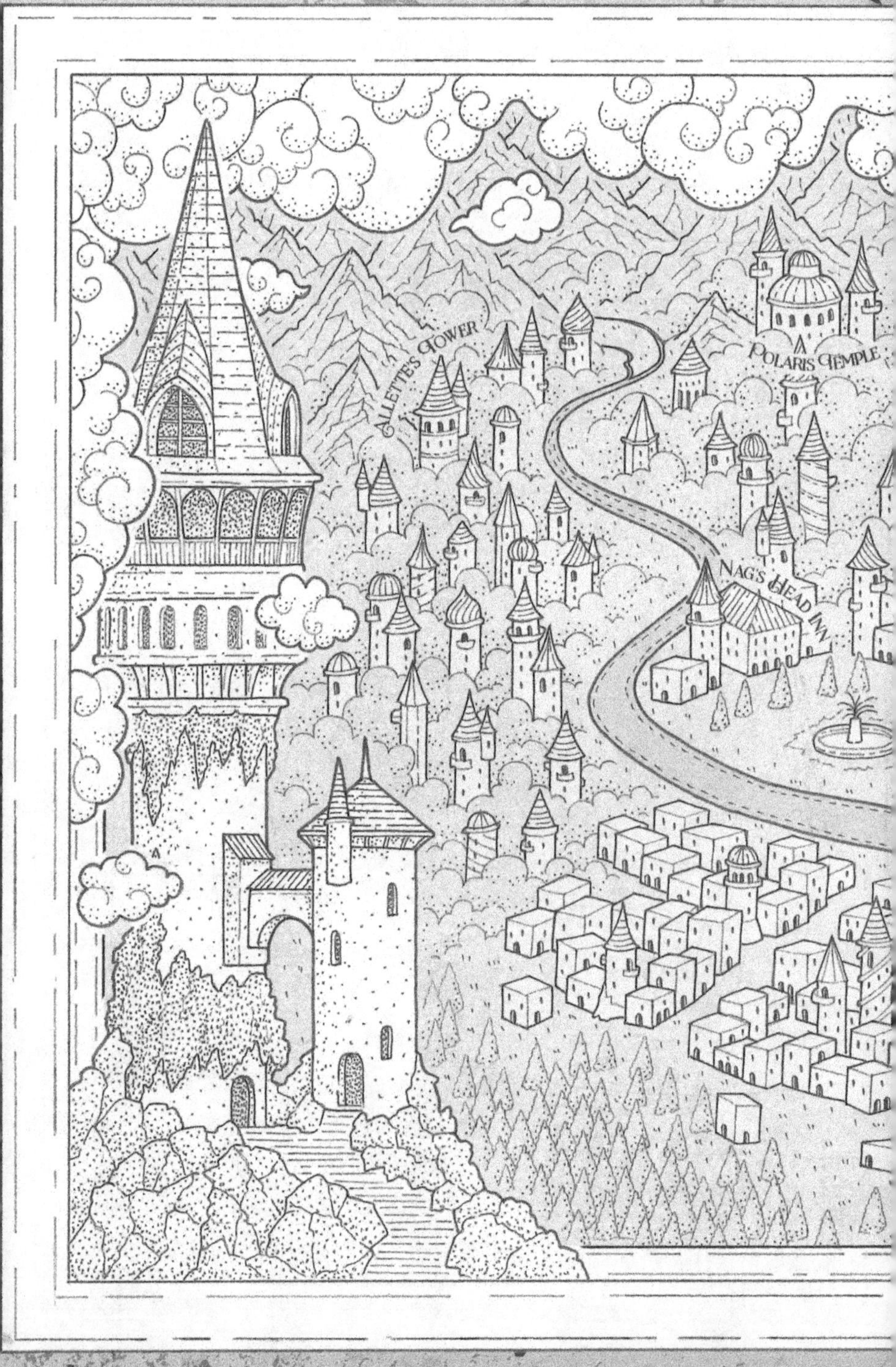
Allette's Tower
Polaris Temple
Nag's Head Inn

Kumulus City
Kumulus Castle
The Black Hole
The Portal
Textile Factory
River Solace
Badger's
Serpent's
Fox's
The Dens
The Burrows

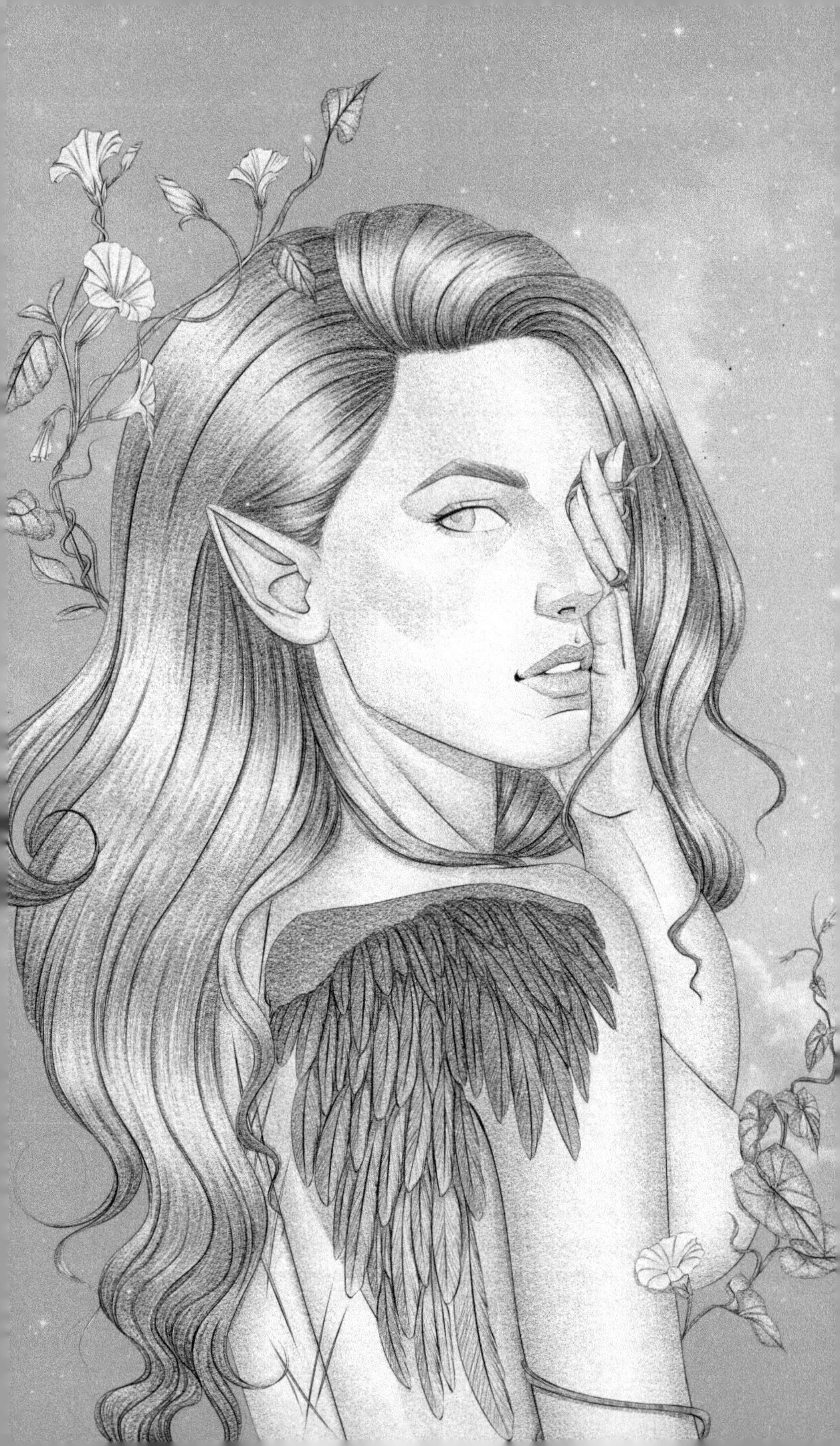

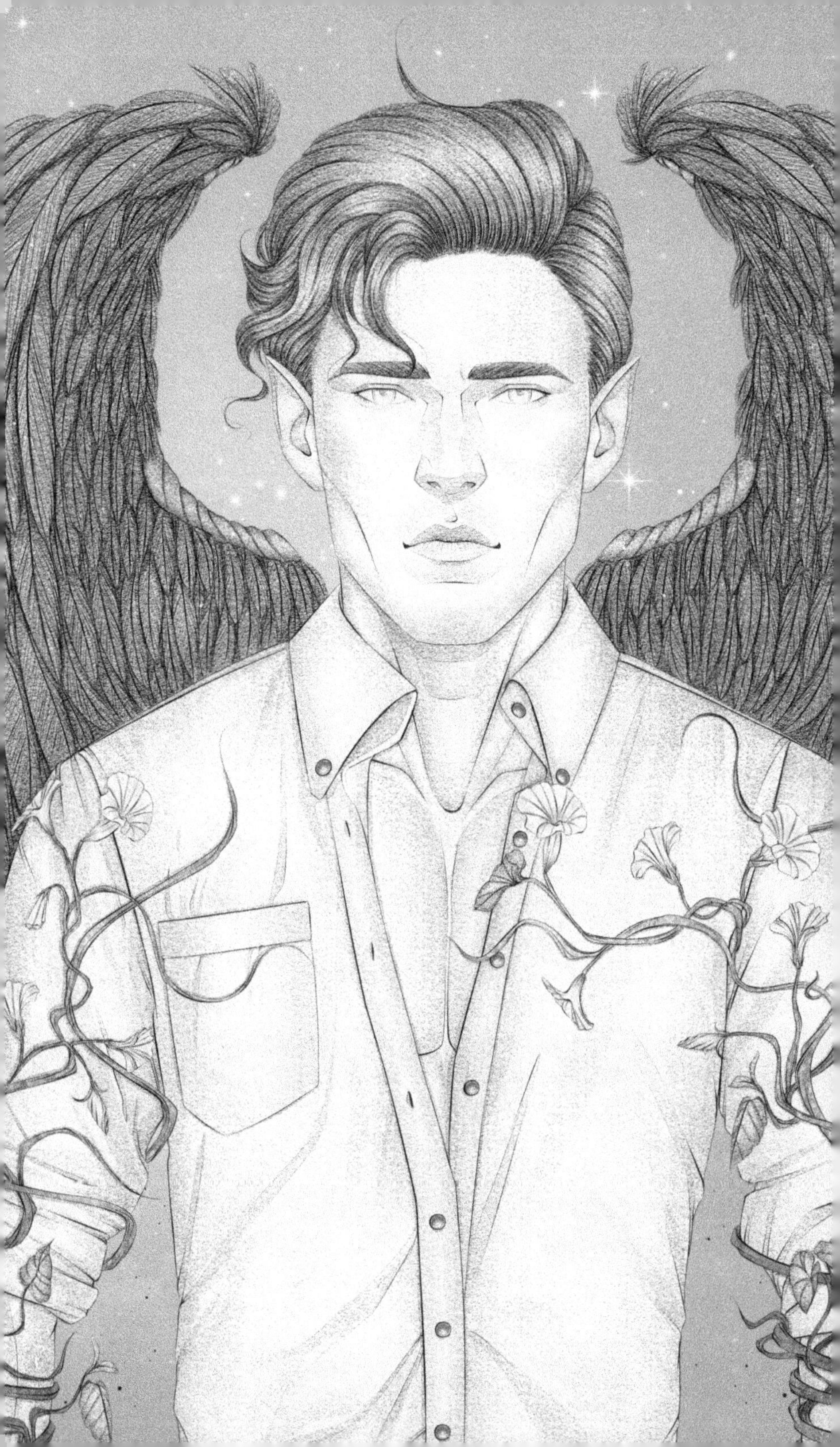

One

ALLETTE

IF I AM TO DIE, I WILL DIE IN THE ARMS OF MY MATE.

That knowledge brings me some semblance of peace as I hurtle through unending darkness, slipping between realms until the portal spits me into a dull gray sky spinning with thick white flakes. Squinting against the sudden onslaught of frozen air, I find my love's body plummeting toward the ground far below, his arms and legs akimbo like the dead raven tattooed across his ribs.

Except in that inky cage, the raven is alone, and this beautiful, broken man has me.

I pin my arms to my sides, making myself as aerodynamic as possible, and lock my gaze on my prince's falling form, praying the speed I gain will be enough. Icy wind stings my tear-stained cheeks, whipping my hair behind me like a dark cape.

The snow-dusted ground draws closer, but so do my love and I, falling like two stars discarded from the heavens.

Senan is as silent as the air around us, his closed eyes facing a world that threw him away.

I reach for him, stretching myself to the point of breaking until my fingers brush his, capturing one limp hand, then the other.

Our bodies collide, as if destiny herself yanked the invisible threads woven between our hearts, binding us as one. I clamp my legs around his waist, racking my brain for some way to rescue us. Some way to defy gravity. There's no point in crying out to the stars; they've done nothing but curse us since the day we flouted fate.

Our survival depends on me and me alone.

If this had happened four years ago, I would've had my wings. Even without wings, I would've had my element. The magic within me used to burn like star fire through my veins, granting me dominion over the very air we breathe.

Now I have nothing.

My love's lashes remain closed, his handsome features contorted in pain.

Nothing but my love for this man.

We're falling too fast, and my whirling mind refuses to cooperate. Fear and terror collide in my heart, sparking something deep within me, and I remember.

I remember how it felt to create chaos with a summer breeze.

I remember how I used to shape and bend that which is invisible.

I remember.

More sparks flicker in my chest, tinder catching fire.

Memories. Hope. Love.

Love for this man who gave everything to save me.

Isn't that the greatest magic in all the realms? Stronger than air or fire combined. An element within us all, Tuath or Scathian. Human or fae.

The love inside me begins to rumble, a slumbering beast waking within my chest.

We've been taught that a Scathian's power emanates from our wings, but what if that isn't true?

My prince and I have endured so many lies. Could this be one of them? What if Scathian power doesn't come from her wings, but from her heart?

Even facing certain death, my heart is full.

I tuck my face into my love's neck, inhaling his essence as I extend a hand toward the expanding earth. My shattered soul, bound with hope, sings to the breeze, calling upon its power. The air doesn't need to catch us, only slow us down.

Maybe it's desperation, but I swear those phantom sparks of magic that once lit me from within begin to stir. Ignite. Fueled by sheer panic and a desperate will to survive.

When I call, the breeze answers. Faint, but its whisper is undeniable.

The breeze becomes a gale, swirling around us, whirling our bodies in dizzying circles until Senan is the one on top of me. I throw out every last ember, slowing our descent, but will it be enough?

Clinging to my prince, I profess my undying devotion to him, praying he can hear me. Vowing to love him forever, whether forever ends today or centuries from now.

We reach the tops of the barren trees, creaking and swaying in the wind.

The standing stones capped with snow.

When I have nothing left to give, we land with a resounding thud against the sleeping earth. The air evacuates my lungs, leaving a searing ache in its wake. An ache as beautiful as it is painful, because if I am hurting, it means I'm still alive.

Snowflakes drift in lazy pirouettes, catching on my lashes.

Stars above, I *did* it.

I saved us.

With throbbing arms, I ease Senan off me, rolling him onto the snowy ground. His pitiful whimper is the sweetest sound to ever grace my ears.

He is wounded but he is alive.

I've never been so happy to hear someone's cry.

We made it. We *made* it!

The heavy layer of clouds far above begins to darken like a bad omen, stealing my elation. We may have landed without breaking our necks, but the panic isn't over yet. If the king sends anyone after us, we won't be safe here in the open. We need to move—and fast.

When I caress my prince's cheek, he does not stir. "Senan? Senan, my love. You must wake up. We need to leave." These standing stones are nothing but beacons to anyone who might venture through the portal, friend or foe.

Right now, all we seem to have is the latter.

What will I do if he doesn't wake up? Even if I manage to drag him to safety, the snow will give away our position. "Senan, please. I know it hurts, but I need you to come back to me. Please."

More snowflakes dust his lashes as I continue to beg, glancing at the ever-darkening clouds. There isn't time. I'll have to find a way on my own. I don't need to take him far, just far enough so that we can hide. But hide where? These woods are nothing but barren trees and boulders.

At least the first would give us some options for cover. Out here in the open, we're as good as dead.

Stumbling to my feet, I slip my arms beneath Senan's and pull with all my might. The slippery ground makes it almost impossible to gain purchase, but somehow, I manage. Snow crunches beneath my boots as I drag him behind the nearest evergreen bush, his bloodstained back leaving crimson streaks across the pristine blanket of white.

Even though my body feels broken, I cannot rest until we are both safe.

Once more, I call on my element, my magic flickering like a candle in a heavy storm. The power is there, but distant. Faint. From my outstretched palms, a breeze twists toward the standing stones, whipping the snow into a frenzy as fresh flakes drift over our tracks, obscuring the blood.

Will it be enough?

Black specks appear high in the sky, hurtling toward the ground at breakneck speed.

Scathian guards—at least three.

The bush's prickly branches jab into my shoulders when I crouch next to my love. If they discover our hiding place, I'll need some way to protect us. I search my prince for weapons only to come up empty. Perhaps there is something of use in his bag.

I slip the pack from my back, finding the clothes stuffed inside damp from the snow. Something sharp slices my finger, too small to be a blade. *Dammit.* I stick my finger in my mouth, the coppery tang turning my stomach as I discard the pack and pry a frozen rock free from the ground.

We did not come this far—survive a fall from the heavens—only to be killed by these blackguards. If I have to bash their heads in, I will.

The ground beneath us rattles when the first Scathian in silver leathers lands, his navy wings stretching wide before vanishing.

Bilson. Senan's personal guard.

Two more follow, but all I can do is glower at the bloody traitor. Senan trusted him—we both did. And he betrayed us.

"Where are the bodies?" the guard with yellow-speckled wings bellows.

Bilson turns in a slow circle, his dark eyes narrowing as he scans the ground. "Fan out. They can't be far."

Don't fan out. Give up. Go home. Please...

"And when we find them?" the other one asks.

The softest breath falls from my lips.

Bilson's head snaps toward where we hide. Although it's impossible, I swear his dark eyes lock with mine through the spiny branches.

Bilson's lip curls, his tone as sharp as the blade in his fist. "Burn them to ash."

The two men take off in opposite directions, one heading across the field and the other toward town. Bilson remains rooted to the snowy ground. When he finally takes a step toward where we hide, my heart leaps into my throat.

Twigs snap beneath Bilson's boots as he creeps into the forest, ducking beneath a fallen branch, still staring directly at me.

My fingers tighten around the stone, prepared to attack.

Oh, who am I kidding? I'm not prepared for anything. I'm shaking in my boots, but surprise is my only ally, my only chance at victory.

Three more steps and he will be upon us.

Two...

One...

Bilson catches the branch hiding us, sweeping it aside.

I spring to my feet and swing, but his massive hand catches my wrist, holding me firmly. I screw my eyes closed, unable to watch as he raises his blade and ends my life in one fell swoop.

I wait and wait and wait, but the pain never comes.

When I finally manage to pry open my eyes, I find Bilson staring down at my love's broken body. He tosses my hand aside, knocking me off-kilter. By the time I right myself, Bilson has crouched next to Senan's still form.

"Don't you touch him!" I shove Bilson's broad back, but he's too bloody big and too bloody strong to budge. "I said don't—"

Bilson's head snaps up, his lips curling in a sneer. "If you don't stop shrieking, they'll find you."

Why does he care? Why isn't he stabbing us with his dagger? Why isn't he calling fire to his palm and burning our bodies as he ordered the others to do?

Bilson cannot be on our side. "You threw me into the pit." I begged and begged for him to release me, but he held fast.

The guard tugs Senan's stained shirt from his waistband. "Only because I knew he wouldn't let you stay there for long."

That's a lie, isn't it? I mean, Senan *didn't* let me stay in the pit, but Bilson couldn't possibly have known the outcome. If he'd been on my side—or Senan's for that matter—he would've taken me somewhere besides that hellish prison. Then Eason never would've found me, and we wouldn't be in this forsaken place, running for our lives.

What choice do I have but to trust him? It's not as if I have any hope of overpowering the man.

I sink onto the ground, watching Bilson lift Senan's shirt, the fabric black from so much blood. My prince's wounds aren't smooth and small like mine, but jagged black stumps.

Bilson reaches for the short sword at his belt. I catch his arm only to falter when he doesn't draw the blade, but a small leather flask.

Understanding flickers through his eyes. "I'm only cleaning his wounds so they don't get infected."

Stars, I never considered the possibility of infection.

Twisting the lid free, Bilson pours clear liquid over what remains of Senan's wings, the water running red onto the snow.

"Why don't you heal him?" At least then we'll have a fighting chance at survival.

"If I return to Kumulus drained of magic, the king will grow suspicious. I'm risking enough as it is." Bilson steals another glance at me. "How did you survive the fall?"

The man may be helping us now, but he could betray us later to save his own skin. Best to keep my secrets, just in case. "The snow cushioned our landing."

He snorts. "You're a terrible liar." Thankfully, he doesn't press for more information as he returns the lid to the flask. "You know this realm, yes?"

"I do."

"Do you have someplace safe to stay?"

Telling him about the cottage is risky, but I can't think of any way around it. I need to move Senan somewhere warm, and while I might have dragged him to this bush, the cottage is over a mile away.

"There is a cottage nearby where we can hide."

Slipping one hand gingerly beneath Senan's head and another under his knees, Bilson stands, the muscles in his arms straining from my prince's weight. "What are you waiting for? Lead the way."

I dart for the path that cuts through the empty forest, finding it quickly enough despite the snow. Bilson has no problem keeping up as we make our way past the old logging road, through the glen, and over the creek. The snow dampens the sounds of our footfalls as we traverse the final stretch of the forest toward the place I once lived but never called home.

A place I inhabited alongside a man who kept me as his unknowing hostage for four years.

A cage of my own.

Bilson remains silent, his mouth bracketed with concern each time I catch him glancing down at the prince. Senan should be awake by now, shouldn't he? I cannot recall how much time passed between when they stole my wings and when I regained consciousness, but this feels too long.

Then again, Eason had healed me. From the amount of blood dripping down Bilson's silver leathers, my love is still losing too much.

I push on, my worry fueling each step forward, until the cottage's bowed roof comes into view, pillowed in pristine white. The place looks even smaller than it used to, with those faded lace curtains pulled. Brown clumps of dead flowers protrude from the window boxes Eason used to fill with flowers every spring.

"Wait," Bilson hisses.

I still.

Bilson sniffs the air, his brow furrowing. "There is death here."

The wind shifts, and I catch a whiff of the same foul stench of carrion that clung to the air outside the pit. Why would it smell like that here? Then I remember. "There's a doe in the shed." I was supposed to dry the meat but ended up leaving instead.

Bilson eases Senan onto the ground, propping him against a stack of wood before pushing the shed's crooked door aside. The deer Eason killed still hangs by its neck from a beam, its hide skinned off and muscles gone a purplish brown.

Bilson inhales once more. "That isn't it." He shoots a glower back at the cottage, telling me to wait with Senan.

I watch the guard slip through the front door and then turn right back around. "You cannot stay there," he says.

"Why not? What's wrong?" When I start for the cottage, he tries to grab me, but I pull out of his grasp. The rotten smell hits me like a punch in the stomach. Not even pressing my hand to my nose makes the stench go away.

What little furniture we owned is in ruins, smashed to bits across the floor. The place was ransacked, the few garments I left behind strewn across the planks, stamped with muddy boot prints.

I bend down to pick up the wool socks I mended, along with the extra shift Eason bought me last Yule. Shards of wood and glass sparkle atop Widow Mae's abandoned scarf. I don't think I've ever seen her without it. I add that to my growing pile, shaking it carefully to remove the debris.

On the far side of the bed, I find the source of the smell. Widow Mae sprawls across the floorboards, her head twisted at a sickening angle, and milky, sightless eyes staring toward the wall. Beside her lies the note I wrote to Eason, telling him that I planned to escape through the portal.

Did she fall? Did Eason come back for me and take his rage out on this innocent old woman?

Is this *my* fault?

A fresh wave of death assaults my senses, and the room starts to spin.

I'm going to be sick.

My stomach revolts, but with nothing in me to expel, I dry heave on the floor.

So much death and pain, all for this star-damned love I've insisted on stealing time and again.

If I'd been strong enough to let Senan go, Wynn never would have been murdered and Widow Mae might still be alive. I would've been there for my aunt when she passed; Senan and I would still have our wings...

Where do we draw the line? At what point do we decide that

our fleeting happiness isn't worth all the pain and destruction we've caused?

Numbness overtakes my bones, spreading like poison through my veins as I collect what little can be salvaged, stuffing the garments into one of the empty grain sacks beneath the broken bed.

Bilson was right; Senan and I cannot stay here.

Perhaps the widow's cottage will be empty. She has no family to speak of, and the place isn't far. It's either that or the inn, and the inn will cost money. While I can hear some coins jingling in Senan's pack, we must save our funds. Besides, I can hardly show up to town with an unconscious man in tow, can I?

The door creaks open, and Bilson steps through the gap, his gaze dropping to the sack in my clenched fist. "Do you have everything you need from this place?"

Unable to find my voice through the tears thickening my throat, I nod.

"Good. Because the prince is awake and asking for you."

Two

ALLETTE

The sack bobbles against my thigh as I race to where Senan stares up at the sky. Relief burns like a fever as hope floods my heart anew. I fall to my knees beside my prince, needing to touch him more than I need my next breath.

When his gaze meets mine, my thundering pulse stills.

His eyes are glassy and glazed, the silver of his irises dull, his pupils no more than pinpricks.

He blinks up at me, first one eye and then the other, before smiling a soft, sleepy sort of smile. "Allette?"

He's alive. He's safe. He knows me. All good things, but why does it still feel as if I'm holding my breath? "I'm here. I'm here, my love." Cupping his stubbled jaw, I bring my forehead to his, taking his breaths as my own.

"He took my wings. He...he cut them off," Senan slurs.

"I know he did. But think of how much faster you can run without them weighing you down."

"Never liked running much. But I'll run with you." His eyes sink closed, and his head lolls to the side.

Still holding tight, I twist toward Bilson. "What is wrong with him?" Could the pain be making him delirious?

Bilson catches the prince's brow, forcing Senan's eyes open

with his thick fingers, revealing no sign of silver, only white. "Still drunk, I suppose. The king gave him quite the dose of barmite. A blessing in disguise, really. Should dull the pain from the wounds."

So that's what the king poured down his throat. A bloody truth serum. "What if the king does the same to you?" Then Boris will find out we survived and send more guards after us.

"I've been taking small doses of barmite for years to build up an immunity. He'd have to drown me in it to reveal my truths."

I want to trust Bilson; really, I do. Heaven knows we could use an ally. But after what Eason did, I don't believe that Bilson's intentions are entirely honorable.

Senan stirs, his head swinging up and eyes pinned, not on me, but on the tiny cottage. "Where are we?"

"In the human realm."

The wrinkle between his dark eyebrows deepens. "This is where you lived…with *him?*"

I hate to admit it, but there's no point in denying the truth. "It is."

Bilson's fingers tap against his thighs, his gaze darting from me to Senan and back again. "Someone else lived here with you?"

"Eason fucking Bell," Senan cuts in, his hands balling into fists on the frozen dirt. "He stole my mate. Took her right from under my wing and kept her for himself."

Heat burns up my throat to my cheeks. "Enough about that. Bilson needs to return to Kumulus before they get suspicious." And before I die of mortification.

The muscle in Bilson's jaw feathers. "Where will you go?"

He must think me a fool if he expects me to tell him my plans. "It's best if you don't know."

With a somber nod, Bilson collects a fistful of snow and then pushes to his feet. "Can you walk, sire?" he asks Senan, scrubbing the blood on his leathers until no trace remains.

"Better than you ever could," Senan shoots back. But when he tries to move, his boots slip on the frozen earth. When Bilson extends a hand, Senan smacks him away.

"You've already done enough," I tell the guard. "Leave us." Bracing Senan's arm across my shoulder, I manage to help him to his feet.

Bilson waits until we're steady to turn on his heel and stomp back into the cottage. He reemerges a moment later with a cloud of black smoke chasing him out the door.

"What did he do?" Senan asks, watching his former guard melt into the forest, becoming just another shadow as smoke continues billowing out of the cottage.

Bilson is covering his tracks the same way Eason once did. If the other guards follow the smoke, they'll find a burned-out shack and the charred remains of a woman. Hopefully, they won't look too closely and realize there's only one body.

The structure groans as the thatch roof and stone chimney collapse, red sparks shooting like fireworks into the sky.

I turn my prince from the flames and start for Window Mae's home. "He's giving us a chance."

"Fuck, that hurts," Senan grumbles, giving me far too much of his weight.

"I know, but we must keep moving. One step at a time. You're doing so well." As soon as we reached the tree line, I managed to use the vestiges of my magic to stir the snow near the cottage, obscuring our fleeing footprints.

Senan's harsh breaths puff white clouds into the clear, cold air as we pick our way over fallen logs and twisted roots through the sleeping forest. We'll be farther from the town and much-needed supplies, but also farther from the stones. I'd put an entire continent between us and the portal if I could.

"Why is it so...c-cold?"

"Because it's winter."

"I h-hate winter."

Right now, with clumps of snow tumbling into my boots, making every step a slog, so do I.

The tall chimneys atop Widow Mae's two-story house rise like beacons on the horizon. No smoke curls from the stone stacks, which bodes well for my plans to hunker down and hide from the world.

"Almost there," I encourage, a little worried to see so much sweat beading on Senan's brow. I hope that's a side effect of the barmite or exertion, not the first signs of a fever.

Senan rests his head against my shoulder, his trembling breath fanning across my neck. "Mmmm... You smell nice."

I'm not sure how that's possible considering I've been to the pit and back, but who am I to call him a liar? "Thank you."

His head droops forward, and he watches my legs as we stomp through the snow. "I like your feet."

"What?"

"Your feet. They're pretty. So are your knees."

"You think my knees are pretty?"

"I think all of you is pretty."

This man. Stars, do I love him. Even on the darkest day, he can bring a smile to my lips.

When we finally reach the front stoop, I ease from under Senan's arm, propping him against the brick wall so I can retrieve the spare key hidden beneath the flowerpot. Unfortunately, this means digging through more snow until my fingers are numb.

A loud, guttural sob wrenches up Senan's throat. I spring to my feet, finding tears streaming down his pale cheeks.

"What's wrong? Is it your back?" What am I saying? Of course, it's his bloody back. The man had his wings sawed off.

Grimacing, Senan drags a fist below his bloodshot eyes. "He did this to you. My own brother did this to you. I have never questioned or d-doubted my love for you, but now I am s-starting to realize that *I* am the c-curse. If you never met me—"

"If I never met you, I would have never known true happiness." I smooth away his tears with my thumbs as my doubts from only a short while ago fall from his lips. "You are not a curse, Senan. You are my purpose, my reason for fighting. For living. Now, let's get you patched up so that we can put all of this behind us and start our life together."

With tears glittering in his eyes, he nods.

I turn the key, twist the knob, and throw the door aside. Peppery notes of clove dance on a rush of frigid air. How is it colder in here than it is outside? Has the frost permeated the stone walls? I'll need to build a fire before we succumb to hypothermia.

Hooking Senan's arm around me once more, I help him through the living room and into the main bedroom on the first floor, where he collapses face-first onto the mattress with a groan.

I hate that it's going to get worse before it gets better.

A few years ago, Eason cut his hand on his axe, and it was my responsibility to stitch the torn skin myself. Knowing what I know now, the blackguard could've easily used magic to heal himself.

He played his part well.

Too bloody well.

The only upside is that I have some experience in mending wounds.

The brass headboard whines when I sink next to Senan's prone form. "I'll need to remove your shirt. It's going to hurt."

"It already hurts," he murmurs, his voice muffled by the quilt.

Tears prick the backs of my eyes. There will be plenty of time for crying, but right now there are more pressing matters at hand.

I leave to gather Mae's sewing basket and a few cloths from the hot press, a bottle of whiskey from one of her cupboards, and a baking dish of fresh water from the sink.

Back in the bedroom, I use the silver shears from the basket to cut away Senan's shirt until I reach the horrific bloodstains. The dried blood is like glue, so I use the water in the bowl to wet the fabric, giving me room to cut through the rest of the way and peel his shirt open.

Stars...

What a mess Boris made of my beloved's back.

Two palm-sized fragments of Senan's black wings protrude from behind his shoulder blades, twisted and gnarled with bits of feathers clinging to them and blood weeping from the broken edges.

I won't only be sewing his back, but what remains of his beautiful onyx wings as well. "Stay as still as you can." My hand trembles as I dip the cloth into the water.

Senan whimpers as I cleanse his wounds. He curses when I douse them in alcohol. And he screams as I sew them closed.

When I finish, he remains still, his breathing unsteady. I assume he's passed out from the agony until he whispers, "I'm so sorry that I married the princess. They didn't give me a choice."

His words are another harsh reminder of what happened.

Boris and all those guards waiting for us at the portal, demanding information about the princess. She isn't just the princess anymore, is she? Leeri Eadrom is Senan's *wife*.

The quilt twists beneath my clenching hands. "Do you have any idea where she might be?" I ask, doing my best to keep the depth of my pain from leaking into my tone.

"No," he says with a small shake of his head, still staring at the wall. "But she was naked so she couldn't have gone far."

Oh, stars... "So you did sleep with her."

It doesn't matter. It does *not* matter. Anything that transpired between them wasn't because Senan wanted her, but because he was forced. I will not take it to heart. I will not punish either of us for something outside our control.

"No. Nope. *Nooo*. Saw her bits though. Not nearly as nice as yours." Senan's long fingers envelop mine, loosening my death grip on the quilt. "How did you survive this pain?"

The pain of having my wings stolen was nothing compared to

the agony of losing the two people I loved most in this world. "I don't know." But I did survive, and so will he.

Senan brings my hand to his soft lips, his warm breath thawing my frigid fingers. "I'm so sorry, Allette."

"Do not apologize. This is no more your fault than it is mine."

The fault for what happened to us falls solely on Boris Vale's villainous shoulders.

If I ever cross paths with the King of Kumulus again, he will rue the day he tried to murder my mate.

Three

SENAN

NINETEEN YEARS AGO

Has anyone ever noticed how, if you lift your legs up in the air and peer through your lashes, it looks like you're walking on the ceiling? My ceiling is pretty nice, with those little swirly things around the fae lights and along the wall. Much nicer than the floor. Marble is so cold and hard. And if you fall on it? That hurts like hell. Why don't they decorate floors like they do ceilings? Come to think of it...why do they decorate ceilings? I've been in this room since I was little and I've never, not once, noticed the ceiling. What a thankless job.

"What are you doing, you bollocks?" My brother Aeron's voice cuts like broken glass, and I drop my feet back onto the bed. "Everyone's waiting."

So am I, but nothing seems to be happening. I thought surely today would be the day. After all, it is my seventh birthday and stupid Aeron got his when he turned six.

"I'm getting ready." I roll off the bed and stuff my feet into my boots.

Aeron snorts. It's his new "thing." He probably thinks it makes him sound like father. I think he sounds like a pig. "Really? Because it looked like you were panned out on the bed, crying like a ninny."

I'm not a ninny. Aeron is a ninny. "I wasn't crying." Even if I was, it's none of his business, is it? I fumble with the stupid buckle on my stupid boot, but the thing won't fasten.

With a roll of his eyes, Aeron kneels to help me even though I don't need his help. "Tell that to your red eyes and all those tears on your face."

What's he on about? I don't have any tears on my face. I already wiped them all away. I kick him off me, biting back my smile when he falls flat on his arse. "Who's the ninny now?"

His perfect black wings appear at his back, and my smile vanishes. Aeron stands up, shoves my shoulder, and says, "See you at the party." Then he takes off from the balcony, his wings spreading like feathered freedom as he shoots into the sunset.

Do I get to fly to my own damn party? No. I get to walk like a big baby.

I'm seven years old. Where are my wings?

By the time I reach Mother's parlor, my legs ache from tiredness. The guards waiting outside see me coming and open the doors with a bow.

"Happy birthday!" everyone shouts in unison, my mother's voice ringing the clearest. Probably because she's the only female in the room.

Rhainn slips off her lap and runs over, throwing his arms around my waist. "Happy birthday, brother," he says, still unable to pronounce his "Rs" properly. Not a good thing for someone named Rhainn.

Must he be so irritating? And why does he always smell like peppermint? "Let me go."

Mother clears her throat. "Senan? What do you say?"

"Let me go, *please.*"

Her pretty black hair glistens in the fae light when she shakes her head. The way her lips press together reminds me of the time I got into trouble for filling Aeron's boots with mud. Which, by the way, he absolutely deserved.

Ugh. Fine. "Thank you, Rhainn."

My little brother grins up at me, a gap where his front teeth should be. When he finally lets me go, I glance around the room, searching for the one person who seems to be missing. "Where's Father?"

Mother's smile wobbles. "He wanted to be here, really, he did. But he got called away for a very important meeting."

Father is always called away for something more important. Thank the stars I'll never have to be king. When I'm a father, I'm never going to miss a birthday. Not even one.

Mother had the servants set the table with the fancy gold plates we save for important occasions, so that almost makes up for it. Maybe she'll let me have some wine with my cake. I am seven now, after all.

I hurry past the table to where Aeron and Boris wait next to the pile of colorful presents. Rhainn trails behind me like a shadow, but I'm way faster because he spends all his time sitting around in the silly library reading books.

"Hi, Boris." My eldest brother is *so* tall—almost taller than Father. I hope I'm as tall as Boris when I'm fifteen.

Boris smiles, tousling my hair the way Father does. My eyes start to burn a bit, but I don't want Aeron to call me a ninny again, so I blink my tears away.

"Hey there, little lad." Boris's voice is so deep too. I hope my voice is that deep one day. Most of all, I hope I have great big wings, just like him.

"Any sign of them yet?" Boris whispers.

"Not yet." I check every morning I wake up and every night I go to bed, and there isn't so much as a feather.

"Chin up. They'll be here soon. I can tell."

Aeron pushes off the wall with a grin. "And when they do show up, they'll probably be piss yellow."

"Aeron Timothy Vale, you apologize to your brother this instant," Mother clips from across the room.

"I'm sorry," Aeron mutters, even though I can tell he doesn't mean it.

Boris slings his arm over my shoulder, pulling me close. "They won't be yellow. They'll be black like the rest of us Vales'."

Black is fine, but I wouldn't mind a different color. Like red. Or blue. Purple could be nice too. Just not piss yellow.

"But Senan isn't a Vale," Aeron says under his breath. "Remember when Mother found him by the rubbish bin?"

She didn't find me by a rubbish bin...did she? Of course she didn't. Aeron is such a lying liar. "At least I was in the castle. They found you in the stables next to a pile of Pegasus shite."

Aeron's smirk vanishes.

"I'm going to pretend I didn't hear any of that," Mother says with a sigh. "Senan, since we're celebrating your birthday, you get to decide what's first: Cake or presents?"

I do love cake, but... "Presents."

"Open mine first," Rhainn squeaks, making me jump.

I forgot he was behind me. "Fine."

He sprints over to the stack of gifts and removes a small square from the very top. I bet it's a book.

He hands it over, and I drop to the floor with all my brothers surrounding me. I tear through the wrapping paper and—oh, look. A book. The same present he gives me every year.

"Thank you, Rhainn," Mother whispers with a stern look.

"Thank you, Rhainn," I repeat so she doesn't scold me.

Rhainn scoots closer. "You're welcome. It's my favorite fairy-tale from all the way in the human realm about an evil witch."

Sounds awful. "I can't wait to read it."

"Mine next!" Aeron's shoulder knocks mine as he drags a present from the middle, sending the rest of the boxes tumbling all over the floor.

He shoves the box onto my lap. Did he wrap this? It's awful.

Why did he use so much twine? The box takes me ages to open but when I finally manage, I throw open the lid and—

The smell hits me like a punch in the face.

What in heaven's name?

Aeron bursts out laughing, clutching his stomach and flopping onto the floor.

A scream tears from my throat as I shove the box away, the sound of my brother's maniacal laughter echoing through my head. He put a bloody fish in a box.

"I hate you." Even when I ball up my fist and punch Aeron in the arm, he still doesn't stop laughing. Let's see how he likes it when I put this box under his pillow tonight.

Mother waves one hand while pressing the other to her nose. "Someone, please remove this!"

One of the servants rushes from the alcove, taking the fish in the box through the servants' stairs.

"That's it, Aeron. No cake for you."

Aeron finally stops laughing.

"You know poor Senan is afraid of fish," Mother goes on.

"I'm not afraid." Did no one else notice how vile that thing smelled? Did they not see its big, bulging eyes? Who in their right mind would *like* fish? They're the mad ones, if you ask me.

Mother pats my head. "Of course not, dear."

Aeron tucks his hands under his armpits and scowls as I reach for the next present.

"That one's from me," Boris says with a nudge to my shoulder. He even put on a silver bow that matches the shiny silver paper. Now this is how you wrap a present.

I take off the paper and sniff—just in case. Not that Boris has ever played a joke on me, but there's always a first time for everything.

No gross fishy smell, thank the gods.

Rhainn pushes closer, peering over my shoulder. "What is it?"

I remove the lid and withdraw a bottle from within. "I'm not sure."

"It's oil. For your wings," Boris explains.

"But I don't have wings."

When he smiles, I find myself smiling as well. "Don't worry. They're coming."

Rhainn grabs my arm and I'm about to tell him to back off when he points toward the window. "Look! It's almost nightfall."

Mother turns, her beautiful face painted in golden light as the last of the sun's rays fall below the pink clouds. "Better hurry. It's almost time for your wish."

The most important part of any birthday celebration—more important than presents and cake combined: the birthday wish. Every year on the anniversary of your birth, you get to go out onto the balcony all by yourself and make a wish on the first star you see.

Boris leaps up, offering to help me to my feet as well. His hand engulfs mine as he leads me to the open doors. "Do you know what you want?" he asks quietly so that only I can hear.

"Yes." I'm going to wish for the same thing I've been wishing since Aeron got his wings on his sixth birthday.

His hand slips from mine. "Go on then. Make your wish."

I step onto the balcony and lift my gaze toward the navy-blue band of night stretching across the sky. My back beings to itch, but I ignore the irritation, searching for the first star.

Something flickers in my peripherals, a shimmering silver ball of light.

"I want wings," I whisper to that star and any of the others hiding in the heavens. "But please don't make them piss yellow." Not sure if that counts as a second wish or not.

Better safe than sorry.

The damn itching behind my shoulders gets worse.

I swear, if Aeron put Toxicodendron on my sheets again, I'm going to cover his bed in spider eggs.

Unable to stand it any longer, I reach behind my shoulder to scratch my back.

That's when I feel a bump.

Not just one bump... *Two!*

"My wings..." They're finally here! I turn on my heel to see my mother and Rhainn and Aeron and Boris all standing in the doorway, their smiles bright despite the fading light.

"They've been there since you came in, you ninny," Aeron says with a laugh.

They have? Why didn't anyone tell me? Then I could've used my wish for something else. "How do I make them as big as yours?" I ask Boris. *Wait...* "What color are they?" *Please don't be piss yellow. Please don't be piss yellow.*

Boris chuckles. "Don't worry, Senan. They're black."

Four

SENAN

NOW

Either someone dropped a load of bricks on my head, or I drank far too much. Is this how I die, felled by a thumping skull? What is with the burning in my back? Did someone stab me? Fuck, it hurts. No wonder I passed out on my stomach.

What the hell happened last night?

I peel open my heavy eyelids, blinking at an unfamiliar room.

Is this an inn?

It doesn't look like any inn I've ever been to. Granted, I haven't been to many, but this space feels too lived in, the patchwork quilt too faded, and the chipping paint too worn.

I did go to the inn though...didn't I?

I did.

And when I arrived, I found Bell trying to steal Allette.

Shit. Where is Allette? I flatten my palms against the mattress and shove myself upright. White-hot agony explodes down my spine, radiating from my shoulder blades. Why am I wearing bandages? Why are they so fucking tight?

"Allette!" My voice is a broken shard, slicing my dry throat. I try to move my legs, but my body refuses to cooperate. The whole room tilts and starts to spin. "Allette!" Tell me she's all right. Tell me this is all a terrible dream—

The door swings wide, and my girl is there, her dark hair a wild halo around her pale face, no sign of my traitorous guard at her back. "There is no need to panic. I'm right here."

Dappled light from the lace curtains plays on her high cheekbones as she steps into the room with a tray in her hands, seeming at ease and not at all concerned for her safety.

I'm almost certain there are quite a few reasons to panic, but at the moment, all I can do is stare at Allette's hips as she sways closer, her skirts swishing with every step.

Perhaps it *was* a dream.

I press a hand to my pounding skull.

Except...it felt so real. That damn poison from all the stardust is really starting to fuck with my head.

Steam curls from a teapot, twisting toward Allette's reassuring smile. "I hope you're hungry. The bread was too moldy to salvage, but the eggs were still good. Do you like scrambled? It was either that or boiled, I'm afraid. I don't know how to make them any other way."

If Allette cooked my breakfast, then this definitely isn't an inn. "Where are we?"

A small wrinkle appears between her arched eyebrows. "You don't remember?"

"I remember going to the inn, but after that, everything gets fuzzy." When I try to shift my body toward hers, my back screams in protest. I've never been stabbed with a red-hot fire poker, but this is how I imagine it would feel. Every move pulls and burns as if some wild beast is clawing at my skin.

The teacups rattle when Allette drops the tray onto the

bedside table and collects a long-neck bottle from the floor. "Here. Drink some of this."

My stomach revolts at the thought of drinking anything, let alone whatever rot is in that bottle. "If it's all the same to you, I think I'll pass."

Her lips purse as I fix my face into a smile. "Suit yourself. I'll leave the bottle here if you change your mind." The brass headboard creaks when Allette sinks onto the bed next to me. "To answer your question, we're in the human realm."

That cannot be right. I don't recall flying us down here.

Come to think of it, I don't remember flying at all. What I remember is falling and...

Wait.

The king. The portal. My *wings*.

Oh, gods...

I reach behind my shoulder and nearly faint from the excruciating pain. *Fuck.* All I feel are bandages that are far too tight and lumps and agony.

So much fucking agony.

"Don't do that!" Allette catches my hand, clasping it in her own. "You'll rip your stitches."

Stitches. The word brings back memories of tugging and pulling as my love sewed together the flayed flesh of my back.

It wasn't a dream at all. Even glamoured, their familiar weight kept me balanced.

A weight that has vanished.

"They're gone, aren't they?" *Tell me I'm wrong. Tell me it isn't true.*

Allette's golden eyes glitter as she nods. "I'm afraid so."

My brother cut off my fucking wings.

When I was little, I waited every day for them to appear. On my seventh birthday, they finally did. Since then, they've been my constant companions, my escape, the only freedom I ever had.

Now they're gone and I'll never fly again. Never feel the kiss of a breeze high above the sleeping world.

The slightest pressure on my fingers halts my downward spiral.

Allette is here with me. Isn't that what truly matters?

It should be.

Except now that I'm looking at her, all I see are pinched lips and bruises beneath her eyes. Does she resent me for all that has befallen us? Has her love for me waned?

I am no longer a prince but an exiled fae living in a strange realm where I have no means of providing for my girl. All those years ago, the disparity of what I could offer her up in the fae realm versus what I had to offer her down here never seemed to matter.

Now I can think of nothing else.

What are we supposed to do if Boris sends guards to find us? How will we protect ourselves? How will we survive on our own? I brought some gold but not enough to sustain us for long. It's not as if I can skip down to the treasury to request more. I'll have to find work, but with this pain in my back, I can barely move. How long will it take to ease?

And Allette…

"Have you slept at all?" Or has she been up all this time taking care of me? If she falls ill, I won't know how to heal her.

"Do not waste your time worrying about me."

As if that's possible. Down here, her wellbeing and happiness are my only concerns. The king could've torn me in two and I'd still be more worried about Allette than myself.

"You must be starving," she says.

My stomach answers with a hollow growl. Although nausea lingers, perhaps some food would make me feel better.

Allette lifts the plate from the tray, stabs a lump of egg, and brings it to my mouth.

I'll be damned if I let my girl feed me like an invalid. "He took my wings, not my arms. I can feed myself."

Something flickers across her face, but she sets the plate down on my lap and hands me the fork. When I lift it to my lips, the stitches at my back stretch, pulling the torn flesh.

Maybe I was too rash. Every time I raise the damn thing it's like being cut all over again.

Allette throws her eyes to heaven. "You are so bloody stubborn."

It's better than giving up, isn't it? Because right now, that's what I want to do.

Four bites in, I've had enough. Food. Pain. Pitying stares. All of it makes me want to tear out my hair. How can she stand to look at me—to be near me? "You needn't stay here." If she wants to leave, I won't try to stop her.

"Where else should I go? Hmm?" When Allette's defiant chin lifts, I glimpse a red line across her throat.

Gods above, is that *blood*? I drop the fork with a clatter, cradling her jaw and adjusting her head to give me a better view of what is indeed a wound. "Someone cut you."

Memories flash like lightning. The guard holding her against her will. The glint of a dagger at her throat.

Maybe it's a good thing I don't have wings, because then I'd be tempted to fly back through the portal, hunt down the bastard, and use his own blade to carve the same mark into his throat.

Allette pushes my hands away. "It's only a scratch."

A scratch? If he pressed any harder, he would've stolen her from me.

Once again, I failed to protect Allette. Now, we are stuck here because of my weakness.

My incompetence.

My uselessness.

Bracing against the searing pain, I prop my elbows on my knees and let my pounding head fall into my hands. "How are we alive?" Heaven knows I didn't save us.

Allette shares the most fantastical story about leaping into the portal after me. I would shout and rail at her, but I'm too stunned

—too fucking humbled by the fact that she would do such a thing. Don't get me wrong. I'm angry as well, mostly because of her recklessness, but damn.

This woman is a true marvel, and I do not deserve her.

"And then I felt it, Senan." Her eyes spark with what looks an awful lot like hope. Heaven knows we need as much as we can get. "I felt my magic stirring in my veins. Somehow, I managed to call to the wind and break our fall. How is that even possible?"

There is only one way it's possible, and with all the truths revealed over the last couple of weeks, the answer is abundantly clear: "We've been lied to our whole lives."

The portal is open year-round.

Scathians can still wield magic without wings.

What if those truths are only the beginning? Princess Leeri had no wings, and yet she swore she was Scathian. Could that be true as well? Does that make her Tuath or something else entirely? Or are Tuath simply wingless Scathians? If wings don't equate to magic, could the Tuath wield magic as well?

"What else do you think they lied about?" Allette asks.

Fire burns deep in my gut as I consider my brother's betrayal and Eason Bell's. About all the clandestine meetings I was never allowed to attend and the books locked inside cabinets in the king's office.

These truths we've uncovered are only the beginning. I feel it in my bones.

"I think they lied to us about everything."

+++

THE EGGS SINK LIKE STONES IN MY GUT. LYING HERE like a useless lump isn't helping either. In the last hour, Allette has carried in more wood, washed my disgusting clothes, and tidied up the mess from breakfast. Now she's sitting in front of the blazing fire, mending a tear in my trousers while I remain in bed "resting."

Talk about torture.

With nothing to occupy my mind, memories from the confrontation at the portal play on repeat inside my head.

"Why couldn't you just take your dust and die?"

Boris *knew* about the poison.

For how long has my brother wanted me dead?

I pick at the corner of the bandage Allette made from an old sheet. My back still hurts, but now it itches worse. Hopefully, I won't have to wear these things for long.

I need to get out of this fucking bed.

Gritting my teeth against the pain, I push myself off the mattress and cross a floor that feels as if it's made of ice, to the pack I threw together before fleeing the castle. I'm almost certain I stuffed in an extra pair of trousers or two, but I had been in a bit of a panic.

When I stick my hand inside, the clothing feels damp. It's probably just the coldness from this damn floor seeping into the canvas. I withdraw two dresses, a shift, three shirts, and a pair of spare trousers. When I place them in a pile next to where I squat, something glitters from the dark fabric. It looks like glass, but I didn't put any glass in my—

Oh fuck...

My pulse roars in my ears as I withdraw the bag of antidote Jeston gave me, finding only shards of broken glass.

This cannot be happening.

"You won't survive until spring."

That's what Jeston told me the day I met him in the pit. Without the antidote, I'm done for.

My throat constricts, and when the coughing begins, it doesn't stop. Blood spurts from my lips, splattering the white bandages.

"Senan? Are you all right?" Allette calls from the living room.

No, I'm not all right. All my efforts to stay alive have been squandered. Boris wins. I'm going to be dead by March.

I clutch the bag against my pounding heart. If I had my wings, I could return to the fae realm for more. Without them, I'm as cursed down here as I was up there.

"I'm fine," I shout back.

If only that were true.

I stuff what remains of the vials back into my pack and shove the evidence beneath the bed.

My lungs seize, unable to draw in a full breath.

These fucking bandages. Wounds be damned, they must come off. Tugging the end until the bindings unravel, I steel my resolve and twist toward the mirror in the corner.

Gods...

No wonder I'm in such pain. Boris didn't even have the decency to take the entire wing. Without access to my magic, I cannot glamour them, so they sit there like mutilated twigs protruding from behind my shoulders.

I try to move them, to flatten them down. *Something*. But all they do is stick out.

Allette comes into the room looking as perfect and beautiful as ever. "Senan? What is it? What's wrong?"

Everything. Everything is fucking wrong.

"Why did you remove your bandages?"

"They were too tight."

She clicks her tongue, the floorboards creaking as she moves closer. "We need to keep your wings bound."

My *wings*? Is that what she thinks these are? "I have no fucking wings."

She jerks back, thoroughly disgusted by my hideous deformity.

I used to love the way she looked at me, as if she saw none of my flaws. But in this moment, all I see is pity in her eyes, and it kills me more than the damn poison coursing through my veins. "Leave me alone. Please. I just want to be alone."

My head falls into my hands, and I can't bring myself to watch her walk away.

Only she doesn't walk away.

She sinks next to me and whispers, "Then let me be alone with you."

Five

ALLETTE

Snow drifts in the alleys and dusts window frames, painting the village pristine and soft. Thick wreaths of holly and pine hang on windows and doors, filling the air with the rich scent of the impending Yule celebrations. As I meander between stalls filled with tiny winter apples, knobby carrots, and dirt-crusted potatoes, my heart remains heavy.

I've never wanted anything more than Senan Vale.

Now I have him all to myself, but he isn't the same man I met five years ago. His grief over losing his wings consumes him, and while I know what it's like to drown under the weight of loss, watching him struggle is killing me.

We have been in the human realm for a week, and the wounds on Senan's back heal a little more each day. The skin has fused nicely, changing from an angry red to a shiny pink, and the stitches no longer weep.

If only I knew how to heal his heart.

I continue to the baker's stall, the scent of fresh bread and sweet pastries making my mouth water. Although I really shouldn't waste the money, I splurge on a fresh loaf of brown bread. When I reach into my cloak pocket and withdraw three copper coins, the bearded man behind the counter accepts them with a warm word of thanks. Unlike in the fae realm, humans have no qualms about taking fae currency, which is a relief considering that is all we have.

I'd love nothing more than to escape this village and the memories it holds, to find somewhere warmer to put down roots, but we cannot leave until the worst of the snow melts. Traversing these roads will be treacherous enough. To do so in inclement weather is beyond foolish.

When in town, I listen for anyone inquiring after Widow Mae. The woman might have been reclusive, but we shouldn't overstay our welcome. There is also the risk of someone from the fae realm finding us, but with Senan's cough getting worse, we cannot allow what ails him to take root in his chest.

The last thing we need is for him to catch pneumonia.

The baker hands me the wrapped loaf, and I add it to my canvas bag along with the potatoes and rabbit I bought for dinner. If we ration, there should be enough left over for tomorrow's lunch as well.

Hefting the bag's strap over my shoulder, I start for the cobblestone path leading out of town. Icy muck covers the stones, frozen in divots from carriage wheels. The muck gives way to snow so high that it falls into the tops of my boots. When the house we've claimed as our own comes into view, the tightness in my chest begins to ease.

I stomp on the stoop, freeing my boots from the chunks of snow clinging to the soles and laces. My wool glove slips on the brass handle, and the door swings wide. The heat from the crackling fire stings my cheeks as I breathe in the most delicious aroma of sugar and vanilla.

Senan hums in the kitchen, a ruffled apron tied low around his hips. The skin across his back is the same rich brown as the counter covered with discarded utensils and—is that a broken bowl?

I let my gaze roam from his trim waist up to his broad shoulders, but then I see his scars and the smile falls from my face.

At least he left the bedroom. That's progress, isn't it?

Senan whirls around, brandishing a wooden spoon like a weapon. "You're back early. I wasn't expecting you for at least another hour." His tanned cheeks flush pink as he reaches for the shirt discarded over one of the two dining chairs.

"The snow is getting worse, and I didn't want to tarry." I set the shopping bag beside the coat rack and tug off my gloves to untie the stiff laces on my boots.

"Probably for the best," he murmurs, fastening the buttons. I wait for a teasing remark or a profession of his undying love, but neither fall from his lips.

Be patient. Give him time.

I'm trying, but with every day that passes it feels as if we're drifting further apart.

Sighing, I peel off my sopping socks, draping them on the fire guard at the edge of the hearth. "You've been busy. What is in the oven?"

"Why don't you look for yourself?" Senan slips on two oven mitts and bends down to withdraw a ceramic pie dish. The top is covered in a light brown crust with a yellowish filling.

"Is that cheesecake?" Heavens above, it *is* cheesecake. Where in the world did he find lemons in the middle of winter? My question falls by the wayside when Senan slides the mitts from his hands, tossing them next to a mixing bowl overflowing with discarded eggshells. "I didn't know you could make cheesecake."

"While I was waiting to return to the human realm, my brother Aeron told me to stop moping and make myself useful. I met with a baker in the city almost every day for six months, soaking the poor man for recipes."

"What sort of recipes?"

Senan stacks the dirty utensils inside the larger mixing bowl and then carries them over to the sink. "Mostly desserts, but also shepherd's pie, almond-crusted chicken, and braised beef."

My hands tremble as I unravel Mae's wool scarf from around

my neck, hooking it over the coat rack along with my cloak. "Those are all my favorites."

The corners of Senan's lips tug up a fraction. "What a coincidence."

Only it isn't a coincidence. This man—no, this *prince*—learned to cook for me.

Perhaps we haven't drifted so far after all.

I finger-comb through my knotted hair and give my cheeks a pinch before crossing to where water splashes into the ceramic sink. Senan glances at me when I turn off the tap, his brow furrowed and a question in his eyes.

How I long to trace the swell of his biceps to his round shoulders. To press my body against his and find his mouth with my own. "Leave the dishes. I'll wash up after dinner." *Let me have you instead.*

"I don't mind—" A chesty cough stifles his protest. Senan grabs the tea towel, holding the fabric to his lips as his body shudders.

Has a more selfish woman ever existed? I am this close to begging him to touch me, to bring me pleasure and comfort, when he is in the throes of grief and sickness.

I take a step back, giving him room to catch his breath. "First thing tomorrow, we are going to the village physician." The man is a hack, but he is the best option we have down here. If he cannot offer any remedy, then we will travel to Dullen City as soon as the roads are clear to seek advice from the hospital there.

"Nonsense," Senan chokes, balling up the towel and carrying it into the bathing room. "I am only getting used to the humans' air," he says when he emerges a moment later. "It's too thick down here."

If that's true, then I should be having trouble breathing as well. The last time Senan and I were in the human realm together, there had been no coughing whatsoever. Then again, he was only here for a few hours. Perhaps he is more sensitive to the environment. After all, he spent most of his life in the highest towers in all the realm.

"If you're not better by next week, we are going—I'll not take no for an answer."

He nods, bracing his hands on the back of a dining chair. "Any luck with the launderette?"

He must know by now that changing the subject won't change my decision. Since he doesn't appear well enough for an argument, I let the topic fall by the wayside. "They offered me shifts on Mondays, Wednesdays, and Fridays." There's no telling how long the terrible weather will last, and we'll need as much money as possible if we're going to move. Don't ask me how we're going to pay rent elsewhere.

All problems for another day.

Right now, we need to celebrate being alive and eat every single bite of this cheesecake.

Lifting onto my toes, I slide two plates from the cupboard, bringing them and the cake to the table. Something is different, but I can't put my finger on it. Wait... "Weren't there four chairs?"

"Yes, but one broke." Senan collects cutlery from the drawer before sinking onto the chair across from me.

"How did it break?"

"Shoddy craftsmanship, I suppose." He slices two helpings onto the plates, handing me the largest one.

"Can we fix it?" Not that we need four chairs when there are only two of us, but it seems silly to throw out something that could be mended.

"I'm afraid I burned it."

There goes that idea.

I cut off a bite of cake and blow until steam no longer curls from the end of my fork. We should probably wait until the dessert has cooled, but it smells too good to delay. "Have you thought any more about what you'd like to do down here?"

Senan stabs a bite for himself. "No, but I will think about it this week. The last thing I want is to be a burden to you."

He cannot be serious. "You're not a burden, Senan."

His mirthless chuckle hits me like an arrow to the heart. "You're not," I insist. "You have many talents; all we have to do is find the one that brings you the most joy." I wouldn't say working at the launderette brings me joy, per se, but I don't mind the sewing. And having a useful skill is quite satisfying.

The second bite burns the tip of my tongue, but I simply cannot wait. "This cheesecake is delicious. Perhaps the bakery is hiring."

"I doubt any baker is looking to take on an apprentice who only knows how to bake one sort of cake."

"You never know until you try," I say, watching him push his cake from one side of the plate to the other. "Aren't you going to eat?" He hasn't even taken one bite.

He sets his fork down on the side of his plate, cheesecake still perched on the tongs. "Not much of an appetite today. I think I'm just tired." The chair scrapes against the floorboards when he pushes back from the table and starts for the sink.

If he's so tired, then he should go back to bed. "Leave the dishes. I'll wash them after dinner."

Inky strands fall over his brow when he shakes his head. "I made the mess, and I will be the one to clean it up."

"You cooked, which means I'm the one who cleans." It's only fair.

He drops the dish with a clatter, yanks the end of the apron string, and tears the thing off, balling it in his fist and tossing the garment onto the sticky countertop.

"Where are you going?"

"Back to bed," he mutters, not bothering to turn around.

How did we go from being madly in love to whatever this is? And how do we get back?

Six

SENAN

I can't look at what's left of my wings without wanting to put my fist through the fucking wall. If Boris had to take them, why couldn't he have taken *all* of them? These black stumps are all I see when I look in the mirror. All I feel when I move. When I *breathe*.

My hands shake where they grip the sink. If this weren't our only privy, I'd rip the porcelain from the wall and slam my fist into the mirror over and over and over again. I'd break everything in this fucking place, from the creaky bed to the drafty, single-pane windows.

I'm trying my best to keep going, but it feels like I'm breathing shards of glass, a thousand tiny cuts stealing my life one inhale at a time.

And Allette...

The only time she comes near me is to change my bandages and clean my disgusting wounds. If there were any way for me to care for them myself, I would.

But like everything else in this forsaken realm, I am completely helpless.

Tonight, I planned on cooking for my girl. It was the least I could do after she spent hours in the village securing work and picking up items to stock our rapidly emptying shelves.

For the first time since we arrived, I did something to contribute. It was only a blasted cheesecake, but I knew it would make my girl smile, maybe even bring the spark back to her eyes.

When she suggested doing the dishes, this thin veneer I've been hiding behind shattered just like the chair I smashed against the wall earlier.

I don't want her to do more. I want her to let me help, to let me take care of her.

Instead, she barely glances my way, like she cannot stand the sight of me.

Meanwhile, I suffer in silence, waiting for some sort of sign that she still finds me attractive. Every time she walks by, my cock gets so hard, even the soft fabric of my trousers makes me throb. The gentle scent of her shampoo haunts the very air I breathe.

These wounds, the pain, this foreign realm—I have survived it all but the distance between us will surely be the end of me. I need Allette to put me out of my misery. For her to confirm that the future we have dreamed of for so long will never come to pass.

I shove the privy door aside and stalk back to where Allette waits by the sink, hands wrenching in front of her, beautiful face fallen in misery. Our gazes find each other as they always do. A silver line of tears clings to her thick lashes.

I take a hesitant step forward, unsure whether she will want my comfort or if my presence disgusts her so much that it only widens this chasm between us. "What's wrong?"

She sweeps a finger beneath those lashes that have brushed my skin so many times, that I can still feel their phantom kiss right over my heart. "It feels as if I'm losing you."

"You couldn't lose me if you tried."

Her huffed chuckle loosens the tears, and they roll like raindrops down her cheeks. "You need time to heal. To grieve. I know that, and yet all I can think about is how desperately I want to throw myself at you."

Wait...

She still wants me? Gods above, why has she waited this long to say so?

"Please, throw yourself at me. I swear I'll catch you every time."

Allette tugs at her littlest finger, her chest rising and falling with every measured breath. "I'm afraid your stitches will—"

"Forget about the stitches." *And the mangled mess they're holding together.* "They're on my shoulders, remember? The rest of me is still in perfect working order." For now, anyway.

Her cheeks turn my favorite shade of pink, like the clouds at sunset on a beautiful summer's evening. "Prove it."

I long to go to her, but fear holds me back.

"This is what I mean, Senan. I am practically begging, and yet you cannot even bring yourself to cross the bloody room. If you're regretting your decision, just tell me."

The only thing I regret is not being able to save my girl from every tragedy that has befallen her since the day we met.

"I'm afraid, all right?" I confess, hating the tears on her cheeks and the terror in my heart. "Every time you look at my hideous wounds, you wince like you cannot stand the sight of me."

She closes the distance between us, her hands gliding up my arms. I can't help but move closer, starved for her touch. "I only wince because I know how much pain you're in. I love your body, but I fell *in* love with your soul." Her fingertips brush against my forehead as she pushes back a lock of my hair, her eyes softening, filling like wells of liquid gold. "You are the kindest man I have ever met. Your capacity for love and joy—and mischief—is endless."

The unease that has gripped my chest ever since I woke without a part of myself loosens its hold as I breathe her into my lungs, into my soul.

Allette's lips hitch at the corners, and her hand drops to the bunched fabric I abandoned on the counter before stomping away like a toddler in a strop. "Would it be too bold of me to say that you looked edible in this apron?"

If my girl wants me in a frilly apron, then that's the way she'll have me. I snag the corner and fasten the ties around my waist. The faded pink material does nothing to distract from my bulging cock. "Better?"

Her smile twists wickedly. "Much." She picks up the fork holding my abandoned slice of cheesecake, bringing it to my lips so I can take a dutiful bite. Sweet, yet tart, but... "Could use more lemon." I'll have to remember that when I bake the next one. Luckily, the woman whose house we've commandeered kept a decent stock of lemon juice and zest down in the cellar.

Allette pops the rest into her mouth, smiling around the too-large bite. "Tastes pretty good to me."

I ease forward, dragging the tip of my tongue along her crumb-dusted lips. "I know something that tastes even better."

Her hands slide up my arms, hooking around my neck, and—*Fuck!*—accidentally grazing what's left of my wing. I bite my lip to keep from crying out, but Allette must recognize the pain on my face.

"I'm so sorry," she blurts, paling as she tries to retreat across the kitchen. "I knew I would hurt you."

I capture her wrists, holding her in place, breathing through the worst of the pain. "I'm fine."

She tries to tug free from my grasp. It's a half-hearted attempt at best, and now that I know she desires my touch as much as I yearn for hers, I'll not be dissuaded so easily. "Ah, ah. You're not going anywhere."

"But—"

"*But* we must do something about these wandering hands of yours." And I know just the thing.

I back her toward the table and shove the baking dish to the side, setting her right in the middle like the dessert she is. Her quiet giggle falls silent when I remove my belt from beneath the ridiculous apron. "Lie back. Hands up there." I gesture to the back of the dining chair.

Wearing a sultry smile, she eases back, her arms lifting and hands slipping between the spokes.

Using the belt, I create a figure eight before sauntering around the table and sliding the makeshift leather cuffs around her wrists, ensuring they're nice and secure. "There we go. Now they won't cause any problems."

I return to the other side, fitting my hips between her spread knees, and kissing her with all the passion she exhumes from my broken soul.

For too long, I've felt useless, but now? Now I am wholly capable and more than ready to be of service to my girl.

I start by untying the laces on the stiff bodice of her brown muslin dress. The material falls to the side, revealing a silken shift so sheer that I can see the rosy pebbles of her nipples straining against the fabric.

"Hello there." My thumb flicks over one of the peaks, and I relish the way it stiffens. "Looks like you've missed me as much as I've missed you." Allette's soft whimper strikes the perfect chord within me. "Now, now. There is no need to be jealous." My free hand falls to her other breast, kneading the pale globe. "I have two hands for a reason."

"Your teasing is infuriating," she grits through her teeth as she writhes on the tabletop, looking every bit like the wanton woman of my dreams.

My head dips, but before I can taste the tantalizing peak, I stop and whisper, "My teasing has only begun."

Her back arches, forcing her nipple against my smirking lips.

How can I resist such a tempting invitation?

Allette's whimper melts into a moan when I take her into my mouth, flicking and teasing with the tip of my tongue. My cock swells, aching and heavy in my trousers, demanding attention. There will be plenty of time for that, I remind it. First, I must attend to this woman who still loves me even though I'm destitute and deformed.

We are meant to be. Meant to live and to love.

If only our time together wasn't limited.

If only we could spend the next century like this.

But we are only playing house, with death waiting on our doorstep, poised to knock.

Suddenly, the week we wasted being at odds feels like a lifetime. How foolish that a problem so simply resolved caused so much misery when all we had to do was speak our truths to one another.

The chair rattles, and her hips buck, but when I said my teasing had only begun, I meant it. I draw back, the dampness from my mouth making the silk translucent, giving me an unobstructed view of my girl's breasts, heaving and trembling with each ragged gasp.

I drop a hand to her knee, gathering the fabric of her skirts in my fist, exposing her pale skin inch by glorious inch until only her lace undergarments remain. The wet patch at her center matches the ones at her breasts, drenched with desire. My thumb slides and strokes, finding the spot that makes her moan, working in tight, fast circles until she's panting my name.

Her chin lifts, exposing the length of her straining throat. "Senan. I need... I need..."

"What do you need? For me to flip up these skirts and fuck you with my tongue? Kiss you right here?" I drag her undergarments to the side, finding that bundle of nerves and flicking faster.

Her mewl of desire drives me to the breaking point. "Yes. Use your tongue."

Kneeling on the floorboards, I bury my face in her wet heat, consuming her the way she has consumed me. Allette's moans become a symphony as I rediscover that perfect spot with my tongue, working her over and over again. The chair rattles as she fights against her bonds, and when I fasten my lips around her clit, drawing the swollen flesh into my mouth, her cries hit a crescendo. I work a finger into her wetness, pumping and curling and twisting as my cock thickens in anticipation.

"Senan, if you don't give yourself to me, I swear..."

The desperation in her voice has me rising to my feet. The delicate flush of her cheeks is the perfect setting for the feral look in her lust-glazed eyes. "Doesn't appear as though you're in a position to make threats, my love."

Allette's legs snap around my back, her heels digging into my spine as she uses my surprise to her advantage, dragging me forward, knocking my apron-clad hips against her soaked center. "You were saying?" she coos, grinding herself on my aching length.

I fall forward, my hands landing on either side of her grinning face. "Minx."

She presses closer, rolling her hips. "I believe you have something for me beneath those ruffles."

"Oh, I do."

Hunger flashes in her eyes, her pupils blown wide, evaporating the gold. "Untie me."

My nose grazes hers, and I pretend to consider her request even as I shift my apron to the side and unfasten the button on my trousers. "Mmmm... No."

A storm descends over her features. "Senan Vale..."

"Allette Vale..." My trousers fall around my ankles.

"I swear—"

"To love me forever?"

"To despise you if you do not—"

Fisting my cock, I position myself at her entrance and thrust, turning her threats into a gasp. "You were saying?" I grit out, blackness spotting the edge of my vision.

Fucking hell, she's perfect. *So fucking perfect.*

Her eyes fall closed as I draw back, her breasts bouncing when I rock forward once more. How does this keep getting better? I will never tire of the way her body cradles mine.

We keep moving together until everything is shaking. The

table. The chair. Her legs. Our breaths. Heels digging into flesh. Hands braced on wood. Stealing whatever pleasure we can find until the world and our problems fade into darkness, cast into shadows by the brightest light shining beneath me.

Far too soon, I'm at my end, but I've spent too much time without her to fall on my own. I slip a hand between where we're joined, working my fingers in tandem with my hips until she cries my name and we're both tumbling head-first into bliss.

My wobbling arms give out, and I collapse forward, my chest pressed to hers as our hearts beat in harmony.

"Until the sun implodes," Allette whispers, her lips like a brand against my temple.

"And the stars no longer shine," I whisper back, praying for more time.

Seven

ALLETTE

The bedroom door flies open, and Senan bursts into the room. He sprints over to the dresser and drags the top drawer open to grab a pair of thick, wooly socks.

I set the book I was reading onto the bedside table, tucking the scrap of ribbon I've been using as a bookmark in between the pages. Who knew Widow Mae had such a scandalous collection of romance novels?

"Why are you in such a hurry?" I ask.

Balancing on one leg, Senan stuffs his foot into the first sock. "Look outside."

I push off the bed and go to the window, drawing the curtains aside. All I see are snow-covered trees. After being here for two weeks, I've had enough snow to last a lifetime.

Senan swaps legs, leaning his hip against the mattress as he dons the second sock. "Do you see it?"

"The snow?"

"No, Allette. *The sun.*"

Sure enough, that elusive ball of light hangs above the trees in a cerulean sky.

Senan takes off like a shot, then skids to a halt when he reaches the doorway. He has officially lost his mind.

"Aren't you coming?" he asks, all sparkling silver eyes and excited smiles.

The first properly excited smile I've seen since we arrived. "Coming where?"

"Outside!" He smacks the doorframe and disappears down the hallway.

Why would anyone want to venture out there when it's so warm and toasty in here?

I drift into the living room, watching him shove his stockinged feet into his boots. When he finishes, he starts for the door in nothing but his trousers, boots, and bandages. "Aren't you forgetting something?" If he steps outside in that, he's going to turn into a fae icicle.

The muscles of his toned stomach flex as he glances down at himself, his brow furrowing.

"A shirt, Senan. And a coat." The sun might be shining but it's still winter. The air will still have a chill.

"I cannot get proper sunlight in a shirt." He sweeps out the door only to come right back with his teeth bared in a grimace. "It's fucking freezing out there."

"I told you so. This realm isn't like ours." In Kumulus, the sun brings heat no matter the season. Down here, you must wait until nearly summer for any sort of warmth.

Senan huffs and puffs, his hands flexing at his sides. "It's fine. I'm strong. I can handle a little breeze."

Strength has nothing to do with it. Down here, you must be practical. Walking around in the dead of winter without proper attire is just plain foolish.

I take my cloak and Senan's coat from the hook, following him out into the bright day. Sunlight glints off the snow like crystals, forcing me to squint against its brilliance.

Senan's boots sink as he stomps away from the house to the middle of the clearing. The color of the sky above reminds me of my wings and hair. Speaking of, I must purchase a bottle of dye the next time I venture into the village. Wouldn't want the humans to realize I'm not one of them.

Senan's lashes fall closed as he lifts his face toward the sun.

Perhaps he is right to try and catch as many of its rays before the clouds return. Restoring his magic could help him heal quicker, and there's no telling if we will need our elements to protect ourselves.

Not that it would work for very long. Unless that's another lie we've been told.

Better safe than sorry, I suppose.

Reluctantly, I set our coats on the ground and unbutton the front of my dress, letting the material fall around my waist, leaving me in a shift and skirts.

Why must it be so bloody cold? Goosebumps pebble my skin, and my nipples are hard as stone.

Five minutes. That's all. I can stand to be outside for five minutes, can't I?

I screw my eyes closed and steady my breathing, searching for the familiar heat of magic inside my chest.

Tell me this is going to work. Heaven knows we need something to go right.

"Can you feel anything yet?" I ask.

"Not yet."

His well would've been depleted from his body attempting to heal itself. *Bloody Boris.* What I wouldn't give to take that bastard's wings—to make him suffer through the same pain he inflicted on us both.

I peek through my lashes at Senan's bandages, hating his brother even more.

Senan peers back, his gaze not on my face but on my chest. Desire burns like fire through my blood. I force my eyes closed once more; otherwise, I'm going to end up abandoning the sun for the heat of my prince's body.

My toes are the first to go numb, swiftly followed by my fingers.

Are any kingdoms in this realm warm, or do they all suffer from the affliction that is snow? What I wouldn't give for a hot, sunny climate. How simple it would be to restore our magic then.

The dregs of my power stir beneath my skin. *Finally.* A few sunny days and I should be fully restored—

Something solid and cold strikes my shoulder.

When I open my eyes, I find the remains of a snowball splatter onto my boot.

Senan grins from across the way, packing a second snowball between his hands.

"Don't you dare." It's already cold enough out here without being covered in snow.

He tosses the snowball into the air, catching it with a single hand. "Or what?"

"Or I shall be the one to tie *you* down and have my wicked way with you."

He draws back his arm and launches the snow directly at me. I duck a second too late, and the snow grazes my temple. I should've known the threat wouldn't be a deterrent.

"You're going to pay for that." I scoop a big hunk of snow with my stiff fingers and throw the ball at my prince, nailing him on the hip. There's no time to celebrate. Senan tosses another snowball, this one barely missing my shoulder.

I'm going to *bury* him.

With each ball I make, I draw closer, throwing them one after the other, barely formed but rapidly fired, giving him no time to launch an assault.

He hunkers down, doing his best to block while creating an arsenal of his own. When he attacks, he does so with no accuracy, mostly hitting my skirts, although there is one that strikes my left breast, soaking the material of my shift.

Senan's hand freezes mid-throw, his gaze trailing down the translucent silk, his tongue darting out across his pink lips. The flush on his cheeks deepens.

It's just the distraction I need.

I hurl my final snowball, hitting him in the dead center of his chest. Clutching his heart with a dramatic groan, Senan falls face-first into the snow.

I steal one of his snowballs, holding it above my head, ready to deal the killing blow. "Do you yield?"

"How can I not, you vicious woman?" When he lifts his head, snow clings to his lashes and eyebrows. "You look utterly terrifying right now. I don't think I've ever been more attracted to you."

My stomach flutters. Leave it to my mate to turn a snowball fight into foreplay.

"And you look utterly frozen." I kneel next to him, clearing the white chunks away. "Can you feel your magic yet?"

He sits up with a shudder. "I'm too cold to feel anything."

I know what he means. Whose idea was it to start a snowball fight, anyway? "Will we go back inside?"

"I'm afraid there is no other option if I want to keep my manhood."

I head straight for the cottage, my teeth already starting to chatter.

Senan collects our coats, keeping a measured pace on his way back to the stoop. When he starts coughing, I whirl, shooting him a glower.

"Don't give me that look," he says with a roll of his eyes. "This is your fault. You're the one who hit me in chest."

"That wouldn't make you cough, you fool."

"Tell that to the hole you put in my lung."

This man. What am I going to do with him?

Once I've changed into a dry dress, I throw on the kettle for tea. Senan pads into the kitchen in nothing but a fresh pair of trousers. Without the bandages, it's almost possible to forget what happened to him.

Until he turns around.

What remains of his wings don't stick out quite as much after being bound, but they still look awfully sore. "Can you feel your magic now?"

His smile wavers, but only a little. "Not even a spark."

That's not surprising. It wasn't until we were hurtling through the sky that I even realized magic still sang in my blood. I rest my hip against the counter, wishing I understood *how* I was able to access my power. For four years I lived in this realm, soaking in as much sunlight as I could, and never felt so much as a spark. It's like in falling, I was able to break through an invisible barrier.

Now it's Senan's turn. "Try to call a flame to your palm."

He holds out his hand with his palm facing the ceiling, his brow furrowed in concentration.

Come on. One little flame. That's all we need.

He shakes his head, his hand dropping to his thigh. "It's not there."

I fold his frigid fingers in mine. My own magic stirs, not as strong as it once was but stronger than it felt before we ventured into the sunlight. I urge the power from my hand to his. "How about now?"

Sighing, he lifts his free hand once more. "I feel nothing."

"Try to focus—"

"I *am* focusing."

"Just try—"

He yanks his hand away. "*Enough*. There's nothing left, Allette. It's all gone."

"It cannot be all gone."

"It is." His hand flexes into a white-knuckled fist. "Every single drop is gone. I don't know why you still have magic, but mine isn't there anymore. Boris stole my power along with my wings, and I'm never getting them back."

The kettle lets out a shrill shriek.

I understand how difficult it is to remain positive, but if we allow ourselves to be flooded by anger and self-pity, what's to stop us from drowning?

He drags his fingers through his hair. "I'm sorry, Allette. I'm just frustrated—beyond frustrated. I thought I'd feel *something*."

I wrap my arms around his waist, drawing him into my embrace. "You will." One way or another, I will make it my mission to help him find at least one of the things the king stole from him.

Eight

SENAN

With my hip braced against the windowsill, I watch the wind tear at Allette's cloak as she stomps through the snow. Her first shift at the launderette begins in an hour. It's a day for celebration.

At least it should be.

Meanwhile, I'm still standing here, counting her footprints.

Pushing away from the window, I head outside into the blustery day… and scream until my voice gives out.

Nine

ALLETTE

FIVE YEARS AGO

"It's such a lovely day, isn't it?" There's something about Tuesdays that makes my heart soar. That "something" has a name: Prince Senan Vale.

Wynn yanks my sheets from the bed, barely sparing me a glance as she rolls the fabric into a ball and adds it to the top of the laundry basket. "It looks quite lovely."

"Why don't you take a break and enjoy the sun with me?" Sunlight is meant to be shared, after all.

She takes a freshly pressed sheet from the pile, stretching it around the corner of the mattress. "I couldn't possibly."

"Come on, Wynn." I venture back inside, grabbing the other side of the sheet and tucking it beneath the mattress. "Just a few minutes. I'll even help you make all the beds, so you don't get behind on your work." I can call down to the kitchens for tea. It's been ages since Wynn and I shared a pot.

Her mask bounces when she stands upright, her lips pursing as she considers the offer. "I promised my parents I would never set foot on one of your balconies. That was their only request when letting me apply for a position here."

That seems silly. Why would they care if Wynn went outside? Unless... "Are they afraid you'll fall off?"

My mother never used to allow me on the balcony alone when I was little, but as soon as my wings grew, she stopped worrying.

"I swear to catch you if you do." I'd hardly let my best friend fall to her death.

"I know you would," she says with a soft smile, collecting the quilt from where she draped it across my chair. "But it's not that." She glances out the balcony door with a grimace. "At least not entirely." She unfolds the quilt, tossing me the other side. "My uncle's best mate was caught on Lord Windell's balcony and the king had him thrown into the pit."

That cannot be true. "Why would anyone care, let alone the king?" Sounds like a tall tale to me. Although if there is some truth to the story, I'd love to hear it.

She shrugs before fluffing the pillows. "I've never thought about it."

When I'm with Senan later today, I'm going to ask.

✦

My heart beats a furious rhythm as I soar over the towers stretching toward the sun. I couldn't hide my smile if I tried.

Senan sent word for me to meet him in the mountain park. I haven't visited the park since my parents passed. After stealing away in my tower for weeks, meeting him somewhere so public feels strange.

The moment my boots meet soft grass, I send my wings away. Wouldn't want one of my aunt's friends recognizing me.

Which is why I've glamoured my hair a sunny blonde. Let's

see if my prince can find me among the crowd of Scathians picnicking on the mountainside.

Males and females lounge on blankets in various states of undress, catching every last drop of sunlight. Tiny children squeal and squawk like the swans they feed down by the pond, as bare as the day they were born.

I unbutton the front of my jerkin and am about to slip out of the leather garment when a deep voice drifts over me, sending chills up and down my spine.

"This is a little too disturbing, even for me," Senan says from behind, his tone laced with smiles.

"What's disturbing?" I ask, biting back my own.

"If people see us together, they're bound to believe we're twins." Warmth from his body presses closer to my back, and I have to fight to stand my ground instead of melting into him.

"Which would be dreadfully awkward if anyone catches me with my tongue down your throat," he whispers against the shell of my ear.

I'm not sure what he means about being twins, but the second part is quite enticing. "Sounds awful. Where do I sign up?" I glance over my shoulder only to burst into a fit of laughter.

What in heaven's name is he thinking? "You look ridiculous."

"Ridiculously handsome, you mean," he counters with a waggle of his dark brows.

"No, I don't."

He runs his finger through his shoulder-length hair, his lips pursing into a pout. "Can I not pull off blonde?"

"That isn't blonde. *That* is lemon yellow."

"Even better. You love lemons."

"In cheesecake, you fool. I don't let them put their tongues down my throat."

In a blink, his hair is no longer yellow, but a dull copper. "Better?" he asks, his brows raised.

I prefer his natural black hair, but at least he doesn't look like a dandelion anymore. "Much. Care to tell me why we're here?"

He loops my arm through his, tugging me farther up the mountain. "Nope. Follow me."

We walk arm-in-arm toward a cropping of trees devoid of blankets. "Are we going for a picnic?" I already had lunch but wouldn't say no to something sweet.

"Gods, no. I can think of nothing worse than sitting on the hard ground eating bug-infested scones. Except maybe swimming in that pond."

"You should probably fire your cook if your food is bug-infested."

He snorts. "Very funny. Do you see all these flies milling around?"

I don't but decide to play along anyway and nod.

"They're waiting for some unsuspecting prince to smear a load of butter atop his scone. And when he does, they'll dive right in, get stuck, and laugh in victory when he unknowingly gobbles them up."

"Are you certain they'd be laughing? Sounds to me like they'd be screaming in terror."

"Either way, the end result is the same: Me with a bug between my teeth and my brother Aeron cackling so hard he nearly chokes on his own scone."

I bite my lip to keep from laughing at the misery on his face. "So no picnics?"

He grimaces. "Not if I can help it."

When we reach the shade of the trees, an unsettling feeling fills my gut. The back of my neck starts to prickle, and I glance over my shoulder, half expecting to find someone following us.

All I see are swaying branches and leaf-dappled sunlight playing on the luscious grass.

Although when I turn back around, the uneasy feeling remains. "Did you come alone?"

Senan catches the lowest branch on the closest tree and lifts himself into the foliage. "Once in the shower this morning," he says, reaching down for me, a wicked smile teasing his lips. "But I thought of you the entire time. How about you?"

My fingers slip into his, and he grips tightly, hauling me up next to him. "I mean to the park, you cad."

He drags a hand across his brow with a chuckle. "Of course, I came alone. The new guard Boris assigned is a pain in my ass though." Balancing himself against the trunk, he reaches for another branch above his head and drags himself up. "It took far too long to shake him. The bastard nearly made me late."

I don't bother asking why we're in a tree or telling Senan that this would be far easier if we flew. All that matters is that we're together.

We climb higher and higher, through the branches fraught with shuddering emerald leaves, until Senan comes to a stop near the top.

He throws a leg on either side of a sturdy limb and then helps me sit in front of him. It's so peaceful up here, with the rustle of the leaves and the sound of laughter drifting from the park. I turn to smile at my prince when I catch sight of something carved into the tree's rich brown trunk.

Senan

I trace the letters of his name, my lips tipping into a smile.

He rests his head on my chin with a contented sigh. "I used to come up here when I was little—before I got my wings. Aeron convinced me it was the tallest tree in the kingdom. Bet me his dessert for an entire week that I couldn't get to the top."

I can picture him now, a little raven-haired boy scaling a tree simply to impress his brother.

Were we ever here at the same time?

As soon as the thought crosses my mind, I push it right back out. The whole park would've been in a tizzy if the queen and her sons had been visiting. "My mother never would've allowed me to climb so high." And she definitely wouldn't have let me bring a blade so I could carve proof of my victory.

His eyes sparkle as he kicks his legs back and forth, shaking the branch. "Who said my mother knew?"

That poor woman. I bet she had her hands full with Senan and his brothers. It must have been nice for Senan to grow up with other children around though. Wynn is the closest thing I have to a sister, and even then, she is almost always working so we don't get to spend as much time together as I'd like.

Thinking of Wynn reminds me of our conversation from earlier, about her uncle's friend. "Can I ask you something random?"

"You can ask me anything. The randomer the better."

"I heard a story earlier today about a Tuath servant being thrown into the pit for stepping onto a balcony. It sounded so far-fetched; I wasn't sure if it was true."

His feet stop swaying. "That's strange." His brow furrows. "Although...now that I think about it, I can't recall ever seeing any of our servants outside. Not sure why he would have been thrown into the pit though. Maybe they're separate incidents?"

"Maybe."

Our conversation drifts to other topics before fading into passionate kisses and greedy hands. We forget about the world outside the branches, losing ourselves in each other until the sun starts to fall, and my prince must return to his castle.

We make plans to meet the following Tuesday, and I hate that it feels so far away. But to love a prince is to watch him leave time and again, hoping and praying he won't forget you between now and then.

Ten

ALLETTE

NOW

Is it possible for a person to die from happiness? If so, I am sure to expire any day now. Even after spending hours hunched over a sewing machine, there is a smile on my face from knowing that I will be spending the evening with my prince. The house will be spotless, and there will be dinner on the table. We will stay up far too late making love and then wake in each other's arms.

This is how our lives would have been if we'd stayed in this realm instead of being ripped apart by a vicious king. It pains me to think of Senan's brother getting away with his crimes, but there is nothing we can do about it now. I have chosen peace and happiness instead of stewing over the past, and it is gloriously freeing. The burden of guilt and grief that I have carried for so long is gone. Although I will always regret what happened to Wynn, she would want me to live my life.

That is what I plan on doing.

The clock on the wall strikes the end of my shift, but before I can push away from my machine, one of my co-workers sweeps into the room, her plain gray skirt matching the hair peeking from beneath her cap. "There's a handsome lad out the front asking for you, Allette," she says.

My heart leaps as I jump to my feet and stretch my hands over my head. When my back pops, I let out a little moan. Perhaps I will be able to convince Senan to give me a massage after dinner.

Who am I kidding? He won't take any convincing at all. The problem will be keeping the man on task after I remove my corset and shift.

A horde of women peer out the launderette's front door, their giggles echoing off the high ceiling.

Senan waits at the entrance; his smile is as brilliant as the pristine quilt of white blanketing the street as he chats with the shift leader. I've never seen the woman smile and yet there she is, laughing and red-faced like a besotted teen.

"Allette, your new man is quite the charmer," one of the women says with a sigh, her head falling against the wall.

They don't know the half of it. If I told them all the things he says and does, they would fall desperately in love with him.

"I don't suppose he has any brothers?" another asks, folding her hands beneath her chin as if sending a prayer to some higher power.

"He has four, actually, but they live far, far away." Senan doesn't speak of his family, but he must miss his brothers fiercely.

Not Boris, of course. No one would miss that tyrant. But the others, especially Kyff.

The woman's face falls. "Pity."

I grab my things and squeeze my way past the other workers as they don their coats and cloaks, tightening my scarf around my neck to keep the wind at bay. When he sees me, Senan's face lights up like it did the very first day we met. The shift leader nods to me on her way back to the launderette, her footsteps crunching in the snow.

"I didn't expect to see you here. Did you come to town for

more lemon juice?" He's obsessed with perfecting his cheesecake recipe. Although I'd never tell him this, I am getting a little sick of eating so much cheesecake. We have it with every meal—the other day we ate cake for breakfast.

His lips purse as he chews on the inside of his cheek. "No."

"Did you forget the way home again?"

"That happened once," he scoffs, shoving the knitted cap he wears to conceal his ears back off his forehead. His voice sounds gruffer than normal, almost hoarse. "And it's not my fault all the trees here look the same and the infernal snow decided to cover my tracks."

I nearly died of laughter when he came stomping back after walking in circles for twenty minutes. He claimed that I didn't care about him—which only made me laugh harder.

The man, for all his brilliance, has a terrible sense of direction.

Senan still hasn't gotten used to the cold, wearing far more layers than anyone normally would. He resembles a stuffed scarecrow, his arms stiff from all the coats. Even so, he is still the most handsome man I've ever met.

"You never answered my question. What are you doing here?"

He takes my gloved hand in his, twirling me around like this is a ballroom instead of the middle of the street. Gathering me into his arms, he dips me back dramatically, his eyes sparkling. "Allette, my love, you and I are going out."

***

The pub near the square has walls painted deep forest green. The owners covered them in all sorts of artwork, from tapestries to paintings to shoes and musical instruments displayed in shadow boxes. There is no rhyme or reason to the decor, but it all lends itself to the eclectic mix of patrons sitting around on low stools, drinking away their cares.

Senan finds us an open table near the back, close to the

fragrant peat fire blazing in the stone hearth. It takes him a comically long time to remove all his layers, leaving on his cap and his sweater to hide what's left of his wings. With the way they're bound, I barely notice the bumps and am certain no one else in here will either. For some reason, he's still self-conscious about them.

With a quick smash of his lips to mine, he skips toward the bar. A few minutes later, we have two foamy pints of ale clasped in our hands and smiles on our faces. Flames flicker in Senan's wide eyes as he takes me in. There's something about him tonight that makes me giddy.

When was the last time I felt like this? Probably the day we had that snowball fight.

Bubbles tickle my throat when I take a sip. "What has gotten into you?"

Senan's grin grows as he glances at his pint, the condensation weeping down his fingers. "Nothing."

Nothing, my foot. "You're acting strange."

"Am I?"

"Yes."

He shifts on his stool, bringing the glass to his lips and taking a deep gulp before setting it down once more. I do the same, waiting on the edge of my seat for him to spit it out. "All right, if you don't tell me this instant, I'm going to scream." I don't care if every single person in here thinks I'm a loon; I simply cannot wait any longer for an explanation.

He glances away, then back at me, scooting himself closer to the table. "So there is something."

I bloody well knew it.

"I have a gift for you."

My heart deflates, the smile falling from my lips. "We agreed not to do Yule gifts this year." Now I feel awful about not having anything to give him.

"This isn't a gift for Yule. It's for your birthday."

"My birthday was months ago."

His dark brows arch. "Your point?"
"You didn't need to buy me anything."
"I know I didn't need to. I wanted to."
"Senan..."
He rolls his eyes. "Do you want the gift or not?"
"Obviously."
He slips a hand into his pocket. "Close your eyes and hold out your hands."

For my last birthday that we spent together, he gave me a child's doll with black hair and large black wings, a "miniature Senan" to keep in my bed when he couldn't join me. Ridiculous, I know.

Whatever happened to miniature Senan and the moonflower paperweight? Were they thrown out with the rest of my things when my great aunt died? Or were they donated? Is some little girl playing with the doll? Does the paperweight adorn the corner of someone's desk?

I screw my eyes shut and extend my hands, waiting until something light tickles my fingers.

"You can open your eyes now."

In my palms sit two cerulean feathers, nearly the same size as each other. They must be the ones he saved all those years ago. The singed vanes have been painted gold, and golden hooks have been fastened to the tips.

He made my feathers into a pair of earrings.

Senan scrubs his hands down his thighs, his expression guarded as he watches me. "I couldn't give you back your wings, but I thought you might like to wear your feathers again."

Has a more thoughtful gift ever existed? "They're perfect."

How did I ever get so lucky to deserve such a sweet, thoughtful man? Swiping away my tears, I push the stems through the holes in my ears. I haven't worn earrings since the first time I came through the portal.

Back then, I felt guilty for relying on Eason to earn all the money, so I brought the pearl studs from my mother down to the pawnbroker in exchange for four pieces of silver.

Senan's warm hand slides beneath my chin, applying the slightest pressure, lifting until I'm staring into his endless eyes. "You don't have to wear them if it's too difficult."

"It's not. I swear. It's just... I love them so much. You give me more than I deserve—you always have."

"You deserve everything good and wonderful, Allette. You are the strongest person I know. You have risen from the ashes like a phoenix, overcoming every challenge this cursed world threw at you." He trails a finger down my feathers, a wistful note in his voice. "*I* am the one who is undeserving. But I intend to hoard your love and attention like a dragon does gold until you come to your senses and find someone better."

"There is no one better." Not in this realm or any other. "Neither of us is perfect, but we are perfect for each other." Of that, I'm certain.

He eases forward, the soft press of his lips slow and savoring. I drink him in, tasting the ale on his tongue and the love in each careful stroke.

"I suppose I'll have to think of something extra special for your birthday this summer," I tease when he draws back.

For some reason, my comment makes his smile falter. "I can't wait to see what you come up with that'll top those." He gives the earrings a playful flick.

"I can think of one thing."

"And what is that?"

Propping my elbows on the table, I lean all the way forward, keeping my voice low. "Let's just say it would involve a new garter belt and a great deal of black lace."

"You know, I just remembered that I was actually born in January."

"Isn't that fortuitous?"

"My thoughts exactly," he says, lifting his pint in salute. When he goes to take a sip, he starts coughing and hacking, splattering the drink all over the table.

I snag the glass before he accidentally pours alcohol all over himself or his pile of coats, setting it well out of the way. "Are you all right?"

Senan coughs into his fist so violently, that the men at the next table throw wary glances toward us. "You'd think at my age I'd be better at swallowing," he manages between fits.

He is the most ridiculous—

What in the world?

Crimson splatters paint his cuff. "Is that *blood*?"

Senan tries to shove his sleeve to his elbow, but I catch him by the wrist. Heavens above, it is. "That *is* blood."

"It was there before."

"No, it wasn't." I've been staring at this man all evening. If he had blood on him, I would've noticed.

"Maybe I cut myself."

He doesn't expect me to believe that, does he? "Grab your coats." I don't care how late it is, we are going straight to the physician and banging on his door until he answers.

Senan goes for his pint instead.

Is he mad? He is coughing up blood, and he wants to keep on drinking? That isn't happening.

I swipe for the glass, but he's faster, holding it just out of my reach. "Put the glass down this instant, or so help me, Senan Vale."

"Will you please stop overreacting?" he murmurs against the rim. "I am fine."

Fine, my foot. "One does not simply cough up blood unless there is something seriously wrong." That is how the wasting starts.

I can still remember the day my mother's decline began. She used to have this handkerchief with her initials embroidered on the corner; she took it with her everywhere she went. That day in the park, she started coughing and pressed the handkerchief to her lips until her fit stopped.

The fabric had been riddled with crimson speckles.

We need to get him to the physician straightaway. I should've pushed the moment I first heard him cough.

With a beleaguered sigh, Senan sets down the empty glass and collects the first coat from the stool between us, slipping his arms into the sleeves and buttoning it closed. Instead of putting on the others, he drapes them over his arm one at a time.

Where is his sense of urgency? Isn't he worried?

Perhaps I am overreacting, but the past has proven that I cannot do this on my own. I need him healthy and by my side.

Snowflakes twirl around our heads as we step into the night. The frosty breeze stings my cheeks, swinging the gas lamps hanging on either side of the pub's door. I head straight for the village square. It isn't until I reach the corner that I realize Senan isn't following me.

"I know I'm the one with the terrible sense of direction, but I'm pretty sure the house is this way." He swings his arm toward the curving road.

For once, his sense of direction is spot on. The problem is, we aren't going home. "You need to see a physician."

His hand falls to his side. "No, I don't."

I stalk back toward the man I love, anger bubbling inside my chest, warming me from the inside out. "Do not fight me on this. One trip to the physician. That's all I'm asking. He might have some sort of tonic for whatever ails you."

Huffing a sigh, Senan's head falls back, and he stares up at the dark clouds hiding the stars from view. "He doesn't."

"You don't know that. Now, come on." I tug his hand, but the stubborn man refuses to budge.

"Yes, I do. I went to see him while you were at work. What ails me cannot be cured by human tonics."

I want to ask what ails him, but the look of resignation on his face keeps me silent as his proud shoulders sink, curling in the same way they did the night the king stole his wings.

"I'm sorry, Allette. I'm afraid I won't make it to spring."

This must be a trick, some sort of twisted joke. My head starts to shake, and yet the words he speaks still find their way to my ears.

"It would seem my years of dusting have finally caught up with me," he whispers.

Not the wasting, then.

Something far worse.

Something that could've been avoided if only the king had left us alone. "You're not dying. I won't let you." I refuse to lose him. Do you hear that, stars?

I *refuse*.

"Technically, we're all dying. It just so happens that I'm going quicker than the rest of you."

"That's not funny, Senan." I can't lose him. "Isn't there anything we can do?"

Downy flakes settle on his hat and wool coat. "Your friend gave me the antidote, but the landing destroyed the vials."

"Which friend?"

"Jeston. In the pit, he was out of his head on barmite and started babbling about hallucinations and me not living until spring. He gave me the five vials I needed right before I escaped the castle."

He's known about his decline for... Stars, he's known for *weeks* and yet he said not a bloody word.

An ache so deep and cold spreads through my marrow, a whirlwind of despair twisting through my chest. Just when I thought we had found peace. Just when I thought we might have earned a bit of happiness.

The rough wool of my coat sleeve scrapes along my cheek as I try to clear these infernal tears from my eyes before they freeze. "Why didn't you tell me?"

"I didn't want to make you sad."

Of all the ridiculous reasons for keeping this secret, *that's* the best he can offer? "Well, now I'm sad *and* angry. How about that?" My hands ball into fists. I want to hit something. Hard. "You aren't allowed to leave me. I won't let you." When death comes for him, I will fight tooth and nail until the bastard takes us both.

Senan traps me in the cage of his arms, pulling me into him, stealing my fight. "It'll be all right."

No, it won't.

If only we knew what ingredients were in the antidote, perhaps the humans would have some equivalent.

Without knowing, my love is doomed.

Unless... "We must return to Kumulus." Then we could find Jeston and get some more antidote.

"Even with wings, I wouldn't bring you back. It's not safe. Besides, Jeston couldn't guarantee that the antidote would work."

"So that's it? You're just giving up?" I push him away, my boots slipping on a patch of ice as I stumble back. "Until the sun implodes and the stars no longer shine, *that* is what you promised me. Last I checked, the sun still rules our days, and the stars our nights." He spoke those very same words to me only a few days ago, when everything seemed so dark and dire.

Senan's hands fall to his sides, the picture of defeat as his glistening eyes meet mine. "I have loved you in this life and will love you in the next, whether there are stars or suns. But I'm afraid this is a battle we cannot win."

Eleven

SENAN

I know Boris isn't standing in front of me with glowing eyes and teeth sharpened into shiny white spikes, yet my adrenaline surges as if the saw in his hand, dripping blood onto the cobblestones, is about to cleave me in two.

I try to skirt back from where I'm sprawled on the ground, but my boots slip in the puddle beneath me, smearing water—

Wait. It's too red to be water.

Shit.

It's blood.

And it's *everywhere*, overflowing the edges of the portal like a river flooding its banks, rising higher and higher, sweeping my body away with the current.

Allette sprints down the alley, her arms outstretched as if she has a hope of reaching me from so far away. I try to scream for her to stop. To turn around. To save herself. But the blood rises to my chin. My mouth.

Thick, coppery liquid gushes down my throat, swelling inside my lungs, stealing my breath, sucking me beneath the surface. I thrash and kick, but there is no light to tell me which way is up. No surface with air waiting on the other side.

Hands clamp down on my shoulders.

Guttural screams flood my ears.

"Senan, wake up."

My eyes fly open, my vision swimming. Allette sits next to me on the bed, pale as the moonlight streaming through the window.

Another dream. That's all. Just another dream.

If it wasn't real, why can't I fucking breathe?

Warm liquid splashes across my thighs, dribbling down my chin onto my chest. The room spins like a kaleidoscope, colors and shapes drifting in and out of focus.

Those soft hands stroke my hair and caress my cheeks as Allette's terrified face comes into view.

Fresh red blood splatters across the stained sheets she has washed and changed every day this week.

Once my breathing steadies, she pushes off the bed and tugs down the ruined quilt, rolling it into a ball and throwing it into the corner with the rest of the soiled linens.

"I'm sor—"

She whips toward me. "Don't you dare apologize."

But I *am* sorry. So very, eternally sorry for what I've done to myself. To us.

The spark of hope that used to light her eyes has turned to golden ash.

If I'd known what a burden I would become, I never would have left the castle. "Go sleep on the sofa. Let me take care of this." As soon as the room stops spinning, that is. It's like I'm on one of those topsy-turvy carnival rides Kyff used to love so much.

Why won't it fucking *stop*?

"How do you plan on doing that when you cannot even hold up your head? Come on, let me help you onto the sofa."

I don't want to sit on the fucking sofa. "No."

"Now is not the time to be stubborn."

Funny she should speak of time when I have so little left. "When is the time, then? Next week? Next month? Next *year*? I'll be dead well before then, so excuse me if I want to be stubborn today. Now, get out."

"Senan..."

"Please, just get out!" I don't want her around when I'm in such a pathetic state. Don't want her anywhere near me.

Allette's short shift flutters as she drifts out the door like a ghost.

I hate myself for turning such a vibrant, promising woman into a specter.

I hate myself for so many things.

The door slams, rattling the sconce on the wall next to the chest of drawers filled with what little we own.

Hurting Allette is the last thing I want to do, but I cannot let these be her final memories of me.

I have only a handful of fond memories of my mother, like when she used to read to us at night or chase us through the nursery. The picnics she used to make us go on in the mountain park. The birthday parties she used to throw us.

The horror of seeing her waste away has eclipsed everything else.

Blood is all I can smell.

Blood is all I can see.

Right now, I'm not even sure I *want* to be alive.

My dry lips crack a little more with each trembling exhale. When I finally summon the strength to push out of bed, it takes forever for me to clear the sheets and the towels Allette placed beneath where I sleep to soak up excess blood. With the amount I cough up every day, it's a miracle there's any left in my veins.

The short pants I wore to bed aren't salvageable, so I change into a clean pair of trousers before stumbling into the bathing room to wash up in the sink. Water swirls down the drain, staining the porcelain a deep pink.

I am so fucking tired of fighting.

After rinsing the vile taste from my mouth and cleaning my

teeth, I step quietly into the living room to keep from waking Allette.

Only my girl isn't sleeping. She is glaring at me from the kitchen, the dark circles beneath her eyes making her look like an angry raccoon.

My beautiful, angry raccoon.

Her knuckles are white from strangling the limp dish towel between her hands. "You will not speak to me like that ever again, Senan Vale. I am your mate. You have given yourself to me, for better or worse, and I will not be pushed away."

"I'm sorry."

"No." She throws the towel onto the counter. "No more apologies, no more feeling sorry for yourself."

I think I've earned the right to feel a little bit sorry for myself.

"We need to find a way back," she says, as if returning to Kumulus would solve all our problems instead of creating more.

My head begins to thump, and it has nothing to do with the poison killing me. Pretty sure my will to live washed down the drain with all the blood.

"How do you propose we do that?" Even if I wanted to return to the fae realm, the moment we set foot in Kumulus, Boris will finish what he started. It won't just be my life on the line then; he will kill Allette as well.

I did this to myself; I deserve this fate.

My girl does not.

She needs to accept this reality like I have. "If you didn't manage to find a way back in almost half a decade, what hope do we have of making our way to a portal in the fucking sky?" It's not like some magical ladder is going to appear.

We're on our own.

Instead of wasting time and energy on something that will never happen, I need to focus on finding ways to help Allette survive when I'm gone.

Except I have no skills—unless you count fucking and baking the perfect cheesecake.

Neither of those is going to help us right now.

The way Allette crosses her arms makes her chest look delectable. Probably not the thing I should be noticing at present considering I can hardly stand, but if I expire here and now, there is nothing I'd rather be looking at.

"I used magic on the way down," she says. "Perhaps I can do the same on the way up."

"What about me?" I've tried everything I could think of since that hour we spent in the sun, but there isn't so much as a spark.

Even if I could access my power, fire does fuck all besides destroy everything in its path. My element certainly can't bring me to the portal.

"You'll wait down here," she says.

"Absolutely not." As if I would let her go on her own.

"You have no right to tell me what to do. If I choose to return to Kumulus, there is nothing you can do to stop me."

No sense arguing with her when she's like this. Better save my breath for when she feels like listening to reason.

Gods, I'm tired.

I cross to the living room and sink onto the sofa before she notices the way my knees wobble.

Allette eases down next to me, her voice breaking. "Don't you want to try?"

What is the point in trying when you are sure to fail?

"It's like you don't want to survive this," she murmurs.

"Of course, I want to survive." I want to build a life with Allette. To make her laugh for the next century. To see her belly swollen with our child. To become a father. To live and laugh and love with her as we always planned.

But wanting doesn't amount to much when fate is determined to fuck you over.

Her fingers capture mine, intertwining like the vines on my arms. "Then let's find a way back home together."

FREED FROM GRAVITY

It's fucking freezing.

What I wouldn't give for a bonfire right now. I'd be sitting smack dab in the middle, worshiping the flames as they consumed me.

But no.

Allette won't let us build a bonfire because someone *might* see us. As if there are any other fools outside at midnight in the middle of fucking winter.

I hate this realm and everything in it, except for the woman waiting in the middle of the standing stone circle.

I stuff my gloved hands into my pockets. "How did you do it before?"

"I don't know."

"Helpful," I mutter, hacking away at a snow drift with the toe of my boot. When I glance back up, Allette is glowering. At least I think she's glowering. It's hard to tell because no moon or stars light this night. It's like the gods have abandoned this realm altogether.

They must hate snow too.

She lifts her gaze to the sky. "I panicked, my adrenaline surged, and it just sort of happened."

My magic was always easier to call on with my adrenaline high. Maybe that's where we should start. "Then let's get your adrenaline up. I can think of one way that we will both enjoy." As a bonus, it would certainly warm us up.

Her chuckle is a puff of white. "You're not strong enough for that."

"If the day ever comes when I don't have the energy to fuck you, you have my permission to stab me in the heart."

"Senan, I need to focus," she groans.

Right. She needs to focus, and I need to—

Oh, wait! I don't need to do a fucking thing because I'm

useless. Might as well flop down onto the ground and let the snow drift over me until I'm buried in an icy tomb.

Seeing no other options, I do just that. At least the ground isn't as hard as usual. The way the white stuff hugs my body is kind of nice too. It's much more pleasant than the last time I laid in the snow. Probably has to do with the fact that I'm wearing four coats.

Allette laughs.

It has been far too long since I last heard that joyful sound.

I ease onto my elbows to find my girl with her arms splayed, snow swirling like a white cyclone around her, lifting her dark locks into the sky.

"You did it... Allette! You did it!"

Her smile flashes as bright as day when she turns to me. "I did it!"

How does she still have so much power? I tear off my glove and hold out my own hand, focusing on the part of my chest where I used to feel my fire, calling on my dormant magic, and—

Nothing happens.

No spark. No smoke.

Not a fucking thing.

Biting back a curse, I stuff my hand back into my glove. It's not like I could do anything with my magic anyhow. "Can you fly?"

I still don't want her traveling to Kumulus without protection, but I wouldn't be much help even if I could haul my ass up through the clouds.

She directs the cyclone toward the ground, disturbing the snow until her boots rest atop a patch of stiff grass.

Come on, Allette. If anyone can do this, it's you. "Make it lift you up."

"I'm trying."

"Try harder."

"I'm doing my best."

The hope spreading through my chest dies before it can do

any more damage. Sometimes trying only to fail is worse than not trying at all.

Still, I force a smile to my lips. "I'm so proud of you."

"Why? I couldn't even lift myself off the ground."

"*Yet.*"

Her hands twist together as she shifts her weight from one foot to the other. "Do you really think I can do it?"

"Allette Vale, I think you can do anything."

Twelve

ALLETTE

Murky light filters through the curtains as I snuggle deeper into Senan's embrace. I would love nothing more than to spend the day lying in bed, but there is a portal to reach, and I cannot possibly do that from beneath these covers.

Senan sleeps peacefully by my side, one heavy arm draped across my waist, his soft breaths fanning against my bare shoulder. It's too cold to be sleeping without clothes, but when your mate spends the entire night worshiping your body, putting clothes back on is the last thing you want to do.

I lift his arm and slip from beneath the covers. The floor is like ice beneath my feet. Although I add a log to the waning fire in the bedroom, it will take some time for the room to heat. I dress quickly, use the toilet, and bank the fire in the living room. Bundled from my head to my toes, I sneak back into the bedroom to check on Senan.

"I'm going to the stones," I say.

He smiles sleepily, his eyes remaining closed. "I might stay here."

That isn't like him. He never lets me go alone.

Perhaps it's for the best. All he wants to do is distract me with his kisses. Without him there, I'll be able to focus on the task at hand.

Outside, the wind whips into tiny tornadoes, tossing powdery snow into the air. Our footprints from the day before have been wiped away by the squall, leaving no trace behind.

The joys of living in the human world this time of year. Darkness brackets each day, with mornings beginning late and the light fading by early afternoon. We are trying to keep our hope alive, but everything is unraveling at the seams.

Curse this season and this precipitation and all the damn clouds blocking this realm's most vital resource.

When I reach the center of the standing stones, I plant my feet in the snow and hold out my hands.

My magic stirs.

A whisper.

Enough to swirl the flakes dancing through the air.

Closing my eyes, I focus on the heat sparking in my chest. The lies we've been told fall away like shackles, freeing me to access the power in my heart. I feel the moment my feet leave the ground but don't dare open my eyes for fear of losing control.

Today.

This *will* happen today.

I squeeze my eyes closed, stoking this fire with every wish and dream that still lives within me, refusing to let any of them die. When my lashes open once more, I can see the tops of snow-dusted trees.

It's going to work!

Smoke curls from distant chimneys in the village. The road on the far side stretches toward the next town over.

I can see it all.

Higher and higher I climb, up toward those clouds that conceal the way, not caring if a random passerby catches sight of me hovering mid-air.

I can do this.

I can do this.

I—

My magic stutters. Fades. Evaporates.

"No!" I scream to the wind, forcing the dregs from my fingertips.

I will not fall. I will not falter. I will save my love. Save us both.

A wicked wind slams into my spine, knocking me out of the circle, spinning me around and around.

Please. *Please.*

I call on my magic once more.

Only silence answers.

I start to fall, slipping through nothing, dropping faster and faster, hurtling toward the blanket of white far below, and slamming into the snow with a pitiful cry. The air evaporates from my lungs, and I lay there gasping, struggling to find my next breath.

When I finally do, each inhale feels like someone driving a dagger between my ribs. Tears freeze on my cheeks as I stare up at an endless sea of white and gray.

The wind whistling through the forest echoes like laughter.

Perhaps it was fool-hearted to believe that I had the power to traverse realms without wings.

What other choice do I have? Am I supposed to sit idly by and watch the man I love slowly pass away?

I feel so bloody helpless, fighting a battle we cannot win on our own.

Perhaps tomorrow will look more hopeful.

One thing is for certain, I won't be trying to fly again any time soon.

Bracing a hand against my sore back, I ease carefully to my feet.

Right now, all I want is to return to the house, strip out of these frigid clothes, curl up in bed next to Senan, and pretend today didn't happen. He'll be upset when he finds out I'm hurt and end up blaming himself. He does that far too often despite my constant reminders that the situation we are in is not his fault.

Each aching step is a slog, all the way back to the home we've stolen. When I open the door, the usual blast of heat that greets me is nowhere to be found.

Is it any wonder? The fire in the hearth has burned down to almost nothing.

I slip the gloves from my hands; my fingers have gone white from the cold. When I call Senan's name, he doesn't answer. Pain lances across my back as I bend down to untie my frozen laces and set my boots beside the hearth, adding a log that hopefully won't smother the few embers that remain.

"Senan?" Floorboards creak as I cross to the bedroom, my damp socks leaving wet footprints behind.

Senan hasn't moved since I left.

The night terrors seem to have abated, and the coughing has eased, which is a blessing for us both. His face, serene in sleep, is too pale. What I wouldn't give for a week of proper sunlight to restore us both.

"My love?" I cup his stubbled jaw, but he does not rouse. His hand tucked beneath his cheek is almost as cold as mine, which makes no sense since the fire in this room blazes as bright as the sun.

His bare chest is as still as the silence around us; his pulse flutters like a moth's wings.

"*No...*" He cannot die. Not today. "Senan, my love. Open your eyes." My thumbs trail along the thick sweep of his lashes.

Unlike the other times I've pleaded with him, his eyelids do not lift.

There is no smirk or smile or soft retort.

Silence envelopes us both, and the aching in my back is nothing compared to the agony in my heart as it disintegrates. I must get that antidote. There is no other option, no alternative.

I either save him today or lose him forever.

I stumble for the door, stuffing my feet back into my boots and racing outside, through the forest, through the snow, panic fueling every jagged breath.

Wind whips and tears at my dress, but I feel no cold.

I feel nothing at all.

Numb to the snow and the pain—everything but the unending emptiness in my chest.

The stones loom, and I swear I can hear the stars cackling from wherever they hide. I cry out to my power but no magic springs from my fingertips. The winds no longer answer my call.

This cannot be the end.

I won't survive losing him.

I fall to my knees, willing the cold to seep into my bones and take me too. To snuff out this cursed life of mine so that we might find each other beyond the veil. So that he does not have to cross into the unknown alone.

We've been damned in this lifetime, but in the next, surely, we will be allowed to love one another.

I swipe at the tears streaming down my face, but they keep flowing.

For Senan. For me. For the family we never created. For the years that have been stolen from us.

The ground shakes beneath my knees, a resounding thump echoing through the stones.

I squint against the harsh white backdrop, barely able to see through the blur of tears.

Before me stands a man with tanned skin, a strong jaw, and silver eyes. I know he cannot possibly be who I think he is because this one still has his wings, and yet he almost looks exactly like...

"Senan?"

The man comes closer, kneeling next to me in the snow. That's when I see the gold rings climbing the shell of his ear. His brow scrunches and eyes narrow as he glowers down at me. "Where the hell is my brother?"

Thirteen

SENAN

FIVE YEARS AGO

I used to wonder why they never put pillows on the chairs in the throne room. The king gets one to cushion his royal arse but the rest of us are left with awkward wooden slabs. Now I realize they're meant to keep us from falling asleep. Because if I was even the slightest bit comfortable, I'd be snoring away until this meeting ends.

Thank the gods for notebooks and ink pens. I was meant to be taking notes in mine but an hour in, my eyes started going crossed and I abandoned that in the pursuit of fine art. Since then, I've drawn a fawn with tiny white spots, a badger with black eyes, and an entire family of mice.

It's some of my best work, if you ask me.

I'm not the only one distracted.

Philip sits beside me, rag in hand, polishing the barrel of a short pistol. A gift from his father's brother's cousin or some shite like that. I stopped listening the moment he pulled the thing from its holster.

Then there's Rhainn. He hasn't stopped paying attention once. I'm not even sure he's blinking. By the time this meeting finishes, the notebook in his lap is going to be filled to the brim—and not with artwork like mine.

Philip's father Counsellor Windell and the rest of the king's jowly council have been yammering on and on about policy and foreign relations and some other topics that bring tears of boredom to my eyes.

Then there's Boris with his hideous crown sitting on his cushy throne, listening intently. He wanted Rhainn and me to wear our crowns, but I outright refused. I'd rather fade into the background than be stared at for wearing a magpie's dream on my head.

I wonder what Allette is doing. Gods, do I wish it was Tuesday. Instead, I have to wait another five days to see her again. Maybe I could find a way to sneak out early during tomorrow's meeting. Or skip it altogether.

I see a terrible stomachache in my future.

Normally, they'd be having this meeting in the privy chamber, but since we have representatives from the other kingdoms in attendance, there wasn't room. Thank goodness. The privy council chairs are even more uncomfortable than these.

The doors fly open, and a man stumbles in, not in fine robes and garments like everyone else in attendance, but in a pair of faded trousers held up by bright red braces. The shirt beneath is yellowed from age—or sweat, I suppose. Either way, between his clothes and the unhealthy gray cast to his skin, he stands out like a rabbit in a den of bears.

The whole place goes silent—which is no mean feat considering there are fifty-six men in here. I know because I counted them twice.

Two guards burst in behind him, their wings protruding from the backs of their silver leathers. The man doesn't fight when they take him by the arms and start to pull him out of the room.

Boris stands from his cushy throne, and even though I cannot see his face from behind, the anger in his voice is unmistakable. "What is the meaning of this?"

The turquoise-haired guard bows his head. "Apologies, Sire. It would seem this intruder managed to sneak in with tonight's performers."

"That is unacceptable, captain. Let's hope he isn't here to murder me."

The man's limp silver hair barely moves when he shakes his head. "N-no, Your Majesty. I would never dream of it. I only came to ask for your help."

The counsellors and foreign dignitaries exchange wide-eyed glances, murmuring amongst themselves.

Boris waves his hand, and the guards let go of the man. The Tuath takes a moment to right himself, smoothing his stained hands down his trousers. Why are his fingers so black?

"Help with what?" Boris asks.

The red-haired guard shoves the man between the shoulder blades. "Out with it."

The Tuath's hands shake when he begins to speak. "The foreman just announced they were closing the northern mines. I've worked there for fifty years."

Fifty years in one place? Sounds awful. Doesn't the man get bored? I've only been in here for a handful of hours and already I'm dying to escape.

"Then you must be thrilled to retire," Boris says.

"I'm afraid I cannot afford to retire, Your Highness. My wife Sarah has an awful case of gout, and the tonic to relieve her pain costs almost an entire week's wages. I was hoping to appeal to your giving nature for a few coins to get us through until I can find work."

Counsellor Windell pushes to his feet and leans close to whisper in Boris's ear.

Boris nods and then asks the man where he lives.

How is that relevant? The man is worried about his poor wife.

Redhead jabs him in the back again. "Your king asked you a question, Tuath."

"I live in the burrows, sire."

The room erupts in curses, and those closest to the Tuath push from their chairs, stumbling back as if the man is on fire and dragging their collars over their noses.

Windell pulls his robes over the lower half of his face as well, his enraged voice muffled by the silken material. "You live in the breeding ground of wasting sickness and you dare to bring your filth near your sovereign? Remove him at once!"

The guards drag the man out of the room, but he doesn't fight. He hangs his head, his hair falling like a curtain, hiding the shame on his face.

The meeting is adjourned so that the servants can clean every inch of the throne room in case the man was infected by the wasting. He appeared healthy to me—as healthy as any of the Tuath look with their gray skin and bulging eyes, anyway.

I abandon my notebook beneath my chair. My body sighs the moment my arse leaves the seat.

"That was exciting, wasn't it?" Philip says, tucking his pistol back in its holster as he trails after me into the hallway.

While I appreciate an interruption to the monotony, I feel sorry for the man. How desperate must he be to climb all those steps and infiltrate a meeting full of self-righteous Scathians simply to ask for assistance? "How sad that you find one man's tragedy exciting."

Look at all of us, rushing for the dining room where there will be more than enough food laid out for everyone in attendance while that man is probably trudging back down the thousand steps, empty-handed and without hope.

When I see my brother's crown glistening up ahead, I push through the others to where he and Counsellor Windell speak in low tones next to a bust of our late father. "Boris? Might I have a word with you?" Windell shoots me a glower. "In private," I add.

The last thing I need is that oaf's opinion on anything.

With a nod, Boris says, "I'll see you inside, Windell." He follows me to one of the many alcoves lining the wall and folds his arms over his chest. The stance used to be imposing back when he was a head taller than me. Now that we're eye-to-eye, it doesn't have nearly the same effect.

"What is it now, Senan?"

He doesn't need to be so snippy. I only have a question. If anything, he should be happy that I'm taking an interest in something that happened during the meeting. "If that man hadn't been from the burrows, what would you have done?"

Boris stands taller, his crown glinting in the sunlight streaming through the windows. "Where he's from doesn't matter. He gained access to the castle illegally—"

"To help his wife." I feel like that's a very important piece of information.

"His reasons don't matter. He broke the law. We were lucky he wasn't an assassin sent to murder us all."

Please, he was hardly going to murder *all* of us. "What if he had arrived on the fifteenth instead?" That's the one day of the month when Boris meets with the Tuath in the throne room.

"Then we would have listened to his woes and sent him on his way."

"How would that help his wife?" Anyone can listen. The man needed *help*.

"You are too soft," he mutters, scrubbing a hand down his jaw. "Beggars are like rats: Feed one and you end up with an infestation. If they thought we'd be willing to empty our coffers for them, there would be a line of beggars from here to Nimbiss. Now, if that's all, I'd like to have my dinner before getting back to work."

It's not all—not by a long shot. But when Boris is hungry, his mood tends to sour more than usual. Still, I must know, "What will happen to the man?"

"If you bothered to study the law, you'd already know." Boris lifts his eyes to the heavens, a heavy sigh passing through his lips.

"He'll either be fined or incarcerated. That's for the courts to decide." My brother starts for the dining room without a backward glance, leaving me to my chaotic thoughts.

Yes, the man broke the law, but only because he needed help for his sick wife. How will he pay a fine if he cannot even afford healing tonic? If he's thrown into the pit, how will his wife manage without him?

Is there any way to keep either scenario from happening?

There's only one way to find out.

Jogging toward the nearest balcony, I call on my wings and leap over the ledge, freefalling toward the downy clouds, plummeting beneath the cottony layer to the grayness that lurks below. By the time I land at the courthouse, I'm no closer to a plan. All I know is that I need to do *something*.

The guards from the castle wait in line with the man, his wrists clapped in manacles and head hanging in defeat.

"You there!" I really ought to learn some of these guards' names. "Guards!"

Both Scathians in silver twist toward me, their scowls almost as menacing as the swords at their hips. When they see me, their scowls vanish, replaced by wide-eyed confusion.

The one with the penchant for shoving bows his head. "Prince Senan, you shouldn't be here. If people recognize you, there could be a mob."

I'm willing to risk it. "I'll leave as soon as you let my friend go."

"Friend?" the other guard scoffs, glancing at the man in their custody. "You mean this Tuath beggar?"

"That is exactly who I mean."

The Tuath's mouth drops open. Does he not realize he should be playing along?

"But he's to be put on trial," the guards say in unison, as if they've been rehearsing together.

"And I'm saying he's to be set free. Consider it a royal pardon."

"Can princes pardon criminals?" the one with red hair says under his breath, as if I'm not standing right here and can't hear every word. The other guard shrugs.

Enough is enough. It's cold and damp down here, and I left without my cloak. The sooner I get back to the sun, the better. "Do you know what princes *can* do? We can have insubordinate guards thrown into the pit with no questions asked. I know that for a fact, because I've done it to three guards before."

Thankfully, my threat seems to do the trick.

One fumbles for the key, dropping it into a grimy brown puddle. The other picks it up, unlocking the manacles and freeing the man.

"Thank you both. You are dismissed."

The turquoise-haired guard reaches for me. "But we can't leave you on your own—"

The *audacity* of this one. I slap his hand away. "I said, you are dismissed."

Although they take off, they don't return to the castle, choosing instead to circle overhead. The people in the line have all turned around to stare at us.

This man has already suffered enough humiliation. He doesn't need these looky-loos gossiping about his plight as well.

I gently take the man by the elbow, leading him to an alley. "I want you to have this." I unhook my purse and hold it out to him.

In hindsight, I probably should have added more coins. How much do miners make, anyway? Hopefully this will be enough to cover his expenses and his wife's medical costs while he searches for work.

The man throws up his hands, slinking deeper into the shadows. "I couldn't possibly."

"Is what you said in the throne room true? Is your wife unwell?"

"Well, yes, but—"

"Then I demand you take the coins."

His hand trembles as he accepts the purse with a quiet word of thanks. "Why would you do this for me?"

Maybe Boris is right. Maybe I am too soft. Either way, I'm here and I refuse to stand by and do nothing when someone is hurting. I offer the man a smile and a clap on the shoulder. "Because anyone who climbs all those stairs up to the castle deserves a reward."

Fourteen

SENAN

NOW

It's snowing again.

I still hate the stuff but tonight there's something peaceful about how each cottony flake pirouettes through the air, stark against the backdrop of night like the stars I haven't seen in so long.

The cold isn't so bad anymore either.

At least it numbs the pain. After years of dusting, I'm accustomed to feeling nothing.

I could get used to this—

Fire rips through my flesh, engulfing my entire chest.

Get it off! Get it off!

I writhe in anguish, but the snow is too deep, a casket of ice and misery. I have no choice but to endure the suffocating torment, hoping it will end.

Knowing it won't.

A pair of glowing hands anchor to my bare chest. I follow the hands to their owner's face, but what I find makes no sense at all.

Not because I don't recognize the man shooting flames directly into my heart, but because I never thought I'd see him again.

My brother Aeron cannot possibly be here.

This is another hallucination. A dream.

The fire burns stronger.

A fucking nightmare.

"Stop!" I gasp.

Aeron removes his hands, and Allette leans over me, the dark strands of her hair falling like a shroud, shielding my face from my tormentor. "You're back," she whispers.

What does she mean, I'm back? I'm in the same bed we've shared for weeks. Where does she think I've been? More importantly—

I nod my chin toward the other person in the room. The one who doesn't belong. "Who the hell is that?"

Allette's hands fly to her pale cheeks. "Oh, stars. Senan, that is Prince Aeron. Your brother."

"That isn't my brother." Sure, he has the earrings and the scowl, but Aeron isn't in the human realm. I left him in Kumulus.

"He doesn't recognize you," Allette says in a wobbly whisper. "Do you know who I am?"

"Besides the most beautiful woman in the world? You are my Allette." Hers is a face I could never forget. I twist my head toward where my brother waits, silhouetted by the window, his arms folded and mouth flat. "But that man is not my brother. Aeron was always the handsome one, the strong one. This weak, weasel-faced person is no relation of mine."

"How can you make jokes at a time like this?" Allette scoffs.

Nothing like death to put a few things into perspective.

Aeron's eyes narrow into slits. "If you weren't dying, I'd kill you."

My brother always did love idle threats. "Go away. I refuse to have your ugly mug be the last face I see." I smile up at my girl, hating the tears glittering on her cheeks but too weak to wipe them away.

Her shaking hands curl against my bare chest, ice cooling the fire that continues to burn beneath my skin. "Stop that talk right now. You're not going to die."

If only she could share some of that hope with me. This poison infecting my veins hasn't gone anywhere. It's still coursing with each beat of my slowing heart whether Aeron is here or not.

"We have a way home," she says.

Do we? Right now, all I have are more questions than answers. "Why is he here?" Aeron shouldn't even know we're alive, let alone where to find us.

Aeron's scowl deepens. "I'm here because I need your help. Minister Donnell abducted Kyff and locked him up in Nimbiss castle. Their king refuses to hand him over until we return their princess."

That fucking prick.

And I thought I hated Donnell before.

I plant my hands on the mattress and force myself upright. Even sitting on this damn bed, I still feel as weak as a kitten.

How the hell could Boris let this happen? Why wasn't our baby brother protected?

Aeron swallows thickly. "If Princess Leeri is not returned by the end of the week, Nimbiss will declare war on Kumulus."

Gods...

What if Aeron is lying? What if he's using this information to manipulate me into returning to Kumulus? Boris used Kyff's well-being far too often to force me to do his bidding. Who's to say this isn't one of those times?

"How do I know we can trust you? That you're not working for Boris?" Everyone seems to be working for Boris nowadays. The king's influence is like this poison, invisible but spreading, tainting everything it touches. He could've gotten his evil claws into Aeron in the weeks I've been away.

Aeron's hands flex into white-knuckled fists at his sides. "Do you honestly think I could ever forgive him for what he stole from me?"

"You don't have to forgive the bastard to be blackmailed." Look at me. I didn't want to marry the princess, but I did anyway because Boris held Allette's life in his corrupt hands.

We need to remain vigilant.

"I haven't been blackmailed," he says. "Boris doesn't even know I'm here."

Maybe. Maybe not.

Aeron grips the back of his neck, his features painted in frustration. "Look, I held up my end of the plan that night, brought the gold to the inn, and drew as many guards as possible so you could escape. When I returned to the castle and found out you'd gotten married instead, I realized something must've gone terribly wrong. I know how Boris works, the way he controls everyone like fucking puppets." Blowing out a breath, his hand drops once more. "A friend showed up to my door two days later. He told me what the king did to you."

So much for keeping my downfall a secret.

There's only one person who would have such intimate knowledge of my whereabouts. "Bilson."

With a nod, Aeron continues his fantastical story. "Boris obviously wouldn't confess to what he did, and with the princess missing as well, he had no choice but to lie to everyone. He told them that you and your new wife left for your honeymoon and had plans to arrive in Nimbiss the following week. Minister Donnell kicked up a fuss but couldn't refute the word of a king. Meanwhile, the guards have been scouring the city for the woman. Until today, there have been patrols watching the portal day and night in case whoever took her tries to abscond with her to this realm."

Until today. What changed?

Aeron grimaces. "I went to wake Kyffin for breakfast this morning and found a note saying Nimbiss took him as retribution for losing their princess. They issued an ultimatum."

From his pocket, he withdraws a piece of parchment and drops it onto the bed next to me. A broken wax seal bearing the Nimbiss crest clings to the folds.

My body begins to shake as I read the damning words.

Nimbiss stole my baby brother, and Kumulus has seven days to locate the princess or there will be war.

"Boris ordered our fastest men to the border to see if they could catch Donnell before he reaches Nimbiss. Almost all the others have been called to arms and are headed north. It's mayhem up there and there's so much fucking confusion. I saw a gap in the guard and took my chance."

While I appreciate the risk he took and the fact that his healing magic might have saved me from death's door, one part of this still doesn't make any sense. "What do you expect me to do about it?" Even if I wanted to help, I'm wingless, powerless, and *dying*.

Aeron sinks onto the end of the bed. "You are the last person to see the princess alive. I thought maybe you would have some idea of where she might be. We're desperate, Sen. Can you think of any details that might help us locate her?"

...see the princess alive.

Gods, what if she *is* dead? What will Nimbiss do then?

What if we never find her at all?

I close my eyes and scour my memories from that fateful night. Memories I've tried to forget. "After the wedding, the king locked us in my chambers. Leeri insisted on consummating the relationship right away. I used a vial of stardust to incapacitate her."

Aeron slams a fist into the mattress, narrowly missing my leg. "What were you *thinking?*"

"I was thinking I never wanted to marry the woman in the first place!" He knows all about being forced to marry against his will. If he were in my shoes and saw an out, he would've done the same fucking thing.

My brother shakes his head, the veins near his temple pulsing. "How did you escape?"

"The servants' stairs. A friend added my blood to the enchanted register so I could cross the wards." I shudder to think of what would have happened if Jeston hadn't come to my aid. If he hadn't given me the first vial of antidote, I could be dead already.

Hold on—

"I wasn't the last person to see the princess." *Fucking hell...* "Jeston was." That's it! He must know what happened to her. I reach for Allette's hand. "How much do you know about your friend?"

"Not much at all, I'm afraid," she says with the smallest shake of her head. "His uncle used to be the House Master before you sacked him. Oh! And he has another uncle who owns The Black Hole."

I'm not sure if any of that information is very helpful, but at least it's a start.

Aeron pushes to his feet. "So, if we locate this Jeston fellow, we might find the princess."

Allette rises as well, her voice so full of hope. "And when we find the princess, they'll release Prince Kyffin."

Maybe it's the weight of imminent death, but I find it difficult to share their optimism. What if we get caught crossing through the portal? What if we make it to Kumulus but spend the next week searching for Jeston to no avail—sealing both my fate and poor little Kyff's?

Nimbiss won't keep him indefinitely.

When a fae kingdom declares war, they send a member of the enemy court to the rival castle's gates...in pieces.

Fifteen

SENAN

Looks like I have a one-way ticket back to Kumulus inside an old trunk. If I wasn't so fucking wrecked, I'd be humiliated.

Everything we own has been packed into two rucksacks. My love helps me tie my boots, and my brother assists me with my coat. If I survive this whole ordeal, I will be in for quite the earful from him. As it stands, he doesn't waste time with reprimands, instead keeping his disapproval between buttoned lips as he waits for me to finish.

The plan is for him to bring me up first in case we only have one shot at making it through the portal. I am the one dying, after all, and Allette is more than capable of taking care of herself in this realm.

It's all shit if you ask me.

"Aeron? Can you give us a moment? I want to say goodbye."

Goodbye.

The word sounds so final; I hate the taste of it on my tongue.

He huffs like I'm an inconvenience, but twists for the door. Once he's gone, I take both of Allette's hands in mine, darting a glance back at the entrance to ensure we're alone. "I'm still not convinced that he can be trusted. For all we know, we could be flying straight into a trap."

I realize that if Aeron wanted to betray me, he could've brought an entire army with him through the portal. Still, one can never be too cautious, especially where one's mate is concerned.

"The moment we leave, I want you to hide in the attic. When he comes back for you, I'll instruct him to call you Allette Vale if it's safe. If he doesn't use that exact name, I want you to stay hidden until he leaves and then run the first chance you get."

Her lower lip starts to tremble as tears fill her eyes. "Senan..."

"Please, Allette. I cannot bear the thought of something happening to you. Promise me."

Her fingers tighten around mine. "All right. I promise."

The thought of leaving her behind, of returning to Kumulus on my own, wreaks havoc on my withered soul. If only we had another choice.

Allette leans forward, pressing her lips to mine.

She tastes of sorrow. She tastes of farewell. "I will see you in a few hours," she murmurs.

Although I return the sentiment, I sincerely hope it isn't a lie.

I CRADLE MY PACK IN MY ARMS AS AERON AND I MAKE our way to a clearing near the house. I tried putting the thing on only to abandon the idea when the strap hit what's left of my right wing. "Where will we go when we reach Kumulus?"

Aeron doesn't bother glancing at me as he lugs the empty trunk across the snow. "There's a small village on the Direc, near the bay. Shouldn't take more than thirty minutes to reach."

With guards on high alert for the missing princess, staying outside the city is the smartest move. The Direc River is the official border between Kumulus and Aeron's kingdom, Stratiss, an ideal hideout if you ask me.

He drops the trunk onto the ground, and the lid falls open. "Come on. In you go."

Puking blood all over myself night after night isn't nearly as mortifying as having to fold myself into a musty old trunk that he found in one of the back bedrooms.

His black wings appear from between the slits in his jerkin. Does he realize how lucky he is that our brother left him whole? Does he appreciate the freedom his wings afford?

"You're loving this, aren't you?" I grumble, sinking down, clutching my knees to my chest and flopping on my side. The way I have to contort my neck hurts like hell.

"Yes. I love the fact that my brother has all but killed himself and now I am forced to carry his sorry ass." Aeron flips the lid closed, encasing me in darkness. I hear him stomping around, fastening the clasps.

"You're a sorry ass."

His muffled chuckle makes me want to punch him. "You mustn't be well if that's the best comeback you have."

The trunk bobbles as he hoists me into the air. Hopefully, he doesn't end up dropping me in the river and saying good riddance.

Whose idea was this, again? I've changed my mind—

The force of his takeoff plasters me to the wood. I feel each pump of his wings as we climb higher and higher.

This is fine. Everything will be fine.

I'm not going to die. We're going to find the princess and the antidote and live happily-ever-after.

"Deep breath," Aeron roars over the sound of beating wings.

Black liquid floods through the keyhole. I press my thumb to the lock, so I don't end up drowning in starlight. Someone shouts, and my brother responds with a deep bellow.

A short while later, the trunk hits the ground, rattling my bones. My heart pounds as I wait to see what awaits me outside this box. For all I know, Boris could be standing over the trunk, ready to run me through.

The lid flips open.

When I dare to stick my head out, I find only Aeron and his scowl waiting in a dark alley. Wooden homes rise on either side, the windows covered in cobwebs.

It's all a bit anticlimactic if you ask me.

Then again, what sort of threat would a dead man be to the king?

A grave one, if I have my way.

A cold, fishy wind drifts over me, turning my stomach. The air down here tastes like licking seaweed—fucking revolting.

Aeron helps me to my feet, keeping a hand on my bicep. "Can you walk, or do I need to carry you?"

"Fuck off. I can walk just fine." I mean, my leg is asleep, but I'm not going to tell him that. The pins and needles will eventually subside.

When I try to take a step forward, my dead leg doesn't get the message, and I collapse into one of the stone walls.

"Just fine, huh?" Aeron hoists me upright, this time refusing to let go despite my protests.

We emerge from the alley and end up right next to a stall selling salmon, the disgusting creatures flayed atop a bed of ice, their eyes bulging and mouths gaping.

A few Tuath mill around, their cloaks and coats pulled tight to their necks to stave off the dampness clinging to the pungent air.

The inn he brings us to is green—and not from paint, but from mold. The sea's damp air rots everything it touches, from the buildings to the boats docked in the bay to the people themselves.

You must be a little mad to live next to the sea.

Give me a quiet mountaintop chalet over these squatty homes any day.

Of course, this is the Tuath part of town. The Scathian homes would be made of thick plaster and painted white, with roofs a thousand shades of blue where they sun themselves.

Aeron keeps his steps slow as we traverse the slick, knobby cobblestones to the inn's front door. The interior bustles with men in knitted caps who look like they've been formed from barnacles and brine.

A man with skin the color of slate greets us with a stern nod, standing from his stool and hobbling forward. When he gets closer, I catch a glimpse of a peg leg protruding from beneath the hem of his trousers.

Fascinating. How high up does it go? How did he lose it?

Probably a fish.

Aeron nods toward the row of bronze keys hanging on hooks behind the desk. "I'd like a room for two, please."

The man's gaze shifts past Aeron to me. The longer he stares, the more his eyes narrow. "What's wrong with 'im?"

Rude.

My attempt at a smile ends in a grimace as sweat breaks across my brow.

Aeron clamps a hand on my shoulder, giving me a bone-rattling shake. "My cousin drank a little too much down at the pub and needs to sleep it off."

At least the lie explains my swaying. Are we on dry land or the sea?

A cough suddenly tightens my chest. I try to swallow it down but end up spluttering into my coat instead. Of course, my luck is shit and the man sees all of it.

His jowls shake as he tucks his nose and mouth into the collar of his shirt. "Get out, the both of you. I'll not have the wasting infecting my patrons."

I don't have the fucking wasting.

"He doesn't have the wasting," Aeron says.

"You'll not play me for a fool, sir. I know the wasting when I see it."

I've seen the wasting too, and it is nothing like what's killing me. For one, I'm upright. Once the wasting strikes, its victims are on their backs for the rest of their too-few days.

"He's a duster, all right? It's the stars that are killing him."

Nothing like coming right out and saying it. I'm too fucking wrecked to be embarrassed. Besides, everything he said is the truth.

Aeron jabs me in the ribs. "Show him."

Show him what?

My brother taps his palm.

I hold up my hand so the man can see the scars I've put there. The innkeeper still doesn't look convinced until Aeron unfastens his purse and tosses it onto the desk, jangling the coins inside.

Damn, that sounds like a lot of gold.

Aeron braces both hands on the edge of the desk, his voice dropping to a low, lethal tone. "For your hospitality...and your silence."

He can be an intimidating bastard when he wants to be. Growing up, it was annoying because he always used it to get his way. Right now, though, it's awfully handy.

The man swipes the purse and opens the top; his mouth drops open like one of those fish from the stalls. "Room 204," he says, still fixated on the purse as he fumbles for one of the keys and slides it across the desk to us. "It's yours for as long as you need it."

It always amazes me how quickly people are willing to turn a blind eye if you throw enough gold at them.

Aeron thanks the man and braces my arm across his shoulders like we're about to dance a reel. The smart comments on my tongue remain unsaid as he hauls most of my weight up the stairs.

The truth is, I'm grateful that he put himself in danger for me. Because of him, I have a chance to live. A chance I don't plan on squandering like I did the last time.

He props me against a doorframe at the far end of the hallway and sticks the key in the lock. The door swings open, the room smelling surprisingly fresh. I stagger forward, my feet catching on each other right before I flop onto the bed. With a muttered curse, Aeron drags off my boots, rolls me over, and tucks the blanket around me.

"I'm going back for her," he says.

For a second, I consider asking him not to bring Allette here.

Consider telling him to pack up as much gold as possible and leave it on her doorstep so that she can be safe.

But the thought of betraying my girl cuts me in two. If the past has taught us anything, it's that neither of us do very well when we're apart. "She's hiding."

Aeron's eyebrows climb toward his hairline. "Why?"

"I didn't know if you were leading us into a trap."

"I would never—"

"I know." I do now, anyway. "When you reach the house, shout for Allette Vale."

He turns and starts for the door.

"Oh, and Aeron? This place is shocking. I expected more from a prince of the realm."

His chuckle, followed by the sound of the key in the lock, are the last sounds I hear as my eyes sink closed. I drift off, praying I don't die without knowing whether or not Allette is safe.

Sixteen

ALLETTE

TWO MONTHS AGO

"This wine is terrible," I say for what feels like the hundredth time. It's important for Braith to understand just how terrible it is so that she knows how good of a friend I am for drinking it with her.

I bring the mug to my lips and take another awful sip.

"It's dreadful," she agrees, gulping from her own mug. "But it's not my fault. Iver gave it to me as a birthday gift."

"Ohhh, *Iver*. Who is he and why is this the first time I'm hearing his name?" Is he a former lover? A childhood crush?

"Gross. He's my older brother."

Not exactly the scandalous story I was hoping for. "I didn't realize you had a brother."

"I have three, actually. Iver and the twins. And two sisters as well, Regina and Lettie. When they found out the castle hired me, Lettie bought me a paint set, and Iver gave me the wine. He's as cheap as they come, though. He probably found the bottle in an alley."

When I peer into the deep purple liquid, my distorted reflection stares right back. "Tell me we're not drinking alley wine."

Braith tilts her mug from side to side, her brow furrowed as she considers. "We might be drinking alley wine."

Oh, well. At least it gets the job done. I raise my mug and so does she.

"To new friendships," I say.

"And terrible wine," she adds.

We clink our mugs together and then take another drink.

How does it keep getting worse? Oh, well. It's not as if we have anything else to drink.

Braith's nose wrinkles as she sniffs the wine. Lord Windell used to do the same thing at dinner. Made him look like a pretentious prig.

"I'm detecting notes of…" She inhales again. "Mold and rat."

"As do I." Channeling my inner Windell, I sip, swish, and swallow. "And there's a bold, crunchy texture. Could it be shards of broken glass?"

"Absolutely. Everyone knows the best alley wine contains plenty of glass."

"So much glass."

We sip between giggles and sip and sip until our mugs are as dry as the wine bottle.

When I've drank the last drop, heaviness settles in my chest, and my eyes start to burn. "Mine's empty." How tragic.

"Mine too," she says with a frown.

"Now I'm sad." I don't want the night to be over.

"So am I."

"Although, now that it's all gone, we don't have to drink it anymore."

"Good point," Braith agrees. "I've never tasted anything quite as revolting."

Another giggle bubbles up inside me. How did I get so lucky to find a friend as wonderful as Braith? When I lean down to set my mug next to the bottle, the room starts to spin.

Drinking so much on an empty stomach probably wasn't the best choice. Not that there's anything I can do about it now. When was the last time I had this much to drink? Stars, I can't even remember. Whose idea was it to open the alley wine, anyway?

With a gasp, Braith grabs either side of my face and pulls my cheeks back as far as they'll go. "Wynn! Your teeth are purple!"

They are? Wait! "*Your* teeth are purple too!"

We erupt into a fit of giggles, gasping and falling back on Braith's small bed. Between spending time with Senan and Braith, this might be one of my most favorite days ever.

I blink up at the ceiling, my heart full to bursting. The mural she painted reminds me of the garden where my prince and I spent the afternoon rediscovering each other. The memory of that picnic is one I'll always cherish.

Braith's finger digs into my arm. "You have that whimsical look on your face. Does that mean you're daydreaming about a certain prince?"

"Perhaps." How can I not? "He's so perfect." When I think of Senan, my heart feels as if it's ready to burst.

Braith snorts. "No man is perfect. Except maybe Jeston."

Please. I can list at least ten of Jeston's flaws here and now. "Jeston is an ass." He and I might have come to an understanding, but that doesn't mean I like him.

"You don't know him like I know him."

Thank the stars for that.

"I'm telling you here and now, Jeston Warnick is the most handsome man I've ever met," she goes on.

I don't see it. Is he handsome? Objectively, maybe. If you're into men with gray skin and terrible manners, that is. But the *most* handsome? Not by a longshot. "I'm sorry, but how can you say that when you've met *the* Senan Vale?" I still cannot believe what transpired only a few hours ago. It feels as if I'm floating on a cloud of happiness.

Then again, that could be the alley wine.

Braith's nose wrinkles. "Senan spends too much time in the sun."

"He does not! You take that back."

"Never. And his black hair is boring."

"It is not! It's regal and beautiful and so thick." If I close my eyes, I can still feel my fingers running through the inky strands.

"I prefer my males with silver hair."

"Good. Because I don't intend to share Senan."

She chuckles. "Except with his wife."

The smile doesn't just slip from my face. It shatters.

How easy it is to forget reality when drowning in alley wine. "He's not married yet," I say, my throat tight as a fist. And if I have my way, he never will be.

Braith takes my hand in hers. "Of course, he isn't. I'm sorry. I meant it as a joke."

"I know."

But that doesn't change the fact that one day, Senan Vale will no longer be mine.

Seventeen

ALLETTE

NOW

Dusty floorboards groan under my boots as I duck beneath the cobwebs clinging to the exposed wooden beams. More webs straddle the rungs of a rocking chair missing an arm.

There's enough broken furniture in Mae's attic to furnish another cottage. It's a variable treasure trove of antiques up here.

The wind wails against the rooftop, singing a haunting and lonely song.

It's difficult to say how long I've been up here. Enough time to go through three trunks of old sheets and quilts and moth-eaten gowns. None of them are salvageable, which is a pity. It would have been nice to find something new to bring back with me.

I've just opened the fourth trunk when the unmistakable sound of footsteps drifts from below. I hunker behind a stack of old books covered in dead flies and listen.

Aeron's deep voice pierces the silence. "Allette?"

My stomach sinks all the way to my toes.

He's not supposed to call me that. Does this mean something happened to Senan? Did Aeron bring him to the castle and hand him over to Boris? Did he even bother bringing him to Kumulus at all? Maybe he murdered my love in the forest and has spent the last hour burying his—

"Allette Vale!"

I stand too quickly, thumping my head against one of the low-hanging beams. *Ouch.* "I'm up here!" I call back, rubbing my sore skull as I pick my way between two chairs and a bedside table.

I kick open the trap door and ease the ladder through the gap. Aeron appears on the floor below, frowning up at me.

"Is Senan all right?" I ask, carefully lowering myself down the ladder to where he waits. With my boots on solid ground, I take a moment to brush the dust from my skirts. Too bad I don't have a clean dress to change into.

"For now," he says, stomping down the stairs to the dark living room.

"What does that mean?" I have to take the stairs two at a time to keep up.

He catches the front door and throws it aside. A terrible wind screams through the gap, stealing my breath. "It means we need to get that antidote. So, if you would kindly hurry up, that would be wonderful."

What an ass. Would it kill him to be kind for once?

I thought perhaps he'd been in a sour mood the night I met him in the castle. Apparently, misery runs through his veins.

I collect my pack and cloak and step into the dark night where the empty trunk awaits. I hate that my first instinct is to search inside for signs of blood. There aren't any, thank goodness. "Is the trunk really necessary?" I wouldn't call myself claustrophobic, per se, but I've never been a lover of tight spaces.

"Get in, Allette."

Fine.

I shove my pack into his chest and then step inside. How did

Senan fit into this cramped box? Even with folding myself as small as possible, I still barely fit.

Aeron knocks the lid closed without a warning, enveloping me in musty darkness.

I'm coming, Senan. Hold on a little longer.
I'll be there soon.

The trunk bobbles as he lifts me up. "Hold on."

Hold on to what? There's nothing in this bloody trunk but me—

The intensity of his takeoff plasters me to the bottom of the box. I force my breaths in through my nose and out my mouth, doing my best to forget where I am and where I'm going. That if the king finds out we survived, the poison will be the least of our worries.

Senan is all that matters.

I'm doing this for *him*.

To save him. To be with him. To reclaim the life that was stolen from us.

The higher we fly, the louder the wind blows, howling like a feral beast. "Hold your breath!" Aeron bellows.

I take a deep breath right as black liquid starts to gush through the keyhole. I press my hand to the lock to stem the flow.

Outside the trunk there's an ear-splitting *crack*.

My body slams into the lid. My stomach drops to my toes.

It no longer feels like I'm flying...

It feels like I'm falling.

Inky starlight gushes through the lock. I try to cover it but there's too much and it's too slippery and—

It's not just coming from the lock. By my feet is a giant, gaping hole.

Starlight floods around me. Reaching my knees. My chest.

"Aeron! Hurry!" I bang my fist against the trunk as starlight closes around my neck. "Aeron!"

Why can't he hear me? I have to get out of here; otherwise, it's going to swallow me whole.

I maneuver my body so that my legs are pressing against the lid. I kick and kick and kick. Hoping and praying and cursing and—

The lid flies open.

My eyes burn as I blink into nothingness, blackness pressing me from all sides, sliding like oil over my sink. I throw out my hands and start kicking for the surface but there's no telling which way is up—

Something clasps my ankle, dragging me in the opposite direction.

I emerge from the portal with a gasp, flopping onto the hard cobblestones and staring up at Aeron's face as he chokes, starlight weeping down his face and wings.

What in heaven's name just happened? "Did you *drop* me?"

"Not on purpose. The fucking handle broke," he rasps.

So that was the crack I heard. Stars above... I press my hand to my heaving chest, willing my heart to slow. "I nearly drowned."

Rolling his eyes, he holds out his hand. "But you didn't, did you?"

No, thank you, asshole. I smack his hand away and push to my feet. There's no longer any sign of the liquid starlight.

Aeron straightens. "If you're finished being dramatic, we should go."

Since when is almost dying being *dramatic?* The sooner Aeron returns to his own kingdom, the better.

The ignorant prince takes off for one of the alleys, not bothering to check if I'm following. I do, of course, because I have no clue where we're going or how to get there. Two minutes later, he comes to a sudden halt in front of a short gray building with a black door barely clinging to its hinges.

I could've sworn Aeron said he was bringing Senan to an inn. This doesn't look like an inn. The windows are nothing but rotting boards and broken glass.

He twists the handle, easing the door open with an ominous

creak. There isn't any furniture in the room inside, and the floor is nearly as dusty as the attic I left behind.

"What are we doing here?"

"Waiting."

I thought time was of the essence. We need to find Jeston. "For what? What have you done with Senan?"

"Don't worry. My brother is safe."

"Forgive me if I don't take your word for it." The words barely leave my lips when the door opens once more, and a man in silver leathers prowls into the room.

My lungs seize, and I'm drowning all over again; not in starlight, but in terror.

Eason?

No... No...

How could Aeron bring me to *him*? Senan was right. We never should have trusted his brother.

The man stalks closer, stepping into a shaft of light breaking through the wooden slats. He can't be Eason because Eason is dead.

My relief is like a gasp of fresh air. "*Bilson?*"

Senan's former guard inclines his head. "Hello, Allette."

Aeron clears his throat. "Enough pleasantries. Bilson, I need you to bring Allette to the inn I told you about. You remember the one?"

"Yes, Sire."

Hold on. That wasn't part of the plan. "Why can't you bring me?"

Aeron's jaw works, like he's chewing on his disdain for this world and everyone in it. "This may come as a shock to you, but your wellbeing isn't my top priority. Right now, I need to return to the castle and sort out this shite with Jeston."

Bilson turns toward the prince. "You mean the new House Master? What do you want with him?"

"He has something I need."

Bilson's chestnut hair falls across his brow when he shakes his head. "But, Sire, Jeston isn't at the castle."

"Where is he?"

"If the rumors are to be believed, someone in his family passed away. All I know for certain is that he's been given three weeks of personal leave and an interim House Master has been appointed."

"Dammit." Aeron rakes his hands through his hair. "Can't one fucking thing go right?"

Now he knows how I feel.

He blows out a breath before stalking toward me. "Do you know where Jeston lives?"

"I'm afraid not."

"We don't time for this. If we cannot find him, all hope is lost."

How can he think I don't understand the gravity of the situation? I have been living this nightmare ever since Senan told me the truth of his fate.

The fact of the matter is, we are pinning all our hopes on a chance.

Even if we do find Jeston, he might not know what happened to the princess. He might not be able to get more antidote.

All of this could have been for *nothing*.

Not that I say as much aloud.

Is there anything at all that I can remember about Jeston? He has two uncles, but I already told him that. Let's see... Braith thought his neck smelled good.

Wait! That's it!

"I have a friend; her name is Braith. She and Jeston were close. If anyone would know where he is, it's her." At least I hope so.

"Wonderful. Do you know where your *friend* lives, or am I going to have to hunt her down too?"

Would it kill Aeron to use a kinder tone? We're all at the end of our tethers; that doesn't give him the right to treat everyone like shite. "She lives in the caverns beneath the castle. She's one of the servants. We were both hired at the same time. I trust her with my life."

"Good for you," he mutters. "Bilson, bring Allette to the inn, and I'll speak to the servant."

"Her name is Braith."

Aeron bares his teeth. "I'll speak to *Braith*."

"I'd watch your tone if you expect her to cooperate. She doesn't like most Scathians, and she likes them even less when they're self-important pricks." I turn my back on him and start for the door.

I've had enough of this prince and his rotten attitude.

Eighteen

SENAN

I wake to Allette beside me, her soft exhales tickling my bare chest as she watches me through heavy-lidded eyes. Is this a dream? If so, I hope to never wake.

She smiles and shifts closer, her arm draped across my stomach squeezing tighter.

This is real. *She* is real.

"When I promised to bring you to the seaside, this is hardly what I had in mind," I whisper, my mouth dry as sand.

"I think it's quaint," she says with another sleepy smile, snuggling closer.

She would find the silver lining in this dark situation. What would I do without her?

Her lips trail kisses across my chest, up my throat. Even on my deathbed, my body stirs for her.

"As much as I'd love to take this further, my brother could return at any moment."

"He won't be back for ages. He stayed in Kumulus to search for Jeston."

"How did you get here, then?"

"Bilson."

At least one of my guards turned out to be a decent male. I

pull my love so she's draped over me like a blanket. "Have you been here long?"

"I don't know. I fell asleep the moment my head hit the pillow." Her fingers trail along my ribs, spreading chills across my abdomen. "What do we do now?"

I run my finger down the slope of her neck to the strap of her shift. If Aeron isn't coming back... "I can think of a few things."

She smacks my chest playfully. "I meant after we save your little brother and get the antidote."

Oh, right. Let me see...

Returning to this realm was never part of the plan, so I haven't thought about what would happen if we ever found ourselves back here. "We cannot stay in Kumulus."

"I know."

"We're right on the border with Stratiss. I imagine Aeron would welcome us into his kingdom. That might be our best option." The farther we are from Boris, the better.

"As long as I'm with you, I don't care where we are in this realm or any other."

I know exactly what she means. Happiness can be found anywhere if you're with the people you love. I'll have Allette by my side and be able to meet with Aeron from time to time. Rhainn would keep my secret, and perhaps at some point in the future I could even see Kyff again.

Assuming Aeron manages to find Jeston and the princess.

I don't want to think about that right now. Not when my girl is in my arms. I need something positive to keep me going. "If you could live anywhere, where would you choose?"

"Let me see," she muses, a smile in her voice as she tucks her cool fingers beneath me. "What about a house on the coast where we could walk along the cliffs and listen to the waves?"

That sounds terrible.

Being so high up without a pair of wings to catch us if a gale knocked us off the cliff? No, thank you. But if it's what my girl wants, I will do my best to make it a reality. There are plenty of small coastal villages in Stratiss that would make perfect hideouts. Who knows? If I manage to get some sunlight, perhaps I'll even regain access to my magic.

Allette and I make plans as though we have time, as though the entire world isn't about to come crashing down on our heads. Plans that cease when my stomach decides to embarrass me with a guttural howl.

"You must be starving." She throws the coverlet aside, revealing long, bare legs that I'd love to have wrapped around me. "I'll find us something to eat."

As famished as I am, I say, "I'd be more than content to have you for breakfast."

Her bubble of laughter is as effervescent as her smile. "Says the man who can barely lift his head."

I tap my fingers against my smirking lips. "Sit down right here, and I won't have to move at all."

"Senan Vale!"

I love it when my girl acts scandalized, but I can see that wicked mind of hers working. "Get yourself some breakfast and we can try it out."

Laughing, she throws a plain gray muslin dress over her shift and slips on a pair of stockings with her worn boots. When she leaves, I hear the turn of the key in the lock, as if she's keeping me locked away, her very willing prisoner.

Turns out I don't mind being caged nearly as much when Allette is my jailer.

Ten minutes later, my girl returns carrying two plates laden with sausages, bacon, and ham—basically an entire pig's worth of breakfast, along with eggs and thick-cut toast.

I give the closet and chest of drawers a cursory glance. "Do you have more men hidden in here that I'm not aware of? That's enough food to feed an army."

"Very funny." Her skirts billow when she sinks down next to me. "You've been so picky lately; I wanted you to have options."

I've only been "picky" because the food in the human realm

never had much flavor. The smell of all that bacon grease is making my mouth water.

We eat as if we haven't been fed in months, washing it all down with a bottle of wine.

Allette dabs her lips with the corner of her serviette, peeking at me from beneath her lashes, and then glancing back down at our empty plates, a delicate pink stain washing over her cheeks. "So... The position you mentioned. How does it work?"

My girl has been thinking about my proposition while we dined, has she?

My body stirs, and although I still don't feel quite like myself, I'm not going to let a little thing like being on the brink of death keep me from missing an opportunity to show her this.

"I lay down nice and comfortable, so you have no worries about me straining myself. Then you spread those pretty thighs on either side of my head and feed me your delicious cunt."

She launches her serviette at my head. "You have the wickedest mind."

"You have no idea." If she knew all the positions I'd love to have her in, the ways I long to take her, she'd probably keel over.

With her cheeks and neck the color of a blush rose, she twists her hands in her lap. "Wouldn't I smother you?"

"What a way to go."

She smacks my shoulder far too hard, clearly forgetting that I am a dying man. "You're mad."

Mad about her.

Now that this is on my mind, I can't seem to get it out. "What if I tell you that it's my dying wish?"

She lifts her eyes to heaven. "You're not going to die."

I will if Jeston cannot acquire the antidote or if the antidote doesn't work. Not that I say any of that aloud. Wouldn't want to piss all over her garden of hope.

I reach down to adjust myself in my trousers. The more I think about it, the harder I get. This is the perfect way to distract ourselves from the direness of our situation. I slide a hand down to her ankle, then slip it beneath her skirts, tracing and trailing until I reach the lace along her undergarments. "Should we take these off? Just in case."

She lifts her hips, allowing me to slide the fabric down her thighs, all the way to her ankles. Once her undergarments are gone, I help her straddle my hips. "That's my girl. Now, get up here and grab the headboard with both hands."

Slowly she complies, her face the perfect shade of pink as she climbs higher, until her skirts fall around my neck. "Up you come. Lift onto your knees."

I grip her skirts, gathering them so I can slip beneath, urging her higher still, until her knees are on either side of my head. "Sit down."

"I don't think—"

"I said *sit down*." I grip her backside with both hands and drag her onto my face. A moan eclipses her gasp when I fasten my lips around her clit and drench my tongue in her slick heat. *What a way to go* is right. This is exactly what I needed, to taste her. To consume her. To fuck her with my tongue.

The way she grinds herself drives me to the brink. I match her pace, licking and sucking and losing myself. Soaking in her heat. Her scent. Her taste.

Not only my dying wish, but my living wish too.

All my wishes from now until forever.

To have this, to have her, to bring her to the edge of climax, teasing, tasting, pulling back when her thighs begin to tremble against my head. Smiling against swollen flesh at her frustrated curse before going back for more. Harder. Faster.

"Senan..."

She's close. Teetering on the edge. Tipping over. Falling.

Squeezing. Pulsing. Fracturing.

Drenching.

I continue working her until she falls way, rolling off me onto the mattress, gasping.

I drag my sleeve over my mouth, the sweet taste of her still clinging to my tongue. "I can die happy now."

"You think I'll let you die after that? You've never been more useful to me."

Two quick raps on the door interrupt my retort.

Wide, golden eyes fly to mine. "Who is that?" she mouths.

I haven't been out of this bed since arriving however many hours ago. How am I supposed to know? "I don't know."

"Should I answer?"

The person knocks again. Harder.

"Probably." They must have the wrong room.

She whips her undergarments from the bed and steps into them on her way to the door. Over her shoulder, she hisses for me to hide. My stiff cock barely fits beneath these covers—how does she expect me to hide? I suppose I could stuff myself into the closet, but it's all the way over there.

I flop onto my back and draw the covers over my head, listening to her bare feet pad across the creaky floorboards. The lock gives way, and she gasps. "What are you doing here?"

Nineteen

ALLETTE

The woman on the other side of the door is the last person I expected to see, especially outside Kumulus City. What the hell is Braith doing here?

Braith launches herself at me, throwing her arms around my shoulders, sending me stumbling back. "I cannot believe it! I thought for sure he was lying."

I pull the door closed behind me and step into the hallway. "Thought who was lying?" What is happening?

She draws back with a grimace. "Prince Pleasant."

Aeron stomps up the stairs, his favorite scowl contorting his features. "That's rich coming from you."

"I am perfectly pleasant to people with manners," she shoots back.

As far as I can tell, Aeron doesn't have any of those. Didn't I tell him that Braith wasn't fond of pretentious assholes? Was it really that difficult to pretend to be nice for one bloody conversation?

"You see her," Aeron mutters. "*Now* will you tell me where Jeston is?"

Braith plants her fists on her hips, glowering right back at him. "That depends. Are you going to tell me why you need him?"

Despite the delay, I love her even more for being so loyal that she wouldn't give over Jeston's whereabouts to Aeron simply because he's a prince. "We can trust her." Braith would never betray me.

Aeron scrubs a hand down his neck, his gaze imploring. "I don't think—"

I don't care what Aeron thinks. He doesn't know Braith like I know her. I trust my friend more than I trust "Prince Pleasant." I throw open the bedroom door, take her by the hand, and drag her into the room.

Senan waves at us from the bed, a smile on his face.

Braith lets out a squeal and leaps back. "Heavens above." Her hand flies to her chest. "I thought the prince was off on his honeymoon."

Senan's smile fades.

Braith's fingers strangle mine. "What's going on, Wynn? Last I saw you, they were hauling you off to the pit."

"It's a long story, and I swear I'll tell you when there's more time. Right now, we need your help finding Jeston. Senan isn't well. We need a very rare fae medicine to heal him. The king thinks he's dead so we cannot let anyone at the castle know."

"And you think Jeston can help?"

"He managed to find us the antidote the last time. We need him to do it again."

Braith whirls on Aeron, her eye blazing. "That wasn't so hard, now, was it?"

Aeron sneers at her.

He is such an ass. It's a wonder he and Senan are related at all and a miracle that he came to our rescue. From what I've seen of the man, he hardly seems capable of empathy.

"*Now* can you tell me where to find Jeston?" he grits through his teeth.

Braith offers him a saccharine-sweet smile. "I'll do you one better. I'll bring you to him myself."

One more piece of this intricate puzzle falls into place. Here's hoping Jeston will come through for us as well.

Aeron suggests leaving straightaway, but the poor man looks like he's ready to fall over. I insist he eat something first, and then try to rest for an hour or two. It would do us no good for him to fall ill before we can find Jeston. Plus, that gives me time to catch up with Braith and hear all about what happened with Prince Pleasant.

Such a perfect name for Senan's brother.

Aeron stalks back out into the hallway, taking the key with him and locking the door.

"What a prick," Braith mutters with a shake of her head.

"I'm sorry. I told him to be nice to you, but I'm not certain he knows how."

"He definitely doesn't."

A moment later, the door flies open, and Aeron slips inside, his silver eyes wild. "There are royal guards downstairs. At least six of them."

My blood runs cold.

Cursing, Senan stumbles to his feet. "You must've been followed."

"I wasn't."

"Then how do you explain a bunch of fucking guards downstairs? Do you suppose they're on holiday? Visiting the seaside for a bit of relaxation?" Senan grabs his shirt.

We don't have time for arguing. We need solutions. "The two of you can bicker later. What are we going to do?" The window in here is too small to climb out of and the only other exit leads to the hallway. Six guards are far too many to fight off, especially with Senan at death's door. Our best bet is to throw them off our scent. "Even if they followed Aeron, that doesn't necessarily mean they know why he's here, right?"

Senan and Braith both nod while Aeron stands there like a scowling plank.

"So, all we have to do is convince them that he's here for something besides hiding us." Then they'll leave, and we can go find Jeston.

"I can think of one reason Aeron might visit the bay," Senan says with a pointed look at his brother.

Aeron's jaw pulses. "No fucking way."

"If they believe you're here for *that*, they'll not bat an eye."

Must these men be so damn cryptic when time is running out and our lives are at stake? "Here for what?"

Senan finishes tying his laces and reaches for his coat. "This village has a reputation for its brothels."

That could work. "We can convince the guards that he's here for pleasure." A good plan—at least I *hope* it's a good plan because it's the only one we have.

Senan nods. "You and I can hide in the closet while Braith and Aeron—"

"Just a minute. You want me to pretend to share a bed with *him*?" Braith scoffs, backing toward the door.

Sneering, Aeron crosses his arms over his broad chest. "As if they'll believe I came all this way to rut with *you*."

"Scathian pig. You would be so lucky."

Aeron bares his teeth, looking far more likely to bite off her head than kiss her.

An ear-splitting bang explodes from down the hall. Screaming erupts and men shout.

The king's guards are coming, and if this doesn't work, we're doomed.

"Please, Braith. I am begging you. I would offer, but one of them might recognize me from the portal."

Although her eyes narrow at Senan's brother, she bobs her head with a curt, "Fine."

Jaw flexing, Aeron starts unbuttoning his shirt and taking off his boots. "Fine."

Senan and I dart into the tiny closet, but instead of closing the door, he suggests leaving it ajar, making it less likely for the guards to come and inspect it. Aeron tosses his shirt onto the floor, and Braith's overskirt follows a second later. Senan drapes them across our legs and feet as we press our backs against the wall.

"You're squishing me," Braith mutters.

"I am not," Aeron growls back.

"Don't put your leg there."

"Quit harping."

Senan and I cling to each other, scarcely breathing as our only hope continues to squabble and bicker in harsh whispers like an old married couple. More shouts echo from down the hallway, growing louder and louder until—

The door bursts open.

Braith's scream tears through me, and I have to press my hand to my lips to keep from crying out.

"What is the meaning of this?" Aeron roars.

A man clears his throat, his voice trembling, "Sire, we...I..."

"Spit it out," the prince demands.

"We are here under the king's orders."

"What is so important that the king interrupted the leader of a foreign nation in his own bedroom?"

"You must forgive my intrusion."

Senan goes stiff as the walls around us. I recognize the droll voice from the night at the portal.

The king is *here*.

"It appears my sources have been misinformed," Boris drawls. Boards creak. Men mutter. Boots shuffle.

What sources? We didn't meet anyone besides Bilson at the portal, and if he betrayed us, the king would know for certain why Aeron is here. What reason would anyone have to follow Aeron from the castle?

"What the fuck are you talking about?" Aeron doesn't sound the least bit cowed by his brother's presence.

"Is that any way to speak to your king?"

Poor Braith. I sincerely hope she still considers me her friend when this is all over.

"She's a pretty little Tuath," Boris says. "If you want to know what real power feels like, I'll be more than happy to show you once my brother is finished with you."

What a bastard. I don't care if he is the bloody king. He has no right to speak to her like that—to anyone.

"Get out, Boris."

And I thought Aeron sounded angry before. He sounds downright murderous now.

The men stomp out of the room, and the door closes with a resounding *bang*.

There's shuffling outside the closet, and the springs in the mattress groan. Senan and I wait for Aeron to collect his shirt and Braith's skirts before emerging. They both refuse to meet our questioning stares as they don their clothes in silence.

When I offer to help Braith with the laces on the front of her dress, her hands drop. Her flushed cheeks are the only color on her face. "I am so sorry. I had no clue the king would be here—or that he would speak to you so abominably."

Her soft sigh fans across my cheek, her gaze flicking toward Aeron. "It's hardly the worst I've heard."

Aeron yanks on his laces, his eyes narrowed at his boots. When he finishes, he crosses over to the far wall and draws the curtains aside, peering out into the murky gray. "The guards have taken up posts outside."

Of course they have. Heaven forbid they make something easy on us. "How are we supposed to escape now?" We might be safe for the moment, but we cannot stay here forever. Not when Boris is already suspicious, and the clock is ticking.

Braith fluffs her hair, freeing the ends from where they were caught inside the high neckline of her wool gown. "I know a way."

Aeron rolls his eyes. "I'm sure they're watching the back door too."

"I never said we were going out the back, did I, you pillock?"

"Where?" I ask, hoping to stop their bickering before it starts again.

Braith's small, mischievous smile gives me more hope than I've had in a long time. "Come with me and I'll show you."

Twenty

ALLETTE

The floors in this inn are far too creaky. Each time one of us places a foot down, it's like a bloody siren wailing. My heart pumps like mad in my chest as we make our way down a tight, turning stairwell to the bustling kitchens. Braith, the angel that she is, went down ahead of us to clear the path.

Workers stop dead to gape at us. Do they know the princes' true identities? Do they suspect? Aeron glamoured his hair a dull copper and they both have their hoods drawn, but their stature alone might give them away.

Senan's breaths come in ragged gasps, but he refuses his brother's offers to help him walk. Stubborn, prideful man. I love him, but right now I could throttle him.

Through the kitchens we go, into a storeroom filled with sacks of grain, potatoes, and root vegetables. Braith waits with a key, her expression sullen as she watches us enter and tells Aeron to close the door. He grumbles about being given orders but follows them all the same.

"What you are about to see is never to be spoken of," Braith says in a whisper. "I want you to swear it to me."

My nerves settle like sediment in my chest. "I swear."

Once the men repeat the vow, Braith turns to the shelf, grabs the corner, and rolls it toward us, revealing a wooden door. After unlocking the door, she hooks the key on a nail fastened to the outside of the frame.

The area on the other side of the door is black as pitch. Braith presses a stone on the wall, and orange fae lights illuminate the tiny space. The term tiny is generous. The men will have to walk sideways to fit their shoulders through.

"Ready?" Braith asks with a gleam in her eyes.

I'm not sure what I'm agreeing to, but I follow her, descending into a damp basement where water weeps down the walls, blackened from time and moisture. It smells as if the sea itself is seeping through the mottled stone floor. A few colorful curses later, Senan and Aeron reach where we wait at the edge of the lit path.

Braith presses another button that switches off the lights above and behind us, illuminating instead another five or six fae lights along a slanted path angled downhill.

After ten minutes of walking, we emerge in a cavern as large as the one beneath Kumulus Castle. Like the castle caverns, there is a river. The only difference is that, in this river, there are boats.

Braith climbs into one, offering me a hand to help me board as well. Aeron follows, but Senan remains on the shore, looking downright terrified.

"What is it?" Braith asks after a glance around at the boat.

Senan swipes his hands down his thighs. "I don't like the water."

Aeron chuckles. "He's afraid of fish. Always was. Used to be terrified of baths as well."

"I'm not afraid of fish," Senan shoots back.

"Come on, my love. You can sit beside me." I pat the wooden bench. "I won't let the mean fish get you."

He takes my hand in an iron grip, squeezing until my fingers go white. "Sure. Make fun of the dying man. That sounds like a wonderful idea."

The poor man really is scared; I probably shouldn't poke fun. "I've got you," I whisper.

Before Senan can settle, Aeron rocks the boat, and my love screeches, throwing his arms around me, clinging tightly. Aeron's booming laughter echoes across the cavern.

I suppose the man can smile, after all.

Senan's death grip slowly loosens, but he doesn't fully let go. "I'm going to fucking murder you," he says to his brother, shooting him a deadly glower.

"I'd love to see you try."

These two. Honestly. Do they ever stop goading each other?

Aeron takes a seat on the back bench, between two oars. "Whoever owns this boat won't be very happy about us stealing it."

Braith lets out a heavy sigh. "Fear not, Prince Pleasant. The boat belongs to my sister. I'll send word and have my brother return it by the weekend."

Senan chuckles, and Aeron kicks him in the shin.

"I swear, if the two of you don't stop rocking the bloody boat, I'm going to throw you both out." I might not fear fish, but it's cold down here, and if they end up capsizing us with their antics, I'll be the one doing the murdering.

With the princes properly cowed, Braith explains that the underground waterways lead just about anywhere in Kumulus you'd like to go.

Still clinging to me, Senan peers over the side of the boat. "I didn't know these waterways existed."

Braith unhooks the thick ropes and uses one of the oars to push off the bank. "You have your ways to get around and we have ours."

A good point, to be sure. We never would have needed the river if Senan and I could still fly.

Aeron insists on taking the oars from Braith and rowing himself. Although she rolls her eyes, I catch her gaze drifting toward Aeron's biceps on more than one occasion.

Perhaps she doesn't dislike him as much as she lets on.

Not that there is any hope for them. He is married to the Princess of Stratiss and they are expecting their first child together.

Still, I suppose there is no harm in looking.

Speaking of looking, even unwell and marginally terrified of water and fish, Senan's countenance seems brighter than before. Each stroke of the oars brings us another step closer to healing him and saving his brother.

My prince's head drifts to my shoulder, and he promptly falls asleep.

Braith nods toward Senan. "What's wrong with him?" she mouths.

This doesn't feel like my story to share, but Braith already knows about Senan's struggle with stardust. When I tell her, understanding lights her eyes.

"There's been a lot of talk lately about tainted dust," she says. "Some believe they poisoned it on purpose."

We were always taught that stardust could be lethal—mostly because it can make you hallucinate and do reckless things. But to think of someone making it deadlier on purpose is abhorrent.

What about all those people who don't have access to the antidote? Who is going to save them?

Aeron nods toward a split in the river. "Which way?"

Braith gestures to the lower cavern of the two, where a bunch of stalagmites shoot up from the dark water. "Left, then when it splits again, take a right." Braith leans toward me, bracing her elbows on her knees. "How are you handling things?"

Honestly? I don't even know. The last few days have been such a whirlwind, I'm only now beginning to think straight. "It's been rough."

Her hand falls to where mine twist together in my lap. "I'm so sorry to hear that, but I'm glad you're back. The castle isn't the same without you, and Jeston has become an unbearable prick altogether."

He was always a bit of a prick, if you ask me.

"The night they took you, we were all down in the caverns and may have had a little too much to drink. I did what you said, told him that he should kiss me, and he did."

"You did not!"

"I did."

"Well? How was it?"

The boat jerks as Aeron steers us around an enormous stalagmite, barely missing the thing.

Braith shoots him a stern look before leaning closer to me. "It was good, but...I don't know. It felt like there was something missing. I've been dreaming about kissing him for so long and I didn't even feel one spark."

"Maybe he isn't the one for you." Personally, I think she could do so much better.

"Maybe. Regardless, everything fell apart that night. First Mari, and then you being hauled away. Then Jeston met with the king and has been a different man ever since. After meeting the bastard myself, I can understand why." She shudders.

Wait... the king already met with Jeston?

If that's the case, Boris must have asked about the princess's whereabouts. Did Jeston lie or does he not know what happened to her? And if he doesn't know, what the hell are we going to do?

"Is there any news in the caverns regarding the Princess of Nimbiss?" She might have heard some detail that seemed innocuous at the time but could point us in the right direction.

"Just that she and Prince Senan left for their honeymoon—which was clearly a lie. Beyond that, I haven't heard any gossip. Then again, I'm not assigned to the family's tower, so maybe one of the other maids has more information."

Where could she have gone? People don't just vanish into thin air.

The king has been looking for weeks and has countless resources at his disposal. What makes us think we can do any better?

No. I refuse to go down that rabbit hole. We need to remain positive.

We *will* find the princess. We *will* save Senan and Prince Kyffin.

We *will*.

I give Braith's knee a reassuring squeeze. "I am sorry things didn't work out with Jeston." Hopefully, we'll get a chance to speak a little more on the matter without an audience.

Braith shrugs and says, "Fate doesn't care about what we want."

THE CAVERN'S LANDSCAPE CHANGES WITH EVERY NEW passage. Fae lights guide our way like shining stars, the ones beneath the water making the surface glow a beautiful turquoise. We fall into an easy silence. Senan's even breaths. Aeron's labored. The steady swish of the oars meeting the water. Other boats pass, their occupants offering friendly nods or the occasional wave, but everyone seems to be minding their own business.

Eventually, we reach a cavern larger than the one we first left, with docks lining both shores and colorful boats bobbing atop an underground lake.

Braith leaps onto the dock with the rope in hand, pulling our boat until it bumps into the post and tying an intricate knot to keep the thing from floating away.

I wake Senan with a small shake.

He blinks at me with a sheepish smile, swiping a hand across his jaw. "Sorry for falling asleep. I hope I didn't snore."

"Only a little," I tease. "I'm glad you finally rested." He slept more peacefully than he has in weeks. "You'll be pleased to know I didn't see one fish."

Aeron stands and stretches his arms toward the ceiling. "No fish, but there were a few eels. Big, slimy ones."

I smack the bastard's knee. "Stop that right now."

Senan cups my chin, his eyes still glazed with sleep. "Don't worry, my love. I will get my revenge when he least expects it. Aeron has an awful habit of falling into Toxicodendron."

"You mean you have a habit of putting it in my fucking bed," Aeron grumbles.

Braith waits on the dock, hands on hips, watching the princes through narrowed eyes. "You two act exactly like my brothers—and they're fifteen."

I must agree—not that I have any brothers to compare them to. Although it's nice to hear them teasing each other. To see Senan smiling again.

"Where are we now?" my prince asks on a yawn.

Braith points to the far wall. "The entrance to the burrows is through there."

I'm not sure what I was expecting, but it certainly wasn't a gate carved into the reddish-brown stones. Twisted vines and whimsical woodland creatures line the arched entryway, as fine as any of the sculptures I saw at the palace.

"You expect us to go into the burrows?" Aeron scoffs, making no move to climb onto the dock.

Braith folds her arms across her chest, her eyes narrowing into slits. "That's where Jeston is."

"Then you can go in and get him for us."

"Oh, can I?"

"Yes."

My legs tingle from sitting for so long. When I stand, I press a hand to Aeron's shoulder. "Calm down."

"You expect me to calm down? This madwoman wants to bring my ailing brother to the breeding ground of the wasting."

"*You're* a breeding ground of wasting," Braith shoots back.

Senan chuckles, seeming unbothered by the rising tension. Am I the only person with a level head today?

"What Prince Pleasant is trying to say is that we have heard the burrows are infected with the wasting," I say. "And with everyone living in such close quarters, it might not be safe for Senan."

Braith's grin returns. "You shouldn't believe everything you hear."

Twenty-One

SENAN

THE BURROWS ARE...BEAUTIFUL.

Cramped, yes. Small, certainly. But they're homey and quaint and far more practical than having to fly half a realm for dinner.

Each home has been built around stones, dirt, and the roots of trees, boasting circular windows fashioned from bent willow branches. These abodes do not insist; they follow the lay of the land, blending in with nature instead of trying to stand out.

As far as I can tell, there doesn't seem to be any sickness here, which makes no sense. We've always been taught that the wasting spreads quickly when living in close quarters. These are some of the closest quarters I've ever seen and yet everyone looks perfectly healthy.

Pale and gray, all right, but laughing and smiling and going about their days as if there is no place they'd rather be.

How many times have I heard it preached that the Tuath are jealous fae, that they would overtake our towers in a heartbeat if given the chance?

No one here appears jealous.

If anything, I am jealous of them.

The children run freely from one house to another, kicking a leather ball in the dirt streets. There is more joyful laughter in these caverns than I have ever heard in the halls of Kumulus Castle.

Unlike in Scathian towers, isolating and tall, these neighbors greet each other with conversations about more than the weather or the latest fashion at court.

The Tuath have created a beautiful life here in the ground, with no sun and no magic required.

Allette's dark curtain of hair sways as she turns in a slow circle, golden eyes scanning the dwellings built into the ground. "This is stunning."

"It is," I agree, relief settling in my bones that we won't be fending off the wasting while we're searching for Jeston. Not sure my body could handle much more fighting.

Aeron looks angrier than usual, and I think I understand why.

We have been lied to, not only about the source of our magic but also about the Tuath themselves. They're not helpless and desperate to serve in our towers. They appear content.

"Come on. This way." Braith waves for us to follow her up the incline, toward where the bulk of the houses have been built. Every single person who passes us stops to speak with Braith, asking after the young woman's mother and father and so many other names of what I assume are either siblings or cousins that I can barely keep track.

They look at us with interest, but not malice, which makes me like every single one of them. Up the hill we go, past a pub and apothecary, a bakery, and a cobbler.

Who knew such a haven could exist beneath the ground?

The home where Braith stops is the same as all the others except for the green holly wreath nailed to the red door. "Mum? Dad?" she calls, throwing the door aside.

We follow Braith into a cramped living room with a sofa, a worn wing-back chair, and a bevy of large pillows tossed haphazardly in front of a stone fireplace.

A portly woman with cheeks as rosy as the berries on the holly wreath bobbles out of a small kitchen. "Oh, Braith, my girl.

What brings you home—" Her gaze lands on us, and her jaw drops.

I wish Aeron would stop scowling for once and try to look amiable. We need these people to help us, not hate us.

"Is that Braith I hear?" A man's deep voice rumbles from a hallway to our right. The moment he sets foot in the living room, he stops dead, the book in his hand tumbling to the ground.

"Mum, Dad." Braith steps forward cautiously, taking Allette's hand and pulling her closer. "This is my friend Wynn. The one from the castle, remember?"

"It's so good to finally meet you, Wynn," says the older woman, although her gaze is still bouncing between my brother and me. "I have heard such wonderful things about you. Our Braith was so worried when they took you away. Such an awful thing to happen."

Allette's open, friendly smile seems to set Braith's mother at ease. "It was awful but ended up being a terrible misunderstanding."

With a deep breath, Braith reaches for Aeron. Although he scowls down at where she grips his wrist, he steps forward. "And this is my friend... Terrence."

Ha! Terrence! Brilliant. Looks like *Terrence* is not impressed by the sudden name change.

Come to think of it, he kind of looks like a Terrence.

Braith turns to me. "And this is—"

"Simon," I say, holding my hand out to Braith's father before she can come up with some terrible name for me like Anton or Filben.

The older man takes my hand with obvious reluctance, giving me the slowest shake in the history of fae kind. "It's nice to meet you, Simon." He nods to Aeron. "And you, Terrence. What brings you to the burrows?"

"They need to speak to Jeston," Braith says. "Have you seen him?"

"I saw him with his aunt this morning," Braith's mother

answers, bending down to collect her husband's book with a groan. "Poor Cynthia. She's in an awful way after losing her Glenn. Such a tragic tale. You know, Glenn Warnick used to be the House Master at Kumulus Castle. What am I saying?" She takes Allette's hand, giving it a sympathetic squeeze. "You worked there, of course; you already know about him getting fired. Anyway, that's when the drinking started, you see."

Braith's father shakes his head. "Josie, they don't need to hear the man's life story."

Josie pays him no mind, continuing as if he hadn't interrupted. "As I was saying, the only place hiring were the mines on the other side of the river—you know the ones. They're not nearly as stable as the ones my Harold oversees here on the eastern bank. *Anyway...*" She takes a deep breath—which is a good thing since her face is starting to turn blue. "My sister's husband's best friend Leonard told her that Glenn was drinking on the job, got lost in one of the ancient shafts, and the roof collapsed right on his head. Killed him stone dead just like that." She snaps her fingers.

At least now we know who to ask if we need any information. Gods, this woman could talk down a stone wall.

"That is tragic," Allette says with a somber nod, shooting me a meaningful glance.

I should feel guilty for my role in the man's downfall, but he brought this upon himself the moment he raised a hand to my girl.

However, this could pose a bit of a problem in convincing Jeston to help us find my missing wife.

"So tragic," Braith's mother agrees with a sniffle, dragging a finger beneath her dry eyes. "We're on our way down to the house now if you'd like to extend your condolences."

"They don't know Cynthia, Mum," Braith says with a sigh. "Can you ask Jeston to come here when he's finished? I'd like to speak to him without an audience around."

The older woman's smile lights up her whole face as she pats her daughter's cheek. "I'm sure he will appreciate that, my dear. I know how close the two of you have always been, and sometimes grief brings us even closer."

"Josie..." Braith's father pinches the bridge of his nose, the ghost of a smile playing on his lips as well.

Braith goes rigid as a post, her expression slipping into a grimace. "Would it be all right if my friends stayed here for a few days? They're only passing through."

Aeron's head whips toward her. If looks could kill, Braith would have expired on the spot. She blinks innocently at my brother like he's an adorable puppy instead of a snarling wolf in a cage.

Makes me like the woman even more.

"Oh, we wouldn't want to impose," Allette says, her hands twisting as she falls back next to me.

"It's no imposition at all," Braith's mother assures. "Simon and Terrence, you boys can stay in Evan & Vaughan's room. My twins are away for their first year at Devin Academy, you see. The house feels so empty without them."

It's been a long time since we were referred to as "boys." I sort of like it. Makes all the trouble that comes with being a "man" feel a little further away.

"Devin is a good school." No wonder she looks so proud. Although I wasn't aware they opened enrollment to Tuath. Good for them. Segregation is such an archaic and asinine practice. Why it still exists in this day and age, I'll never understand.

"It really is," Josie agrees. "Wynn, you can have Lettie's room. She won't be coming back here with the new baby for a little while. My first granddaughter—of many, I hope."

By the time Josie finishes speaking, I feel like I need another nap. Braith urges her parents out the door and then ushers us down a dark hallway that smells suspiciously like cabbage.

The last thing I want is to share a room with my brother, but I say nothing out of respect for these people who have so kindly given us refuge.

Braith opens a door at the very end. Here I thought this might not be comfortable.

Boy was I wrong. There are bunk beds attached to the wall! I've always wanted bunk beds.

"I call top bunk."

Aeron shoulders past me, tossing his pack onto the top mattress. "Fuck off with that shite. You're younger, so you're on the ground."

"That's hardly fair. I called it first."

When I go to grab the knobby wooden ladder, the prick slides it out of reach so he can climb up instead. "Stop acting like you won't be sneaking down the hall to your mate every chance you get. At least this way I won't have to listen to you going up and down the ladder all fucking night."

A valid point. Wonder where Allette's room is? Must check it out when I get a chance.

Like the other rooms in the house I've seen, this one is small but cozy. Blue quilts on the beds, a matching rug in the center of the stone floor, and two desks along the far wall beneath two round windows. Someone painted the ceiling to resemble the night sky, complete with golden stars that look like they're made of tiny crystals and a crescent moon. As stunning as the mural is, the constellations are all in the wrong places.

I throw myself onto the bottom bed. The mattress is a little firm, but I can make it work. When I'm tired, I can sleep anywhere. One time, I fell asleep in the middle of dinner. Granted, I was about four or five, but still. "I like it here."

Aeron snorts. "You would."

I kick the underside of his bed, biting back a laugh when he curses. This is going to be fun. "What's that supposed to mean?"

"It means you live in a fantasy world where you think what we want matters."

"I wish you'd stop grumbling for two minutes and admit you like it too." I saw the want in his eyes as he took in the simple furniture. This isn't a tower, nor is it a house. It's a *home*.

A home in a nice cozy hole.

"I'd like you to shut the hell up so I can sleep. Some of us didn't take a nap."

As if he'll be in a better mood when he wakes up. He's as grumpy in the mornings as he is in the evenings. He could sleep for an entire day and still wake up like a briar.

I give the top bed another kick. "What does your wife think of all this?"

"You think I told my wife? I haven't seen her since I came to town for your wedding. And before you call me a heartless bastard, I did send word that I would be staying to help with diplomatic relations. She's busy decorating the nursery and probably doesn't even realize I'm gone."

How...sad. What should be the most joyous time of his life, and he talks about it as though he couldn't care less. No doubt, if I were stuck with Leeri, I'd feel the same.

Silence falls between us, and I try to close my eyes, but they keep popping back open.

It's cold down here.

I miss Allette.

I bet she misses me too.

I roll off the mattress and consider doing something to my now-snoring brother, but figure he's earned a reprieve since he saved my life.

Leaving him to his slumber, I tiptoe down the hallway, passing the tiny kitchen, the wooden counters overflowing with baskets of veg. There is only one other door closed on this end of the hallway, so I assume it's where Allette is staying.

When I open the door, I find my girl curled on a white bed beneath a mural of an exquisite rose garden. I slip in next to her, wrap my arms around her, and promptly fall asleep.

Twenty-Two

SENAN

Sunlight glints off the glass cabinets along the wall in the king's private office. I scan the titles on the faded spines until my eyes go crossed. Where is Boris? It's not like him to be late to his own meeting. When I try to open one of the cabinet doors, the thing doesn't budge. What's the point in locking up books? It's not like anyone wants to read about Fae History. Talk about boring.

Boris's wide mahogany desk sits in front of the balcony. Our father used to keep a bottle of whisky in the bottom drawer. I wonder if Boris has kept up with the tradition.

I sink into his chair. At least this one is comfortable.

Maybe a little too much so.

With all this warm sunlight stretching over the desk, I could lean back and go straight to sleep. Especially if I had a drink—

"What do you think you're doing?" a deep voice clips from the balcony.

I leap out of the chair and shoot my eldest brother a grin. His black wings vanish, but his irritated scowl remains.

"Sorry. You were late, and I got tired of waiting," I say, rounding the front of the desk to make room for him.

"That means you can sit at my desk and go through my things?"

"I didn't go through anything." Not yet anyway.

Boris drags out his chair and sinks down on the plush cushions. "Have a seat—in one of the other chairs."

I drop down a little too quickly, and my arse immediately regrets it the moment it collides with unforgiving wood. Next time he suggests a meeting, I'm bringing my own pillow.

Boris removes a stack of parchments from the corner of his desk, tucking them safely into one of the drawers.

"What are those?" And why does he need to lock them up?

He grimaces as he fastens his shoulder-length hair into a leather queue. "Records from The Pit. The guards arrested five stardust dealers already this week, yet there seems to be more dust than ever in the city."

How is that possible? "I thought William Felt was dead." One of our father's last acts as king was to execute the infamous dealer. I still remember the wet sound of the man's head thumping on the balcony outside the throne room.

"There are rumors of a new operation near Dread Row, but no one can find the culprit. The man is like a fucking ghost. Whoever he is, he must be producing more dust at a much quicker rate."

"Is there anything I can do to help?"

Boris snorts. "Come now, Senan. We both know you're better at causing problems than fixing them. Leave the ruling to those of us who know what we're doing."

That's not fair. I can fix problems too. Look at what I did for that Tuath a few weeks ago. Not that Boris knows about that.

Then again, maybe he's right. It's not as if I'll be expected to do much in Nimbiss. The role of ruling will fall on my wife's shoulders. I'll just be there to provide their kingdom with heirs.

My stomach churns at the thought.

A man with brown and white wings lands on the balcony, and I resist the urge to groan. Counsellor Windell stalks into the room, his jowls swinging in time with his black robes. Sunlight reflects off his bald head as he comes to a halt next to Boris.

What is that twat doing here?

"Pardon the intrusion, Your Majesty, but these are urgent." He

sets a folder on the corner of Boris's desk. His dark eyes land on me, and his lips twitch, no doubt wanting to pull into a sneer. "Did you tell your brother the good news?"

Boris blows out a breath. "I'm about to."

"Good news" to Windell inevitably means bad news for me. I'm almost too afraid to ask. "What news?"

"Counsellor Windell has graciously agreed to accompany you to Nimbiss in three weeks' time."

Three weeks? Is he fucking joking?

If I'm in Nimbiss, I'll miss Samhain. I've never been that concerned about the holiday before, but this year Allette is going through the portal, and I had planned on joining her. It'll be our first time.

Maybe our only time.

Not that I can say as much aloud. Wouldn't want my brother growing suspicious. "Why do I need to go to Nimbiss?"

Boris's smile tightens. "To meet with your betrothed. Speaking of Princess Leeri, she has written to you again." From the top drawer, he withdraws a letter bearing the Nimbiss seal and hands it across the desk.

I don't want to meet the woman, let alone read her simpering letters. As soon as I get back to my room, it's going straight into the fireplace like all the others.

Not once have I written back. You'd think by now she would have gotten the hint.

"What's the point in meeting her?" It's not as if I'll be able to call off the betrothal if we don't suit. Boris has told me in no uncertain terms that his word on who I am to wed is final.

"Gods save me..." Boris mutters, rubbing his temples. "To woo her, you fool."

I'll save my wooing for Allette, thank you very much.

"Can we do it after Yule?"

"No."

Shit. Shit. Shit.

There's that infamous Windell sneer I loathe so much. "I'll

leave the two of you to your meeting," he says. "But before I forget, my son's marriage contract is in the folder as well. If you could sign it sometime this week, I would greatly appreciate it."

Which poor woman has the misfortune of marrying Philip Windell? Maybe I should send her a card with my condolences.

I BLINK AT THE SHADOWS, WAITING FOR MY EYES TO adjust to the darkness while Allette's soft, even breaths tickle my neck. My dream hangs like a low fog over our bed, the memory a stark reminder of the way things used to be before Boris wanted me dead.

Inching out of the bed, I shuffle to the door and run a hand through my hair to try to tame the wild strands.

We both know you're better at causing problems than fixing them.

That statement has never been as true as it is today.

Look at the mountain of problems on our doorstep, all thanks to me.

Time to stuff the depressing thought as far down as it will go and let it marinate in the anger I keep locked deep inside.

This place is a good deal larger than it appears from the outside, unlike Scathian towers, where bigger and bolder is "better." Maybe there will be an open burrow for us, and we can live here in peace for the rest of our days, unbothered by the outside world.

Imagine that, living out our happily-ever-after right under Boris's nose.

Too bad I would never be able to rest or relax for fear of him finding us.

Quiet conversation drifts from the living room where Braith and her parents speak in low tones. Everyone twists toward me when I pop my head into the balmy space. "Is there room for one more?"

Braith's mother launches off the sofa, stumbling a little over her black skirt. "Simon! You're awake! Here. Take my seat."

"There's no need to move on my account. I don't mind sitting on the floor in front of the fire." The rug looks almost as cozy as the sofa, and there isn't a scowling woman there.

From the armchair, Braith's father shakes his head, his deep chuckle warm and welcoming. Firelight dances across the glass of amber liquid clutched in his large hand.

"No, no. Sit next to our Braith. I insist." Braith's mother crosses the room, sinking onto her husband's knee like a rotund little bird perched on the edge of a thin limb. She nudges a plate of biscuits toward the empty spot.

Short of offending our host, I have little choice but to sit on the sofa next to a glowering Braith. I get the feeling that Allette's friend doesn't like me. Who can blame her? Look at what has happened to Allette because of me.

I forego the tea but snag a biscuit for myself and lean back against the cushions. Gods, I'm starving. Breakfast feels like it was ages ago. When I take a bite, I expect sweetness, but whatever is in my mouth tastes like turnips and dirt.

Everyone is looking at me, so I can't spit the thing out.

Has anyone ever noticed how loud it sounds when you chew in complete silence? My mouth is closed but all I hear is the grinding of my teeth and the occasional clink of Braith's teacup against the saucer.

After a good deal of struggling, I manage to swallow the bite.

What should I do with the rest of the biscuit? I can hardly put it back on the plate with a giant chunk taken out of it. Would I get away with slipping it between the cushions?

Maybe I will take some tea, after all. Anything to wash away the dust in my mouth.

I pour myself a cup and set the rest of the biscuit on the edge of the saucer. This time, I have the foresight to sniff the tea before drinking it.

It's a good thing too, because the muddy liquid smells like unwashed feet.

Braith's mother claps her hands dramatically, her glassy, bloodshot eyes narrowing as if she's having difficulty focusing on my face. "So, Simon, where do you hail from?"

"Kumulus City." Hopefully, she doesn't ask me *where* in the city—or why I'm putting the teacup right back down without drinking a drop.

"And how do you know our"—*hiccup*—"daughter?"

"Oh. Um... I met Braith in a pub one night. She and Wynn were out drinking and dancing." At least that part is true.

"Did she tell you that she is working at the castle?" Another hiccup. "We are so proud of her, our Braith. The king doesn't hire very often, but he wanted our girl."

Braith's teacup rattles when she slams it onto the coffee table. Her father presses a hand to his mouth as if to keep himself from interrupting.

"I did hear that," I say.

Josie preens. "I'm not sure if you know, but she is quite the artist as well."

Groaning, Braith massages her temples with her fingertips. "Mum..."

"Did you do the mural in our room?" I ask Braith.

"Of course she did! Isn't it beautiful?" Josie says. "My boys are obsessed with the stars. You should see the one in her sister's room. It's a rose garden."

I shouldn't mention that I *did* see the other room, in case Josie takes issue with it. Wouldn't want to be put out on our asses with no place to go.

Braith hides her face behind her hands. "Mum, please."

"What? Am I not allowed to be proud of you, sweetheart? You're such an accomplished young woman; I don't know why you're still single—"

"Simon and Wynn are mated," Braith grits out.

So *that's* what is happening here. Braith's drunk mother is trying to find her daughter a mate.

Turns out, matchmaking is quite entertaining when my love life isn't involved.

"It's true," I say, hoping to save the poor young woman from her mother's meddling.

"Well, I didn't know that, now, did I? You must tell me these things." The older woman clicks her fingers. "What about the other one? Terrence, was it?"

If my brother didn't already have a wife, I would absolutely be taking advantage of this moment.

Braith's father pats his wife's thigh, a smile tugging at his lips. "Calm down, Josie. Can't you see you're embarrassing the poor girl?"

Once again, I come to Braith's rescue. "Terrence is married, I'm afraid." I am a wonderful brother, and Aeron doesn't even appreciate me.

"Not all marriages last forever," Josie counters, swiping her husband's drink for a gulp.

"Mum!"

To be fair, the woman does have a point. But where royal marriages are concerned, it's either annulment or death—and the former isn't an option for Aeron considering his wife is pregnant.

"He and his wife are expecting their first child in the next couple of months," I add. Not sure if that was meant to be a secret, but I must deter this woman somehow. She is as tenacious as a terrier that spotted a squirrel.

Josie's shoulders sag, her disappointment palpable. Braith's father takes back his drink, sipping slowly as his wife starts chattering again. "I keep telling my Braith that she needs to find a nice partner with a good occupation so she doesn't have to work so hard."

Braith throws her head back against the cushions. "I thought you were proud of me working at the castle."

"I am proud, dear. But I'd be just as proud if you gave me grandchildren. By your age, I was already married with your sister and brother in nappies and you on the way."

How many Nightingales are there?

"You remind me of my mother," I say, doing my best to shift the focus off Braith. "She always wanted grandchildren." Instead, she got saddled with five rowdy boys who, at the time, insisted they were never going to settle down. The headaches we used to give that poor woman with our antics.

Josie blinks at me, her glazed eyes wide. "And are you and your mate trying to start a family?"

Braith's father finally lets his smile free. "That's a little difficult when you put them in separate rooms, Josie."

Josie gives him a playful smack on the shoulder. "Well, I didn't know they were mated, did I, Harold?"

"I would like a family someday." One exactly like this one, where Allette sits on my knee, and I can stare at her anytime I want. Where my children feel comfortable enough to bring a whole host of strays into my home and we welcome them with open arms. "Once we're a bit more settled." Assuming I survive this poison, and the king doesn't find us.

As if she could hear me thinking about her, Allette drifts into the room, yawning into her fist. "Sorry about that. I didn't realize how tired I was."

Braith gets up and moves to the rug. Although Allette tells Braith it isn't necessary, she falls onto the cushion next to me, sitting so close that our thighs press together. When she reaches for a biscuit, I capture her hand and give a subtle shake of my head. Her brows come together, but she doesn't reach for another.

The conversation moves on from talk of relationships to what Josie is planning to cook for dinner. Something called fish pie, which is just fucking wonderful.

I might end up starving before the poison has a chance to kill me.

Allette nudges my shoulder. "Simon doesn't like fish. He's afraid of them."

I am *not* afraid of fish.

"I don't blame the boy," Harold says. "Those beasts have razors for teeth and there's no telling how big they can grow. Be glad you didn't arrive by river. There are some real monsters down there. A few weeks back, Martin Fletcher pulled out a walleye as big as himself."

There were fish in that river? Oh, gods... I'm going to be sick.

Josie leans forward to pat my knee—so far forward that she nearly falls off Harold's. "Don't worry. There's some leftover veggie pie just for you."

Thank the gods.

An impatient rap of knuckles rattles the door.

Josie doesn't bother getting up. She simply calls out for the person to come in, and the door swings open.

When I see who it is, I sit up straighter, schooling my features into an impassive mask so the silver-haired man who steps inside doesn't realize how relieved I am to see him.

Jeston greets Braith's parents with a warm smile. "Josie. Harold." His gaze lands on Braith sitting alone by the fire, and his shoulders tense ever so slightly. "Braith."

Her cheeks flush. "Jeston." She looks away before he does, her gaze swinging toward me.

Jeston follows her line of sight, stilling when he finds us on the sofa.

I give him a wave. "Hello again, old friend."

From the wild look in his eyes, I wouldn't be surprised if the man took off right out the door. "What are you doing here?" he clips, adjusting his grip on the basket in his hand.

Guess he isn't happy to see me. Such a pity because I am beyond thrilled to see him.

"They've come to offer their condolences," Josie slurs. "So sad about poor Glenn. Such a terrible way to go. I've tried convincing Harold to retire from the mines, but he's too stubborn to quit."

"Now is not the time, love," Harold whispers in her ear.

Allette strangles my fingers. "We're very sorry for your loss, Jeston."

Jeston bobs his head. "Thanks, Goldie."

Have I mentioned lately how much I fucking hate that this prick gave my girl a nickname?

Aeron comes around the corner, and Jeston's gaze widens, glancing between the two of us with worry furrowing his brow.

Nice to know my brother's scowl is good for something.

Harold must sense the tension in the air, because he nudges his wife's hip and says, "Let's give these young ones a little time alone together."

"Nonsense. Jeston only just arrived, and I need to start dinner—"

"Sleep off the wine first, then we'll discuss food." Harold pushes to his feet, forcing Josie off her perch, and laces their fingers together, hauling her down the hallway despite her protests.

Aeron slides into Harold's vacated chair, his narrow-eyed stare boring into Jeston's forehead. "Why don't you have a seat so we can chat?"

With a final glance toward the exit, Jeston skulks over to the fireplace, dropping next to Braith on the cushions.

When he leans in close to whisper in Braith's ear, the funniest thing happens: Aeron's jaw starts to pulse in time with the clock above the mantle, which I find *very* interesting...

"What else was I supposed to do?" Braith hisses back.

I suppose Jeston is giving her shite about bringing us here. There's no telling how Braith's parents would react if they were to learn the truth of who they are harboring. Come to think of it, why don't they know us? Between my black hair, our silver eyes, and the golden brown of my brother's skin, surely, they must at least suspect we aren't Tuath.

Jeston scrubs a hand down his cheek with a weary sigh. His features appear sharper than they did before, his eyes warier.

"What do you want? And don't give me some shite about mourning the loss of my uncle."

I appreciate the directness. There is no time to waste.

Aeron sits forward. "I want to know what you did with Princess Leeri Eadrom."

I didn't think it was possible, but Jeston's gray complexion turns even paler. "I don't know what you're talking about—"

"Bullshit," Aeron snarls.

Jeston's hands ball into fists in his lap, his jaw working as he glares daggers at my brother.

"You forget that we have witnesses, Jeston. Senan left her in the room with you, which means you were the last one to see her alive."

Braith's mouth falls open. "Is that true, Jes?"

"You want the truth? Fine. It doesn't matter now anyway." He jabs a finger toward me. "That fucking prick doused the princess in poisoned stardust."

"To subdue her." And I didn't know for certain it was poisoned, did I?

"You subdued her, all right. Subdued her so fucking much that she started convulsing on the bed."

Shit...

Allette presses a trembling hand to her lips. "She's dead?"

Jeston shakes his head. "No, because I gave her the antidote."

If he gave her the antidote, then she should still be in the castle.

She isn't in the fucking castle, so something else must've happened. Jeston is being too cagey, and we don't have any fucking time to waste. "Did you leave her in the room?"

Jeston's eyes darken before he glances away.

He knows what happened to her. He must.

Aeron launches to his feet, no doubt ready to tear the Tuath limb from limb.

We don't need Jeston in pieces. We need his help.

Apparently, our mother never taught Aeron that you attract

more flies with honey than with vinegar. Unfortunately, my darling brother pisses vinegar.

I catch Aeron by the sleeve. "Sit back down."

He turns his glower on me. "Excuse me?"

"You heard me. Ass on the seat or go back to bed." Although he grumbles, Aeron rips his sleeve from my grasp and falls back onto the chair, his face red as he silently fumes.

How can Jeston trust us with the truth when we aren't willing to trust him with ours? It's not enough to threaten him—that's what Boris would do. We need to appeal to his heart. Assuming he has one. "Nimbiss took my littlest brother hostage, and if Princess Leeri isn't found by the end of the week, they're going to kill him."

Jeston's gaze snaps to mine. Beside him, Braith's hands fly to her cheeks. Allette's hand falls to my knee, warm and steadfast, giving me the strength to continue.

"He's only nine years old, Jeston. *Nine*. If you know *anything* about the princess's whereabouts, this is your chance to help Kumulus avoid war."

Jeston gives an almost imperceptible shake of his head. When he speaks, his voice is all gravel. "If I tell you, he'll kill me."

"If you don't tell us, *I'll* kill you," Aeron says under his breath.

"Who will kill you? Boris?" If that bastard knows where she is and something happens to Kyff, I swear to the stars—

"Not the king. Someone worse."

Who could be worse than Boris Vale?

Jeston's head falls. "Cadoc Carew has her locked in his secret vault."

Well, *fuck*.

Better get your shovels out and start digging.

If our brother's fate is in the hands of Cadoc Carew, he's as good as dead.

Twenty-Three

ALLETTE

It would seem as though I am the only person in this room who doesn't know who this Cadoc Carew fellow is. From the crestfallen look on Senan's face, Carew mustn't be an upstanding citizen. When I ask, the men exchange narrowed-eyed looks, as if daring one another to be the first to tell me.

In the end, it's Braith who comes to my aid. "Cadoc Carew is the largest dust dealer in the realm."

What does a dust dealer want with the princess? The obvious answer would be for ransom, but if he sent ransom demands to Nimbiss, then surely the King of Nimbiss would realize Kumulus had nothing to do with her disappearance.

Senan turns toward his brother. "You need to tell Boris. He can send the guards—"

Jeston throws up his hands. "Absolutely not. If Carew catches wind of an attack, he'll kill the princess himself. Believe me when I say he *will* find out. The bastard has eyes and ears everywhere. Guards on his payroll. Spies in the castle."

"We can't just leave her there," Braith says.

She's right. If we cannot trust anyone but ourselves, then... "Is there any way we could save her without the king's help?" I ask.

Aeron groans, his head falling back against the chair. "What would you suggest? Waltzing up to Carew's front door and asking nicely?"

"Watch the tone, *Terry*," Senan growls, shooting his brother a warning glare.

While I appreciate my prince coming to my defense, I do not need his help dealing with Prince Pleasant.

"She needs to know what we're up against," Aeron says. "Cadoc Carew decorates his rooftop with the severed limbs of fae who have crossed him."

"Does that mean you know where his hideout is?" Or is this man's infamy yet another one of the many lies we've been told?

"It's not much of a hideout, my love," Senan says. "Carew owns the tallest tower on Dread Row."

Not a lie then. A terrible truth.

It's no surprise that someone with such dark dealings would set up operations in the seediest neighborhood in Kumulus City. I might never have heard of the man, but I have heard of Dread Row. Tales of the wickedness there would be enough to make a grown woman afraid of the dark. "If they know where he is, why hasn't the king done anything to stop him?"

Jeston chuckles, then sobers as quickly. "Sorry. I thought you were making a joke. Carew has been lining the king's pocket for years. In exchange, the royal guards turn a blind eye to his less-than-ethical way of doing business."

Braith stares at him, mouth agape. "How do you know all of this?"

I'd love to know as well. Who is Jeston that he would have such intimate knowledge of a very dangerous man?

"When my mother got sick, I couldn't afford her medication. I was already working two jobs and barely had a few hours for sleep. I heard Carew was looking for help, and I offered in exchange for coin. It was only supposed to be a few vials, but once he gets his claws into you..." Jeston drags a hand through his hair. "The king may rule above the clouds, but Carew owns the streets below. I'd hoped to escape with the staff going to Nimbiss but when that didn't happen…" He shrugs.

Now that he mentions it, I recall him saying something about being part of the household staff sent to Senan's new kingdom. How awful, to be in such a situation where your only choice is to watch your mother succumb to illness or be forced to work for an evil man like Cadoc Carew.

Senan eases forward, resting his elbows on his knees. "That's how you knew about the antidote."

Jeston nods.

That's right. The antidote… With all this talk of the missing princess, I almost forgot. "If we needed more, would you be able to get it?"

Jeston rolls his eyes. "Sure. Why not? I mean, if you're planning on saving the princess, you can just swing by Carew's safe on your way out and grab some yourself."

Senan's head falls back against the cushion as if he has already given up.

"Fine," Aeron clips, frustration bracketing his pinched mouth. "Jeston, you and I will go to Dread Row to retrieve the princess and the antidote."

"I'm sorry, but are you serious?" Jeston presses a hand to his forehead. "They'll know who you are the moment they see you. And me? Carew would hunt me down, tear me limb from limb, and add me to his rooftop. Not to mention what he'll do to my mother."

"What if we offer you protection?" Then he can be safe.

"No offense, Goldie, but you can't even protect yourselves. That is what you're doing here, isn't it? Hiding so the king can't find either of you."

"They can't offer protection, but I can." Aeron flattens his palms on his thighs, his expression tortured like the kind offer physically pains him. "Help us and I will give you sanctuary in Stratiss."

Silence stretches as Jeston stews for a moment, his jaw working. "You must give my mother sanctuary as well."

"Done."

"And I want a house far from Kumulus along with a decent wage for the rest of my days."

"*Fine.*"

Jeston pushes to his feet, holding out a hand. Aeron gives him a firm shake.

Now that they have the details of the agreement squared away, we need to figure out a plan.

Senan sits up, a determined set to his jaw. "This is my fault. I'll be the one to go with you—"

"The duster prince?" Jeston chuckles. "Pretty sure Carew commissioned a portrait in your honor from all the gold you've given him."

He's right. Not to mention, if the king's guards stumble upon Senan, there's no telling what will happen. I would never ask Braith to risk her own life, which leaves only one other person. "I can do it."

The thought of being able to help instead of remaining on the sidelines sends a jolt of adrenaline rushing through my veins.

"No," Senan and Aeron blurt in unison.

Surprise, surprise. The men have an issue with a woman coming to the rescue. Well, that is too bad, isn't it? "You don't get to tell me what to do." I am free to come and go as I damn well please.

Braith's chin lifts in defiance. "That's right. She is her own woman." To me, she says, "I would volunteer, but if I'm not back at the castle by sunrise, I won't have a job."

While I appreciate the sentiment, this isn't her fight. Besides, she has already done more than enough by offering us a safe place to hide.

"It's too dangerous," Aeron counters, looking every bit like a man used to getting his way. I can't wait to disappoint him.

"Life is dangerous. Does that mean we must stop living it?" I spent four years in the human realm being cowed and told what to do. That season of my life has passed. It is high time I take back some of the power they stole from me.

That starts by saving my prince and his little brother.

Bracing my elbows on my knees, I lean forward, looking to Jeston for direction. "Do you have a plan?"

Jeston stares down at his boots, the wrinkles across his brow deepening. "The princess is locked in a cage, so we'll need to retrieve the key before going to Dread Row. Cadoc is a paranoid bastard and always keeps it on his person. He spends most of his nights in Serpent's, so finding him won't be an issue."

What is Serpent's? Is it a bar? A gaming hall? Either way, it sounds seedy.

Senan drags both hands through his hair, his face draining of color as he pulls me back against him. "No fucking way."

Braith grimaces, and Aeron, well, he is scowling but his eyes are murderous and trained on Jeston. This Serpent's place must be awful.

"What is Serpent's?" I ask.

Senan's mouth clamps shut, his jaw pulsing. I hardly expect his brother to be forthcoming, so that leaves Braith or Jeston. I pin my hopes on my friend, giving her shoulder a poke.

Braith's cheeks turn as rosy as her mother's. "Serpent's is... It's a...um... Well, it's a den."

That doesn't sound too terrible. The burrows are dens as well, aren't they? Perhaps this Serpent's place won't be as bad as everyone believes.

"A fucking flesh den," Aeron growls. "Only the most elite criminals in the realm can gain entry."

Jeston holds up a finger. "Elite criminals and *workers*."

Senan's arms begin to tremble. "Over my dead body is my girl going into that hellhole."

"It will be over your dead body if we don't get the bloody antidote," I say. "And have you forgotten your little brother's life is at stake as well?" I haven't.

If sneaking into some seedy establishment can save them both, I'm going to do it. "So we go to this den, and then what?"

"Then I find a way to steal the key."

Steal a key from a murderous dust dealer. Sounds like a bloody brilliant idea to me. "Do you think he'll let you get close enough?"

"Being the House Master at Kumulus Castle has its advantages. I'll tell him that there's news from the castle. The only problem is that I'll be searched on the way in and on the way out," he adds with a poignant look in my direction. "I'll have to give the key to you."

The *only* problem? I can think of about a hundred, the most pressing being that we are plotting to steal from a man with a garden of severed limbs on his rooftop.

"What makes you think they won't search me?" I ask.

"They never search the women in Serpent's."

"Why is that?" Women can be thieves and assassins too.

Aeron curses. "Because the women in Serpent's are usually naked."

Twenty-Four

SENAN

IF THIS BASTARD THINKS I'M GOING TO LET MY GIRL waltz into one of those flesh dens without a stitch on, he has another thing coming. While I appreciate that Allette is willing to put her life on the line to save Kyff and me, I cannot allow her to sacrifice herself.

This is where dancing with darkness leads: To a bottomless pit where every option is worse than the one before.

I glance from Allette's wrenching hands to her flushed cheeks, my chest feeling as if someone pried my ribs apart and ripped out my heart.

"Do I *have* to be naked?" my girl asks, forcing her hands to her sides.

There's fear in her eyes. She's right to be afraid. Carew is on par with Boris in his villainy—hell, he might be worse given his penchant for dismemberment.

"I know someone who works in the dens," Braith says. "I can ask if she owns an extra...uniform."

Is that what we're calling the scraps of fabric those women wear? I cannot believe our lives have come to this. Anything could go wrong down there, and if it does, the person I love most in this world will suffer the consequences.

I'm not worth it. If it weren't for Kyff, I'd downright refuse. Still, I need her to know: "You don't have to do this." We will find another way. "If we tell Boris—"

"The king might be able to save Kyff, but he won't lift a finger to save you," Allette says, her gaze softening as she takes my hand. Everything about her is so soft, so warm and welcoming. Far too good for the likes of me. "This might be our only chance to save you both."

"It'll be dangerous." More dangerous than she can fathom.

"Maybe I like danger." She wiggles her eyebrows suggestively. "I fell in love with you, didn't I?"

Although I smile at her attempt at humor, the truth is like a vise around my chest: Compared to these men, Aeron and I are fluffy fucking ducklings.

✦

It's been two hours since Jeston hatched this harebrained plan, and I still cannot believe Allette is going to be spending her night in the Serpent's Den.

They couldn't have thought of a more conspicuous name. Might as well have a big fucking sign above the door saying: "Certain Death Awaits" and a bunch of arrows pointing to the entrance.

I pace the hallway, wearing a hole in the stone floor. This isn't going to work. We need to come up with another plan. We need to—

The door to Allette's room creaks open, and my girl steps out looking like the star of my deepest, darkest fantasies.

Her hands shake as she smooths down the red silk of her skirt, the gaps on either side revealing the sinful length of her pale thighs. The top hardly covers her breasts. If she were to bend over, her nipples would slip out. The only thing holding the dress— and I use that term in the loosest sense of the word—together is a twisted sash with a hole right below her navel where disgusting men will drop coins in exchange for all manner of perverse requests.

Her painted lips lift into a knowing smile. "Modest, isn't it?"

I have to pick my jaw off the floor to respond. "If anyone so much as looks at you, I will take their eyes and cleave their heads from their bodies."

"I can handle myself."

Ordinarily, I'd agree, but these men will be unlike any she's ever encountered.

Jeston waits for my girl in the living room in a set of black leathers that make him look like a villain. "Are you sure we can trust him?" The whole story about his sick mother could have been a lie. For all we know, Jeston could be Carew's right-hand man. He could be stealing Allette to take her hostage as well.

Allette flattens her hand down the front of my shirt, straightening the wrinkles there. "We don't have any other choice. I'm not going to lose you, and if that means I have to wiggle my arse for a few monsters, then so be it."

"There shall be no arse wiggling for you." For the first time since we met, her laughter makes me uneasy. She is joking, isn't she? "Allette..."

My warning is met with a placating pat on my chest. Braith offers my girl a cloak to wear and a word of good luck before she leaves for her shift at the castle.

All too soon, it's time for Allette to leave as well.

I kiss my girl goodbye and watch her slip into the darkened cavern behind Jeston. My heart isn't even in my throat but gone completely, tucked safely into the silk clinging to my girl's body, hidden beneath a cloak as black as my mood.

Aeron drops onto the chair, letting his head fall into his hands. "It isn't fucking fair. I should be the one doing this."

"And risk leaving your unborn child fatherless? You know as well as I do that this is the best choice among a host of shite ones." Even if we wanted to go and keep an eye on things in the den, I can't be seen alive, and his presence would jeopardize the entire mission. "Besides, your hairy arse wouldn't have looked half as good as Allette's in that silk."

His lips twitch. "I don't know. Women always tell me how pretty I am. I reckon I could've pulled it off."

"And when the customers reached beneath your skirts and found a cock?"

A chuckle. "They'd be too stunned by how big it is to say a fucking word."

The night may be upon us, but the only stars I see are the ones painted on the ceiling in this tiny bedroom. For some reason, the inaccurate positions of those constellations irritate the hell out of me. Not because they're not beautiful. Braith is an incredibly talented artist. Rather, I assume the reason she painted them like that is because she has never actually seen the stars. Which is a tragedy in and of itself. Yes, they're vicious and vindictive, but they're also one of the most profound sights one can ever experience.

As lovely as it is down here, there are some clear disadvantages to living underground or beneath persistent clouds. I'm not sure how I would feel about never seeing the stars ever again, or the sun, for that matter. That the Tuath themselves are not allowed to own towers or step onto the balconies in the towers where many of them work, is an offense of the highest order.

Not long ago, Kyffin caught Allette sunning herself on the balcony outside the castle and said something that struck me as funny at the time.

She's stealing our sun.

I thought he was joking and told him the sun was too large to fit into her pockets. Now, I realize he was serious. Someone taught him that the sun belonged to those of us with wings. It's an absurd notion, that any of us could own the sun—or the stars.

Yet keeping these people from rising above the clouds has made it true.

I shake the heavy thoughts from my head.

Look at me, coming up with more problems instead of attempting to solve the ones at hand.

Like what we're going to do if Allette and Jeston fail in their mission to retrieve the princess.

There's only one option left, I'm afraid. Aeron will have to go to Boris and tell him the truth about who has Leeri. Then we'll have to pray he can save the princess himself.

When I lean back in the chair behind the desk, the hinges creak. The stiff wood is terribly uncomfortable, but it's better than the bed. If I lie down now, I might fall asleep. Not because I'm tired, but because this damn poison has leached the energy from my bones.

I refuse to rest until Allette returns unharmed.

Aeron lays on the top bunk, bouncing a small rubber ball off the ceiling and catching it over and over again. The constant *thud, thud, thud* is irritating as hell, but if I tell him that, he'll only keep it going forever.

As if he knows I'm thinking about him, he says, "What are we going to do about Boris?"

Thud thud.

Thud thud.

Fucking Boris. King of ruining everything.

I prop my feet up on the corner of the small desk stacked with books on astronomy and astrology. The idea of a Tuath studying something he might never see in person fascinates me. What's the point?

"I cannot think about Boris when Allette is trapped in a pit of slithering vipers. I hate sitting here like a useless plod."

"Then do something useful and help me figure out what we are going to do about our eldest brother."

Why is he bothering to ask me? Every plan I've ever hatched has gone up in flames.

I collect an ink pen from the top drawer and a piece of parchment to keep my hands busy. "What can we do?"

The infernal thudding stops. Aeron turns the ball around in his hand, his eyes narrowed at the ceiling. "He cannot be allowed to keep the crown. There's no telling how far his treachery reaches."

Knowing the extent of Boris's villainy doesn't mean we'd be able to stop him.

Something flies toward me. That damn ball. Good thing Aeron is a terrible shot; it only grazes my shoulder. "Are you even listening to me?" he grumbles, propping himself up on an elbow.

"Hard not to with you shouting," I shoot back. "I agree that knowing Boris could be ruling this kingdom for centuries is a truly terrifying thought, but what other choice do we have?"

"We could find a way to remove him from the throne."

I never pegged Aeron for a comedian.

"Think of Kyff," he goes on. "Do you want him growing up in that castle with Boris and his cronies as his only mentors? The boy is young and impressionable. If we don't do something, he will turn out just like him."

That's assuming Kyff makes it back from Nimbiss alive.

Fucking brilliant. Now I'm picturing our baby brother being chopped into pieces. They wouldn't hurt a child, would they?

I hope he isn't scared, that he doesn't even realize he is a hostage. Maybe he's been told he's on holiday and given sweets to keep him occupied.

One can only hope.

The circles I draw intersect, looking a bit like a cross-eyed squirrel. I decide to lean into it and give the animal some buck teeth and an acorn. And a tail—a big, fluffy one.

"Let's say, for argument's sake, that Boris vanished in the morning. Who would take his place?" The squirrel needs a home. Time to draw a tree. "Rhainn?"

Aeron shakes his head. "He's been sent to Allto."

"Already? He isn't supposed to wed until next year."

"After the shite you pulled, Boris wasn't taking any chances."

Right, so not Rhainn. "You have your own kingdom, so you can't do it. Which leaves Kyff ascending with Counsellor Windell as his head advisor." Lord Philip Windell's father is so far up Boris's arse, he's practically his shadow.

Aeron says nothing.

I stop doodling long enough to glance over at the top bunk only to find my brother staring at me.

"What?" Is there ink on my face? I check my fingers for smudges, but they're clean.

"There is one obvious solution." My brother clears his throat and nods toward me.

What the hell does he want? Is he trying to see what I'm drawing? I hold up the picture, but that only makes him glower. Clearly, he doesn't appreciate fine art.

I grab the pen and add my signature to the bottom corner, next to the pile of acorns.

Senan Vale

"Senan."

When I glance back up, Aeron is still staring.

Wait... Surely, he isn't suggesting... "You want *me* to do it?" My heart begins to race, a cold sweat breaking across my brow. The ink pen tumbles from my fingers, rolling onto the stone floor.

Aeron sits up fully, his long legs dangling off the end of the bed as he scrubs a hand down the back of his neck. "Gods, you're slow."

"Just one of the many reasons I should not be king." Yes, my parents raised me to sit on a throne, but all the lectures we were forced to endure went right over my head. See this squirrel? He is only one of a whole host of woodland creatures I've created instead of studying. I never took any of our lessons seriously because I knew I wouldn't be the one making the decisions.

That responsibility would fall to my wife, the Queen of Nimbiss.

"Did you forget that I already have a wife?" If she survives this ordeal and I were to return from the dead, I'd be expected to go to her kingdom.

"Did you forget that the two of you never consummated your marriage? You can file for an annulment. No one would blame you after they abducted Kyff."

True, but that doesn't change the fact that I am not equipped to rule a kingdom. Not only that: "I don't want the throne."

He climbs down from the top bunk and snags his boots from where he discarded them earlier. "And you think I did? If I had my way, I'd be sailing the Folly with Madelynn. But we are meant for something more. I, for one, think you would make an excellent king."

"Oh, fuck off." Now isn't the time for jokes.

"I'm serious. You have lived the life of a prince and the life of a pauper." He takes a break from fastening his buckles to tick each nonsensical reason off on his fingers. "You have soared through the clouds, freed from gravity, and now you are bound by it. You have struggled and fought for yourself. For the woman you love. You have suffered great loss. There isn't a person in this kingdom who cannot sympathize with at least one of your many plights. Our people have always loved you, and if you tried, I have no doubt you would earn the respect of the Tuath in the burrows. Look at how you convinced Jeston to help us."

"Aeron..."

His extended hand clenches into a fist, silencing my protest. "The law states that a Vale prince must sit on the throne. Even if we wanted to change it, that could take years—and I can guarantee the current Scathian council would not allow it. You are Kumulus's only hope."

This kingdom is doomed if *I'm* its only hope.

I appreciate his vote of confidence; really, I do. But it is entirely misplaced. "If a Vale prince must take the throne, then Kyff can have it. We'll fire Windell and find a worthy advisor."

Who's to say I would be better than Boris, anyway?

Any time I picture my eldest brother, all I can think about is killing him in the most gruesome way imaginable. Those sorts of thoughts belong to a villain, not a hero.

And what Kumulus needs is a hero.

"Are you fucking kidding me? You would let our nine-year-old brother take on this immense responsibility instead of stepping up and doing it yourself?" Aeron rips his coat from where it hangs over the small ladder. "I never pegged you for a coward."

"Sorry for wanting to live my own life and not be tethered to that castle or a fucking crown." To be locked back in a gilded cage.

Then there is Allette to consider. She had her life—and her happiness—stolen from her for far too long. She deserves to decide what she wants for her future.

And I'll not give her up for this kingdom, for my family, for anything.

Aeron stalks forward, towering over where I sulk. "That castle and that 'fucking crown' gave you this life. Hate it all you want, but I think it's high time you gave back instead of taking."

I know I owe my life to the castle, or, more accurately, to the treasury. That I have incurred debts that can never be repaid, but I just...I can't do it.

Maybe Rhainn hasn't married his princess yet and can be brought back instead. If not, Kyff will surely find his way under the right advisor. But who? For all we know, everyone in that castle has been tainted by Boris.

There is no telling who we can trust.

I never pegged you for a coward.
You would make an excellent king.

Unfortunately, Aeron is wrong on both counts.

Twenty-Five

ALLETTE

Jeston and I don't speak as he swipes the oars through the black water, the heaviness of what we're about to do hanging like a dark cloud above us. The dock he stops at ten minutes later is no different from the one in the burrows, with colorful boats tethered to wooden pegs. Jeston hoists himself onto the dock, and I hand him the thick braid of coarse rope.

Once we're both on dry ground, he glances around the dark cave before stepping closer. "Let's go over the plan once more."

I nod, my heart already in my throat, and I haven't even shed my cloak.

"I'll go and speak with Cadoc," he says. "While he is distracted, I'll retrieve the key. Before we leave, I'll pass you the key to hide in your sash. You'll leave first, and I'll follow you out shortly after. If for some reason we get separated, we meet here at the boat."

A simple plan at face value, but if there's one thing the last four years have taught me, it's that plans rarely go smoothly.

We only have one shot to make this work.

If we're caught, we'll end up as rooftop ornaments.

I'm still shocked that Senan didn't put up more of a fight over me leaving. That he trusts me to do this means more than he will ever know.

Together, Jeston and I follow a well-worn path toward a small tunnel that spits us out in a tiny shed. We emerge onto a grimy street cloaked in shadows. Each inhale of the damp air feels like a sip of cold tea. There are far more people out and about than I expected. Almost all of them are men in leather trousers and jerkins, like Jeston's attire. A few women loiter in doorways, but they are wearing...considerably less.

With my head down, I focus on keeping up with Jeston's long strides until we round the corner, where a large mound rises like a boil from the ground. A black snake carved into a wooden sign hangs from a stake, staring at us through ruby-red eyes.

Jeston stops and turns to me, his shadowed eyes searching. "Are you ready?"

No. But will I ever be?

I reach for my cloak, unfastening the clasp. The chilly night air prickles against my skin. Jeston balls up the fabric and hides it around the corner while I take a deep breath...and head inside.

✦

Part of me thought perhaps the Serpent's Den wouldn't be as bad as everyone assumed. I mean, look at the Black Hole and the burrows. The former wasn't so different from any other pub and the latter is downright lovely. If they had a bit of sunlight, I'd happily live there for the rest of my days.

This place, however, is exactly as awful as its name. My slippers stick to the drink-splattered floor, and every time I try to breathe, the cloying air, ripe with sweat and perfume, swells in my throat.

Bodies writhe in corners and atop stools. Some women wear clothes similar to my attire, and others wear nothing at all. There are a handful of male workers wearing tiny leather shorts, their bare chests painted in black and red whorls, glowing gold from the dust in their veins.

This place makes the Black Hole look like a children's funfair in comparison.

Card tables and dealers in black and red masks fill the center of the room, surrounded by men hunched over their cards with sweat leaking from their brows.

Some glow. Some don't.

Their eyes feel like scales sliding across my skin. What I wouldn't give for my maid's uniform and mask as I meander through the tables, trailing Jeston without making it obvious that the two of us are together.

Occasionally, I stop at a gaming table or throw a flirtatious smile at an unsuspecting male who doesn't seem to be getting as much attention as the others. It's what all the other workers are doing, after all, and I don't want to stand out. Nearly all of them have hair as dark as mine, but there are a few blondes in the mix who appear to be in high demand.

Then there are the three women at the back with fuchsia, emerald, and ochre colored hair. Their skin glows brightest, like they've been painted by the stars. One turns to open the curtain at her back for a man as tall as a tree.

My chest tightens.

Behind her shoulder blades rest two scars exactly like mine.

Did the king exile her as well or did someone else steal her wings?

I would love nothing more than to ask but now is neither the time nor the place. Not when Jeston just entered a section along the far wall, cordoned off by black velvet ropes. A tall man sits on an onyx throne carved with the heads of serpents. Two bare-breasted women sit atop tufted red pillows on either side of him, rubbing his toned chest and feeding him grapes, while a third kneels between the man's spread thighs, her head bobbing beneath the table.

The sight is enough to make me blush to my toes.

The guards pat Jeston down before allowing him to approach the man.

They're too far away for me to overhear their conversation, but from the rigidity of Jeston's back, I assume Cadoc isn't happy to see him. Perhaps if I move a little closer—

A hand lands on the back of my thigh, sliding up to my arse. My body freezes in place, the air leaving my lungs with a tremble.

"Ten quid for a lappy," the man slurs, leering at the pale skin of my exposed thigh through glassy eyes.

"You know the rules, Daffid," a chiming voice croons. "This den is worker's choice." A dainty hand slips around the wrist connected to the hand *still* on my arse. "And no one in their right mind would choose a pig like you." The woman jerks his hand. A sickening crack rings through the crowded space, followed by the man's howl of pain.

I'm grateful for her assistance, but now everyone at the table is staring at me.

"You all right, pet?" she asks, the sash at her waist laden with coins.

"I'm fine. Thank you."

Her perfectly arched brows come together over flawlessly made-up green eyes. "Don't put up with any shite from this lot, yeah? Give 'em a chance and they'll ruin you." She glances down at my sash. "This your first shift?"

I nod, slowly trying to distance myself from the now-whimpering man clutching his trembling hand to his chest.

I hope she broke it.

"How long have you been exiled?" the woman asks, twisting to show me the marks on her back as well.

After hiding them for so long, it feels strange to wear my scars so boldly. "Four years." Four long, exhausting, grief-filled years.

A breath whistles through her gapped front teeth. "Impressive. I only made it six months without mine before burrowin' down here. Hardly an honest livin', but at least it puts food on the table and a roof over your head." Leaning forward, she whispers in my ear, "You don't have to sleep with 'em. Sit on their laps, give a few wiggles, show a tit or two. That'll earn your dinner. But if you do decide to go the whole hog, make 'em wash first. Showers and bedrooms are upstairs." She jerks a chin toward those velvet curtains where the emerald-haired woman is now missing from the bunch.

Imagine *this* being your life. Coming to this underground den of heathens, night after night, letting men look at you and touch you in exchange for coins.

No one should be forced to decide between starvation or life in a flesh den.

I'm not judging this woman or any of the other fae for doing what they must to survive. If I hadn't found my way to the castle, I very well could've ended up somewhere like this as well. I only wish there was a different way for them to support themselves if this is not the life they want.

I thank the woman and then turn back around, only to find the man on the serpent throne watching me.

He lifts a hand and crooks his finger.

Nausea roils in my gut.

The naked women with the grapes have left, and Jeston sits on one of the cushions, his already pale face white as bone and his eyes bulging as I step forward. At least the woman beneath the table is...um...finished, and the man's pants appear to have been pulled up. She's still sitting on the ground though, her head now resting on Jeston's knee as she strokes his leg.

Scars adorn her back as well.

Two burly men as big as the king's guards unhook one of the ropes to allow me past.

Cadoc is far handsomer up close, with a hint of gray kissing the dark copper at his temples and striking brown eyes. "You're new," he says without inflection. "What's your name?"

My voice only wobbles a little when I respond. "Wynn."

Cadoc pulls a heavy purse from behind him, dropping it onto the tabletop. "How would you like to make a bit of gold, Wynn?"

What do I say? I don't want to get caught, but I am not going to sleep with this man or let him touch me or sit on his lap and... *wiggle*.

"What would I have to do?" That's a perfectly valid question, isn't it? Surely no person here is so hungry for gold that they would agree blindly.

His lips twitch as he withdraws something else, slamming a dagger next to the purse, the silver blade gleaming where it sticks out of the wooden tabletop. "Kill the man who touched you."

My heartbeat roars in my ears, screaming for me to run far and fast. I lick my trembling lips as tension coils at the base of my spine.

He cannot be serious. "I'm not going to kill anyone."

His thick black brows rise toward the sweep of his copper hair. "Why not? Don't you want to? He put his hands on you without your permission. Now I'm giving you permission to kill him."

Who does this man think he is? He cannot give me permission to take someone's life. Yes, I may be angry and indignant, but I refuse to let that anger control me. Besides, that woman already wounded the blackguard. Surely, he learned his lesson and will never let it happen again.

"I'm not a..." I'm about to say killer, but that isn't true, is it? I've killed two men, haven't I? First, the guard in the caverns and then Eason Bell. "No, thank you."

Cadoc shrugs. "Suit yourself." With a click of his fingers, one of the guards at the entrance stalks toward the man who touched me. He whips out a dagger and carves the blade along his throat. Blood sprays like a fountain across the cards on the table. The dying man's mouth falls open, and he slumps onto the floor, convulsing a few times before falling still.

No one bats an eye.

The women step over the body as if it isn't there, and the men who were playing cards with him divvy up his chips and continue their game. One of the guards next to Cadoc carries over a saw to cut off his arm, wrapping it in brown paper once the limb has been severed.

A new rooftop ornament, no doubt.

Death is nothing to these people.

And if Jeston gets caught slipping that key from the man's pocket, there is no doubt in my mind that Cadoc Carew won't hesitate to end him.

Twenty-Six

ALLETTE

Cadoc resumes his discussion with Jeston while I'm led back to the main part of the den, where the overwhelming scent of sweat clings to the air. The longer I'm here, the harder it is to breathe. It doesn't help that my gaze won't stop straying to that body.

That could be Jeston.

It could be me.

With my heart in my throat, I meander through the crowded tables, doing my best to act like the other men and women earning their keep. Trailing a finger along a shoulder, offering a flirtatious smile, lingering near the patrons with the most chips. A few slip coins through the gaps in my sash. Others leer, expecting more for their money.

Eventually, Jeston stalks away from Cadoc. One of the guards calls him back, but he ignores the man, coming right up to me, the toes of his boots brushing my slippers as he leans in close to whisper in my ear. "Smile at me and touch my face. Quickly."

Forcing a smile to my lips, I bring both hands to his cheeks, smoothing my thumbs along the harsh stubble on his jaw. He steps even closer, his nose grazing my ear. "I'm sorry for this," he murmurs, the words slurred. Without another word, his mouth finds mine. I'm so shocked, that I freeze. Then I feel the press of something cold and sharp against my lip.

The key.

My mind screams at me to pull away, that this isn't right. My body leans in, allowing Jeston to pass the key from his mouth to mine. The metallic taste turns my stomach as I tuck the key into the side of my mouth.

Jeston steps back, his pupils blown wide as he stares down at my mouth. He swipes his thumb along my lower lip, then whispers, "I want you all to myself. Meet me outside, and I'll make it worth your while."

One of Cadoc's guards waits behind him with a smirk, his beefy arms crossed over his broad chest. "Someone's eager tonight."

"You know how it is, Boone," Jeston says, his gaze still pinned to mine. "You see something you want...you take it."

I give Jeston a saucy wink and start for the door.

We did it. Now, all we have to do is make it out of here—

"Leaving so soon?" Carew waits with a casual shoulder propped against the doorframe, blocking the exit.

How am I supposed to hold a conversation with a key under my tongue?

He knows. He knows and is going to chop off your arm too.

Except... He would look angry if he knew, right? He certainly wouldn't be smiling.

I need to get this damn key out of my mouth.

Pretending to cough, I lift my hand to cover my mouth and spit the key into my fist. A false smile finds my lips as my heart hammers against my breastbone. "Just needed some fresh air."

Carew watches me like a predator sizing up his prey, the muscles in his shoulders tense, ready to pounce. "Not much of that to be found down here."

"No, there isn't."

He pushes off the frame, stalking close and raising his hand. "May I?"

No. No. No.

I nod.

Cadoc drags his knuckle down the scars on my right shoulder. Bile singes up my throat. Burning. Scalding. Bringing tears of indignation and revulsion to my eyes.

"Who took your wings?" he asks, his voice low. Seductive. A tone reserved for secrets and lovers.

"Does it matter?"

Dark eyes bore into mine. "It could if you want it to."

There is something intoxicating about this man, something that defies logic. I can practically feel the malice crawling beneath his skin, and yet part of me yearns to give him the king's name just to see what he would do.

"Someone more powerful than you."

Cadoc's eyes widen, sweeping down my body. Assessing. "I see. And what did you do to piss off the king?"

Tell him nothing.

Keep your secrets.

This man—no, this *monster*, forced Jeston to serve him in exchange for saving Jeston's mother. He kills people and chops them up. I want nothing to do with him—least of all his help. There's no telling what price he would expect in return.

I swallow my response and shrug.

He might be able to take my life, but he will never have my truths.

Carew's brows lift as he traces my scar once more. "You wouldn't happen to be the same Wynn who had an affair with Prince Senan, would you?" Darkness flashes in his eyes, giving me a glimpse of the villain lurking beneath. "King Boris is awfully protective of his brothers."

My fists tighten at my sides, the key hidden within biting against my palm. How does he know? "What do you want?"

His hand drops. "You mistake my intentions. I'm here to offer my services to you. What do *you* want, Wynn?"

Men like this don't do anything out of the goodness of their hearts. He's trying to force me into his debt, just like Jeston. If I only wanted one thing, perhaps it would be worth the risk, but I need two: The princess freed *and* the vials of antidote.

"When I decide, I might just let you know," I say.

His deep chuckle rumbles over me as he steps aside. "Then I hope we see each other again soon."

I don't. If I never hear the name Cadoc Carew again, it would still be too soon.

Broken glass litters the streets, glittering across the cobblestones. The fae light on Dread Row burns green, as if the light is tainted by the evil infecting this place. The short, squatty houses have boards in place of windows. Fat chimneys pump thick black smoke into the too-sweet air while cats scream down alleys with sludge-lined gutters.

I thought the community surrounding my great-aunt's tower west of the river was bad. Imagine growing up in such a hopeless place as this.

Amidst the small homes looms a lone gray tower with two men guarding the door.

Jeston blows out a harsh breath, tucking me behind him in an alley so small, if I reach out, I could touch the slimy stone walls on either side. He gives the dark wool covering my form a swift tug. "Time to lose the cloak again, Goldie."

With a deep breath, I unfasten the clasp at my throat and roll up the wool, tucking the garment onto a nearby windowsill. Gooseflesh bubbles across my bare skin.

Jeston drapes his arm around my shoulder, his bark of laughter echoing through the streets. The men jolt to attention, scanning the night. When they see us coming toward them, their mouths twist into sneers.

The first man pats Jeston down, then nods at me. "On the pull tonight, Jes? She's a right looker."

Jeston's lips remain pressed in a flat line. "Keep staring and you'll have no eyes to close, Wells."

Their chuckles feel like phantom fingers sliding down my spine, but neither of them touches me as they wave us into the tower.

Inside, golden veins run through the black stone floors, and the walls have been painted a deep, emerald green. The hallway leads to a parlor of sorts, with opulent gold and black furniture. It feels as if there should be people sitting on the sofas or having drinks over at the bar.

With the slightest pressure from his hand at the base of my spine, Jeston steers me deeper into Carew's lair. The hallway gives way to other corridors with walls of raw, unpainted stone where golden crystals sparkle in mine carts for as far as the eye can see.

"What is all of this?"

"Stardust. Grind it down and add a few more ingredients, and it's ready for a vial and an empty soul."

"There's so much of it." I might not be well-versed in the ins and outs of stardust dealing, but I do know that dusting is an expensive habit that has put more than one unfortunate fae onto the street. The amount of money these men are dealing with is impossible to fathom.

We continue to a door as black as midnight, with serpents carved into the frame.

I expect terrible things on the other side: a dungeon with instruments of torture on display or an actual pit of vipers. Instead, the large room is filled with shelves of books.

I turn in a slow circle, taking it all in. If I didn't know who owned this tower, I would be enamored by this room. None of this finery seems to fit with what I saw of the monster earlier tonight.

A throne like the one from the den sits behind an imposing

desk of black marble with thick golden veins. It's as if the dust has infected everything in this place.

Framed maps of the kingdom and the realm hang between golden sconces. Stunning oil paintings fill the wall on either side of the door. A fine gallery and ancient library combined.

As beautiful as everything is, there does appear to be something vital missing.

"Where's the princess?"

Jeston walks to the bookcase along the rear wall and pulls a thick tome. The ground begins to rumble, and the entire shelf slides back, revealing a set of stairs curving into the ground, lit with that same eerie green light from the streets.

We descend into a cavern the size of the office above, where a safe has been set into the far wall. On the other wall sits a large iron cage.

A young woman with dark violet hair waits inside the cage, curled on top of a small bed with a pile of books stacked on the stone floor.

We found the princess.

And from the way she glowers, she doesn't look very happy about it.

Twenty-Seven

ALLETTE

Princess Leeri shoves back the curtain of her dark violet hair and darts a glance toward the entrance.

So this is my mate's wife, the woman who has been given everything I've ever wanted.

Even dirty and with dark bruises beneath her eyes, she is still one of the most stunning females I've ever seen, which is both infuriating and depressing. How could Senan choose me over someone like this? She's so *perfect*.

Jeston holds out his hands like he's trying to keep a wild animal at bay and takes a cautious step toward the cage. "Please don't scream. We're here to rescue you."

The princess's eyes narrow and her lips flatten, but she nods. The simple dress she wears hangs off her thin frame, the skirt falling over her bare feet when she rises.

Jeston turns to me. "Give me the key."

I withdraw the key from where it hides within the twisted fabric of my sash.

We need to free the princess, but that's not our only mission. Kyffin isn't the only Vale prince who needs to be saved.

Stepping back, I clutch the key to my chest.

"Allette, please. Give me the key." Jeston's eyes search mine, panic tinging his voice.

"Allette?" the princess gasps, her Nimbiss accent harsh and grating against my ears. Her ice-blue eyes widen as her head swings toward me. "*You're* Senan's Allette?"

Hearing my love's name on her lips makes me want to rip out her hair. She looks down her nose at me as if I am beneath her. Without me, we wouldn't even be here.

"Give me the damn key," Jeston demands.

How can I free Senan's *wife* knowing her claim to him is a hundred times more valid than mine?

Remember Prince Kyffin.

None of this is for the princess, but for the littlest prince.

I am going to give Jeston the key, but first... "I want the antidote."

His expression darkens, but he stalks over to the safe and dials in the combination. I don't ask how he knows it and he doesn't offer an explanation. The lock releases and the door swings wide, revealing vials of every color.

I step toward the translucent rainbow of glass and liquid. How are there so many shades? This cannot all be stardust...can it? What else might Cadoc be mining and creating in this terrible lair?

It's a shame I'll never know. "Which ones do I need?"

Glass *clinks* as Jeston sorts through the vials, collecting a handful of light blue ones from the very back. He gives them to me and then waits with his hand extended.

"I want five more." Better to have too much antidote than too little.

Sighing, Jeston withdraws an additional five vials. "The key, Allette."

I walk toward the cage, doing my best not to compare myself to the future Queen of Nimbiss. Even in the clothes of a peasant, she still manages to look regal.

She will leave this place and return to her castle, living out the rest of her days surrounded in luxury. Meanwhile, I'll be here, praying she never seeks out her wayward husband.

I won't let her have him.

Senan Vale is mine—he always has been. There is only one way to ensure that he remains that way. "If I agree to let you out, I want your word that you will file for an annulment the moment you reach Nimbiss."

The princess stands taller, her eyes igniting. "I want to be married to that wretch as much as he wants to be married to me."

What she wants doesn't change the facts: As long as the two of them are wed, he is tied to her. Those ties must be severed. "Your word, princess."

"You have it," she clips. "The moment I reach my father's castle, I will file the paperwork."

Can I trust her? At this stage, I don't have much of a choice. It's either believe her or leave her in the hands of these monsters, sealing Prince Kyffin's fate as well.

Reluctantly, I place the key in Jeston's outstretched palm. He unlocks the door, and the heavy iron bars swing open with an ominous *creak*. The princess falls into his arms with a broken sob.

"It's all right. You're going to be all right," he murmurs, smoothing her dark hair back from her face. She clings to him like a lifeline, and I feel a little guilty for considering leaving her behind.

But only a little.

I carefully tuck the small vials into my sash, ensuring each one is properly secured to keep them from dropping out.

Jeston murmurs something low and quiet to the princess before lifting her into his arms and cradling her close. Tears glisten in her eyes as her head drops to the crook of his neck.

I cannot wait for this awful night to end. "How do we get out?"

"When we leave the office, take a right."

We hurry on silent feet back up the stairs to the office and out into the hallway. I turn right as instructed, but then shouts erupt from down the corridor. It sounds like they're coming this way.

With a curse, Jeston adjusts his hold on the princess and nudges his chin toward a black door at the opposite end of the hallway. "We need to take the staircase to the roof."

The bloody roof? Doesn't he remember what's up there?

More shouting jumpstarts my trembling limbs. Seeing no other option, I sprint toward that doorway and throw the barrier aside. Jeston sets the princess on her feet, but keeps an arm around her waist, helping her up the stairs.

Into the darkness we go, the curving staircase growing more compact the higher we climb. More bellowing sounds from below. At the very top, another door awaits.

A door that refuses to budge.

"Open it," Jeston hisses.

Why didn't I think of that? Probably because it won't open. I throw my shoulder into it, and the thing gives a little. I ram my shoulder again, opening it a little more.

Cool air rushes through the gap. I make the mistake of taking a deep breath. Stars...it reeks like the cottage in the human realm.

Like death.

One more hard shove and the hinges give. The door scrapes open, and I tumble onto a flat rooftop blanketed in a thick layer of fog.

Fog and pikes.

Pikes topped with arms and legs and...*heads*.

The princess stumbles out, and when she straightens, her face blanches. Jeston closes the door swiftly, appearing unfazed by the macabre graveyard. I scan for a ladder or a nearby rooftop but there doesn't seem to be a way down. "What now?"

Jeston cards a hand through his silver hair.

The princess blinks at the decaying body parts, her complexion as gray as the fog.

Wait a minute. She can save us. "Call your wings and fly us down."

"I can't."

"Why not?" Her skin is still tanned, so she must have some sunlight left in her veins. Unless... "Did they take them?"

Her gaze drops to where her bare feet peek from beneath her skirts. "No."

Jeston stalks between pikes, stepping carefully over the puddles of entrails and blood. "She has no wings, so we need to find another way off this roof."

I remember seeing the princess with wings on more than one occasion. "She does have wings. White ones."

The princess winces. "The wings you saw were prosthetics commissioned by my father."

Wait... the Princess of Nimbiss is Tuath? *Dammit.* How the hell are we going to escape this bloody rooftop now?

"How do we get down?" For all we know, Cadoc could be on his way right now. Hell, he could be combing his tower as we speak. He could be climbing the stairs.

Jeston presses his fingers to his temples. "Give me a minute to think."

We don't have a bloody minute.

He's going to find us and kill us.

A thump rattles across the rooftop. A shadow emerges from the fog. Wings flare from the shadow's back as the man steps forward. There's a flash of silver by his thigh. *A blade.*

I assumed Cadoc was Tuath. Apparently, I was wrong.

Then I see the color of his wings.

Black.

Aeron Vale is here.

Relief spills through my chest. Say what you want about his scowls and lack of manners, Senan's brother has impeccable timing.

"I am so happy to see you." That is until I notice the large crimson stain spreading over his abdomen.

"I would've been here sooner," Aeron grits out, clutching his middle, "but three men attacked me in the alley."

"Are you all right?"

"I will be. Unfortunately, this means I'll only be able to carry one of you at a time."

How I wish I could tell him to take me. To take me away from this nightmare and return me to my prince. Unfortunately, that cannot happen. "Take the princess first."

Aeron stalks toward Princess Leeri, lifting her into his arms. His wings flare, and he takes off into the clouds. He mustn't bring her far, because he returns a few minutes later, landing on the far side of the roof.

I run toward him, then come to a skidding halt. This man's wings aren't black.

They're red.

Cadoc Carew isn't Tuath after all.

The man's evil grin is a flash in the fog. "I didn't expect to see you again so soon, Wynn. What a pleasant surprise."

Shit. I stumble behind a hairy arm, the fingers at the end bent and broken. Cadoc's gaze tracks down to the glowing blue vials inside my sash, and his nostrils flare. "Looks like you figured out what you wanted after all. Didn't anyone teach you that it's not nice to take things that don't belong to you?"

Leaning down, he catches the base of a pike topped with a head, the gray skin melting off the skull. He gives the thing a shake, and the head pops off, landing with a wet *splat* next to his boot. "I wish you would have come to me. We could've reached an agreement."

I grab for the closest pike, intent on defending myself, but there's too much blood coating the wood. *Dammit.* I can't get a decent grip.

I swipe my hands down my thighs, leaving dark smudges on silk and skin. The next pike isn't slippery but refuses to budge.

I continue inching back toward the edge of the roof, praying for Aeron to reappear.

Cadoc is so focused on me, that he doesn't seem to notice Jeston creeping closer... or the pike in his fist.

It's up to me to distract the bastard so that Jeston can run him through.

"I would never bargain with a monster like you," I spit.

"Strong words coming from a woman at the wrong end of a pike." Cadoc lifts the pike like a spear, a twisted smile on his face.

The breath leaves my lungs, bracing for impact.

He whirls, driving the pike through Jeston's stomach. My accomplice collapses to the ground with a wail, blood gushing from the wound, spraying over the rooftop.

Cadoc pins Jeston with a boot on his chest. "Jeston, Jeston, Jeston." He clicks his tongue. "What would your poor mother say if she saw you now?" He yanks the pike from Jeston's torso, and my friend lets out a rattling gasp.

With Jeston's blood dripping from the end of the pike, Cadoc turns back to me. "Such a waste," he mutters, adjusting his grip on the wood.

My heels hit the edge of the slate tiles.

I try to call to my magic, but my element is as silent as the air around us.

Even if my power decided to cooperate, there's no way I'd be faster than Cadoc with his wings.

I need to stand my ground.

I need to fight.

I lunge for a pike holding a skewered arm, catching the dismembered wrist and tugging the limb free, throwing it aside. Gripping the wood in both hands, I yank until I hear a crack.

Only the top breaks off.

When I turn, Cadoc is there, his pike aimed at my heart. He lunges, and I pivot. The spear flies through the air, tumbling into nothing. His hand snaps out, wrapping around my throat, choking me. Lifting me off my feet.

Blackness speckles the edge of my vision.

Senan's face flashes before my eyes, wearing his roguish smile.

His laughter fills my ears. My heart.

I'm coming, my love.

I'll be there soon.

Splinters pierce my palm as my fingers tighten around the wood. I stab the stake into Cadoc's forearm. His howl of rage floods the air. His grip loosens. Vanishes.

A scream tears from my throat as I slip through the fog, flailing for the edge of the rooftop, my fingers scraping nothing but mist. My body drops through the clouds, plummeting toward the cobblestones. Darkness flashes in my peripherals and a pair of arms bands around my waist, ripping me sideways through an alley.

A hand clamps over my mouth, stifling my scream. "*Quiet,*" Aeron hisses, darting between two buildings and pressing me against the hard plaster.

I listen to the ominous flap of Cadoc's wings as he searches for us, the cacophony of his vicious curses rising in the darkness.

A sob climbs my throat. I swallow it down, closing my eyes and envisioning my prince's face, praying Cadoc cannot hear my thundering heart.

The pressure against my lips begins to ease. Aeron drops his hand, peering from between the buildings. "I think he's gone. Stay here—remain hidden. I'll go back for Jeston."

In all my panic, I completely forgot. "Jeston is... He's d-dead."

The world starts to spin, my legs threatening to give out as terror grips my heart. We managed to save the princess and retrieve the antidote...

But at what cost?

Twenty-Eight

SENAN

If this poison doesn't kill me, all this waiting will.

The problem with lying around like a helpless infant all fucking night is that it gives you the chance to think. With worry spilling from the edges of my mind, plagued by every terrible mishap that could have befallen my girl, the last few hours have been torture.

Don't get me started about the shite Aeron brought up regarding the king. My mind is on fire and the only way to dampen the flames is to keep moving.

My bare feet make no sound as I pace back and forth between the fireplace and the wall, my trembling hands stuffed deep inside my pockets.

I still cannot believe Aeron wants me to take the throne.

Gods... Could you imagine? *King Senan.* Sounds like a curse if you ask me.

Who would want someone like me telling them what to do? Leading an entire kingdom when all I've done is lead myself and my love astray? Perhaps if I'd had more self-control and been better able to manage my grief, then I'd feel up to the task.

Instead, I squandered my life away.

I was right to turn him down—

The door bursts open, and Aeron races through the gap, cradling my girl in his arms. All the warmth in my body drains away as I lunge for her, my hands meeting the pale skin of her waist between the scandalous panels of her scant red gown.

Her hands look as if they've been painted in blood.

"What happened?" For the first time, I wish I did have the crown if only to exact revenge on whoever harmed my girl.

My brother's haunted eyes meet mine. "Carew found them. I managed to save the princess and Allette, but Jeston... He didn't make it."

Shit.

Allette's lashes flutter open, her gaunt cheeks pale as her vacant eyes find mine. "Senan?" She twists and wriggles out of my brother's grasp.

Aeron sets her on her feet, and she throws herself into my arms. I hold her as tightly as I dare, cradling the most precious person in my life.

"Where is the princess now?" I ask my brother.

"She's safe."

Allette slips a hand inside her sash, withdrawing a blue vial. "And so are you."

Gods above...

She did it.

It's not that I doubted her. If anyone deserves my faith, it's this woman in my arms. I doubted this world. Doubted that the stars would allow me another chance to live and love and be free of all my terrible misdeeds.

Allette pops the cork with her thumb, and it tumbles to the ground, rolling toward my boot. "Here."

Why do I deserve to live when Jeston died trying to save Kyffin and me? That should've been *my* fate. I should've been the one to die, not him.

"Don't let his death be for naught," she whispers.

My death won't bring him back. Nothing will. All we can do for Jeston now is live.

I throw back the antidote like a shot of whiskey. Whatever magic it contains instantly quells not only the ache in my chest, but also the darkness shadowing my mind.

Allette's cool hand falls to my chest. "How do you feel?"

"As if I will live forever." All because of the sacrifice of a man I'm almost certain hated me as much as I despised him.

One by one, Allette sets the vials on the coffee table. This should be more than enough to rid my body of the poison.

Aeron sighs. "I must get the princess back to the castle. The two of you need to remain hidden until I can find a way to bring you to Stratiss."

Jeston had hoped to find sanctuary in Stratiss as well...

What about his mother? Perhaps Braith will know where to find the woman so that we can offer her the protection and the life her son had hoped to secure for them both. It's the least I can do after all he sacrificed.

Allette shakes her head. "We can't leave now. Cadoc must be brought to justice."

"Men like Carew live beyond the law," Aeron explains. "If we were going to take him out, tonight would have been our best chance. You heard what Jeston said: The man is in the king's pocket. Boris isn't going to raise an army over the death of one Tuath servant, and anything short of that won't work."

I love Aeron, but he's never been what I would call an optimist. He thinks everything is going to go to shit no matter what, which often leads to him giving up when he should fight.

If anything is worth fighting for, it's this. Carew needs to pay for his crimes.

It's the least we can do for Jeston.

"Then you don't give him a choice," I say. "Cadoc didn't just kill Jeston, he kidnapped the Princess of Nimbiss. He is the reason a Kumulus prince was stolen by a foreign kingdom. Present the evidence to the king in such a way that his only option is to retaliate with the full force of the kingdom's might. And do it with a big fucking audience."

Aeron scrubs a hand down the back of his neck. "*Shit.* You're right. I need to go. Stay hidden. I mean it, Senan. I'm done saving your ass." With that, my brother stalks back out the door.

Alone in the living room, I turn to find my girl looking up at me with tears limning her lashes.

When I reach for her, she steps away.

"I'm sorry. I just... I think I need a moment alone." She folds her arms around herself, her shoulders curling inward as she drifts into the hallway toward the bathing room.

I wait until the door closes to follow her. I'm going to give her space but want to be close in case she changes her mind. Soft sobs drift through the barrier, the broken sound crushing my soul.

Let me be alone with you.

My girl spoke those words to me only a few weeks ago.

Why wouldn't I do the same for her?

Before I can talk myself out of it, I twist the knob and open the door.

Allette stands at the sink, her hands coated in suds as she scrubs the blood from the front of her dress.

"Allette?"

Her red-rimmed eyes meet mine in the reflection of the mirror above the sink. "It's not fair. Love is meant to triumph over evil. That's what all the stories say. But evil keeps on winning, and it's *not fucking fair.*"

I step behind my girl, my chest meeting her back. "I know." Gods, do I know.

"I was so frightened. I thought I'd never see you again. I thought he was going to..."

"Shhh... I've got you. You're safe now." I reach for the cloth, and she lets me take it. I twist off the tap, hang the cloth on the edge of the sink, and untie the sash at her waist. With a few tugs, she's bare before me, the drenched silk in a puddle on the stone floor. I remove my shirt and slip the soft cotton over her head, pulling her hair from the collar so the midnight strands fall down her back.

She continues staring at her reflection, a frown on her lips. "What if he finds me?"

"He won't." *I would never let that happen.*

"You weren't there. You didn't see the madness in his eyes. He won't stop until I'm impaled on a pike."

"Aeron will take care of it." *And if he doesn't, then I will. Don't ask me how, but I would move the sky and the sea to ensure her safety.*

If I were king—

No. Those are the thoughts of a selfish man, one who wants to use the throne for revenge. A man exactly like Boris Vale.

Allette's lower lip starts to wobble, and a single tear rolls down her cheek.

I turn her toward me and cover her trembling lips with mine, breathing her in. *My life. My world.* "You are the bravest person I know. I am humbled by your selflessness. In awe of your strength. I'm so sorry you had to risk your life for mine. That my foolishness cost Jeston his," I murmur between kisses to her lips, her face, her throat.

Love is meant to triumph over evil.

Maybe it has. Maybe the fact that we are both here, both alive, clinging to one another is evidence of that triumph.

"Make me forget," she begs, her nails tattooing crescent moons on my shoulders. "I want to forget it all."

How can I deny her this escape?

My hands come around her hips, trailing down to grip her backside and lift so her legs can wrap around my hips. Allette's arms come around my neck, pressing our bodies closer as she pants into my mouth, her fingers dragging through my hair.

Losing our minds. Suppressing memories. Finding only each other. Stealing what we can in this frantic moment.

She tastes of salty tears and bittersweet hope.

Of love and loss and life.

Make me forget...

I set her on the ground only to watch her drop to the floor without a word. She leans back on her elbows, knees raised and spread for me, my shirt riding up her bare thighs.

I kneel in front of her, unable to fathom how a man who has made so many mistakes could ever get so lucky. I drag my knuckle along the swells of her breasts, my mouth as dry as the cotton covering them. My hands slip to her waist. Her hips. Her thighs. Tugging my shirt to reveal her red silk undergarments. I trace my thumb along the wet patch covering her core. "Is all this for me?"

"All for you." Her hips tilt upwards, pressing her closer to my touch. *So fucking wet.*

"Would my heroine prefer I lick her clean or mess her up?"

Her teeth drag along her bottom lip. "Why can't it be both?"

Both it is.

Off comes the scrap of lace hiding her center, abandoned on the stones along with reservations and decorum. I throw her legs over my shoulders and go to work, lapping at her sweetness, searching for the spot that makes her hips buck. Her hands tear at my hair and her pelvis grinds against my face as I drown in her. Relief and misery have me setting a frenzied pace, clawing at her unblemished skin, flicking my tongue against her clit, coaxing her to the edge until she's panting my name.

She is still pulsing when I yank down my trousers and bury myself inside her, the stones biting my knees with each punishing thrust. Pleasure and pain. Our love and this terrible, beautiful life described in two words.

With one hand firmly planted on the stones, I relish the way her breasts bounce as I thrust into her. The way her stiff nipples strain. Has a more beautiful sight ever existed?

This woman is my undoing. My detriment. My salvation.

A low, tingling sensation starts in my stomach, and my balls tighten. I don't want this to be over but can't bring myself to slow. If Carew succeeded, Allette wouldn't be here, writhing beneath me. She'd be gone.

Gone. Gone. Gone.

"You are mine."

"Yours," she whispers, eyes closed and chin raised, exposing the smooth column of her throat as she strains for another release. "All yours."

I palm her breast, teasing the tip with calloused fingers until her walls tighten around me, pulsing as she comes once more. It's not enough. It will never be enough. I withdraw before I spill into her, and my body screams its protest. "Get on your knees."

Her thighs tremble as she rolls to her front and presses back into me, thighs still spread and round ass lifted. I fist my cock, soaked from her sweet honey, and take her from behind, watching her face flood with ecstasy in the mirror leaning against the far wall.

I twist the thick curtain of her hair in my fist, tugging her head up until our eyes lock in the reflection. "See what I see? The power you have over me?" I reach around to toy with her swollen clit, teasing her until she's pushing back against me, meeting each buck of my hips, begging for more. When I've reached the end of my tether, I pull out, spilling onto the globes of her ass.

With my trembling hands still anchored to her hips and my heart pounding an uneven song in my chest, I force the breath back into my lungs. "Gods, Allette. You are a sight to behold."

She peers over her shoulder, her eyes glistening with unshed tears. I retrieve the cloth from the sink and clean my spend from her skin.

"Come here." I pull my girl onto my lap, cradling her in my embrace. She melts into me, her body fitting like the key to my locked heart. How did I get so damn lucky to have such a strong, fierce woman loving every dark and broken inch of me?

Make me forget...

Our bodies may have been sated, but in the silence, those dark thoughts tend to creep back in. I should know; I spent the last four years drowning in them.

I don't want my love to drown as well.

Love is meant to triumph over evil.

The only way for that to happen is if we never stop fighting. Hoping. Dreaming.

My head falls back against the wall, the floor cold beneath my bare ass, and yet I have no desire to move from this spot. "Let's dream together."

Her voice wobbles. "How?"

"Close your eyes and I'll show you." My fingers sweep along the small of her back, tracing her spine. "Are they closed?"

Her lashes sweep against her name inked over my heart. "Yes."

"Do you still want to live by the coast?"

"More than ever."

My little air wielder, always searching for the breeze. "Imagine we've finally reached our seaside destination, the breeze rife with stinky seaweed and fish urine. What happens next?" My lips twitch into a smile. "Please, don't tell me I'm a fisherman."

Her whole body vibrates with her watery laughter. "Heavens, no. You will obviously have the most successful cheesecake business in the village."

Obviously. "What about you?"

"I'll mend the villager's clothes. That way I can sit and watch you bake all day long and taste everything to make sure it meets expectations."

"Sounds like the perfect dream."

"The perfect dream," she mumbles, her breaths evening out as sleep steals her away.

Love is meant to triumph over evil.

I only hope Aeron succeeds in taking down Cadoc Carew before the bastard finds us so we have a chance to make those dreams come true.

Twenty-Nine

ALLETTE

I WEAR MY GRIEF LIKE LEADEN ARMOR BENEATH MY skin. Heavy. Cold. Unforgiving.

My eyes cannot shut for any length of time without picturing Jeston's lifeless body impaled by that pike, Cadoc standing over him with a victorious sneer before turning his sights on me. Suddenly, I'm back on that rooftop, dodging pikes and dismembered body parts, a madman with bloodred wings breathing down my neck. Squeezing my throat until I'm on the brink of death. When I fall off the rooftop, Aeron isn't there to catch me.

It's been three days of restless nights and heart-stopping panic every time someone knocks at the front door. We have yet to hear a word from the castle, waiting with bated breaths for news of Kyffin and the princess. As much as I would love to explore the burrows as a distraction, we cannot leave for fear of someone working for Cadoc recognizing us.

This beautiful home so full of love and life has become another cage, the walls slowly closing in.

Despite it all, Senan remains upbeat, doing his level best to make me laugh every chance he gets. Still, I see the shadows cross his eyes when he thinks I'm not looking.

Josie ambles by the bedroom I've been given, glancing in as

she passes. Her brows come together when she finds me sitting on the edge of the bed, staring at nothing. Remembering everything.

"I'm so glad you're awake," she says. "How would you like to join your handsome mate in the kitchen?"

That had been the plan, but this is as far as I've gotten.

After suffering through three barely edible dinners, last night I offered to help Josie cook. She waved me off, said she was used to cooking for far more people, and didn't mind the task. I couldn't find it in my heart to tell her that I wasn't only offering for her benefit but for ours as well.

Apparently, she changed her mind.

In the kitchen, Senan stands at the counter, a gingham apron tied around his waist, a peeler in one hand, and a sweet potato in the other. When he sees me, he offers a quick smile and a wink.

Swallowing my misery, I attempt a smile in return. "Nice apron." The last time he wore similar attire, we made love on a kitchen table.

Senan knocks his hip against Josie's, saying in a conspiratorial whisper, "Told you she'd love it."

"You wouldn't catch my Harold dead in one of my aprons," Josie replies with a giggle. "This lad all but insisted."

Sounds like Senan, always finding brightness even on the darkest of days.

I glance at the pile of vegetables on the counter, half of them peeled, half still covered in dirt. "What're you making?"

Josie grabs a potato. "Braith's favorite. She sent word from the castle that she'll be coming by for dinner."

My stomach sinks even lower. How am I supposed to tell Braith what happened to the man she has pined over for so long? She's going to be devastated when she learns of Jeston's fate—assuming she hasn't already.

I should've fought harder to save him.

Now I'm here, alive and breathing while he's probably still on that rooftop.

In pieces.

My throat constricts, making it impossible to swallow as I blink back the tears that never seem to go away.

Josie nods toward the cupboards, oblivious to my spiral. "There's a peeler in that drawer there. Grab one and get to work. Be sure to cut off any bad parts or mushy bits you see." She sets down the potato to collect a handful of peels from the pile, dumping them into a bucket next to the bin. "Do the two of you have any idea how long you might be staying with us? Braith never mentioned."

"We'll be leaving as soon as Terrence gets back," Senan says, rinsing the potato he just peeled and adding it to the four others next to the sink.

"There's no rush now. Stay as long as you'd like; the more the merrier in this burrow, that's what I always say." A rosy flush stains her cheeks, and she clears her throat. "Although, if you could keep your cavorting down after eleven, I'd appreciate it. My Harold has to be out at the mines by half past six every morning and needs his rest."

She can *hear* us? I wish the floor would open and swallow me whole.

Senan doesn't have the decency to appear embarrassed, puffing his chest like a strutting rooster. "Our apologies, Josie. We will try to be quieter."

"Thank you. It'd do no good to anyone for Harold to end up falling asleep on the job and tumbling into some pit. Oh! Speaking of pits..." Josie scurries into the hallway, leaving Senan and me alone with the potato mountain.

"I am going to die of mortification." When I glance over and catch Senan still grinning, I snatch a handful of peels and throw them at his irritating face. "*Stop* smiling."

He dodges them easily enough, his laughter echoing around the room. "Maybe I like the idea of everyone knowing how loud I can make my girl scream."

He would. "Tonight, I'll be silent as the grave."

"Will you, now?"

"Yes. Not even a peep."

He eases forward and just when I think he's going to kiss me, he nips my neck. A startled squeal bursts from my mouth, and Senan draws back looking as smug as ever.

I take my potato as far from him as possible, ignoring his chuckle as I swipe my peeler over the rough brown skin, shaving away the layers until only coppery orange remains. There are quite a few bad spots, so I cut those out as well, adding them to the pile of skins.

With each potato I peel, my embarrassment slowly melts back into worry. What am I going to say to Braith when she arrives? We'll need to make time for a private conversation.

Setting his potato aside, Senan snags one of the leafy greens draining in the sink. "Do you see this? This is grass. Do you know what eats grass? The food I want to be eating."

The Nightingales do eat a lot of vegetables. "Don't let Josie hear you say that. She might take offense. I'm pretty sure Braith's parents are vegetarians."

Senan slumps against the counter with an exaggerated huff. "Well, I'm not."

Neither am I, but beggars don't dine on steak; they eat whatever they're given.

Josie appears in the kitchen once more, a canvas bag draped over her shoulder. She's not alone, either. A tall, scowling man waits at her back. "Look who I found outside," she says, beaming up at Aeron. "We'll have a full table tonight."

Senan's brother ducks through the door. For the first time since I met the man, he doesn't look as if he's on the verge of collapsing or murdering someone, and if I'm not mistaken, he's had a haircut as well. The sides appear freshly shaven, the dark strands at the top trimmed so they skim the tops of his gold-lined ears.

The leaf in Senan's hand floats down to the floor, his smile fading away. "You're back."

Aeron nods. "I returned as soon as I could."

Josie sets down the canvas bag and then practically skips back out the door, leaving the three of us standing in tense silence.

I'm almost too afraid to ask, but I must know… "What news from the castle?"

Aeron's silver gaze slides to where I strangle the peeler. "The king's guards raided Dread Row last night. They arrested almost fifty men."

Senan cards a hand through his hair. "And Carew?"

Aeron's lips twitch. If I didn't know better, I'd say he was about to smile. "In the pit where he belongs."

Did he just say Carew is in the pit? Heavens above! He did.

Carew is in the bloody pit!

"There's more." Aeron glances over his shoulder, searching up and down the hallway before stepping closer. When he speaks, his voice is no more than a whisper. "Jeston isn't dead. They found him locked in a cage beneath Carew's office. He was unconscious, but the healer says he should make a full recovery."

My heart damn near leaps from my chest.

Jeston isn't dead!

How is that even possible? This feels too good to be true.

What if it is? Could this be another lie told by the king? "You're certain? You saw Jeston with your own eyes?"

"I did."

A sob wrenches from my throat. Thank the stars and the gods and the fates for watching over him. I throw my arms around Senan's neck, my tears soaking his soft cotton shirt. *We're safe.* Carew is locked away where he cannot hurt me or anyone else I love, and Jeston isn't gone.

Could this day get any better?

Squeezing me tightly, Senan presses a kiss to my temple. "And Kyff?"

What's happening to Aeron's face?

Is he…*wait*. Is he *smiling*?

No. That's not a smile. It's an impish grin.

Although Senan holds my heart, I finally understand why women claim Aeron is the most handsome of the Vale princes.

"Our baby brother is on his way back to the castle as we speak."

Love is meant to triumph over evil.

I said those words to Senan only a few days ago. After what happened on Dread Row, it felt like all hope was lost. Now, I can see the light at the end of this dark tunnel. Our dreams are waiting right around the corner.

We still need to remain vigilant. To guard our secrets and remain hidden from the king.

But those are all worries for tomorrow.

Tonight, we're celebrating a miracle.

Thirty

SENAN

Josie's grin feels foreboding as she saunters into the dining room with a gigantic crockery dish propped against her hip. Who would've suspected such a jolly woman was actually a harbinger of doom?

"I hope you boys are still hungry. You look as if you could use a little meat on those bones."

Exactly. *Meat* on my bones, not fucking vegetables.

If I eat one more leafy green, I might keel over and turn into one myself. The last few days, I have consumed more carrots and parsnips and cabbage and fucking sprouts than any person has a right to.

Not by choice, mind you.

Braith's mother puts them in *everything*. And by everything, I mean desserts as well.

That's right. I've had carrots in fucking cake—a place no vegetable has any business being.

And let's not forget the sweet potato "pie" she served last night.

I ate all of it—wouldn't want to be rude to our host—but I did not enjoy one bite. Pie should not be the color of mucky clay or the texture of cold mashed potatoes. Positively vile.

The problem with clearing your plate is that the cook mistakenly believes you enjoyed the dish and is prone to cooking it over and over and *over* again.

I'd kill for a steak right now. Or a juicy chicken, slow roasted over a fire, stuffed with sage and rosemary. Or a pig. Sausage, bacon, ham—I'm not picky. Give me any part of a pig and I'd be in heaven.

Aeron hasn't grumbled under his breath or complained once tonight, and it is infuriating. Probably because he has been dining at the castle the last few nights and has been spared the worst of it.

Braith's mother sets a dish between us, removing the lid with a flourish.

Another pie. How exciting.

Josie hums a happy little song as she cuts each of us a slice as big as our heads and flops them onto plates with a sickening *splat*. Aeron thanks her and collects his fork from beside his empty dinner plate. She cuts one for Braith as well, sliding the plate in front of her daughter. Braith's face gives nothing away as she takes a small bite.

According to Josie, this dessert is Braith's favorite.

Either the woman's tastebuds are broken, or she is an excellent liar.

Allette was the only smart one of us, telling Josie she couldn't eat sweet potatoes because of an allergy. I don't have a clue if that's an actual allergy but figured it would look a little suspicious if I revealed a fake allergy to the same thing. Last night I ate my pie like a polite guest, but tonight I just cannot stomach it.

Josie tells us to enjoy, collects a handful of dishes, and then leaves us to our *delicious* dessert.

Allette hides her smile behind her glass of mulled wine as she leans back against her chair.

"How can you eat that?" I whisper under my breath to my brother.

With his eyes narrowed on me, Aeron hacks off a huge bite and stuffs it between his lips. "What do you mean? It's good."

What a load of bollocks. He winces every time he swallows. The man went through at least four pints of water trying to choke down his dinner, for stars' sake.

He makes it about halfway through the pie before finally abandoning his fork and guzzling what's left of the water in his glass.

Good, my arse. "Then why don't you finish it all?"

Braith smiles from her chair, seeming oblivious to the grief we've endured since she left us. The news at the castle is all sunshine, with Kyff set to return by the end of the week. Allette asked her about Jeston, and Braith said she heard he wasn't feeling well but that his position as Head Master meant the king allowed him access to the royal infirmary.

We've decided it's best to keep the truth of what happened to him a secret—for now, at least.

"Yes, Terrence," Braith says. "Why don't you finish it all?"

Turning his glower on Braith, Aeron abandons his empty glass and stabs another chunk. "I plan to." Down the hatch it goes, followed by another gulp of water—this time from my glass.

He's going to break. It's only a matter of time before the potatoes turn to cement in his gut.

I nudge his plate toward him. "Go on, then. Still, a few bites left. Eat up."

A humming Josie saunters back into the room. When she sees my untouched dessert, her smile falters. "Do you not like tonight's pie?"

I don't want to hurt her feelings, but if I try to take a bite of that, it's going to come right back up, along with the salad greens and sweet potato cakes from dinner.

Aeron smirks at me, his jaw pulsing with each chew.

I can think of one way to wipe that infuriating look off his smug face. "The pie is wonderful, but my brother asked if he could have my slice. I'm full from dinner, so I've agreed."

Aeron chokes on his bite, his eyes blazing like star fire. One of these days, his head is going to explode from all the pent-up rage. He really should find an outlet for it.

I scoot my plate across the table with a grin. "Here you go, Terrence. It's all yours."

Josie refills his water glass from the jug in her hand. "My, you're a thirsty boy, aren't you?" Smiling warmly, she pats Aeron's cheek and then returns to the kitchen, probably coming up with a new recipe to torture us with for breakfast.

"You're some prick," Aeron mutters, fork poised as he stares down at the second helping of pie, his face downright green.

Allette and Braith giggle, while I sit back and watch him shovel in my slice as well.

FOR THE FIRST TIME SINCE WE ARRIVED, I DARE TO venture outside the house. Without access to a glamour, I'm forced to hide beneath the hood of my borrowed cloak. No matter. At least I'm outside. The damp air down here isn't fresh, but I have space to breathe.

That is until Aeron follows me out and sinks onto the stone ledge next to the house with a beleaguered sigh. "We need to talk."

I fall next to him, just out of reach in case he plans on exacting revenge. "If it's about the pie—"

"It's not about the damn pie," he clips. "Have you given any more thought to what we discussed?"

If he hasn't noticed, life has been a little busy of late. "No."

"Senan, look at me. If Boris is allowed to keep the throne, there's no telling what—"

Braith's father steps out of their burrow, a bucket and shovel in his hand. "Terrence? Would you mind helping me for a bit? I've to clean the grass from the gutters, and Jones took my damn ladder."

I'm so happy for the interruption, I could kiss Harold's balding head.

Aeron grimaces.

Biting back a smile, I give my brother's shoulder a nudge. "Go on, Terry. The man needs help cleaning his gutters."

Aeron levels a finger at me. "Don't you fucking start."

"Why not, *Terry*? What are you going to do to me?"

"Remember the gift I bought for your seventh birthday?"

Not the fish in a box! I had nightmares about those bulging eyes for weeks afterward. "You wouldn't dare."

"Try me." He pushes to his feet, dusts off his trousers, and heads up the hill.

Part of me is tempted to offer a hand as well—mostly to avoid the fish-in-a-box—but that part is overshadowed by the need to sit here and stew over what Aeron said.

I don't want this kingdom to go down in flames, but I cannot fathom taking the throne for myself. Besides, who's to say we would succeed? We aren't the only people who hate Boris Vale, and yet he remains king. More than likely, we'll all end up getting killed trying to remove him from power. What's the point in joining a suicide mission? We have fought too hard to live to give it all up now.

"Heya," a high voice trills, interrupting my spinning thoughts.

I glance toward the burrow below where I sit, finding a small girl peeking from a round window. Her silver ringlets remind me of tiny springs. Her eyes are so large, they take up far too much room on her dainty face.

"Hello," I say with a small wave.

The girl drags a chubby fist beneath her nose, her little mouth turning down in a frown. "I never seen you before. What's your name?"

Her lisp is the cutest I've ever heard. Reminds me a bit of Kyff before his elocution lessons. "My name is Simon. What's yours?"

"Dahlia."

"That's a pretty name."

"I know."

Modest. I like her already.

The longer she stares at me through those wide eyes, the more her little brow furrows. "Why did you let someone draw on you, Simon?"

It takes a moment for me to realize that she's referring to the tattoos on my hands. "Because I wanted to." I splay my fingers, giving her a better view of the words inked there, and shove up my sleeves so she can admire the moonflowers as well.

Her head tilts and springy curls sway. "That's odd."

Nothing like a child to give unsolicited, unfiltered opinions. Sure, the tattoos put some people off, but there is only one other person whose approval matters to me, and she loves them. "Maybe I think it's odd that you haven't let anyone draw on you."

Dahlia's pink lips purse into a pout before she ducks out of view.

"I was only joking," I call toward the open window.

Her head pops back out the window a moment later. This time, she doesn't stay inside the burrow but climbs out onto the rocky knoll and skips right up to where I sit.

In her grubby hand, she clutches an ink pen that she extends toward me. Her other hand lands on my knee with a smack. "I want a bunny."

All right. That's random. "I hear bunnies make good pets."

"I can't have pets because Mummy says they shite everywhere." My startled laugh makes her smile, revealing two missing bottom teeth. "I want you to draw one. Here." She taps the back of her dimpled hand.

I really shouldn't...but this ink will wash off, right? Against my better judgment, I draw a bunny on her hand, not too large of course. "There you go. All finished."

Her face falls. "What is that?"

"What do you mean? It's a bunny." Although now that I'm looking at it, he looks a bit rabid.

"Bunnies don't look like that."

"Fine." I pass her the pen. "Show me what a bunny looks like." I stretch out my hand, giving her free reign over my bare forearm. Her tongue peeks through the gap in her teeth as she focuses on her drawing, which is, admittedly, a hundred times better than mine.

"Dahlia! Time for your tea!" a woman shouts.

The little girl's curls slap my cheek when she whirls toward the window. "Coming, Mummy! Goodbye, Simon!"

I wave goodbye, watching her disappear into that hole.

What would it be like to have grown up somewhere like this? Are the Tuath here happy with their lot in life or do they wish for more?

I glance back to where Aeron is shoveling dirt and clumps of grass from the gutters, Braith's father directing him like a foreman on a building site. They seem to have their business handled just fine without me. Besides, I don't have a lot of spare clothes, so I can't afford to get covered in dirt.

Quietly, I rise and slip between two burrows, heading down toward the river.

The Tuath have everything here—everything except sunlight, that is. Their light comes from large clusters of fae lights attached to the ceilings and walls of the caverns. What I saw of the servant's quarters beneath the castle during my escape is similar in that regard. There's even a market selling fruit and veg, although the carrots are kind of puny. The potatoes look half-rotten as well.

I pick up an apple, its flesh pink and crisp on one side and mushy and brown on the other. "What's wrong with these?" I ask the woman behind the baskets with her feet propped on a stone. "Why are they all brown?" Are those worms? *Eew.* I drop the apple back into the basket, scrubbing my hand down my trousers.

She lets out a throaty chuckle. "Have you been hiding under a rock? Everyone knows the apples on the trees go to the Scathian markets, and the ones that have fallen arrive here."

That doesn't sound fair at all. Then again, neither does the fact that Scathians live in the sunlight while these folks are forced underground. Although, if I'm being honest, I think I'd rather live here, together with my family, instead of having to fly from one balcony to the next to visit them.

Imagine growing up sharing a bunk with Aeron. The trouble we would've gotten into.

Maybe it's for the best that we were separated. Our poor mother would've lost her mind otherwise.

Speaking of mothers, Josie must be exhausted from cooking for us. Maybe I can finally convince her to take a break. Heaven knows my stomach could use one. If I can find all the ingredients, perhaps I can cook dinner. And dessert. "Do you have any lemons?"

The woman points to a stall across the path. "Old Jonesy is the one you'll need to see for the citrus fruits, but they're usually the first to go."

I thank her and head for Old Jonesy. He doesn't have any lemons or limes, but there are a few oranges that have those gross brown patches on them. Not that I can make much with oranges.

I've only baked one apple pie but can probably remember enough to make it edible. Although if the last few days are anything to go by, something being edible isn't a requirement for meals in the Nightingale house.

I return to the woman's stall for a dozen of the least rotten apples available. "Is there a butcher's nearby?"

The woman pauses. "For what?"

"For meat." Obviously. What other reason would there be to visit a butcher?

"The closest butcher is in the city near the clinic, but they'll fleece you for coins. My husband wanted to buy a leg of lamb as a surprise for Yule and they wanted twenty pence!"

Is twenty pence a lot? When I think of how much gold I've squandered through the years on the most frivolous things...

And these people cannot even afford to buy meat for Yule.

Do the Nightingales eat only vegetables by choice, or can they not afford anything else?

"How much do I owe you?" I ask.

"Two pence."

That's all? I mean, the apples are half-rotten but that seems like a steal. "Do you have change?"

"Of course." From her pocket she withdraws a purse that looks as if it barely holds any coins at all. Aeron only gave me gold.

Gold I'll probably end up squandering on something silly like new boots or shirts when the ones I have are perfectly fine. Unlike this woman, who would use it to buy her family dinner. In her face, I see the man I helped all those years ago. Why wouldn't I help her as well?

"Here." I take out two pieces of gold and place them in her lined palm. "Keep the change."

She sucks in a harsh breath. "I couldn't possibly—"

"I insist. Get yourself that leg of lamb."

I return to the elderly man across the way to buy some oranges and then I purchase a handful of carrots. Josie can use them to bake another terrible cake if she wants. By the time I leave the market, I have an entire basket full of produce. Don't ask me what we're going to do with it all. Maybe that little girl would want some apples—the ones without the worms, of course.

On my way back to the burrow, the sharp clacking of wood draws me off the path.

Two boys around Kyffin's age spar with sticks in a dirt patch between a dress shop and a weaver. Their form is all wrong and if they keep hacking at each other like that, one of them is going to break a finger.

I set the basket down beside a bench carved in stone. "You're holding it too high," I call.

They whirl, and when they see me, their massive eyes widen even more. The sticks hang limply at their sides as they gawk.

Keeping hold of my hood, I jog over to them. I motion for a stick, and the smaller of the two hands me his. I show him how to grip the bottom properly only to realize why he was holding it so high. The "hilt" is riddled with splinters. "Where did you find this?"

"Don't tell him nothin'," the other boy sniffs, his dimpled chin lifting as he watches warily.

"We was just borrowing it from Milton," the first one blurts.

"Tommy!"

Sounds like they're using the term "borrow" in the loosest sense of the word. "Does Milton have sandpaper?"

They both nod.

Guess I'm going to make some swords.

✦

Turns out, Milton is a carpenter here in the burrows, and once I hand over a few coins, he is more than helpful, fashioning twenty wooden swords in under an hour.

That's right. *Twenty.*

When one is commissioning weapons, word gets around.

Now I have amassed an army of children, all of whom have been sparring for the last fifteen minutes with their new swords.

Children aren't the only ones who have gathered, either.

Five young men sit on the stone bench, eating my apples, worms and all. I don't warn them about the creepy crawlies hiding within. Consider it their punishment for stealing another man's fruit. Besides, I can't begrudge them a bit of protein.

When I eventually return to retrieve my basket, only two apples remain. Why couldn't they have eaten the oranges instead?

So much for my pie.

The silver-haired man in the middle folds his arms, smirking up at me in silent challenge. When I don't take the bait, he nods toward the children playing with faux swords. "You're going to get into right shit for that."

In hindsight, giving a bunch of children weapons without

their parents' permission wasn't the brightest idea, but it's too late to take them back now.

Look how happy they are.

At least they won't go home tonight with splintered hands.

The mousy-brown-haired one to his left nudges his shoulder. "How tall would you say he is?"

"At least a head taller than our tallest man," responds the one perched on the knoll behind the bench, rolling an apple between scarred hands.

The fourth man snorts, his pierced eyebrows lifting. "What's your mum been feeding you? Magic beans?"

The man in the middle, the one with the silver hair and a few golden rings in his ears, smirks and answers before I can. "Nah. This one's been eating too much birdseed."

"Excuse me?" Who in their right mind would eat birdseed? Gods above, *do* the Tuath eat birdseed? Those potatoes Josie made the other night did have a strange, almost crunchy texture.

"Are you all blind?" the one who made the birdseed comment scoffs, throwing a hand toward me. "The man isn't Tuath at all."

The five of them murmur amongst themselves, heads pressed together as they cast wary glances my way.

"If he's Scathian, he's the palest I've ever seen," the short one says, pulling away from the group and running a hand along the patchy hair on his weak jaw. "You think he's one of the birds, Nightingale?"

Wait a minute. "Are you by chance related to Braith *Nightingale*?" I ask the silver-haired one with the earrings.

The man launches to his feet, squaring up to me. "Why the fuck do you want to know?"

"Calm down." You'd swear I just told him I slept with his mother. "Braith and I are friends."

I barely have time to smile before his fist slams into my jaw.

Thirty-One

ALLETTE

For the first time since we arrived at the burrows, I have more energy than I know what to do with. Back when I had my wings, I would have soared high above the city, watching the sun paint the sky as it descended below the horizon. Here, all I see are paintings of beautiful things.

I miss *real* rose gardens. The sweet perfume of flowers and the sound of bees buzzing from one bloom to the next. The kiss of a breeze drenched in sunlight.

Sunlight...

What I wouldn't give for some right now.

There's a knock on the bedroom door, followed by Braith's high voice. "Wynn? Would you like to go for a walk with me?"

Is she serious? A walk sounds like heaven. There might not be gardens in the cavern, but at least there would be people and life and something to see besides these four walls. It's safe enough, isn't it? Cadoc isn't a problem anymore, and the king believes us dead.

Surely if I wear a cloak, I should be able to join her.

"Just a minute!" I snag my cloak from the back of the door and join my friend in the hallway.

"We have so much to discuss," Braith says in a conspiratorial whisper. "I want to hear all about what transpired on Dread Row."

Perhaps I don't want to go on a walk after all.

Josie appears from the kitchen, brandishing a basket and a smile. "Did I hear you say you were going for a walk? Would you be a dear and drop these leftovers to your sister?" To me, she explains, "My eldest daughter gets so busy with her work that she sometimes forgets to eat."

Sounds like the perfect distraction from talking about Dread Row. "Does she live far?"

Sighing, Braith takes the basket from her mother. "Only down by the river."

For some reason, her shoulders slump as we make our way to the front door, the basket resting at the crook of her arm. With my hood pulled over my hair and my face cast in shadows, I follow Braith out into the wide caverns.

She links our arms, the basket swinging on her other side as we hurry down the path toward where the river snakes through the center of the cavern. "So, tell me. How did everything go with Carew?"

It takes every ounce of my willpower to keep my smile from slipping into a grimace. "We managed to save the princess and find the antidote, so I'd say the mission was a success."

"I'm relieved to hear it. I was so worried about you. The stories I've heard about that man are things of nightmares."

Sounds like the stories are probably true. "Enough about that. How are things at the castle?"

She throws her head back and groans. "It's so bloody boring without you and Jeston. I understand work isn't always meant to be exciting, but the monotony is killing me. I don't know how I'm going to keep it up for the next month, let alone forever."

"You could always quit."

"And work where?" she snorts. "At the mines with my father and brother? Not all of us are mated to a prince."

I know how lucky I am, but it wasn't always like this. Look at what has befallen us since we met. If I could make Senan a carpenter or a baker instead of a prince, I would. While we are incredibly fortunate that Aeron is willing to provide us with funds to live now, it wasn't meant to be that way. "It's not all roses and sunshine, you know. I had to work in the human realm."

"I'm sorry. That sounded spiteful, but it wasn't meant to be. I'm truly happy that you found your other half. I think I'm just tired of being on my own, you know? Not that I need a mate to find happiness. I don't." She nudges a small stone with her slipper. "But sometimes I think it wouldn't be so bad to have someone to lean on."

I understand exactly what she means. Even though we had very little in the human realm, Senan and I had each other. "Perhaps when Jeston recovers, the two of you will make a go of it."

Her lips purse. "Perhaps."

Or maybe she will meet someone better, someone who doesn't need as much coaxing. Someone whose kiss sets her on fire. As long as she finds happiness, that's all that really matters.

The homes grow smaller as the paths twist downward toward the market. How lovely it feels to stretch my legs. Men and women nod and wave hello, everyone wearing the same contented smile.

When was the last time I felt content?

Probably the day Senan met me at work and brought me to the pub. Those few precious hours before I found out about the poison were magical.

Stars, I need to think about something less depressing.

"Tell me about your sister." I always wanted a sister growing up, someone with whom to share memories and adventures. Someone to turn to in times of need or sorrow.

Instead, it's just me, holding all the memories of my parents and my aunt inside my heart. Of Wynn.

Braith's arm stiffens where it links with mine. "Regina and I don't get along."

"Why is that?"

"It's complicated."

We come to a halt outside a burrow with the words "TATTOOS & PIERCINGS" scorched into the door.

This is where her sister lives? The place is so dark and sullen compared to the brightness of her parents' burrow. Not that I say that aloud.

"I've always wanted a tattoo," I confess.

Braith frowns up at the sign. "So have I."

A little thrill zings through my blood. Wouldn't Senan be surprised if I came back with a tattoo? I can picture the look on his face, the way his eyes would turn molten. "I'll get one if you do." I could get something to celebrate surviving Dread Row.

"And give my poor mum a stroke? You should've seen what happened when Iver got his ears pierced. Every time he walked into the room, she broke down crying, asking where she went wrong."

That sounds a little dramatic over earrings. "I bet she loves the princes'."

"Oh, she doesn't seem to mind anyone else's piercings—or tattoos for that matter. Only her precious children's. She thinks we're all perfect as we are and believes wanting to alter our bodies in any way means we don't love ourselves or some nonsense like that."

An interesting opinion, I suppose. "Did your brother take out his earrings then?"

Braith's teeth flash with her grin. "No. He told her to stop being a crazy old biddy and got another two to spite her."

How could anyone do anything to spite Josie Nightingale? She has been a saint, bringing us into her home as if we were her own.

Then again, perhaps this is Braith's brother's way of rebelling.

During my rebellious phase, I decided to sneak off with a certain Vale prince.

The door swings open and a man emerges, too enthralled by

the red and black ink curving around his forearm to notice us, and nearly bowls Braith over.

"Apologies, ladies." He catches the door, holding it open. "Going inside?"

"Don't be silly, Ollie," a smoky voice says from within. A woman with rings through her lip and both eyebrows appears from the darkness, leaning a tattooed shoulder against the door frame. "Princess Braith doesn't frequent places like this."

Braith's spine goes rigid as a post. "Nice to see you too, Regina."

Besides Regina's silver hair, I see no resemblance to my friend. Unlike Braith's fresh face, her sister wears heavy shadow and black kohl around deep-set brown eyes that snap with anger. Her face is thinner as well, her cheeks sunken. Gaunt.

The man looks between them, his brow furrowing.

Regina waves him off, saying she'll see him next week, and he practically sprints down the street.

Braith is too busy glowering to introduce me, so I step forward and extend my hand. "I'm Braith's friend Wynn. Your mother sent us with leftovers."

Regina's palm slips into mine, her pierced brows climbing her forehead as she glances down at the basket still on Braith's arm. "I suppose I should invite you in then, shouldn't I? Wouldn't want Princess Braith telling Josie how rude I am." She lets go and shifts to the side, a challenge in the stubborn lift of her jaw.

Braith stomps through the gap, her head held high, looking more confident than I imagine she feels. The sweet smell of incense hangs in the air. Orange fae light illuminates intricate drawings scrawled on the stone walls, everything from ferocious striped tigers to nonsensical symbols.

Regina takes the basket from her sister, bringing it over to a high table. "You should've told Josie not to bother." She opens the top with a grimace. "But I know how hard it is for you to disappoint our mother." One by one, she removes the dishes and scrapes every scrap of food into the rubbish bin.

Braith's hands clench into fists at her sides. "There are people starving on the streets, and here you are, wasting an entire meal."

"I wouldn't eat this slop if I were one of them." To me, Regina says, "Our mother is a terrible cook. She shouldn't be allowed in the kitchen."

"I wouldn't say she's terrible." Then again, I wouldn't call her good, either.

One eyebrow arches, and a wry smile plays on Regina's lips as she piles the plates back into the basket. "So you've been subjected to Josie Nightingale's cooking then? Some friend you are, Braith. Did she make her 'famous' sweet potato pie yet?"

Don't get me started on the "pie." Thank heavens I told Josie I was allergic. "Twice."

Regina's laughter booms through the tight space.

Enough about their poor mother. Clearly, the woman tries her best, and from the way Braith's fists bang against her thighs, she is this close to fighting with her sister.

Shifting closer to the wall, I trace a drawing of a colorless feather. "Did you draw these?"

"Most of them. Although, my mate did the ones over there." She points to the far wall.

Braith shifts awkwardly in the middle of the room, her hip bumping into the table, rattling the dishes inside the basket. "Where is Carolynn?"

"She went across to Coill to visit her father."

The ring in Regina's lip glistens when she speaks. It's fascinating. "Did that piercing hurt?" I wouldn't have the nerve to let someone put a hole in my lip.

"Everything hurts." Shrugging, Regina runs a finger down the thin gold ring. "At least this is pain I can control. Mum hated them at first, but she's gotten used to them since. I'm not perfect like Braith, so she doesn't really care what I do."

A pink flush stains Braith's jaw. "I'm far from perfect."

With a harsh chuckle, Regina sinks onto a backless stool next to a padded table and starts putting the lids on the tiny pots of ink. "What brings you down from your castle, *Princess* Braith?"

"Stop calling me that. I'm a servant, nothing more."

"You sure? From the way Josie goes on, you'd swear her little girl is mated to the king himself. I think you might be the only one of us she's proud of. Well, you and the twins of course. And now Lettie since she gave Josie her first grandchild."

Braith reaches for my arm, her fingers trembling where they dig into my skin. "Come on. Let's go."

"That's right. Run back to your castle and hide behind your mask. Because heaven forbid they have to look at your face."

"It's a job, Regina; nothing more."

Regina bares her teeth, her dark eyes hard as flint. "It's a fucking betrayal, that's what it is. How can you stand to work for Scathian scum?"

I stiffen.

So *that's* why there's friction between them. Does Regina hate all Scathians or only the ones in the castle? What would she say if she found out her parents were harboring two Vale princes? If she learned I was once Scathian myself?

"You know what they stole from us," Regina goes on.

Hold on. Did Boris take something from Regina as well? Heaven knows he's stolen enough from me. "What are you talking about?"

Braith pulls me harder, but I stand my ground. "It's nothing," she insists with an exasperated groan.

"It's *everything*," Regina counters. "Did you know that we used to have magic?"

Unease stirs beneath my skin. Given all the lies we've been told, her claim isn't outside the realm of possibility. I turn toward my friend. "Is that true?" If it is, this could change the very fabric of our realm.

Braith's eyes narrow on her sister, her cheeks an angry red. "No, it's not. My darling sister prefers fiction over fact. She always has."

Regina slams the lid on another pot. "You've never read the ancient texts—"

"Neither have you!" Braith hisses. "How many times must we have this conversation, Regina? Just because you want something to be true does not make it so. Come on, Wynn. We can go into the city for a tattoo."

Wait...what's happening?

Regina pushes back from the padded table. "*You're* getting a tattoo?"

"I was hoping to. But since you can't keep your mad conspiracy theories to yourself, we'll go elsewhere."

Regina folds her arms over her chest. "I can keep them all to myself. Go on, then. Tell me what you want. I have plenty of time and ink right here. How about a mask? Or a tower? Wait! I have just the thing: a crown of your own, *Princess Braith*."

Enough is enough. I don't care that Regina is Braith's sister. No one speaks to my friend that way. "Leave her alone. I'm the one who asked about getting a tattoo, all right? Braith said you were the best and I asked her to introduce us. But now that I've met you, I'm not convinced."

Regina's jaw falls open. "You said that about me?" she asks in a quiet voice, like the wind has been taken from beneath her wings.

Braith bobs her head. "It's true. You are the best."

It could just be the lack of light, but I swear Regina's eyes sparkle with tears. "What were you looking for?" she asks.

That's easy. "I want a tattoo on my back."

Braith's eyes widen. "I don't think that's a good—"

"It'll be fine, Braith." Patting her hand, I slip out of her grasp. "I promise."

Regina bobs her head. "How big?"

"My *whole* back."

"That'll take a lot of ink."

"If you have the time, I have the coin." Senan told me to use the gold to buy myself something nice. He probably meant a new dress, but now that the idea has taken root in my mind, I cannot think of anything I'd like more than this.

Regina slaps a hand to the padded table. "Then take down your dress and hop on up. What are you thinking?"

I unbutton my dress and peel down the cotton, exposing my scarred back.

Braith's sister curses when she sees the marks. Her gaze flies to mine.

"If you can forgive the fact that I'm Scathian scum, I would like you to give me back my wings. Ones the king cannot steal."

Thirty-Two

ALLETTE

Braith hides her face in her hands, muffling her words as she trudges up the hill from her sister's burrow. "What was I thinking? My mum is going to have my head."

While my friend is overcome with dread, my stomach leaps with giddy anticipation over showing Senan the start of my tattoo. After Regina picked her jaw off the floor and muttered an apology for her rude comments, she got straight to work on the lines for my new wings. With the special ointment she applied, they should be ready for color in a few days.

"Don't worry. Your mother will never know," I assure her.

Her hands fall but her head still hangs. "She always knows. It's like she can smell when I've done something wrong."

"But you haven't done anything wrong. You're a grown woman, and you got a tattoo—a beautiful one at that. It is small and discreet, and as long as you avoid stripping naked in front of Josie, she will never suspect a thing."

Braith's eyes swim with emotion, a smile playing on her lips as she seems to stand a little taller. "Do you really think it's beautiful?"

"Yes. Don't you?"

"I love it," she says with a nod, sending her hair swinging. "Who knew being rebellious was so thrilling?"

So true. I'm not sure what my parents would have thought about my little act of rebellion, but Aunt Marjory would have loathed everything about my tattoo. I can almost hear her saying that no man would ever choose a wife who disgraced her body in such a way.

Clearly, she never had the pleasure of meeting Senan Vale.

We take a circuitous path back to the burrow, past a bustling pub built into the cave wall, through the empty marketplace, and between two knolls where a bunch of men shout and children squeal.

An entire cache of tiny wooden swords has been abandoned, presumably by the handful of children jumping up and down, screeching.

I'm about to turn away when I realize what they're cheering for.

Senan hunches in the center of the mayhem, his face splattered with blood and one eye swollen shut while a silver-haired man wearing matching wounds circles him.

The basket I offered to carry tumbles to the ground.

What is he thinking? Everyone in the bloody burrows can see his face!

Braith forces her way through the crowd, shouting for folks to get out of the way. Aeron catches her arm, halting her mid-step. She glowers up at him with such venom, it's a wonder he doesn't let her go immediately.

Instead of shrugging him off, she twists back toward the altercation. "Iver! What in the heavens do you think you're doing?"

Iver? Don't tell me Senan is fighting Braith's brother. I leave him for a few hours, and *this* is what happens? I never liked the fact that the king saddled my prince with a guard, but it's clear Senan needs a babysitter.

"Stop this instant!" I bellow.

Senan's head snaps up, and when our gazes connect, the fool winks his only good eye.

My traitorous stomach flutters until Braith's brother punches my mate in his. Senan bowls over, clutching his middle, his vicious curse sending a flash of anger through my chest.

Iver's laughter booms through the cavern.

Senan catches him in a headlock, throwing all his weight into the move. They both crash to the ground, but Senan doesn't let go and doesn't ease his hold, keeping Iver face-down in the dirt until Iver's hand starts tapping his knee.

They both fall onto their backs, staring up at the stalactites on the lofty cavern ceiling with smiles on their faces.

My prince has truly lost his mind.

Did he forget that we were meant to be lying low and *not* drawing attention to ourselves? Thank goodness Cadoc was taken into custody; otherwise, he'd probably hear the ruckus from Dread Row.

With the fight over, the crowd starts to disperse, giving me room to run to Senan's heaving side. I drop to the rocky ground beside him. I don't know whether to throttle the man or kiss him. "Are you all right? Your eye is swollen."

His tongue sweeps across his teeth, clearing some of the blood there. "Is it? I hadn't noticed."

Braith stomps over to her brother, jabbing him in the ribs with the toe of her boot. "You are some gowl, Iver Nightingale."

"The fuck, Braith?" Iver grunts, clutching his ribs.

Senan starts chuckling, and Iver rolls, punching him in the arm.

If this is what it's like having brothers, I'm glad I have none.

I press a hand to Senan's thigh, keeping him from retaliating. Although he glowers at Iver through his good eye, his fists remain firmly on the ground. "Why are the two of you fighting?"

Senan drags his forearm across his busted lip. "He thought I was sleeping with his sister."

Iver's face flushes. "Because you said you were, you bollocks."

"No, I said that your sister and I were friends."

"It's not *what* you said, but *the way* you said it."

All this carnage over a simple misunderstanding? I give Senan's leg another nudge. "Did you not set him straight?"

A grin. "Look at his eye. You tell me."

With a shake of her head, Braith presses her palm to her brow. "I will never understand how men rule this world with their epic stupidity."

Senan's hand curves around my waist, urging me closer, tugging me down to where his split lips wait. "This is what happens when you leave me to my own devices," he murmurs against my mouth, tasting of blood and sweat. "I'm no good without you."

"Can you not do that in public?" Aeron grumbles.

"I think it's sweet," Braith counters.

"You would."

"What's that supposed to mean, *Terry*?"

Senan's burst of laughter flutters my hair where it falls like a curtain around our faces. "*Ha*. Terry. That will never get old."

Aeron levels a thick finger at his brother. "Don't you fucking start or I'll close up that other eye."

Senan pulls me down for one final kiss. "Where have you been?"

"We went to see Braith's sister."

"We got tattoos," Braith adds.

Iver uses the hem of his shirt to dab at his bloody nose. "No fucking way. *You* got a tattoo?"

Aeron's silver eyes widen. "Where?"

"As if I'd tell you," she says with a roll of her eyes.

Senan's face lights up like a child with a new toy, his hands burning like fire where he squeezes my hips. "I can't wait to see yours." When he tries to waggle his brows, only one moves.

I can't wait to show him—after he's cleaned up. Honestly, this man attracts trouble like a bloody magnet.

Aeron offers Senan a hand up, muttering something about his

right hook being pathetic, to which Senan replies, "You're pathetic," and all seems to be put to rights.

My prince leaves to collect an enormous basket of fruit and veg. When I ask about it, he only shrugs and says he wanted to help.

On the walk back, Iver sidles up next to me, hand extended, bloody knuckles and all. "Iver Nightingale. And you are?"

"Save your breath," Braith says, trailing behind us. "She's not interested."

"She might be," Iver counters.

"She's not," I say. Still, I take his hand if only to keep the peace. "My name is Wynn."

His grip tightens as he twists toward his sister. "Your friend from the castle?"

"One and the same," Braith confirms.

I slip my hand from Iver's, hoping that he doesn't take offense when I scrub the blood from my palm onto my skirts. Yet another dress ready for the wash.

Iver jerks his chin toward where Aeron scowls. "Who the fuck are you?"

"My worst nightmare," Braith says under her breath.

Aeron's gaze snaps to her, a wicked twist to his lips. "Been dreaming about me, Braith?"

"Ways to kill you," she says with a bat of her lashes.

To my dismay, Iver doesn't seem inclined to leave. Instead, he follows us all the way to his parents' home. Hopefully, he doesn't try to make more trouble. We've had enough to last a lifetime.

Senan's fingers dance along the small of my back, sending chills tingling down my spine. "So, about this tattoo of yours. Where is it?"

"Behave, and I'll show you."

Iver appears on my other side, like a stray dog desperate for a pat on the head. "Does that go for everyone, or...?"

Senan leans forward, his eyes narrowed. "Speak to her again, and I'll use your head for target practice."

"If your aim is as poor as your right hook, I'll be just fine."

These two. What is with them? "No more fighting. I mean it, Simon."

Senan's jaw snaps shut.

Iver snorts. "Cowed by a female. Pathetic."

What's pathetic is the way he keeps pushing Senan's buttons. Is he this way with everyone? If so, Josie must've had her hands full with him growing up. Speaking of Josie, the front door swings open and Braith's mother steps out, her hands flying to her heaving bosom as she lets out a tiny wail. "Saints above! What happened?"

Senan jabs a finger at Braith's brother. "He attacked me for no reason."

"Iver James Nightingale," Josie clips. "Have you lost the run of yourself altogether? I taught you better than this."

"Now who's cowed," Senan murmurs under his breath.

"Come in, you poor thing." Josie takes Senan by the hand, cooing at him while her own son trails behind, looking fit to explode. "Have a seat there next to my terrible boy and let me find you something for the pain before the bruising sets in."

Senan sinks onto the sofa, fighting a smile, no doubt loving being pampered. Josie whirls on her son. "On the couch, Iver."

"I'm not sitting next to that Scathian bastar—"

"Get your arse on the bloody couch, or so help me..."

Iver drops like a stone, glancing away as his mother bustles into the kitchen. Seeming satisfied that his brother isn't going to cause a ruckus in here, Aeron stalks down the hallway toward the bedroom he slept in last night. Braith leaves as well, heading in the opposite direction.

Josie returns clutching a bowl to her chest. She goes to Senan first, and when he sees what's inside, he tries telling her that he's all right.

He might as well be speaking to the wall for all the attention she pays him. Using her fingers, she carefully smears green goop over his eye.

What did she put in the stuff? It smells rotten.

Satisfied by her work, Josie steps over to her son and slaps the goo over Iver's wounds.

"Ouch, Mum! That hurts."

She dips her hand into the bowl for more, this time smearing it across Iver's broken lip. "Good."

Thirty-Three

SENAN

After thirty minutes of breathing in the disgusting muck on my face, Josie permits me to take a shower. I hurry as quickly as possible, anxious to find Allette's new tattoo. What would she have gotten? I scrub the bar of soap over my chest, the suds bubbling over her name. Imagine if she got "Senan" inked across her lovely arse.

The thought makes me scrub a little faster.

By the time I return to the living room, Allette has taken up residence on the armchair while Iver sits across from her, munching on one of Josie's terrible biscuits, gawking at my girl's profile as she watches the flames dance in the fireplace.

I can't blame the lad for staring; she is a sight to behold.

Aeron steps into the room behind me, shouldering his pack.

Why does it look like he's leaving?

Iver's head swings toward us. "Where are you going?"

Aeron bares his teeth. "As if I'd tell you."

Iver launches to his feet, what's left of his biscuit tumbling to the floor. "You want to go, bird boy?"

Why is this man so mad for a fight?

Braith sweeps into the room, tucking her short hair behind her ear, her gray skirts swaying. "He will kill you, Iver. And think of how upset Mum will be when she finds out you're dead."

It's true. Aeron doesn't pull his punches—I found that out on more than one painful occasion. He has this fiery rage burning inside of him that keeps the masochistic bastard coming back for more. He nearly lost an arm during one training session, and still didn't accept defeat. The guard sparring with him was the one to concede.

If only he had fought our brother with the same fire, perhaps his fate would have been different.

Iver folds his arms over his chest, tucking his hands beneath his armpits, his face twisted like he just bit into a lemon.

Maybe he's smarter than he looks.

A knock on the front door breaks the tension in the room. Braith saunters over and proceeds to speak in low tones with the person. She glances over her shoulder at me. "It's for you, Simon."

How can the door be for me when everyone I know down here is in this burrow?

A woman I've never met before waits on the path, her bulging eyes peering from beneath her hooded cloak. One of the little boys from earlier hangs his head by her side, swiping his nose with his shirtsleeve.

"Did you give this to my son?" She thrusts a wooden sword toward me. Good thing the blade isn't sharp; otherwise, she would've cut me with it.

"Yes?"

"Who the hell do you think you are?" she clips. "We are a people of peace. Are you trying to get my boy dragged off to the bloody guards?" The sword clatters at my feet. The little boy's sobs make his shoulders shake.

Kyff would've been the very same if our mother had taken his weapons. "Of course not," I say, but she's already hauling him away by the arm, past a man carrying another wooden sword.

He speaks not a word, throwing the weapon at my feet and stalking back down the road. I'm not sure where they all come from, but men and women and a handful of children all return the swords until there's a pile of play weapons outside Josie and Harold's door.

Iver appears beside me, glancing down at the swords with his lips pressed into a flat line. "Told you that you'd get into right shit, didn't I?"

He did say that, but I'm still confused as to why. "I don't understand."

"Ignorant pheasant," he mutters, collecting an armful of swords and dumping them onto the living room floor. "Tuath who show any aptitude with a sword are forced to serve in the king's guards."

"So?" While I would never wish to be a guard myself, they're paid handsomely and are given housing and meals in the barracks while they train. A man could do worse.

Iver blows out a breath, returning for another stack. "*So*, do you know where the Tuath guards serve? On the front lines. We're nothing more than fodder for Scathian cannons."

I twist to find Aeron turning over one of the swords in his hand. "Did you know this?"

He shakes his head. Allette looks horrified while Braith appears nonplussed. Being Tuath, she would have known the rules, but I'm still in shock.

"That's wrong." So fucking wrong.

Iver dumps the last of the swords onto the pile and then closes the door, sliding the lock into place. "Welcome to life under the clouds. No weapons. No power. And no sunlight."

I cannot believe I thought these people were content. I *am* an ignorant pheasant.

Braith steps around the pile to remove the fireguard. She picks up a sword and adds the weapon to the blazing logs within. Flames eat the wood, destroying the evidence of my ignorance.

"Has it always been this way?" I ask.

With a shake of his head, Iver hands Braith two more swords. "Just since our 'benevolent' king took the throne. The week after his coronation, he sent his guards around to the cities and villages collecting new recruits. Our best fighters were drafted and never heard from again."

More swords are reduced to ash.

People should have the right to learn how to protect themselves. They shouldn't be afraid of being forced to sacrifice their lives for a king who doesn't care about them.

It would seem Boris has forgotten that he isn't just the king of the Scathian fae but of the Tuath as well. Being born without wings doesn't make someone "cannon fodder."

"Simon?" My brother's voice cuts through my muddled thoughts. He watches me with an unreadable expression. "I need to go back."

Although I don't want him to leave us, staying any longer might draw the king's attention to this peaceful place. "I'll walk you out."

I follow my brother into the wider cavern, my stomach twisting with dread at having to say goodbye. "When you reach the castle, give Kyff a hug for me?" I hope he isn't too traumatized after all that's happened.

What I wouldn't give to see him myself, to wrap him in my arms and keep any more harm from befalling him.

"I'm afraid I won't see him. I'm going back to Stratiss."

Wait. What? "You can't go back yet."

"I've been gone long enough. It's time I return to my own kingdom. To my wife."

"What about us? We're supposed to go with you." We haven't even discussed our escape plan. How long has he known he was leaving? Why didn't he tell us sooner? Maybe he won't mind waiting for us to throw our things into a bag. We could be ready within the hour.

"In light of all that's happened, I hoped you'd given our discussion some more thought."

I have but my decision remains the same.

While my heart goes out to these people, what could I

possibly do to change their future? Why should this be my responsibility? Haven't we already sacrificed enough?

Even if we managed to remove Boris from power, becoming king would mean accepting the reality I've fought for so long: I have a wife and a kingdom waiting for me.

I'd rather the world think me dead and continue hiding in the shadows than give up my girl.

I steel my spine, steadfast in my decision. "Nothing has changed."

Shaking his head, Aeron blows out a breath. "You are unbelievable. Do you have no sense of duty?"

I do, but I'm fucking terrified of everything that could go wrong if I were to ascend. I could be killed trying. I could be a shite king and let down not only everyone in my family but also everyone in the kingdom. It's too much to ask of anyone, let alone someone like me. A man who couldn't even deal with his own grief without drowning.

"My duty is to Allette alone."

Aeron refuses to meet my gaze as he withdraws a heavy purse from his pack. "Then I suppose I'll send word when I have arranged transport to Stratiss. Until then, stay here and keep out of trouble." He twists toward the underground river and stomps away, leaving me feeling like a scolded child.

"What was Aeron talking about?"

I whirl, finding Allette in the doorway, her golden eyes dancing with fae light.

How long has she been standing there? How much did she hear? "Nothing important," I say.

"It sounded important to me."

This is neither the time nor the place for this conversation. "It's chilly out here. Let's go back inside." To my surprise, she listens. Instead of stopping in the living room, she continues to the room we've been sharing, her shoulders stiff as stone.

I close the door, waiting for the inevitable.

Allette turns, her eyes alight with fury and her dark hair

cascading like a shadow behind her thin frame. "You still don't trust me, do you?"

That isn't true. "I trust you more than I trust myself."

"Then tell me what is going on with your brother."

I rake a hand through my hair, the strands at the back of my neck still damp from my shower. I want to be finding Allette's tattoo, not arguing with her about something that's never going to happen. Still, I've learned my lesson about keeping secrets. It's time to come clean.

"Aeron thinks we need to kill the king."

Thirty-Four

ALLETTE

We need to kill the king.

That isn't what I expected Senan to say. Not at all.

When I overheard the princes arguing, I assumed they were talking about Senan's marriage to the princess. That Aeron wanted Senan to reconsider his duty to his wife.

I hate that I'm relieved, but killing the king?

That's impossible.

Not only does Boris Vale occupy the realm's tallest towers, but also he is always surrounded by highly trained guards and wards.

Don't get me wrong—the man is a villain in every sense of the word and needs to be brought to justice for the terrible crimes he has committed, but at the end of the day, he is too powerful.

I don't want Senan getting hurt, or worse, getting himself killed. Not that I'd ever tell him that if this is something he feels he must do. People have tried to control my prince from the moment he was born. I'll not have my name added to the list.

Misery lines his brow; conflict dances in his eyes.

"What do you think?" I ask, prepared to support him however I can, no matter his choice.

"Gods, Allette. I don't even know anymore. The answer

should be simple. Boris hurt you and broke me. The crown and throne shouldn't give anyone a free pass to commit such terrible atrocities. If no one is willing to stand up to him, the atrocities will continue."

My stomach sinks at the truth in his words. Boris could rule Kumulus for centuries. How much worse will life become for those who've made their lives beneath the clouds?

"I have fantasized about his death more often than I care to admit, about making him pay for what he has stolen from us. And yet," he says on a heavy sigh, "when it comes down to it, I don't know if I have it in me to take his life. What kind of man does that make me?"

"A *good* man." The best man, really. A man whose compassion knows no bounds.

For a moment, I allow the scenario to play out in my mind. We manage to overthrow Boris and all of us survive. What would happen next?

"Who would take his place?" Aeron said their younger brother Rhainn is gone and Prince Kyffin is only a child, not to mention how distressed he must be after being held hostage.

Aeron is responsible for Stratiss, so he cannot take the crown.

Senan's grimace returns, and my chest tightens when I realize the only option left. "He wants you to do it, doesn't he?"

His somber nod brings tears to my eyes. "If I file for an annulment, my ties to Nimbiss will be severed, leaving me free to ascend in Kumulus."

If the princess keeps her promise, the first part of that statement should already be in motion. But if Senan is crowned king, where does that leave us? What of our plans to escape to the seaside and live there for the rest of our days?

It's selfish to yearn for such a simple life with a man raised to wear a crown, but that's all I've ever wanted.

The man, not the title.

Is it possible to separate the two, or are they one and the same?

How easy it is to ignore reality here beneath the ground, to forget we're living in a temporary fantasy.

Senan cards a hand through his hair, mussing it even more. "Aeron thinks I'd make a good king. Can you believe that?"

"You would make a brilliant king." I would follow him anywhere, and once people saw that he had their best interests at heart, they would as well.

His head shakes. "Kumulus deserves someone who hasn't given in to the darkness."

That's not true. Not at all. "How can one understand the value of light if he has never seen darkness?" He might have given in before, but he has also fought tooth and nail to drag himself from the shadows.

"It doesn't matter. You didn't sign up for this. This was never meant to be our life, our fate."

"I know that. But dreams are allowed to change."

"Have your dreams changed, then? Do you dream of being Queen of Kumulus? Of having every decision in your life dictated by others? Of being scrutinized and spoken about in whispers? Hated as much as you are revered?"

"Well, no…" The thought of taking on that responsibility makes my knees quake.

"Exactly. I don't want any of those things either. And that is why you and I will retire by the seaside like you've always wanted. We'll have a modest house with a garden for lemon trees, and our fourteen children will know a simple life and happiness."

"Fourteen?"

He presses a tender kiss to my nose. "The number is negotiable. But your happiness is not."

Senan leans closer, whispering against the shell of my ear, "Now, where is this tattoo of yours?"

My stomach flutters, and as much as I yearn to give in to temptation, there are more important matters at hand. "We need to sort this out first—"

"There's nothing to sort out." He traces a finger along my collarbone. "You and I are going to Stratiss. End of story."

If that's true, then why does it feel like this is only the beginning?

"Your tattoo, Allette..." His teeth graze my neck. Nipping. Teasing.

I turn around, offering Senan the buttons at the back of the dress I borrowed from Braith. It seems like nowadays all we do is borrow. Clothes. Shelter. Gold. *Time.* It feels like nothing belongs to me, not even the man peeling away the gray fabric covering my body.

Senan's breath catches. "Gods..." Warm fingertips trail down my shift, tracing the outline of my tattoo.

Nothing belongs to me except for the new wings inked upon my skin. "Do you like them?"

Senan tugs my shift off one shoulder, then the other, letting the garment fall to my waist. "Like them? They're almost as beautiful as you are." He sketches his fingertips ever so delicately over the ointment Braith's sister applied to set the ink. "How far down do they go?" His feather-light touch drifts to my ribs.

"You're welcome to find out."

My dress falls to the ground, followed by the shift as Senan traces the wings all the way to the base of my spine.

"Stunning." Bracing his hands on my hips, my prince presses a kiss to my shoulder.

Our conversation hangs in the air between us like a ghost, haunting my mind and his eyes.

"Senan..."

His head falls against my neck, the dark sweep of his hair tickling my bare skin. "Not tonight, Allette. Please. Just give me tonight to love you. Let the only decisions we make be how many times we lose ourselves."

How can I deny Senan the same escape he has given me time and again?

He turns me around, stealing my next breath as his own,

consuming my thoughts with his kiss and ruling every beat of my heart. Our lips crash, our bodies fueled by instinct as we strip out of the clothes keeping us from each other. Mouths seek skin, teeth graze, and tongues discover.

Senan lifts me onto the bed, nudging my knees apart with his thigh, settling between them. His hips punch forward, his stiffness gliding through my folds, sliding over my most sensitive spot.

My exhale leaves on a gasp, my back arching, begging for more.

"Tell me what you need," he says against the shell of my ear.

I need you to choose me. Over this kingdom and everyone in it. A selfish request that never makes it to my lips. "Do that again."

He rocks forward, his hips grinding harder.

"Right there. *Yes.* That's it. Just like that."

We don't rush, making love as if we have all the time in the world. As if this fantasy will never end. Losing ourselves and finding each other, gripping, gasping, flying and falling as one. Nothing stands between us, no words, no space, no clothes, yet this choice looms like a devious shadow, waiting to pounce the moment we pull away.

Thoroughly sated, we cling to each other, determined to keep this connection even as sleep drifts over us like a warm blanket.

Senan is the first to succumb, his soft, even breaths matching mine.

My love.

My mate.

My prince.

A man who could be so much more, if only he would let himself. Tears spill from my lashes, soaking into the pillowcase as I think of all the good he could do for this kingdom—for this realm.

If he truly doesn't want to be king, then I will support his decision.

But if he wishes to take the throne, then I will stand and fight by his side.

Thirty-Five

SENAN

Allette sleeps soundly on her side of the bed, her soft breaths a balm to my tortured mind. All I want is to give her the life she's dreamed of for so long. A quiet, peaceful existence, far from castles and problems, just the two of us.

So why does Boris's vile smirk appear every time I close my eyes?

Instead of being bent over me, he pins little Kyffin to the ground, blood dripping down his fists as he saws off Kyff's small black wings.

Wasn't the antidote supposed to rid me of these terrible visions?

Boris wouldn't dare harm Kyff.

What am I saying? Of course he would. If Kyffin shows even a glimpse of my rebellious spirit, Boris will break him the way he broke me.

Afraid of tossing and turning and waking my girl, I roll out of bed and grab my wrinkled clothes from the floor. They're in desperate need of a wash, but my others were destroyed in the fight with Iver.

After hearing how the Tuath are treated, I can hardly blame

the man for his rage. If I had to watch children be stolen away and forced to serve a tyrant against their will, I'd be angry too.

Hell, I'm angry and I'm not even Tuath.

I shuffle through the silent house, finding Braith's father sitting on his worn-out chair, a short glass of amber liquid clutched in his hand.

It's the middle of the night. What's he doing awake?

Josie's request from earlier plays through my mind, and my face starts to burn. I sincerely hope we didn't disturb his sleep.

When Harold sees me, he offers the same welcoming smile he gave us the very first day we showed up out of the blue. "Trouble sleeping?"

I nod.

"Why don't you grab a cup from the kitchen and join me?" he says with a tilt of his chin toward the sofa.

It's not as if I have anything better to do. Plus, a drink might be the only way to get any sleep tonight.

In the kitchen, I retrieve a blue mug whose handle looks as if it's been reattached more than once. Back in the living room, Harold hooks a bottle of liquor by its long neck and pours me a generous helping.

I sink onto the sofa before taking a sip. Gods, the stuff tastes like turpentine.

Harold's lips tilt into a smirk. "Good, right? My buddy down in Corva made it."

"Very good," I choke. Some of the tension in my muscles starts to unwind. I suppose I'll find a way to force it down.

"The eye giving you grief?" Harold asks.

"No. It hardly hurts at all." That paste of Josie's must've been laced with magic.

He sips his drink, his Adam's apple bobbing with each swallow. "Want to talk about what's keeping you up then?"

"Not really." Like I told Allette, there's nothing to talk about.

I take another burning gulp, blinking back tears. How is the second drink worse than the first? This reminds me of the rot Aeron used to sneak from our father's office when we were around Kyff's age—far too young to be drinking.

Dammit. I don't want to think about Aeron or Kyff, but my mind is insistent tonight. Maybe it would help to speak with an impartial person to help me sort through all this shite.

Let's see... How do I talk about becoming king without talking about becoming king? "My brother wants me to...take over the family business."

Harold watches me from over the rim of his glass. "I assume by 'family business' you mean the Kumulus throne."

My jaw falls open. *Fucking hell.* Harold knows who I am.

"Don't look so surprised." Harold chuckles. "Those silver eyes gave you away the moment you set foot through the door, *Simon.*"

"Why didn't you say anything?"

He shrugs. "You clearly had your reasons for keeping up the ruse. Who am I to question a prince of the realm?"

Right now, I don't feel like a prince of anything but nightmares and bad decisions. What would my mother say if she could see the disappointment I've become?

I cannot believe Harold has known the truth this whole the time. "I'm surprised you helped us at all." With the way my family has treated the Tuath, it's a wonder he didn't stab me on sight.

"It's true that folks down here aren't very fond of Scathians—and for good reason. I've had friends hauled away for protesting the conditions in the mines. For getting turned around in a tower and stepping onto a balcony to find their bearings. Hell, they arrested young Jonesy for taking the apples from the trees instead of the rotten ones on the ground. Until a few years ago, you wouldn't have been able to set foot in the burrows."

"What happened a few years ago?"

"Henry Caplin."

The name doesn't ring a bell. Then again, why would it? I

only know a handful of Tuath, and most of them live in this house.

"Henry was a friend who worked alongside me in the northern mines before they shut them down. We were all laid off and desperate for any bit of work going. Unlike Josie and me, Henry and his wife Sarah were never blessed with children. When the eastern mines said they could take six men, Henry managed to secure the last spot. He knew I had more mouths to feed, and gave up his position so I could have it."

That was incredibly kind, but I'm still not sure what this has to do with Harold opening his home to us.

"I felt guilty as hell, especially since Henry's wife suffers from gout."

My head snaps up. *Impossible.*

Harold's lips curl into a smile before he takes a long sip from his glass. "I imagine you know the rest of the story."

The man who worked in the northern mines with a wife suffering from gout...

Henry must be the same Tuath I helped all those years ago.

"You saved him from the pit that day," Harold goes on. "He came back to the burrows singing your praises to anyone who would hear them. It was the first time any of us heard of someone from the castle being willing to help one of us. And a prince, no less."

I hardly deserve his praise. "He never should've been punished for needing help."

"Yet he would've been punished all the same. So in case you were wondering, *Simon*, you and your mate are safe in the burrows. We won't let anything happen to you. Unless Iver gets another burr in his britches," he chuckles.

My heart swells in my chest. To think all these people would put aside their disdain for Scathians for something so small. Now I wish I could've done more—not just for Henry but for the rest of the Tuath suffering under the clouds. "Thank you. If it weren't for you and your family, I hate to think what might have happened to us."

"It's our pleasure. Not many folks can say they've hosted two princes." Harold's nail taps against the glass as he watches me. "Back to your predicament. If you take over the family business, I assume that means you'd be ousting the current king."

I grimace. Ousting sounds a lot nicer than assassinating. Because that's what this boils down to: Assassination. *Murder*.

"Doubt he'll go quietly," he murmurs into his glass.

"I suspect not. But he's...he's not a good man. Neither am I, but he's done horrible things. I feel like this should be a simple decision. That I should be angrier over all he's done to me and the people I love. Don't get me wrong, I am angry, but...more than that, I'm fucking scared."

Gods, I cannot believe I confessed that out loud.

"I don't know much about ruling a kingdom, but I do know a thing or two about fear." Harold sets his glass on the low table next to the bottle. "Providing for the family has always fallen on my shoulders, and with seven mouths to feed including my own, that responsibility can make you feel like you're suffocating. When I feel like I can't breathe, I remind myself that my fear isn't as strong as my love. That love is what keeps me going."

Before being cast into the human realm, I'd never been responsible for anyone besides myself, and we all know how that turned out.

I love Allette and long to give her the life I promised, but I also love Kyffin and don't want his life to be in danger. And damn it all, I'm starting to care for these people down here, about how the king's decisions have created so many hardships for the Tuath.

The problem is, even if we were guaranteed victory, I still don't know if I'm strong enough to take that leap.

You're better at causing problems than fixing them.

How can someone like me be worthy of a crown?

"I don't know what to do," I murmur, more to myself than Harold.

He grips both sides of the chair and pushes himself to his feet. With an empty glass in one hand, he claps my shoulder with the other, giving me a gentle squeeze. "Sometimes we convince ourselves that we don't know what to do when really we're just too afraid or too stubborn to do what needs done."

Thirty-Six

SENAN

WITH THE SECOND DOSE OF ANTIDOTE HUMMING through my veins, I should feel better than I have in years. Instead, my breakfast is about to make a second appearance. A letter arrived from Aeron this morning saying that a carriage would be waiting outside the burrows at noon, ready to take us to Stratiss. We've spent the last few hours packing what little we own and helping Josie wash and hang the sheets from our bed, so they'll be ready for any unexpected guests that may arrive.

We came to the burrows a little over two weeks ago and already it's come to feel like home. Leaving is going to be more difficult than I anticipated. What pains me most is that I won't have the opportunity to tell Harold goodbye. He left for work this morning before any of us were out of bed and won't return until dinnertime.

Tears sparkle in Josie's eyes when she hugs us, still referring to me as Simon as she bids us farewell. Did I mention she gave us a basket of snacks for the long trek to Stratiss Castle?

Come to think of it, maybe the turn in my stomach has to do with the smell of the two sweet potato pies and dishes of stewed vegetables she packed for us.

Allette's hand slips into mine, her head falling to my shoulder. "I'm going to miss this place."

"So am I." Josie's cooking, though? That I can live without. This basket is about to be donated to the first beggar we come across.

We make our way to the mouth of the cave where the burrows open into Kumulus City. What we find when we finally reach the entrance makes my knees quake.

Men and women wail alongside tiny huts of straw, wearing little more than rags. Muck covers their faces, and the whole place reeks worse than a privy. Who knew such poverty and horror awaited so close to such a beautiful, peaceful place? No wonder no one in Kumulus wants to visit the burrows. If we'd come this way, there is no way anyone would've convinced me to enter.

My stomach twists, and I find myself wishing I could do something to help these people. That I had the money or the land to offer them a place to live and earn an honest wage instead of begging for coins from passersby.

With my heart in my throat, I step around a small girl with mud streaked through her ringlet curls. Her piercing yowl echoes off the low ceiling. When I look down, I recognize the little face staring back.

Dahlia, the Nightingale's neighbor, the one who wanted the bunny.

I kneel in the dirt, Josie's basket tumbling onto the ground next to me. "Are you all right?" I ask, taking her gently by the shoulders.

She grins back at me. "Hi, Simon."

The knife in my gut twists a little deeper. Why is she out here? Did something happen in her burrow? "Hello, Dahlia. Where are your mother and father?"

"Mum's right there." She points a dimpled hand toward one of the huts, where a silver-haired woman hunches over an iron pot, stirring with a wooden spoon.

Why are they here when they have a home inside?

Dahlia glances up to where Allette watches us through tear-filled eyes. "Who's she?"

"This is my wife."

Dahlia cups her hands around her mouth but whispers loudly enough for anyone within earshot to overhear. "She's really pretty."

Allette smiles down at the girl. "I think you're pretty."

"I know." Dahlia beams, gripping the sides of her skirts and doing a little twirl. "Do you like my costume?"

"Costume?" Allette and I say in unison, trading wide-eyed looks.

She nods. "Today's our day to play pretend. Mummy says I'm the best actress."

Allette sucks in a breath.

Play pretend...

I take in the entrance with fresh eyes, recognizing some of the faces from deeper in the burrows. The woman who sold me the apples. The man who made the swords.

None of this makes any sense. "Why do you need to play pretend?"

Dahlia's face scrunches and she raises her arms in the air, her fingers curling like tiny claws as she stomps toward me. "To keep the bad men away."

"Who are the bad men?" Allette asks.

"The ones with the wings, of course."

Bloody hell...

All of this is a ruse.

Whoever thought of using sickness as a deterrent might be a genius. I certainly wouldn't want to go past these people if I didn't know the truth of their "ailments."

Does anyone from above the clouds know the truth?

Not that it matters. We're leaving today and I cannot see us returning as long as Boris holds the throne. If nobody stops him, that could be a very, very long time.

"Not everyone with wings is bad," I tell her. "I had wings before. Do you think I'm bad?"

Her mouth twists as she considers, her gaze falling to where my shirtsleeves meet my forearms. "Just bad at drawing."

I chuckle. She has a good point.

Dahlia's smile slowly fades. "What happened to your wings?"

"Someone stole them."

"Mummy says stealing is bad."

"Dahlia!" The woman with the spoon shouts, gawking at me with a horrified expression.

I smile at Dahlia, silently wishing her a long and happy life. One full of bunnies where all her wishes and dreams come true. "Better go to your Mum."

"Bye, Simon. Bye, Simon's wife." The girl takes off running, leaping over mounds of dirt, her stained skirts billowing behind her.

Allette folds her arms over her chest. "Bad at drawing, huh?"

"I can't be good at everything."

Her laughter warms my soul as I collect the discarded basket. With her hand in mine, we traverse the well-worn path together, the mud so deep it slurps at our boots.

"It's fascinating, isn't it? Going through all of this just to keep people out," she muses.

"It's genius, that's what it is." The Tuath keep to themselves, and the king and his guards avoid the place like a plague. Everyone wins.

The gray light of day grows brighter as we near the mouth of the cavern. Outside, a carriage waits on a dirt road. The driver leans against one of the oversized back wheels, pipe smoke like a cloud around his head.

I've never travelled by carriage before. Those cushions look comfortable, and if we close the curtains, my girl and I would have plenty of privacy.

Perhaps today won't be so bad after all.

When the man sees us, he nudges his cap higher, his jaw dropping as he gawks at Allette.

I have to clear my throat twice before he turns toward me. "Are you Tallin?"

A nod. "Simon, I presume?"

"That's right—"

A deafening boom of thunder rumbles in the distance. The ground beneath my boots shakes and shudders, throwing me off balance.

Allette yelps, gripping my arm with both hands. "What's happening?"

Tallin catches himself against the carriage wheel, his pipe clattering to the ground. A plume of black smoke billows into the sky, mixing with the low-hanging gray clouds on the horizon.

"What's up there?" I ask.

"The mines," Tallin says.

The ground shakes again, the violent rattle knocking my girl and me to my knees. Is it the same mine where Harold works?

It doesn't matter.

We need to leave.

What if he's hurt? What if he needs help?

It's not safe for us out in the open.

Aeron is expecting us in Stratiss by nightfall.

More smoke billows over the treetops.

Allette clutches my hand. "Harold."

Screams echo through the valley.

You're better at causing problems than fixing them.

I have no business getting involved. Hell, I'll probably make it worse. Yet, I find myself shoving the basket at the driver. "Wait here." I take off up the hill, sprinting toward the smoke.

"I have other fares, you know!" Tallin shouts at my back.

I hear Allette tell him that we'll pay double if he doesn't leave us behind. When I glance over my shoulder, I find her running behind me.

The mines aren't difficult to find on account of all the screaming.

Men painted black with soot stumble from a hole cut into the ground, coughing and gasping as inky clouds surge from behind them like living shadows. They fall onto the stones and dirt, chests heaving as they fight for air. Some have gashes dripping with blood while others seem relatively unscathed.

"Is that Iver?" Allette points to two men carrying a third.

Shit. It is Iver. I'm there in a blink, helping them ease the unconscious man onto the damp grass.

Not just any man.

Harold Nightingale.

Allette kneels next to Braith's father, taking his hand in hers. "What happened?"

Iver sinks onto the ground, his eyes glazed and hands covered in deep cuts. "Cave-in..." His throat bobs. "Dad... He... He went back in to help drag men out when the ceiling fell on top of him." Tears track down his face, streaking the soot on his cheeks.

"Harold? Harold, can you hear me?" Allette cups his weathered cheeks, but Harold remains silent. Her fingers shake as they unfasten his shirt.

When I see the black and blue bruises mottling his torso, my heart stops. Years ago, I remember one of the servants being dragged from the stables, his chest and stomach looking the very same. Internal bleeding, the physician said. The man would've succumbed from his wounds if Boris hadn't healed him.

It's one of the few times I recall Boris helping someone.

I hold my hands against Harold's chest, begging for my missing magic to return, but it's no use. Not even a spark remains. "Allette? Can you try?"

She tries for a moment only to shake her head in defeat. "There's nothing there."

Dammit. "Are there any other Scathians nearby?" Surely there must be someone else who can help him.

Iver's eyes narrow into slits. "What do you mean? You're Scathian. Heal him."

"I can't."

"Why the fuck not?"

"Because I haven't seen the sun in months." Not properly, anyway.

"Then fly through the clouds and find the fucking sun."

I would if I could, but I can't.

With a humorless chuckle, Iver shakes his head. "Just when I started to think maybe you weren't all a shower of bastards... You're just like the rest of them, aren't you? Using us and then casting us aside when we need help."

"I'm not—"

"Save it."

I will not *save it*. He needs to understand that I'm doing everything I can—which is fuck all. "I cannot fly because I have no fucking wings. The king cut them off."

Iver's jaw drops.

"Now, are there any *other* Scathians nearby?"

"The foremen are Scathian, but they only come by every couple of days to ensure we're meeting our quota."

Allette raises her head toward the thick layer of clouds, as if begging the sun to appear. "There must be someone nearby who is willing to help."

"There's a clinic near the textile factory," Iver says.

Right. The textile factory. That's not too far, is it? Gods, I'm so turned around, I don't even remember.

I glance over at Allette. "Can you run down to the carriage and have Tallin drive it up here? It'll be quicker than trying to carry Harold." Not to mention safer.

She nods and pushes to her feet, running like the wind she wields, her hair and cloak billowing at her back.

Harold groans. Iver clutches his father's hand to his chest. "You're going to be all right. We're going to heal you."

More whimpers and moans fill the air.

How can we only help one man and leave the others behind? "Iver, can you find those with the gravest wounds and bring them here?" We might not be able to save them all, but at least we can help some of them.

With a reluctant bob of his head, Iver places his father's hand in mine and takes off toward the entrance of the mines.

"Senan?" Harold gasps, peering up at me, his eyes glazed with pain. "You..."

"Shhh... Save your energy. Once you're healed, we can have all the chats you want."

Wincing, he shakes his head. "You...shouldn't be...afraid. You... You would make a great...king."

A great king would have the strength to heal this man's wounds. Me? I am sitting here in the dirt doing *nothing*.

Harold's lids flutter closed, and his hand grows heavy.

"Hold on just a little longer." Just until we can find someone to help.

You're better at causing problems than fixing them.

I might not have caused the cave-in, but I'm certainly not fixing anything.

Even knowing it's useless, I can at least try, can't I?

Forcing Boris's taunting voice from my mind, I close my eyes. With my hands anchored to Harold's chest, I call on my absent magic, attempting to coax it from nothing. I saw the sun in the human realm. Briefly, but I felt its rays on my bare skin. There must be *something* there.

Come on. Please. Let me fix this.

I squeeze my eyes tighter, searching deep within myself.

Harold begins to convulse beneath my palms.

No. *Please.* I don't give a shit about my element. The gods can keep my fire for the rest of my days. All I need is a spark of healing magic, just enough to save this man who gave us refuge when he could've turned us away.

Where the hell is it?

Allette can access her power, so where is mine?

It feels as if I'm staring into an abyss as big and wide as space itself. Fathomless, cold, empty, and dark—

Dark except for one speck of light, like the farthest star in a midnight sky, barely glowing.

I call to that star, begging it to grow brighter with every part of my blackened soul.

You're better at causing problems than fixing them.

NO.

I might have caused problems in the past, but now all I want to do is make up for the many mistakes I've made. To do something to help instead of drowning in sorrow and guilt.

The speck grows a little brighter.

Don't you think it's time to give back instead of take?

I will.

Give me this, and I'll stay and fight. I swear.

Something stirs in the center of my chest. *Magic.* I force every last drop of power from my body to Harold's. When I dare to pry open my eyes, I find the bruises on Harold's chest have faded. They're not gone, but it's a start. At least he isn't convulsing anymore, and his breathing seems to have evened out.

The carriage finally rolls into view. Allette leaps down from where she sits next to the driver at the front and sprints toward me. "Tallin said he can bring six more."

I call a man over to help me maneuver Harold into the carriage. Allette climbs in next to him, holding his hand and speaking in soothing tones. We manage to fit in four more, with wounds ranging from lacerations on their heads to what looks like a broken leg.

Iver refuses to take up a seat that could be given to one of the wounded men, choosing instead to run behind the carriage. I climb up next to the driver, gripping the edge of the seat as the mammoth horses lunge for town. We drive to the tune of wails and curses, racing to save Harold and heal the rest of these men.

It feels like forever before we're pulling in front of a squatty stone building with the word "Clinic" painted in faded white letters above the door.

Women and a handful of whimpering children huddle beneath the overhang, staring at us with blank expressions, as if they cannot see us at all.

The carriage barely comes to a halt before I leap from the seat. "We need a physician," I bellow, pushing through the door and stopping dead in my tracks. More women sob on tables, clutching blood-drenched hands while men and women dressed in blood-stained white robes pace between them, working furiously to heal the wounded. To my right, shoeless feet protrude from beneath a white sheet.

Gods... "What happened?"

"Fire at the Textile Mill," a stern-faced woman says as she passes, an armful of white gauze clutched to her chest.

There isn't a spare table in sight, and with so many patients already waiting, how can we expect them to help us first?

Outside, Allette and Iver speak in low tones, their expressions grim. When I explain the situation, Iver curses, dragging a hand down his grimy face.

There's only one way I can think to help now.

"We need sunlight." Curse the thick blanket of clouds above us. Why did Boris have to take my fucking wings?

Iver holds his head between his hands. "If we're caught in the sun, they'll throw us into the pit."

"There might not be time for us to restore our magic and return." Hell, by the time we find a way above the clouds, it still might be too late to save Harold.

Allette's gaze finds mine. "Isn't Lord Windell's tower on this side of the city?"

Shit. She's right.

Except showing up at Philip Windell's tower is akin to announcing myself to Boris himself.

Behind me, a girl no older than Dahlia starts to cry. This one isn't in costume. This one isn't pretending.

Allette's hand finds mine. "Senan?"

Iver chokes. "Did she just call you *Senan*?"

Looks like not everyone in the burrows was in on my little secret. There's no time to explain. "Philip Windell will go straight to the king."

"What other option do we have?"

The only other option is to leave these men behind.

Even as the thought crosses my mind, I know we cannot abandon these people.

You're better at causing problems than fixing them.

Fuck off, Boris. I'm going to fix this.

"We'll go to Windell."

Thirty-Seven

ALLETTE

I can sense Senan's nervousness from where he trudges behind the carriage, the trek slower through the city due to the number of Tuath on the skinny streets. Thankfully, the drive to Lord Windell's tower isn't far. I've only been here once, back when my aunt believed Philip and I would make a fine match.

Feels like a lifetime ago.

The base of the tower looks the same as all the others in this area, cream sandstone mottled together with thick plaster, a single door with no windows, and green moss creeping along the base. I never used to wonder why there were no windows below the clouds. Now that I've lived down here, the distinction strikes me as odd. Even if there isn't much to see, the people working inside still deserve some sort of view instead of being cooped up in a stone cage.

Senan glances at me from the stoop, his trepidation written on his face as he raises his fist to pound on the door.

The barrier opens, and a woman with a black mask over her face appears in the entrance. "May I help you?" she asks in a weak voice, her head turning to where Iver and I wait next to the carriage.

Senan straightens to his impressive height. "Is Lord Windell here?"

"Who's asking?"

"Prince Senan Vale."

She shoves her mask onto her forehead, her eyes narrowed as she studies my prince. "You expect me to believe a prince of the realm is knocking all the way down here? Be gone with you before I call the guards."

Senan raises an arrogant black brow. "And have them haul you away for refusing me entry? Go on, but don't say I didn't warn you."

The woman looks him up and down once more, her lips pursing. "If you are the prince, then why aren't you up there?" She jerks her chin toward the clouds.

"Because up there, people will see me, and I would rather speak to Philip in private."

The use of Windell's given name seems to give the woman pause. "I'll tell the master, but if you're lyin' and he has me whipped, I'll hunt you down and whip you." The door snicks shut in Senan's face.

He turns to us and drags a hand through his hair. "What do we do if he doesn't come?"

Iver glowers at the barrier, his hands balled into fists. "We beat down the door and force our way inside."

In light of all that's happened, I wouldn't put it past the man, and I certainly wouldn't be the one to stop him.

"Iver?" a weak voice calls from the carriage.

We all rush over to find Harold awake, clutching his chest. The man beside him looks as if he's asleep, while the one farthest from the door sucks in a sharp breath and winces.

Tell me we didn't drive these men all the way up here only to have them die in this alley.

Iver reaches through the window, taking his father's weathered hand. "Save your energy. Help is coming."

A dark shadow appears high above, speckled wings displacing

the clouds as Lord Windell lands next to where Senan waits with his hood still pulled. Windell doesn't spare the rest of us so much as a glance, his brow pinched until Senan eases down his hood.

Windell's boots catch on the cobbles as he stumbles back. "By the gods, it is you. Why are you covered in blood? Did Carew take you hostage as well?"

My prince shakes his head, his lips pressed into a grim line. "There was a cave-in at the mines and some friends were badly wounded. I brought them here, hoping you could help me heal them." Senan starts for the carriage just as Iver swings open the door.

"Why were you at the mines?" Windell's voice trails away as he gapes into the carriage. "They're Tuath." He grabs the front of his shirt, dragging the material over his nose like a makeshift mask.

"They need help, Philip," Senan insists.

"Then let them go to the Tuath clinic on the edge of town. My wife is with child, and if any of them have the wasting—"

"We don't have the fucking wasting," Iver grits out.

Windell's eyes narrow on Braith's brother before he twists back to Senan, as if Iver isn't worth addressing. Why did I think for a second that this vile man had changed? That he would have grown a heart?

"I should've known you'd bring trouble to my doorstep," Windell clips. "Whatever this is, I want no part of it." His wings flare as he takes a step back.

Senan stalks forward, his hands flexing at his sides. "We don't have fucking time for this. If you don't help, they'll die."

"If you ask me, there are too many Tuath to begin wi—"

Senan's fist slams into Philip's nose with a terrible *crunch*. My former admirer falls back, his hands flying to cradle his face. Whimpering pitifully, he removes one, staring at his palm as if he's never seen blood before. His face drains of color, and he crumples to the ground.

Senan doesn't look the least bit repentant as he turns to me. "We need to get everyone inside."

This time, he doesn't knock on the door but twists the knob and steps straight inside. "Tallin, help Iver carry Harold up to the main floor. Allette, help anyone else who can walk."

Two servants emerge from the kitchen, their gasps muffled from beneath their masks.

The one at the back lifts his mask, revealing his pale face. "Iver?"

"Heya, Twig." Iver eases his father down the carriage steps. "Can you help us? There was a cave-in at the mines."

Twig nods and rushes out to where the other men climb gingerly down the carriage steps.

"What about him?" I point to Lord Windell still sprawled on the ground. If we leave him there, he's liable to fly straight to the king.

Senan's nose wrinkles as he glances down at the fallen man, then he turns to the servants. "Is there somewhere we can keep him where he won't cause trouble?"

The woman who first answered bustles over to a door. "What about the broom closet?"

Senan's grin widens. "Perfect."

+++

WITH THE HELP OF WINDELL'S SERVANTS, WE MANAGE to bring all the wounded up the ten flights of stairs to the main parlor. Golden sunlight washes from the balcony over the fine furniture I once sat on drinking tea.

Reaching behind his neck, Senan drags his shirt up and over his head, letting it fall onto a velvet settee on his way to the balcony. The whimpers and murmurs grow quiet as everyone in the room stares at the remains of his wings. Questions hang in the air, but there is no time for answers.

Senan cannot do this by himself. I'll need to refuel my magic as well.

I ease the man still leaning on me onto the cushions and start unbuttoning my dress as I make my way from the shadows into the light. The wool falls away, leaving me in nothing but my shift. I raise my face toward the sun's healing rays, letting its warm kiss seep into my weary bones.

When I open my eyes, I notice the Tuath standing at the edge of that arc of light, staring down at the floor as if it would set fire to their toes.

Have they truly never dared to venture onto a balcony?

Iver takes the first step, his father braced at his side. I help him lay Harold on the rust-colored tiles. Senan kneels next to him with his back to the sun and places his hands on Harold's shoulders. My prince's fingers start to glow, and the bruising beneath Harold's almost translucent gray skin begins to fade.

I'm so bloody proud of him. He didn't question whether or not he could do it; he took charge and made it happen.

One of the miners limps toward the balcony. I hold out my hand, and when the callouses covering his palm scrape against my fingers, I urge my magic toward him, healing the wound across his face until it's no more than a faded pink line.

One at a time they come, sinking onto the marble, removing their shirts and letting the sunlight bathe their bodies.

"It's so bloody warm," one says with a shudder, lifting his face, his eyes closed.

"Feels like the fire," another remarks.

Iver stares down at his own grimy hands, his brow furrowed. "The wounds on my hands," he whispers. "They're gone."

Sure enough, the cuts have been replaced by tiny silver scars.

We haven't healed him yet.

Stars...

Does that mean he somehow healed himself?

Removing their masks, the servants shuffle toward the light, their eyes wide as they study Iver's hands.

Senan stands from where he kneels next to Harold, his jaw tight.

"They have magic," I whisper. There is no other explanation. These people who have been kept out of the sunlight have the power to heal themselves. Stars above, Braith's sister Regina was right.

"Have any of you ever been in the sun before?" Senan asks, a command in his deep voice that I haven't heard in far too long.

The Tuath trade worried glances before shaking their heads.

The servant who knew Iver steps forward, stopping right on the edge of the light. "None of us want to risk the pit."

What if the kingdom doesn't keep the Tuath below the clouds because they're wingless...but because they don't want them to discover they have magic?

Do they only possess healing magic, or can they wield the elements as well?

Of all the lies we've been told, this one rocks the very foundation of our realm. If all the Tuath knew the truth, there would be riots in the streets. Hundreds—*thousands*—of people could lose their lives in the upheaval.

No one in the kingdom would be safe. The king has guards and wards, but what about the rest of the Scathian nobility? Who would help protect them if the Tuath decided to rebel?

We're on the crest of a wave, hurtling toward the shore.

And the wave is about to break.

Senan and I cannot abscond to Stratiss now. The Tuath need someone who will stand up for them, who will fight for them instead of doling out punishments for something that should be their right.

Scathians do not own the sun; no one does.

We cannot allow the king to continue hoarding the realm's most valuable resource.

We cannot stand by and do nothing.

I turn to the man I love, recognizing the same realization in his quicksilver eyes. "We cannot leave now."

Grimacing, Senan nods. "I know."

Iver steps forward, peering over the balcony's edge to the tops of the clouds. "What do we do about the lad you struck?"

I forgot about Windell. *Dammit.* That man has been a thorn in my side ever since the day he brought me that disgusting rabbit foot. "When he comes to, he'll go straight to the castle."

Senan scrubs a hand across his stubbled jaw. "Then we bring him with us until we can figure this out."

Who would've thought when we found out the princess had been taken by Carew, that only a few days later, we'd be taking a hostage of our own?

Thirty-Eight

SENAN

CARRYING A MAN BOUND AND GAGGED INTO THE burrows garnered surprisingly little interest from the Tuath who live down here. Granted, we had the foresight to throw a sack over his head, but still. While I didn't want to bring trouble to Josie and Harold's doorstep, we had nowhere else to go and the revelations made back in the tower aren't the sort you can forget.

The front door opens, and Iver saunters into the living room, looking chuffed with himself.

"What did you do with him?" I ask.

"He's in one of the old caverns. And don't worry, I wore the mask so that he didn't see my face."

Do I feel guilty? Not in the slightest. Philip Windell is an unfortunate casualty of this problem that none of us wanted to be part of. If he hadn't been such a heartless bastard, maybe today would have played out differently for him.

Harold doesn't move from the sofa where he stares down at his hands. The skin peeking from beneath his shirt has gone red from the sun.

I remember the one and only time I experienced sunburn. I'd been five years old and sick with fever for weeks, unable to leave my bed of my own accord. Although the physician had carried me outside to refuel my magic, my lower half remained covered in blankets to keep me from shivering myself off the balcony ledge. This was before my wings grew, so falling from that height would have been a death sentence.

Yet another reason *not* to live in a tower above the clouds.

Anyway, when I recovered, I spent a whole day sunning myself in nothing but a pair of briefs.

My legs were so burnt that my skin peeled off.

Needless to say, it was not a pleasant experience.

Iver drops onto the sofa next to his father.

Allette leans back on the chair across from them, her head resting against the cushion, her eyes a million miles away.

I sink onto the arm of Allette's chair, searching the two Tuath for signs of their magic. Besides their red skin, they don't look any different. "How do you feel, Harold?"

His head lifts, and his eyes meet mine. "Better than I have in years."

Iver turns his hands over and back again, staring at them like he's never seen hands before. "Regina was right all along. She's going to be unbearable now."

Harold chuckles.

"Who is Regina?" I ask.

"My eldest daughter. She's always been interested in history. A few years back, she stumbled upon some old documents that claims we used to have power. Apparently, there's a book in the king's library that holds all the details."

Too bad Rhainn isn't still at the castle. I bet he'd know about the book. Hell, he probably read the thing.

Not that it matters when we know the truth: Tuath have healing magic. "The king must know about your magic." Boris might not understand the particulars, but he must suspect the reason behind keeping these people out of the sun.

Allette sits up. "I had the same thought. But why would he care that the Tuath can heal themselves?"

She makes a good point. If anything, it would be more efficient for the Tuath to have access to healing magic, especially given some of the more dangerous occupations they have. Look at what happened at the mines today and the textile mill.

I look back at Iver through fresh eyes, wondering... "Do you feel any different?"

Iver shrugs. "Maybe? Warmer. A little...tingly?"

"Give me your hand." Despite my wings being reduced to pitiful stumps, my well of magic stirs beneath my skin. When I call it forth, heat expands through my chest, humming in my veins. Taking his hand, I send some of my magic toward my palm the same way I once did with Kyff.

Iver's eyes widen.

"You feel it, don't you?"

A nod.

"Hold out your other hand."

He extends his palm face-up toward the ceiling. I force more magic from my hand to his, waiting for a spark to appear.

Beads of sweat tumble from Iver's hairline, down his furrowed brow. *Come on.* Why isn't this working?

Perhaps he possesses the power of air.

I don't love the idea of him touching Allette, but I cannot think of any other way for us to—

"Senan?" Allette's shaking voice cuts through my frustration.

When I turn toward her, she isn't looking at me, but at the floor.

A thick brown vine curls from between the stones; tiny green buds emerge from the stem. I drop Iver's hand, but the vine keeps growing, pushing the stones aside, twisting all the way to the ceiling.

Harold stumbles off the sofa, his jaw hanging as he gawks at the vine twining around Iver's legs.

Allette moves closer, reaching out as if to touch one of the leaves. "Can you control it?"

Iver's gaze narrows in concentration. The bud nearest Allette's fingers unfurls, sprouting a lavender flower.

"Bloody hell..." Harold shakes his head.

They don't just have healing magic. They can control elements as well. I've only ever heard of wind and fire elementals. Clearly, Iver isn't either one of those.

Gods above. This is monumental.

"Harold?" I extend my hand toward him.

His dry, calloused fingers wrap around mine. "What do I do?"

I send my magic toward him, already feeling my power start to wane. If only we had more sunlight. "Do you feel the magic in my hand?" When he nods, I explain what I want him to do. The stones beneath us begin to shake. I expect another vine. Instead, water bubbles up through the cracks, gathering around Harold's boots but never getting them wet.

Beside him, Iver's vine spreads across the plaster in every direction.

"We need more sunlight." But how do we get more Tuath into the sun without the king or the guards finding out?

"Surely, there must be at least a few vacant towers. Perhaps the owners are on holidays?" Allette suggests.

Gods, my mate is brilliant. "Iver? Can you ask everyone you know who works in the city if there are any free towers? Tell the servants to try to access the sun if they can."

Iver nods, then grimaces. "What if they're caught?"

If they're caught, then we will have to find a way to save them. "They can't stop all of us."

Allette's grip on me tightens. "You know what we need to do, right?"

May the gods save us...

I know exactly what we need to do.

We need to kill the king.

Thirty-Nine

SENAN

P*lip*.

Plip.

Plip.

Water drops from the stalactite in the corner, landing in the puddle beneath with quiet little *plips*.

A few days ago, Allette called me a good man, but it's just not true. In that moment, I might have agreed with her.

Not anymore.

Because as soon as I step into the crevice where we've stashed Philip Windell, I'm overcome with such loathing that it clogs my throat and snarls in my veins.

How could he stand by and do *nothing* while so many people were hurting? I'm glad we took him. Glad he's tied up like a pig on a spit, a dirty rag taut across his mouth so he can't spew anymore hate toward the Tuath.

When he sees me, his eyes widen, darting toward the two males at my back, their faces hidden by hoods and masks. Windell might know who I am, but if things go awry, I don't want my actions to hurt anyone else.

My boots slip along the shale floor as I climb down into the shallow pit where our hostage slumps. Someone brought Windell a blanket, a pillow, and a plate of what looks like sweet potato pie.

I hope Philip chokes on it.

The coarse ropes binding his hands cut into his skin, leaving red marks where they've rubbed his wrists raw. His wings have been bound as well. Even if he tried to fly away, they'd have him skewered before he reached the entrance.

Turns out, Iver's rage is good for something, after all.

I hook my finger beneath the gag and tug the material down. "Hello, Philip."

Philip's jaw hinges as he glances around the cavern. The blood from where I punched him has dried on his upper lip like a mustache. "Where the hell—"

"I'd keep my voice down if I were you. Wouldn't want to wake your housemates." I point to the ceiling.

Slowly, his gaze climbs the weeping walls, landing on the army of black bats hanging high above us. The color drains from his face. "Where am I?" he whispers.

As if I'm going to give him any information. "There's no need to concern yourself with that right now." I nod toward the Tuath waiting at the mouth of the cavern, swords and pistols stolen from Windell's tower clutched in their fists. "My friends have promised to take good care of you."

"You cannot keep me here," he splutters. "There isn't even a proper privy."

The lack of facilities is my favorite part. Let him see how difficult life can be for those who aren't lucky enough to live in their father's tower. Who have no homes to return to.

"I'm afraid we don't have much of a choice. If I let you go, you'll fly straight to the castle."

"I won't. I swear."

Does he honestly believe I would take him at his word? I've had the misfortune of knowing Philip for most of my life. If he thinks he can use this situation to his advantage, he will. The Windell family will stop at nothing to align themselves with our crooked king. Hell, Philip's own father sold out his best friend for a position on the King's Council.

Tears roll down his grimy cheeks. I'm not proud to say that I'm taking far too much delight from his misery.

"I'm sorry, all right," he whimpers. "P-please, just let me go and I s-swear I'll make it up to you."

He blew his one and only chance to prove he was worth something. Maybe next time he won't be such an intolerant asshole.

Still, I want to hear him say he feels guilty for not helping the Tuath. It would be good for my soul. "Sorry for what?" I ask.

His dark brows lift toward his thinning hairline. In a few years he's going to be as bald as his father. "For telling the king about Allette."

The world falls silent except for the thump of my heart and Windell's words pulsing through my skull.

Telling the king about Allette.

Telling the king about Allette.

TELLING THE KING ABOUT ALLETTE.

My vision goes hazy, my arms and legs shaking from the rage swelling in my blood.

Windell skirts back against the wall, his boots slipping on the loose stones. "Hear me out, Senan. *Please.* She was meant to be my wife—the contracts were all signed. Then you stole her right from under my nose."

Don't kill him. Don't kill him. Don't kill him.

"When?" I demand through clenched teeth.

"What do you mean—"

"When did you tell the fucking king, *Philip*?" It's not that difficult of a fucking question, is it?

"F-five years ago."

All this time, I assumed one of my guards had betrayed me to the king and it was this fucking weasel.

"I didn't know he was going to have her killed. I swear. H-he promised he'd take care of it," Philip blubbers, sniffling as if he gives a shit.

What a load of bollocks.

Philip damned the woman I love because she wounded his fragile pride. Because she chose me over him. He never cared about Allette. He only cared about himself.

"I-I thought he was going to give her back to me."

Give her back? He acts as if Allette is a fucking bauble to be bought and traded.

"How did you know?" We were so careful...

"I could feel her starting to slip away, cancelling plans, refusing to make new ones. One day I decided to follow her. She flew to the Nag's Head." His throat bobs when he swallows. "You arrived twenty minutes later."

He saw us together and went straight to my brother instead of coming to me. Instead of giving me a chance to explain—to cover my tracks. To run away with Allette before everything could go to shit.

Fire burns my palms, demanding release. I could light him ablaze, and no one would stop me.

I should.

For his role in my love's downfall—in my own. It's the least this rat deserves. I'd be doing the kingdom a favor, ridding the land of this filth.

"Simon?"

Reluctantly, I turn toward the familiar voice. *Fucking Iver*. Can't he see that I'm busy contemplating murder? My jaw aches as my teeth continue to grind. I force myself to breathe. In. Out. In. "*What*?"

"Your presence has been requested outside."

Allette.

She wouldn't want me to kill the man she was meant to marry.

Is that even true? She mentioned Philip was a suitor, not that they were betrothed. To think of her ending up with him...

His hands touching her perfect body...

His mouth claiming hers...

His child in her womb.

If I don't get out of this room, I'm going to do something she might never forgive me for.

I climb out of the hole and stalk toward the masked Tuath. "I want guards on him day and night. He doesn't leave your sight until I say otherwise. And if he tries, run him through."

The man beside Iver bobs his head, his mask muffling his response. "Done."

My ire refuses to wane as I step into the wider cavern where Allette waits, her golden eyes wide with worry and hands twisting in front of her.

She was meant to be my wife.

I can't get Windell's words out of my head—the image of the two of them together. *Shit.* I think I'm going to explode.

"Senan, are you all right?"

"Were you going to marry him?" I gasp, vibrating with the force of my jealousy.

Her dark brows come together over worried golden eyes. "Excuse me?"

"Windell. He claimed the two of you were betrothed."

"My aunt wanted me to marry him, but nothing was ever formalized, and he never proposed."

As if that matters. I didn't propose to Leeri and still ended up marrying the woman. *Shit.* Why am I so angry about this when *I'm* the one fucking *married*?

"Senan, calm down."

I can't... "He's the one who told Boris about us."

Her lips part in surprise.

Tell me to kill him. Tell me to gut him like the vermin he is and feed his entrails to the monsters that lurk in the river. Tell me you never cared for him.

With the smallest shake of her head, she says, "It doesn't matter who told the king. We have more pressing issues to address."

What can possibly be more pressing than murdering our hostage?

"Come with me." Allette's hand slips into mine, and I reluctantly follow her down the steep slope. Instead of going to the left where the burrows sleep below us, we take a right at the river, following a slender path on the highest bank. A path that comes to an abrupt stop at a wall of reddish stone.

We're almost upon the dead end before I realize it's not a dead end at all, but the entrance to a cavern the size of Josie and Harold's burrow.

Ten Tuath mill around within, their skin no longer gray but the telltale pink of fae too long in the sun.

Allette's fingers squeeze mine. "These people just arrived from Kumulus. They want to know how to access their power. I thought if we split them up, it would take half the time."

"This isn't something they can learn in a day." It took me months to master my element.

"I know. But if we can help them identify their power, perhaps we can pair them up and teach them how to practice with one another while we search for vacant towers."

She has a good point. We brought them to the sunlight; it's our responsibility to keep them moving in the right direction.

I wave the first fae forward. A man with a drooping jaw steps up to me. "What's your name?"

"Sean Mahaffey, my prince."

"There's no need to call me that." If I could shed the whole "prince" nonsense altogether, I would be a much happier man. "I am no different from you."

He scrubs his hands down his trousers. "What'll I call you then?"

"Simon works. Now, how long were you in the sun, Sean?"

"Ten minutes? Maybe fifteen. We caught sight of the guards and went back inside straightaway."

I'm pleased everyone is being cautious. It would do no good for us to get caught before we've begun. "How do you feel? Any pressure or warmth here?" I tap the left side of my chest. The other fae in the room inch closer, their hands finding their own hearts.

Sean's head tilts. "Feels more like a swarm of bees, buzzin' and such."

"Have you ever felt it before?"

He shakes his head.

That must be his magic, then. "Take my hand."

He may be shorter, but Sean Mahaffey has shovels for hands.

Calling on my magic, I urge my power toward our connection the same way I did for Iver and Harold. "Do you feel anything?"

Sean's wide brown eyes fly to mine. "The buzzin' is gettin' stronger."

The other Tuath take another step closer.

"Close your eyes and focus on your free hand. Try to draw my magic to your fingertips."

The stones start to vibrate and crack beneath my boots. A handful of tiny green shoots burst from between the fissures. "You're a terra elemental."

His eyes fly open, falling to where the tiny shoots are beginning to unfurl. "Hold that feeling for as long as possible; see if you can grow anything else." There's still so much that we don't know about their powers.

I let him go, and the plants continue to grow for another ten seconds before falling still. "Well done. Try it again on your own. When the buzzing stops, speak with Iver about where to find some more sunlight. Who's next?"

"I'd like to try."

We all turn in unison toward the cavern entrance where a silver-haired woman waits with her hands on her hips, tattoos peeking from beneath the sleeves of her billowy white shirt. Golden rings glint from her brows and lower lip.

Five more fae enter the cavern behind her, their gazes darting around the room.

Allette's skirts sway as she hurries over to the newcomer.

"Regina. I was hoping you'd come." She takes the woman's hand, bringing her down to where I stand.

So this is Harold's eldest daughter. "I'm a big fan of your work, Regina." The wings she inked on my girl's skin are something else.

Regina's brows lift. "Thank you."

Holding out my hand, I wait for Regina to stop glaring. When her hand finally slips into mine, I call on my magic.

The color on Regina's cheeks darkens as she concentrates on my commands.

The puddle by her boots begins to bubble like a pot set to boil.

"A water elemental—like your father."

Her grin flashes. "I knew it. They all said I was mad, but I fucking *knew* it!" She yanks her hand from my grip, splaying her fingers toward the puddle. The bubbles grow larger, and the water starts to foam.

Unlike with Sean, Regina doesn't seem to have any difficulty maintaining her power without me.

"Can you shape it?" I call a flame to my palm and then form the fire into a flickering sphere.

The water starts to rise, higher and higher, shimmering and glittering as it, too, tightens into a small sphere. With a flick of Regina's wrist, the sphere soars between us, colliding with my fire with a loud *hiss*, extinguishing the flames.

"Incredible."

Her chin lifts. "I know."

I'd love to see what she could do down by the river. But since we're trying to keep this as quiet as possible, that can't happen. At least not yet. "There's more water at the back of the cavern. See what you can do with that."

She bobs her head and saunters through the gawking crowd.

"Who else would like to try?"

A man emerges from between two Tuath. "I'll give it a go."

There's no need to ask his name. The two of us met five years ago. "Hello, Henry."

Forty

ALLETTE

Water collects in puddles and vines sprout from nothing, turning the practice cavern into an underground jungle.

Do you dream of being Queen of Kumulus?

Senan's question from a few days ago plays on repeat in my mind.

I rarely allowed myself to dream of being with Senan beyond our stolen moments, let alone to dream of ruling an entire kingdom, but that doesn't mean I don't want that future.

When Senan asked me, I couldn't help thinking of how ill-equipped I am to become a queen.

At least Senan was raised a prince, given lessons in warfare and diplomacy. I have more experience cleaning privies than anything else. If the people of Kumulus were to discover my background, they would never accept me as their leader.

But Senan... *He* is the man this kingdom needs. Look at what he has done down here with the Tuath, garnering their support in such a short amount of time. There must be plenty of Scathians who would back him for the crown as well.

The throne of Kumulus is Senan's destiny.

And after helping him these last few days, I'm starting to wonder if maybe it might be my destiny as well.

My prince refuses to speak about the issue, instead throwing himself into helping the Tuath find sunlight as quickly and quietly as possible.

Meanwhile, I've been teaching those who have found the sun to wield their powers. They're split almost evenly between water and terra elementals. Not a fire or wind elemental among them.

Iver's friend Twig can make trees grow from nothing. Iver himself can shape the very rock beneath us, crumbling the stone into dust with the clench of a fist. Only one woman has been brave enough to sneak above the clouds: Regina Nightingale.

From what I can tell, she might be the strongest of the lot—not that Iver would ever admit it.

With a twist of her wrist, Regina can draw water from the ground and form it into anything from a perfect sphere to a spear sharp enough to pierce stone.

More and more Tuath arrive each day, anxious to hone their skills. It's only a matter of time before they're truly a force to be reckoned with.

When Senan steps into the cavern, the entire room goes so silent, you could hear a mouse scurry. Everyone stares at him with such reverence in their eyes.

I cannot blame them; he is a marvel to behold. Color has returned to his cheeks and his smile is bright enough to light up the darkest of caverns. Because of us, these people have found a way to heal themselves. They have discovered their power. Their *magic*.

Think of all the good he could do from the throne. He could give them access to sunlight without having to worry about being incarcerated. He could harness the Tuath's ability to manipulate stone and commission affordable housing for those less fortunate. The list is endless.

How am I supposed to get through to him when his only concern is about me and my safety, my happiness? I love him for his selflessness, but, stars above, do I want to throttle him.

Not in front of all these people, of course. Better that I return to Harold and Josie's so we can discuss our future in private. That is, if I'm still awake by the time he comes home. All this teaching is draining and no matter how much I try to fight it, sleep always wins.

How Senan keeps going, I'll never know.

With my cloak around my shoulders, I slip from the smaller cavern, through the tight hallway, and into the larger cave where all the burrows are located. When I hear quick footsteps at my back, I glance over my shoulder, expecting to find Senan.

Instead, Braith is there, her eyes wide and face flushed as she rushes to meet me. "Is it true?" she gasps, pushing her silver hair back from her forehead. "Do we have magic?"

"How did you hear?" Has the news reached the castle? If so, I sincerely hope the Tuath are being careful. If the king or the guards find out, they'll throw all of us into the pit—or worse.

"Stars... so it is true?" Her head shakes even as her smile grows. "I met Regina down by the river and had to come see for myself. She was right all along."

The stone beneath our feet gives a bone-rattling shake, cracking right between us. Braith throws out her hands, steadying herself against the wall.

There's only one fae who has been able to master the element of terra so well. "Come out, Iver."

Braith's brother steps from the shadows wearing a wide grin. "What'd you think of my new trick, Princess Braith?"

"Don't call me that," Braith snaps.

With a careful twist of Iver's wrist, the fissure closes itself. Braith's jaw falls open as she stares down at the healed stone.

"What'd I tell you about doing that out here?" I warn. "We don't want the ceiling caving in on us."

"I won't let that happen," he says with a confidence I wish I shared. We still know so little about their powers, I'd rather take all precautions to keep the people down here safe.

"Does anyone else at the castle know?'

Braith shakes her head. "Not that I've heard."

I'm about to inquire about Jeston when I realize Iver used his magic to reshape a stone into something that looks an awful lot like male genitalia.

At his snort, Braith whips around. "Iver Nightingale!" She slams her fist into his arm. "Mum is going to kill you if she finds out what you're up to."

"Oh, hush. You're just jealous that you and Regina aren't the only artists in the family anymore," he teases even as he rubs his bicep. When he catches me staring, he waggles his brows. "Impressed, Wynn? It's to scale, in case you were wondering."

I bite back my smile. Wouldn't want to encourage the man. "I wasn't." Give a man the power to build anything he can imagine, and he makes a penis. Why am I not surprised?

Together, the three of us meander through the cramped paths toward Josie and Harold's, falling into excited conversation about all our plans. Once we have enough Tuath trained, we'll send them out into the kingdom to spread the good news. By then, it won't matter if the king finds out.

There will be too many of us to stop.

One of the Tuath we helped at the mines tears down the road, a sword bobbing in his fist. If he's not careful, he's going to fall and impale himself.

"He's gone!" he shouts.

"Shit..." Iver races to meet him.

"He's gone!" the man wails with a wheeze. "Chadwick went for a piss, and I only turned my back for a second—"

"Who's gone?" Braith asks.

I know the answer before the man says another word. "Windell." We need to find him before he escapes from the burrows.

"The bastard hit me with a fucking rock." The man raises a shaky hand to trace the lump on his forehead. "Knocked me clean out."

"How long ago?" Tell me this just happened.

"I don't know. I'm sorry."

There isn't time for apologies or placing blame. We need to sort this out. "Can you run to the entrance as fast as you can, see if you can catch up?"

The man nods. "What if he's already gone?"

"Then tell everyone you meet who has seen the sun to hide." If Windell reaches the king, Boris will stop at nothing to get to Senan. If the guards show up here and find the Tuath have been accessing sunlight...

The man takes off for the entrance, sprinting around the corner and out of view.

Braith catches my trembling hand. "Tell us what you need."

"Iver, run back to the practice cavern and warn the prince. Braith, I need you to help me gather our things."

We split up, Iver taking the high road and Braith following me to her parents' home. Josie's humming drifts from the kitchen, the warm sound so at odds with the chaos in my heart. I spring down the hallway and into our bedroom, grabbing our rucksacks from beneath the bed. I toss one at Braith and tell her to throw in everything that will fit.

We don't have many clothes, and after Senan's shopping spree in the market a few days ago, there isn't much gold left. Hopefully it'll be enough to get us safely to Stratiss. Once we reach the castle, we can let Aeron know all that's happened and plan from there.

I grab my shifts from the drawer, along with my undergarments and stockings. Braith drags out the four dresses I own, rolling them tightly and stuffing them into her bag.

Outside the burrow someone shouts.

Braith's head snaps toward the window. "What was that?"

"It doesn't matter." I need to finish packing and get to Senan.

More shouts follow. Louder. Angrier.

Braith rushes over to the window, drawing the curtain aside. "Shit."

"What is it?"

"There are guards in the caverns."

Already? How did they get here so fast? *Shit*. There's no more time. "I need to get to Senan."

I go to grab for the pack still clutched in her hand, but she pulls it out of my grasp. "Have you lost your mind? You can't leave the burrow. If one of the guards recognize you, they'll take you straight to the king."

They won't recognize me.

Senan, on the other hand...

A scream echoes through the house.

We both lunge for the door and fall into the hallway, where two guards in silver leathers drag a kicking, cursing Josie from the kitchen. Black masks cover the lower halves of their faces, making them look even more sinister.

When they see Braith and me, they bellow for us to vacate the premises at once.

My heart hammers and sweat drips down the back of my neck. I should've known this was too good to be true, that it wouldn't last forever.

That fate would find us no matter where we hid.

Outside, the acrid stench of smoke fills the cavern, reminding me of a different time, a different fire that set this whole terrible reality into motion. Broken glass litters the paths and black clouds billow from homes down the street.

Children scream and wail, clinging to their mothers' skirts. The guards dragging Josie drop her unceremoniously to the ground next to Braith.

Josie pushes to her feet, swiping the dirt from her skirt, her face twisted in fury as she glowers at the guards.

How are there so many?

They stand at least a head taller than the tallest male, their eyes narrowed into slits over their masks.

"It has been reported that you have been harboring a fugitive," a deep voice booms.

Any warmth remaining in my body leaks from my bones.

That familiar tone should belong to a ghost.

I shift to the right, peering between Josie and Braith to where Eason Bell stalks across the street, gripping a sword with crimson blood oozing down the blade.

He should be dead. I stabbed him when he tried to take me. He fell to the ground in a pool of his own blood.

The Tuath lined up on either side of the street remain close-lipped, returning the guards' scowls with every bit of venom shot their way.

Across the path, a little girl with silver curls sobs against a woman's chest while a young man tries to console them both.

Eason stalks forward and drags the man to the center of the path. "Where is Prince Senan Vale?" He presses the tip of his sword to the man's throat, the blade biting against pale skin.

No one speaks up.

"Don't hurt him," the woman begs through her tears. "Please, don't—"

Eason carves the blade across the man's throat.

The little girl screams, wriggling from her mother's grasp, her silver curls bouncing as she hurtles toward her fallen father, her feet bare beneath her night dress.

Eason catches her by the hair, and his blade flies to her tiny throat.

He wouldn't dare kill a child.

What am I saying? Of course, he would. The man is a monster. I must stop him. I must speak up. I cannot let him take anyone else—

"I'm going to ask one more time. Where is—"

"It's nice to see you again, Bell."

I whirl, watching in horror as my prince descends from between two burrows.

Senan...no...

My mate strolls down the street, his dark cloak swaying with each step. People gasp and gawk; hands fly to chests as curses ring through the hollow cavern.

There is nothing kind about the grin on Senan's face as he

comes to a stop in front of Eason. "Here I thought you were dead."

"I could say the same thing about you." Eason adjusts his grip on the little girl, her lips quivering and tears spilling onto her chubby cheeks. "Where is Allette?"

"You tell me. You're the one who stole her from me."

"You honestly expect me to believe that you don't have her?"

"If I found her, would I be standing here talking to you?" Senan drawls, slipping his hands into the pockets of his trousers. "Might I ask how you found me?"

Windell steps from between two guards, his fine clothes covered in dirt. I hate these men with every stitch of my soul. Perhaps if I stole their attention, that would give Senan enough time to escape—

Braith's hand finds mine, her clammy fingers gripping tightly. "Don't. Please."

How am I supposed to sit back and watch them steal my prince?

I glance down at the man's unmoving body.

What other choice do I have?

They'll kill anyone and everyone who gets in their way. I cannot help Senan if I'm dead.

Senan does not fight as a guard clamps his wrists in iron manacles. Eason lets the little girl go, and she falls forward, splattering blood on her hands and nightgown as her screams flood the air.

The guards lead Senan through the streets lined with Tuath. Some bow while others appear too stunned to move.

I don't let myself cry until the guards are gone and all that's left is the smell of smoke and grief. When the tears come, they run like twin rivers down my cheeks.

This is our fault.

All this death and destruction is on our hands.

We should've left the night we got the antidote.

We never should've stayed in the first place.

Braith folds me into her embrace, her tears wet against my own. "I'm so sorry, Allette."

The king took my love from me for the last time.

I refuse to let that bastard steal away my life once more. Refuse to let him destroy these kind, gentle people whose only "crime" was to be born without wings.

If Senan cannot kill Boris Vale, I will.

I'm so sorry, Allette.

I'm not sorry.

I'm angry.

What's more? "I'm going to get him back."

Forty-One

SENAN

THAT FUCKING BASTARD.

Windell is lucky he's walking so far ahead; otherwise, I'd bash his head into the stone wall. I should've killed him the moment he mentioned Allette.

Every few steps, he glances over his shoulder with a sneer, and if I were quick enough, I'd steal Bell's sword and run the prick straight through. Hell, I'd love to kill them both.

So many innocent people are dead because of me. When I saw them grab Dahlia, I knew I couldn't hide anymore.

Now I'm being frog-marched out of the burrows, my eyes burning from the smoke pouring through broken windows, consuming peaceful homes. The people who wail at the cavern's entrance aren't pretending anymore.

The guards look as if they cut and burned their way into the underground paradise even though I'd bet none of the dead Tuath put up a fight. How could they? They have no weapons.

The man who sold me oranges lies next to the carpenter who made the swords, their limbs akimbo, staring up at the ceiling through sightless eyes. Such senseless violence all because of me. At least Bell and Windell don't know Allette still lives. I only hope it stays that way.

My former guard lifts me into his arms like a damsel in distress.

I'm in distress all right.

"Just like old times," I quip, racking my brain for some way to escape. But even if I manage to, I cannot come back here for fear of leading them straight to my girl or the Tuath hiding in the back cavern, their skin almost as tanned as the guards'.

Eason's eyes narrow and he tugs down his mask, his smile beneath a vile twist of his lips. When his glamour drops, his gray wings spread wide from his back and we take to the skies.

"What? No, 'Welcome home, Senan. I've missed you?' No hug?" Maybe I'll get lucky and he'll drop me. Not that I have a hope of surviving a fall from this height, but at least it would be better than whatever fate my dear brother has in store for me.

No words pass Bell's tight lips, but his working jaw proves he heard me over the roaring wind.

The clouds seem heavier as we pass through them, the familiar sweet smell more pungent than I remember. I hope the Tuath will continue to find ways to rise above them. That they'll reclaim the power that has been hidden from them for so long. That they'll fight for the life they deserve.

And Allette...

I only wish we left on better terms. I've been avoiding her since our conversation about me becoming the next king. Not that any of it matters now. Once Boris gets hold of me, I won't be anything.

In no time at all, the castle comes into view.

Part of me wondered if they'd bring me straight to the pit. Unfortunately, it looks like I'll be paying my brother a visit before passing beyond the veil.

Boris waits on the balcony outside his office, his hands resting on the balustrade and eyes blazing with fury. Bilson stands at the door, his arms crossed over his chest.

"Hello, brother," Boris says with a victorious smile.

I straighten my shirt to keep my bound hands from bunching

into fists. From letting him know how desperate I am to flee. "Fuck you."

"Is that any way to greet your king?" The chiding way he clicks his tongue makes me want to cut it off. "It's been far too long. I'm surprised you aren't happier to see me."

"After you sawed off my wings and threw me into the portal?" What a fucking joke. What I wouldn't give to throw this chain around his arrogant neck and twist until all the air left his body and he died on this floor.

Actually, no.

That's too quick a death for him.

I want to watch ravens pluck out his eyeballs, see his entrails spilled and then burned while he remains conscious. To see the life fade from his eyes as I regale him with exactly how much darkness lives within me.

Darkness he sowed.

Boris sniffs, flattening a hand over his collar. "Ah, yes. That. Well, it is unfortunate, but all's well that ends well." He snaps his fingers, and a maid slips through the door, head to toe in white, brandishing a golden tray of drinks. "Champagne?"

As if I'd take a glass of what is more than likely drugged champagne. "Pass."

Boris picks one up by the stem, turning the glass between his fingers. "Do you not wish to celebrate the good news? Oh, wait. You might not have heard. Thanks to your little shenanigans with the princess, our baby brother was kidnapped by the Nimbiss minister. Can you believe that?"

We both know that what happened with Leeri wasn't my fault, but there's no sense correcting him.

"Thankfully, Prince Kyffin was returned—along with annulment paperwork from Nimbiss Castle." He stares into the bubbling golden liquid, a frown tugging at his lips. "Such a pity. The two of you made quite the match."

His throat bobs when he takes a sip, and all I can think about is dragging a blade across his gullet the way Bell killed Dahlia's father. Boris finishes the drink and returns it to the tray, sending the servant away with a wave of his hand.

"Oh, Bilson?"

My former guard steps forward, chin held high, and gaze fixed to mine. "Sire?"

Boris rips his dagger from its scabbard, whirls, and carves the blade across Bilson's throat. Blood sprays from the gash, and he crumples to the marble. None of the other guards move a fucking muscle.

Boris plucks a handkerchief from his pocket, dabbing the blood from his face and hands, then cleaning his blade before letting the stained cloth fall into the puddle of blood. "Do you remember when I asked what happened to my brother, and you swore you burned his body?" He digs his boot into Bilson's ribs, and Bilson lets out one final watery gurgle. "I think that might have been a lie." Boris turns to the rest of his men. "Let this be a lesson to all of you. Betrayal will not be tolerated."

Bilson's gaze meets mine once more before his eyes fall closed forever.

I'm sorry, my friend.

He put his life in jeopardy to save mine—and for what? To be murdered in cold blood a few weeks later?

Boris steps over my guard's fallen form, waving for me to follow. "Let's go inside, shall we?"

Bell shoves between my shoulder blades, and I stumble forward, somehow managing to move my leaden limbs.

The brightness inside Boris's office belies the darkness lurking within the king's soul. Familiar shelves rise toward the ceiling, the golden text adorning the spines glinting. In the corner stands an ornate cage that wasn't there the last time I came into this room.

Dread tightens like a noose around my neck as Boris withdraws a key from the desk's top drawer and fits it into the cage's lock.

The hinges creak as he swings the door open with a gallant

bow. "Go on. In you go. Can't have you flying off on me again." He snorts.

Shame burns through me as I duck beneath the bars, what's left of my wings aching from his cruel joke. When I go to turn, my arm bumps against the bars, and my skin burns like the fires of the sun.

Boris kicks the door closed, locking it once more. "Fine workmanship, isn't it? Made by the kingdom's finest craftsmen." His lips twist. "I borrowed it from someone who no longer had any need for it."

I don't give a shite where he got the fucking cage. "What do you want from me?" If he wanted me dead, I'd be lying on the balcony next to Bilson. If he wanted me punished, he would've sent me to the pit.

Boris's dark brows climb his forehead. "From you? Oh, nothing. Not anymore at least. No, you have proven yourself quite useless."

"Then why don't you just kill me and get it over with?"

His eyes narrow but his smile remains, twisted and vicious. "Make no mistake, you will die. But after your little foray into the burrows, too many people have seen you of late. Meaning we must do this the correct way, with trials and such. Must appease my people, you see. Although, I doubt any of them will be too sad to see you go."

At least this gives me some time to escape. And I *will* escape.

Boris practically skips over to his desk, returning the key to the top drawer. *Fool.* His own arrogance will be his downfall. All I have to do is convince a servant to retrieve it for me. As far as I know, my blood will still give me access to the wards, and I can slip through the servants' caverns once more.

"Before I forget, I have a gift for you." Sauntering back toward the cage, Boris unsheathes his dagger. I retreat until I have nowhere else to go. Unfortunately, it's not far enough. A terrible hiss screams through the air when he thrusts his blade between the bars, tearing through my shirt and skin. The explosion of pain sends me to my knees. Blood gushes from the wound, soaking my shirt and trousers, pooling on the white marble floor.

From his pocket, Boris withdraws a glowing vial of stardust. I'm in too much agony to fight as he thumbs off the cork and dumps the contents over my wounds.

Heat replaces the cold, racing through my bloodstream toward my thundering heart. I don't need to ask to know if the vial was poisoned. I can feel each drop stealing away the life the antidote returned to me.

My head spins, and the last thing I see before my eyes close are the king's shiny boots as he turns and walks away.

Forty-Two

SENAN

When I try to stand, my legs refuse to hold my weight. How long have I been out? My skin still glows, so it mustn't have been very long. Why is my thigh so fucking sore? Why are my trousers ripped? When did I cut myself? Gods, that gash looks bad.

Why does it look like Kyffin is standing on the other side of these iron bars?

The mirage leaps back with a squeak like a tiny mouse. I saw a mouse in the burrows once. Scared the shite out of me at first, but its fuzzy little face and twitchy whiskers were kind of cute.

"Kyff? Is that really you?"

He inches closer, so close I can see my drawn face reflected in his blown-out pupils, the silver in his eyes no more than a thin ring.

He's really here.

And I need his help.

Help with what, though? I shake my head to try to clear some of the fog, but it only sets the room spinning. "The door. I need you to open the door."

Kyff glances up at the door, then back to me, his small brow creasing. "I can't."

Of course, he can't because the thing is locked. "There's a key in the..." In the what? *Dammit*. Why can't I remember the word? "Behind you." His head swings toward the... "Desk!" That's the one I'm looking for.

My baby brother shifts back, his hand falling to the pommel of the bejeweled blade Boris gifted him for mastering his element.

Why does he look so afraid of me? Does he think I'm going to hurt him? "I won't hurt you." I would never hurt Kyff.

Kyff's eyes narrow as he takes the smallest step away. "You lie."

"No... No, I don't."

His knuckles turn white where he grips his dagger. "Yes, you do. You said you'd never leave me, but you did. You left and someone took me."

Someone took him? Wait. That sounds familiar.

Nimbiss.

So much for him not realizing he was being held hostage. "I know. I'm sorry."

"You should be. It's your fault. They said you stole their princess."

"I didn't steal anyone." Except Windell, but that was only because I didn't have any other choice. Gods, do I hate that sniveling weasel.

A lock of Kyff's onyx hair falls across his furrowed brow when he shakes his head. "That's not what Boris told me."

Don't even get me started on our fucking king. "You shouldn't trust Boris."

"Why not? He's the one who saved me. Who brought me back. Who helped me when you left!" Kyff shouts, his small face painted red with anger.

All right. No bad-mouthing the king in front of Kyffin. Noted.

I inch closer to the bars, my heart breaking when I see my baby brother take yet another step away from me. "I'm sorry I left. Sorrier than you will ever know. But I'm here now, aren't I?

Stay with me. We can talk about what happened, if you think that will help?"

If I can find a way to rebuild the trust I broke, *then* he'll see the truth.

Kyff drags his sleeve under his nose, his eyes red-rimmed. "It won't help. You got married and didn't invite me."

"Only because there wasn't time. I wanted you there, Kyff. I swear I did."

He glances away. "I missed you so much." Quieter, he mumbles, "I didn't know he lied until it was too late."

"Who lied?"

"The really grumpy man with a big belly and tiny eyes."

Minister Donnell.

"With you and Rhainn gone, there was no one left to play with," he says. "Even the guards were too busy to train with me. When the man asked if I wanted to visit you in your new kingdom, I was so excited."

Here I thought I couldn't feel worse.

Kyff only went with Donnell because he thought he was coming to see me.

"I packed my sword and jam and everything," he goes on, his tone brightening for a moment. "They let me fly on a Pegasus with one of the guards too. His name was Titan, and he had black and white wings."

"That sounds like quite the adventure." Kyff always wanted his own Pegasus.

"It was. And when we got to the castle, the king gave me a whole basket of sweets." A frown finds his mouth as he stares down at the floor, tracing the veins in the marble with his boot.

I can see where this story is headed. "You ate too many, didn't you?" Kyff has an awful sweet tooth.

A nod. "My stomach hurt so badly, I thought I was going to puke in front of everyone. The queen told me I would feel better after a nap. She was nice but the room they gave me was too dark. I tried to be brave, to look for the stars like you told me to, but the sky was empty. I didn't want to be alone, so I asked if you could stay with me, just for one night, until I was used to it, you know? The guards didn't listen. I kept asking, but they wouldn't even let me talk to you."

Because I wasn't fucking *there*.

"I'm so sorry, Kyff. I should've been here to protect you."

"But you weren't." His lips flatten as a fat tear rolls down his round cheek. He wipes it away with a small fist. "They locked me in my room and wouldn't let me out, not even when I screamed and cried."

He must've been terrified. When I think of what would've happened to him if we hadn't found the princess— "I hope one day you'll be able to forgive me." *Not that I'll be around to see it.*

"I won't," he says. "Not ever." Kyffin turns and dashes out of the room, leaving me all alone.

The same way I left him.

Forty-Three

ALLETTE

How?

That one word haunts me as I pace my room. When I told Braith I planned on getting Senan back, she'd asked me how and I had no response. The truth is, I don't know how I'm supposed to save him, or if I even can.

However, if I let myself believe I'll fail, I'll never leave this burrow. Never try.

But *how?*

I sink onto the mattress and force my breathing to steady. To think.

Stars, I'm so bloody tired, weary down to the bone from fighting.

For my love. For my life.

Just a little bit longer, a phantom voice whispers.

You're almost there.

If our roles were reversed, Senan would already be storming the castle gates, tearing apart the towers stone by stone to get me back. How can I give him any less?

Swiping my hands down my damp cheeks, I steel my shoulders and head back to where Iver sits on the sofa, holding his head in dirt-smeared hands. He spent the last hour burying friends and neighbors lost in the attack, too many innocent fae murdered because we sought refuge among them.

Regina sits beside him, fixated on the flames shuddering in the fireplace.

"I'm sorry," I manage past the lump in my throat, the words seeming so insignificant in light of how much suffering these people have endured. "If we hadn't come here, none of this would have happened."

Iver's hands drop and his head lifts, his dark eyes swimming with unshed tears. "The king did this. Not you."

"I'm still sorry all the same."

Sniffling, he drags his sleeve under his nose. "What are you going to do?"

"Find a way to get him back." Or die trying.

Regina turns toward me, her brows raised as she scans me from head to toe. "And if he's in the pit?"

"Then I go to the pit."

Slowly Iver rises, the dirt caking his knees tumbling to the ground as he adjusts his dark trousers. "I'm going with you."

"It's too dangerous." I very well might not come back.

"No more dangerous than it is to stay here."

"He's right." Harold comes into the living room, Josie trailing behind him, both wearing the same solemn expressions, dirt from their friends' graves lining their creased hands. "As long as men who care nothing about us remain in power, we will never be free. We want more than we've been given. We deserve more."

They do deserve more, but if I don't succeed, they may never get it. And when Boris learns they've been stealing sunlight, their fates will be dire, indeed. Still: "I cannot ask you to help me."

Josie takes Harold's hand, her eyes hardening. "You're not asking. We're offering."

Regina slowly rises from the sofa. "You cannot do this on your own."

While I appreciate their support, I'm not sure how they can

help. I'll need to be stealthy, and showing up to the castle with half the Nightingale family in tow isn't exactly inconspicuous.

A knock rattles the front door. Harold ambles over, his shoulders stooped as he answers, revealing a whole host of Tuath with sun-kissed faces. I recognize the fae who weren't too afraid to claim their power, the ones we've been training deep in the caverns.

They continue pouring into the room, some looking angry while others wear streaks from tears on their cheeks. Despite the array of emotions, all of them possess the same determined glint in their eyes.

"Why have you come?" I ask, a tremor in my voice.

Henry's deep voice rings through the silent air. "We're here to save our prince."

My knees begin to quake beneath my skirts.

Boris Vale threatens the very existence of these Tuath. He has made it impossible for them to rise above their station, to unlock the magic hiding within their hearts, and that ends today.

"You all feel this way?" I scan their faces for signs of doubt. All I see are nods; all I hear are shouts of affirmation.

These people are willing to fight. They are ready. Do I have it in me to be the one to lead them to victory?

I suppose there's only one way to find out.

"Then we're in agreement. We free Senan and help him take the throne."

Cheers erupt, fists raised in the air, magic and hope in our hearts.

I hold out my hands, waiting for the noise to die down. Enthusiasm is all well and good, but for us to succeed, we will need a solid plan. "First, I need a volunteer to go to Stratiss Castle." If this is going to work, we could really use Aeron's help.

One of the men to my right raises his hand.

"Thank you. Do whatever it takes to let Prince Aeron know what has happened to Senan." Now to figure out how to save my prince. "Second, we need to know where they're keeping him."

A woman standing beside Josie raises her hand. "My cousin says the guards brought the prince to the castle."

Brilliant. Now, all we need to do is find a way to breach the gates without getting caught.

The door opens once more, and Braith pushes through the fray, coming to a stop in front of me, her white mask hanging loosely at her neck, rising and falling with her heaving chest. "The king is...putting Prince Senan...on trial."

I press my hands to my ribs, forcing myself to take a breath. This is a *good* thing, right? It means Senan is still alive. That we have time to save him.

Cursing, Iver rakes a hand through his hair. The rest of the Tuath begin to murmur, trading heavy looks.

"You're certain?"

Braith nods. "It's all anyone in the castle can talk about."

Can it even be called a "trial" if the whole thing is a farce? Trials are meant to be fair and unbiased. Senan's fate will be decided by the same man who has imprisoned him, who has wished him dead for who knows how long.

I clutch the top of the armchair to keep my legs from giving out. "How much time do we have?"

"Five days."

Thank the stars it's not tomorrow. "Do you know where they're holding him?"

Her hair sways as her head shakes. "Not for certain, but one of the women assigned to the family's tower claims there have been two guards posted in the servants' stairwell leading to the king's office."

"Have there ever been guards there before?"

"Never."

That must be the place. Two guards would be easier to handle than a whole army.

Hope seeps through the cracks in my broken heart. I have access to the family's tower—at least I used to. "Have they changed the wards?"

"Not that I know of."

If that's the case, then I might be able to get into the tower. Now to figure out how the hell to infiltrate the castle.

Even if I found someone to carry me to one of the balconies, there will likely be so many guards, we won't be able to enter without notice. Which leaves the caverns. Except there are guards at the entrances who would raise the alarm if we tried to go through the lower gates.

My gaze falls on the clumps of dirt sprinkled across the stone floor.

Unless...

Unless we make our own entrance. "Iver? Do you think you and the other terra elementals could create a tunnel that links to the caverns beneath the castle?"

His eyes fill with something akin to excitement. "If we have enough sunlight."

Harold scrubs a hand across his jaw. "It'll take more than magic to break through that much rock. There used to be a few mines north of the castle. Henry and I can check the old maps to see if one of the shafts will get us close."

"Do you have access to those maps?" Because that would be damned convenient.

"Give me an hour." With a pat on the back from his wife, Harold moves through the crowd to the door.

Burrowing through the stone to the castle is all well and good, but that's not our only challenge. "We'll need to find a safe place to breach the servants' cavern." Somewhere no one will notice and raise the alarm.

Braith steps closer. "You can tunnel to my room."

"If the guards find out that you helped us—"

"It's the only way, and you know it. Any of the public spaces will be found out. Don't worry about me. When Senan is crowned king, I'm sure he'll give me a royal pardon."

A few Tuath chuckle, but her words are like cement, weighing me down. This isn't just a rescue mission. This is an assassination.

One thing at a time. "Can you get your hands on an extra uniform?" It's the only way I'll be able to slip in and out of her room undetected.

Braith's eyes flash as she slides her pack from her back and unbuckles the top. "Already done." In her hand, she clutches a white uniform and mask.

One more piece of this intricate puzzle falls into place. I hug her close, thanking the stars that Braith and I found each other. "You are brilliant."

Her huffed laugh tickles the hair at my neck. "I know."

So we have a way in, but now we need a way out. I draw back, my mind racing with possibilities. "Can you steal one for Senan as well?" If he were dressed as a servant, then we should be able to leave the same way we arrived.

"That shouldn't be a problem."

Josie worries her lips, her eyes glittering as she watches her daughter. "What about the guards?"

Right. We need to dispense of two guards as well.

"Could you poison them?" Josie adds.

I'd rather not kill them if we can avoid it. Is there a simple way to incapacitate them? Wait... I think I know. "Does anyone have access to stardust?"

Three of them slowly lift their hands.

Perfect.

"Right. I need the three of you to get me as much dust as you can. The rest of you need to spend as much time in the sun as possible; we're going to need all the power we can get."

Forty-Four

SENAN

Don't ask me how long I've been in this cage. It could be a couple of hours or a few days. The only time I'm allowed out is to relieve myself, and even then, I'm chained to within an inch of my life and escorted by no less than three guards. Maybe I should be flattered that Boris believes me capable of escaping, but the truth is, I'm outmatched, out-magicked, and so fucking tired, passing the hours in a golden, dust-fueled haze.

Every time my vision clears, Boris returns with another vial, and I know in my heart that this is the end. I have no friends to speak of, my brothers are all gone, and Allette…

I'd die a thousand times over to keep her from this cursed castle.

Blinking my weary eyes, I stare up at the iron ceiling overhead. This cage may be large enough for me to stretch out fully, but it's impossible to get comfortable on the cold, stone floor. I curl into a ball and hug myself, pretending my arms are my girl's and that we're in her bed in the burrows.

Boris's desk taunts me with the prize concealed inside the top drawer.

That's right.

Boris is still keeping the key in there, and every time he lets me out to use the privy, he drops it back in with a flourish and a smile, like he's proud of dangling that bit of hope in front of me. I've tried begging the handful of servants who've come and gone to retrieve it, but I may as well have been a ghost for all the attention they paid me.

I have nothing to offer them except certain death for their assistance.

No one in their right mind would take that deal.

If I want to get my hands on that key, I'm going to have to be the one to make it happen.

I ease onto my elbows, my head spinning like a cyclone and stomach revolting. I wouldn't put it past Boris to have drugged my drink and food as well as the dust he pours over the wounds he inflicts.

How do I get to that desk?

Perhaps I could strip bare and tie my clothes together, using them as a sort of lasso.

No, that won't work. I have no hope of reaching that far, let alone having enough material to loop around anything.

If only I held the power of the air. Then, I'd have some way of knocking the desk on its side. The drawers would spill their contents all over the floor, and I could carry the key on a breeze.

If there's no way to bring the desk to me, maybe I could find a way to bring myself to the desk.

The cage isn't bolted to the floor, which means, if I shove hard enough, I should be able to move the thing along the marble. There's only one way to find out.

I back up as far as I can and take a deep breath. This is going to hurt like hell.

Not as bad as the death my brother has planned.

I give myself a shake.

I can do this.

My legs wobble as I charge forward, slamming into the iron bars. The metal hisses against any bit of exposed skin it can find, but, fuck it all, the bastard moved! Sure, my shoulder feels like it's been shattered, but that's a minor detail because... The. Cage. Moved!

I rear back and hit the bars again and again and again, gaining ground inch by inch. The thing makes an awful racket, screeching against the marble, but there's nothing I can do about that. After ten hits, I have to swap shoulders, and when I'm too sore to continue, I strip out of my shirt and tear the tattered fabric to wrap around my hands so I can grip the bars.

When I try to push, the soles of my boots slip, so I take those off as well. Every single muscle in my body strains.

It's not enough. Boris is going to walk through that door at any moment, see what I'm doing, and put an end to this pathetic escape attempt.

What's the alternative? To sit on my ass and wait for death to claim me?

No, thank you.

I've already come this far. I cannot give up now.

I clasp my hands behind my back and lift, stretching my sore muscles. The skin of my shoulders has turned a mottled black and blue. What little magic is still coursing in my veins will be working overtime to heal me today. I grip those bars again and push with all my might, my muscles screaming until I can push no more, and I collapse in a puddle of sweat.

What have I done to deserve this fate? I've only ever asked for one thing for myself, for one person. Why have I been punished for falling in love?

Beads of sweat trickle down my brow, splashing onto my wrapped hands.

If I hadn't found the woman who makes my soul sing, I would've had a longer, simpler life, but even a day without Allette isn't worth living.

Closing my eyes, I picture my girl's smiling face and imagine the sweet trill of her laughter filling the air. My fingers wrap around those damn bars, and I push. It could be my imagination, but the cage feels like it moves a little easier. I'm almost to the rug!

If I can get a little bit closer, I could grab the corner and drag the desk over to me. It must be lighter than this damn cage.

I shove with all my might, creeping closer and closer... Close enough to reach the rug.

With the fabric clutched in my fists, I give the rug a yank. After moving iron, the desk feels like a fucking feather. My biceps bulge and ache and my hands start to cramp, but I ignore them both as I pull and pull until I can reach through the bars and touch the edge of the desk. The thing is facing the wrong way. Still, I'm closer than I was an hour ago. So close, I can taste the sweet air of freedom on my—

"You are a determined bastard; I'll give you that."

I whirl, finding the king waiting in the doorway, arms folded and a smug smirk on his lips. There's no telling how long he's been standing there; I haven't looked back, only forward, toward a freedom that will never come.

He doesn't hurry to the desk. He saunters over, as if he has all the time in the world, easing onto the corner where his stack of papers would have been if they hadn't spilled off.

I would rake my fingers through my hair in frustration but cannot lift my arms at all. "Why don't you just take the damn key?"

Boris's smile curls higher. "Because I like to watch you hope."

Hope in a hopeless situation is enough to kill a man, and I'm a dead man walking.

My body sways, and I fall to my knees. Tears prick the backs of my eyes, but I'll be damned if I let him see me break.

Boris pushes the desk all the way to the fucking balcony. When he rounds the front, I expect him to withdraw the key. Instead, he brings out a dagger and another glowing vial. "Time for your medicine."

I fall onto my ass in my haste to retreat, curling at the far side of my prison. "No...I don't...I don't want it."

His brows arch as he stalks toward me, the sunset reflecting off the silver blade. "Are you sure about that?"

The madness is, part of me does want the dust. At least then I can blame my inability to break free on something besides myself. It gives me a spark of life in this relentless darkness.

Boris reaches through the bars and drags the blade down my thigh, flaying my trousers and the skin beneath. When he adds the dust, I welcome its warmth.

Unlike the other wounds, this one does not heal; it weeps crimson and gold down my skin, dripping onto the cold marble. All my magic must be gone, along with all my hope.

Boris wins.

But why? What have I done to make him hate me so much that he is willing to go to such lengths to kill me?

"Why?" The question pounds in my skull like a hammer as my veins glow brighter.

The king stills. Turns. Walks back to the cage to kneel next to me. "Everyone loves Senan Vale, don't they? So *carefree*. So *charismatic*. I once overheard our mother say it was a pity you weren't born first."

Our mother had said that? Even if she had, how is that my fault?

"I never understood why, you know. You never followed the rules, believed you were above them, that there would never be any consequences for your actions." A mirthless chuckle falls from his sneer as his head shakes. "Do you remember Scarlett Tilden?"

"Who?"

The king's nostrils flare, his eyes narrowing into slits. "Scarlett fucking Tilden. She and I were courting when you set your sights on her."

I don't know a Scarlett—*wait*. I *do* know her. Scarlett Tilden was the reason Allette avoided me when we first met, the reason she called me a cad. "I had no idea the two of you were courting." Boris kept his private life private. Hell, I didn't meet his wife until the day of the wedding. "And for the record, Scarlett came on to me." Yes, I kissed her, but that had been her idea. Then she tried to sneak into my room during a ball. When she was found out, the scandal ruined all social standing she or her family had. Last I heard, they moved to a new kingdom.

Boris lunges, grabbing the bars with both hands, rattling the whole damn cage. A sickening hiss fills the air from the iron burning his palms. "Liar! She told me the truth of what happened, how you seduced her. You ruined her—just as you ruin *everything*." His hands fall away, the skin of his palms a brutal red. "Despite it all, I tried my best with you, tried to keep you from wasting yourself on some low-born filth who only wanted you for your crown—"

"Allette loved me."

"Really? Because I heard that she fucked your guard two days after you left her in the human realm."

"Stop... That's not... That's not true..." She mourned me. She loved me. She still does...

"I was disappointed when I found out she wasn't dead, but I think this is much more fitting, don't you?" His lips curl back. "Gods, you are pathetic. Can't even handle a bit of disappointment without breaking. How could you ever hope to rule a kingdom?"

A bit of disappointment? "I thought you killed my mate!" Men have broken for less.

"And you destroyed yourself and made our family look like a bunch of fucking wasters. You are a disgrace to the Vale name. Luckily, I recognized you for the drain you are." He stands, looking down at me as if I'm a worm to be squished beneath his boot. "I cannot wait to finally be rid of you."

Forty-Five

ALLETTE

Darkness surrounds me on all sides, the sort of dark that makes you feel completely and utterly alone. After gathering all the terra elementals, Harold brought us to one of the old mines on the north side of the city. The Tuath went in one at a time, using their magic to cut through the stone until every last spark was gone.

Then Iver and I made our way through the twisting, turning shaft, burrowing deeper and deeper underground. Both my shoulders scrape stone as I feel my way through the cave.

What am I saying? This isn't a cave; it's a crevice. With the castle so close, Harold didn't want to weaken the ground any more than necessary for fear of causing another cave-in. Not that they had enough magic for anything larger.

Don't ask me what color the weeping walls are because I wouldn't be able to tell you. Down here, neither color nor light exists.

Braith went ahead to the castle to prepare for our arrival. We have one chance to get this right. If we break through anywhere besides her room, the guards will surely find us.

There are no fae lights to guide us. We have candles in our pockets, but Iver worried they'd disturb the bats.

That's right. There are bats somewhere in this cave. I'd shudder, but there isn't room for that.

We've been walking for fifteen minutes, and it feels as if this tunnel is never going to end.

High-pitched squeaks echo from overhead, turning my blood as cold as the stones beneath my palms. When I speak, even my whisper seems to echo. "Are those the bats?"

"Yes." The way Iver's voice drifts from the darkness makes him sound very far away.

"Are they close?" I can't see my own hand in front of my face, let alone anything above me. For all I know, the flying rats could reach out their clawed wings and scrape my hair. Or land on my head.

"Probably not."

How comforting.

Our feet crunch against stones, each perilous step bringing me closer to victory.

I'm coming, Senan.

What if the king had him moved from his office?

I'll just have to find him, won't I? I will not rest until my prince is free and the king is no more. For what Boris Vale has done to us—to the people of this kingdom—he deserves to die a slow, painful death.

I still don't know if Senan will take the throne or let the responsibility fall to his youngest brother. All that matters is that, when this is over, Boris Vale will no longer hold any power over this place or these people.

If Senan is the one to ascend in his stead, then I will be by his side if he'll have me.

I might not have been raised in a castle or taught diplomacy, but I love my newfound family and friends—I owe them my life. I want to help those who haven't been able to help themselves. Who have suffered under the crown's tyrannical laws for centuries. To—

My chest collides with something rigid and warm.

Iver's back.

"We've reached the end," he whispers.

The scrape of a striking match fills my ears. I squint against the sudden brightness of the flickering orange flame as Iver lights his candle before turning to hand it to me. A wall of solid black waits on the other side.

"Where do we go from here?"

From his pocket, he withdraws a compass. After some shifting around, he points to the wall to our right. "Through there."

"Are you certain?"

"You're welcome to check for yourself if you don't believe me."

I wouldn't know the first thing about reading a compass. "I trust you." What other choice do I have?

His cheeks puff as he blows out a steady breath, glaring at the wall as if it's his nemesis. "You should back up in case something goes wrong."

I retreat a few steps, giving him room to work. With both palms flat against the wall, his eyes fall closed. The slightest shudder trembles beneath my boots, growing stronger and stronger until the walls quake. A split appears in the rock, directly between his hands. Shards of stone break and tumble toward his boots.

The crack becomes a gap large enough to squeeze through. The walls shake and the ground quavers as Iver carves his way through the stone, making a path where there was none. Will he have enough magic to make it through? The sun should be setting by now, which means we'll have to wait until tomorrow to—

A thundering *crack* rings through the cave. One moment Iver is there, the next he's gone, swallowed by darkness.

A ferocious wind rips at my hair, extinguishing the flame. Lost in darkness, I reach my foot forward, feeling for my next step. "Iver?" Tell me he's not hurt. *Stars...* Tell me he's not dead. "Iver?"

A groan echoes through the blackness.

Thank the stars. "Are you all right?"

"Turned my fucking ankle, but I'll be fine," he calls back, the sound reverberating all around me.

I shuffle forward over the coarse ground.

"Stop moving!" he bellows.

I freeze.

A match strikes. A tiny orange flame flickers from far below, illuminating a wide cavern with a ceiling too high for the light to reach. Iver struggles to his feet, holding the candle aloft. Light glimmers off the water weeping down muddy green stalagmites.

If I'm careful, I should be able to lower myself to where he hobbles. I tuck my candle into my pack and then turn around to kneel on the ledge. With my chest flat on the stone, I ease myself over the edge, feeling for a foothold.

Something solid presses against my slipper.

Iver waits with his hands outstretched; a lump of stone protrudes from the smooth wall just large enough for me to stand on. With his help, I manage to climb down into the wider cavern.

Dusting the dirt from my dress, I offer my accomplice a smile. "Thank you."

"You're welcome." He lifts his candle higher into the air, turning in a slow circle.

"Is your sister's room nearby?"

"Let's find out." Iver hands me the candle and drags out his map and compass once more. The compass face must've been cracked by the fall. "Bring the candle a little closer."

I lift the candle but then something along the far wall catches my eye. I must be seeing things, right? "Are those...*stairs*?"

Iver glances up, squinting toward the wall. "Oh, shit."

Sure enough, a set of stairs climbs toward the ceiling, too symmetrical to be natural. These are fae made. "Where do you think they lead?"

"Into the castle, anyway. Maybe right here?" He points to a spot on the map. The room is right off the canteen. Is that the House Master's office? Is *this* how Carew stole the princess?

"Where do we go from here?"

He twists the compass, turning around until he's facing away from the staircase. "Braith's room should be..." His gaze slowly climbs to the darkness lurking above us. "Up there."

How in the world are we supposed to get all the way to the ceiling? "Can you use your magic?"

Iver stuffs the map and compass back into his pack. He kneels to the ground, presses his palms to the stone beneath his boots, and—

Nothing happens.

"What's wrong?" I ask.

"I don't know. I was sure I had plenty of magic, but now there's nothing left."

Iver spent more time in the sun yesterday than any of us. How could he be out already? Unless... "How's your ankle?"

He rotates his foot this way and that. "Feels perfect."

"Your magic healed you." Meaning he doesn't have anything left to get me to Braith's bedroom. I turn back toward the far wall. Either we wait and come back tomorrow after he's had more sunlight... or we climb those stairs.

"Tomorrow will be soon enough," Iver says, as if reading my mind.

Will it, though? Every hour that we delay is another chance for the king to move Senan. We're so close to the end, and there's a way into the castle *right there*. "No. We need to go now."

"Wynn—"

"He's waited long enough. We have to save him tonight." There's no telling what sort of torture my mate has been forced to endure. I'll do anything to spare him pain.

I cross the cavern with Iver on my heels, climbing the staircase built around stalactites, higher and higher until I reach the very top. A wide door has been cut into the stone, the wood completely smooth, no sign of a lever or lock. "Where's the knob?"

Iver slides a hand down the knotty wood, feeling for something that clearly isn't there.

We did not come all this way just to reach a dead end. "Do you have any magic left at all?"

The candle's flame dances in his dark irises when he peers over my shoulder at the door. "I can't feel anything."

Right. It's down to me then.

I pass the candle to Iver and hold out my hands.

"What if there's someone on the other side?" he asks.

"Then I'll deal with him." We knew this mission would not end without bloodshed, and I am prepared to blacken my soul to save Senan.

I call on the spark of magic within my heart, commanding the flickers to burn brighter, stronger. Concentrating on the barrier, focusing all my power, and shooting a bolt of wind at the door.

The wood explodes, flying into the room with a resounding *bang*.

A set of stone stairs and more darkness awaits on the other side.

I clutch my skirts to keep from tripping on our way up another staircase. If someone heard the noise, there won't be much time. Iver hurries behind me, his footsteps silent as we approach a second door. Thankfully, this one has a knob and a lock. He breaks the latter and eases the door aside.

I step into a quiet, empty bedroom, listening for signs of life. A thud sounds behind me, and I spin to find Iver's hands raised. "What's wrong?" I whisper.

The wrinkle between his brows deepens. "It's the wards. They won't let me through."

Strange. I didn't even feel them.

"I suppose this is where we part ways."

"Be careful, Wynn. And good luck."

"Thank you, Iver. For everything."

He closes the door, leaving me alone in the House Master's

bedroom. I throw my pack onto the ground and quickly change into the uniform Braith gave me.

Now all that's left to do is find my prince.

Forty-Six

ALLETTE

The servants' cavern might look the same as it did before, but the woman behind this mask couldn't be more different than the one who arrived all those weeks ago.

My mission hasn't changed: To find my prince.

Only this time, my eyes are wide open. The countless lies we've been fed since birth have become steppingstones, a staircase of deceit leading me closer.

This time, I know what must be done to ensure we are never again cast into darkness.

No one stops me or calls me back as I make my way through the cavern and down the hallway to the staff rooms where Braith waits. The other servants and handful of guards pay me no mind, their attention on their duties, not the traitor in their midst.

Braith answers on the first knock, opening the door only a sliver to peer through.

"It's me," I whisper.

Gasping, she swings the door wide, catching my arm and pulling me inside. The room looks the same as it always did, save the two laundry baskets piled high with sheets and pillowcases. Braith raises her mask, the dark circles ringing her eyes matching my own. "I wasn't expecting you so soon. How did you get in?"

"The House Master's office." There isn't time to explain further. After we save the prince, we'll have all the time in the world. I nod down at the baskets. "Did you find a uniform for Senan?"

"I stole two—one for each basket, just in case."

Then I suppose there is nothing left to organize. "Are you certain you want to do this?"

"Certain I won't let you do this alone."

We collect our baskets and slip out of her bedroom. The hallway is clear; no doubt everyone has already been given their assignments and are hard at work earning their wages.

Our slippers make no sound as we navigate our way through the maze of passages to the family's tower. Two guards who look vaguely familiar wait at the base of the staircase. After a quick perusal, they step aside, allowing us past. I hold my breath, wondering if the wards might have changed, but they let us through. The king must've been too busy making everyone's lives miserable to worry about safeguarding against a "dead" woman.

Up we go, turn after turn, stair after stair, past the level leading to Senan's private chambers. I hope he's all right, that he hasn't been wounded.

What if the rumors of the trial are a lie and he is gone already? I force my legs to move faster, bringing me higher and higher, until I can hear the deep rumble of a quiet conversation up ahead.

My footsteps still, and I turn to face my accomplice. "You know what to do."

Braith slips into one of the alcoves that houses cleaning products and supplies.

Here goes nothing.

I set down the basket and toss some of the laundry onto the steps. Then I sink onto the stairs and begin to wail.

The conversation ends, followed by footfalls.

A silver-clad guard sprints around the corner, sword drawn. When he sees me, he stills.

"Dammit," I sniffle. "I tripped over these bloody slippers and turned my ankle."

The man hesitates for only a moment before sheathing his sword and kneeling to help me up. He had to be a nice one, didn't he? I almost feel bad for what's about to happen to him.

Braith tiptoes from the alcove and clobbers him with a shovel made for scooping ashes. The man crumples beside me with a groan.

Memories of killing that blackguard in the launderette come barreling back.

This isn't the same.

There's no blood and I'm not alone. He's not dead, only incapacitated, and if we don't act quickly, he's going to wake up. "Do you have the dust?"

Braith withdraws one of the vials I sewed into her skirts before she left the burrows. I hate doing this, but we cannot take the risk of this man waking up.

Using his own dagger, I cut his palm and pour dust on the wound. The gash heals before the vial is gone, and his veins start to glow, throwing wicked golden light across the stairwell walls.

Together, we manage to drag his heavy body into the storage closet.

One down, one to go.

"William?" the other guard calls. "Everything all right?"

I hold my breath, counting the seconds until the second guard emerges from around the corner, but we're ready. I've cut my hand and smeared the front of my dress in blood. He curses and bends down to check on me, then Braith whacks him as well. This one is smaller, so his body is easier to move. In the alcove he goes, next to his glowing comrade. Another dose of stardust and he's no longer a problem.

I clamber for the stairs, Braith's quick footsteps chasing me as I climb, my heart pounding a steady rhythm, calling for my mate. When we reach the door to the king's office, I grab for the knob and turn—

The damn thing doesn't budge. No. NO! "It's locked."

Braith drags down her mask, her flushed face glistening with sweat. "The doors are never locked."

"Well, this one is."

"Maybe one of them has a key? I'll go check." She runs back down the stairs, and all I can do is stare at the final barrier separating me from the man I love. What if there is no key? I could use my magic, but that would make too much noise. What if we came all this way only to fail?

The stars have cursed us, so why would I think this time the ending might be different?

Braith returns brandishing a key, and I'm so happy, I could scream. Since I can't do that, I stick the key in the lock and turn. Pressing my ear to the wood, I listen for signs of life on the other side.

Braith's hand falls to my shoulder, her whisper giving me strength. "Go on. Open it."

I can do this.

Unfortunately, I'm on my own from this point forward. Braith is to return to her room in case the plan goes awry. It was the only way I agreed to let her assist me. As she makes her way back down the stairs, fear floods my core.

I can do this.

For Senan. For me. For us.

The brass warms under my touch, and when I turn the knob, my racing heart thumps faster.

Golden sunlight washes over a wide desk sitting in front of open balcony doors. Shelves of books line the far wall, opposite more windows.

Down from the windows sits an iron cage.

Inside that cage is my prince.

Forty-Seven

ALLETTE

Not only is this the second time that I've stumbled upon someone inside a cage, but also, this cage looks almost identical to the one from Cadoc Carew's office. Not that it matters right now, because, not only is my prince in a cage, but also he is glowing like a fallen star, the light in his veins reflecting off the wall at his back.

Thank goodness I stole so much antidote. Something tells me that we're going to need it.

Now to get him out of here so he can take it.

"Senan?" I step farther into the room, expecting a ward or something else to stop me. The only resistance I meet is the wall of my own fear.

I can be afraid tomorrow, when we're safe and sound. When all of this is over.

"Senan, can you hear me?"

My prince's eyelashes flutter open, but only for a moment before falling back to his cheeks.

"Allette—" A fit of coughing catches in his throat, and when he swipes his arm across his lips, blood dribbles down his forearm in a terrifying stream. There's no telling how much dust the king has forced upon him since his capture. By now, his poor body must be ravaged by poison.

It's a wonder he still lives.

I cross to the cage on shaking limbs, my aching heart pinching at the state of him. His trousers have been shredded to ribbons, dried blood painting the tanned skin peeking from beneath. "Do you know where the king is keeping the key?" There's no hope of releasing him without it. Even if I have to sneak into the bastard's bedroom, I will.

Senan squints up at me, brow furrowed and chapped lips pursed. "Key?"

"To the cage."

What little spark of life I saw in his eyes dies out, leaving his irises dull and gray. "You shouldn't be here. He'll catch you."

I don't give a rat's arse about being caught. "The key, Senan."

A sigh. "In the desk."

That feels too good to be true. Surely, the king would've been smarter than to leave a key where it could be found so easily. My skirts slap my ankles as I hurry over to the desk, opening the top drawer to find a key resting atop a stack of letters bearing the king's signature.

The small piece of brass feels like victory in the palm of my hand as I carry it to where Senan slumps on the floor.

He rests his chin on his knee, a lazy sort of smile playing on his lips. "You're beautiful. I never told you that enough."

"Stop speaking about yourself in the past tense. You're going to come out of this just fine."

"I love your optimism."

Optimism? This is a fact. I refuse to accept any other outcome.

With a twist of the key, the door unlocks, swinging wide on groaning hinges. We will survive this just as we have survived every other obstacle the stars have thrown at us.

I take a knee next to my glowing prince. Although he smells of sweat and blood, I've never known a sweeter perfume. "Put your arm around my shoulders, and I'll help you stand."

His arm comes around me, heavier than it should be as he tries to rise on shaking legs. It takes four attempts, but eventually he manages to stand. Getting him out of the skinny door is another matter. Somehow, we make it with only touching the bars once. His sluggish movements slow us down, but we reach the door to the servants' stairs, and I can taste the sweet air of freedom waiting on the other side. "I have a spare uniform for you to change into. At the bottom of the stairs, you'll have to walk by yourself. Do you think you can manage?"

He grunts.

"Hold tight. We're almost there."

Something behind us clatters.

"Where are you taking my brother?"

The small voice nearly brings me to my knees. Thank the stars it's only the youngest prince, not Boris. A tray of chocolate cake lays at his feet, and a bowl of strawberries has spilled across the rug.

Senan's face crushes up, his voice breaking. "Kyff..."

Prince Kyffin withdraws his dagger, the blade quivering as he aims the tip in my direction, his face pale as moonlight. "I'll not let you steal him."

"I'm not stealing him. I'm saving him. If he stays here, he'll die."

His eyes widen, but the blade does not falter. "That's not true."

"It is," Senan breathes, the pressure of his arm around my shoulders growing harder to bear.

"The king gives him poison to make him sick," I say, praying this poor, confused little boy believes me.

"You're lying. You're both lying. That's what happens when you glow. You lie. Boris is helping him get better. He promised."

"Kyffin, please—"

"Guards!" Kyffin bellows.

The door bursts open, and three men in silver leathers dash into the room, their swords drawn. A man trails in behind them, walking at a measured pace, as if strolling through the gardens.

Black hair. Silver eyes. Menacing smile.

The king has found us. "Where do you think you're going?" he drawls, folding his arms as if we are a mere inconvenience.

The door to the servants' stairs is the closest exit, but even if I weren't shouldering Senan's weight, I'd have no hope of beating these men to the bottom of the tower.

The king's hand falls to the littlest prince's shoulder to give the little boy a tender squeeze. "Well done, Kyffin."

Silver tears line the poor lad's lashes, and his lower lip quakes.

The king extends his free hand. "Allette Rittey, I presume?"

As if I'm going to shake hands with that lying, manipulative snake.

"Or should I call you *Wynn*?" A smile. "You are a tenacious woman, I'll give you that. I can see why my brother and Sergeant Bell were so enamored. It really is regrettable, what had to happen to you." His eyes gleam with satisfaction.

None of this *had* to happen. He orchestrated it all, wielding his power like he alone is the conductor of fate.

"Let us go, and we won't be a problem." It's a useless plea, but I have to try.

"I wish I could. Unfortunately, because of my brother, we were very nearly at war with our northern neighbors."

Kyffin's shoulders curl as he presses himself into the king, his eyes haunted.

"Senan had nothing to do with that. Cadoc Carew kidnapped the princess."

Boris heaves a beleaguered sigh, but there is a wicked gleam in his eyes that he cannot hide. "I am sorry to say that all the evidence points to my poor brother colluding with Carew to rid himself of his new wife. The princess herself made a statement."

After we saved her? No. That cannot be true. Boris is lying. He must be.

Senan's body shudders with a chesty cough, the gold in his veins fading to a dull glow. "I'll...confess to everything...if you just...let her go."

"You're asking me to jeopardize my kingdom's safety by setting a murderer free?" Boris clicks his tongue. "Here I thought you couldn't be more disappointing."

Kyff's head swings toward me. "That lady killed someone?"

"One of my personal guards," the king says with feigned sympathy. "The two of you make quite the pair, don't you? When I found out my brother was rutting with some Tuath maid, it wasn't all that difficult to figure out who you were, traipsing around the caverns in such finery. Although it was quite a shock to find out the murderous maid and the woman my brother foolishly bound himself to in the human realm were one and the same."

Senan sways, knocking me off balance. In the time it takes me to steady him, the guards have surrounded us, and although they sheathe their weapons, there is no point in fighting.

The battle is over...

Our victory stolen.

"And now, you will both pay for your crimes." Boris gestures toward the cage. "Put them in there for now, then find out what happened to the guards in the servants' staircase. Have more posted before we collect any more unexpected visitors." Our gazes meet and my stomach sinks even lower when the king's smile returns. "Someone get Sergeant Bell in here. I want him on the first watch."

Forty-Eight

SENAN

My traitorous guard saunters into the room like he's the king himself, head high and proud, wings on full display, as if mocking us for having ours cut from our bodies. Beside me, Allette goes still. My arm around her waist does nothing to soothe the worry lines on her face.

I try my best to focus on her despite the stardust in my veins willing my eyes to close so I can drift off to somewhere far more pleasant than this cage.

My girl slips from my grip, walking right up to those bars and staring down her nose at the bastard who could've saved us both, but chose to damn us instead.

"I'm surprised the king let you in the room, given our history," she says, her hands folded at her waist.

Why isn't she shouting or railing at him?

It would seem I'm not the only one surprised by her soft, warm tone.

Bell's brow furrows, his gray eyes narrowing as he returns Allette's stare. "The king knows my loyalty is to him."

Her head tilts. "Then why did you save me instead of killing me as he ordered?"

Must she dredge up the past? If I hadn't left her side that morning, perhaps our fates would have been different. If I hadn't been so fucking complacent and taken her farther from the portal, somewhere no one would ever find us, we would still be whole. *Happy.*

I drop to the floor, unable to hold myself upright. The golden light sparkling through my skin plays on the marble like leaf-dappled sunlight on a forest floor.

"You know why," Bell grits out, fists tightening at his sides.

"Because you love me."

Please. He never loved her. And even if he did, he never loved her half as much as me.

He stole her. He's a thief.

And in Kumulus, the punishment for theft is death.

Wonder if he thought about that when he took her.

What I wouldn't give for a blade and five minutes alone with Eason Bell.

My former guard says nothing, but the muscle ticking in his jaw speaks volumes.

Allette drifts closer to the bars, her voice a warm, honeyed balm. "Do you love me still? You saved me from the pit...you could save me again. All you have to do is open this door. Let Senan free, and I'll go with you without a fight. You and I can live wherever you choose, in this realm or among the humans. I could make you happy."

Fucking dust. Playing tricks on me. Allette would never go with him willingly. I try to push myself to my feet, but my legs have abandoned me as well.

She can't leave. She can't go with him. She can't—

Except...

If she did, she would be safe. Bell could take her far away from the king and the castle. I want that for her, don't I?

Life. Happiness. Hope.

What can I offer her besides certain death?

Warm tears trickle down my cheeks as I consider letting go of

Allette once and for all. Sending her off into the sky with my well-wishes. Even if Bell fulfils his side of the bargain and sets me free, I won't be leaving this place.

I'd rather die knowing she is free than live knowing she is with someone else.

Bell's fist knocks against his thigh as he considers. "We did have a good time, didn't we?" A hint of a smile ghosts across his lips when Allette nods, and he edges closer to the cage. So close that, if I had the energy to stand, I could almost reach out and grab him by the throat.

"I remember the first day I saw you. The king found out that his brother was sneaking off to meet a woman, and he ordered me to follow. You were walking through the park. Your hair was the most stunning shade of blue. I remember thinking how good it would look wrapped around my fist."

Stop. Stop. Stop.

Bell draws even closer, his voice dropping. "I remember the first time you let me into your bed. What was it? A week or two after the prince abandoned you? You spread your legs for me and cried my name when I made you come so hard your body shuddered."

Allette goes utterly still, the color in her face draining away. *She only waited a week?*

Lies. Lies. Lies.

Surely her grief would have kept her from taking him as a lover for longer than that. We were mated—desperately in love.

She thought you were dead.

That knowledge doesn't make the truth hurt any less.

"Eason…" Allette's eyes glisten with her quiet plea.

"You used to love the way I licked your cunt, didn't you? Let me put my head between your knees whenever I wanted. I bet you'd let me do it right now if I promised to let your prince go free." He shifts to the side, his gaze locking on me. "Maybe I should."

Tears splash on my chest. No. *No.* She wouldn't let him do that. Not in front of me.

Rage vibrates through my bones, making the stardust glowing in my veins flicker.

Allette swipes at her tears. "Eason, stop."

"Why should I? Don't you want me to help you? To *save* you?"

"Yes, but—"

Eason slams his boot into the bars, rattling the cage around us. "You might have made a fool out of me before, but never again." He levels a finger at where I slump on the ground. "You chose him, and now you'll die in the bed you made. A fucking duster…" He shakes his head with a mirthless chuckle. "Did he tell you about the time he went to Fox's for his birthday? He fucked four different whores all at once—didn't even use a private room to do it."

No. No. No. No.

My hands shake as I drag them through my hair. "Stop. Please."

I don't want her to know how low I fell. Don't want her to realize she wasted her life loving me.

But he doesn't stop there. He tells her about so many of my dark misdeeds, and no matter how hard I screw my eyes shut, all I see are the faces of the people I've used and those I've let use me.

There is no longer anywhere peaceful to drift, only dark shadows with teeth that slash and sever.

Warmth caresses my cheeks, and when I peer through bleary eyes, I see my girl's golden gaze, her hands holding my face as she sinks onto my lap. "Don't listen to him," she whispers, her hands sliding from my face to cover my ears, pressing close until all I hear is the unsteady beat of my own heart.

She flinches, and that's when I realize Eason is still on the other side of the bars, no doubt spewing more hate. I bring my hands to my love's ears, pulling her close.

"Think of the house by the seaside," I say against her temple, hoping she cannot hear anything but me.

A smile touches her lips even as wetness streaks down her cheeks, gathering into fat drops on her jaw, falling onto her blood-stained uniform. "And the fourteen children."

Fourteen children that will never have names because these are dreams, and in this cruel world, dreams don't come true.

The cage around us rattles, and from the corner of my eye, I see Bell kicking the base, his red face contorted in fury before he stalks onto the balcony.

Allette's forehead presses against mine, and the sounds outside our cocoon fade until it's only our mingling breaths and pounding hearts. "You know, I think I've changed my mind," she whispers. "I no longer want a house by the sea."

"Then what do you want?" I ask, pretending for a little longer that it is within my power to give it to her.

"To be Queen of Kumulus." When she draws back, I see such a fierce determination on her face, that if our fates weren't sealed, there is no doubt in my mind she would get what she wants.

But our fates are sealed and sitting here dreaming of what could have been might kill me before the king gets that noose around my neck.

"Allette—"

Her fingertips press against the seam of my lips, stopping my protest. "And you shall be king."

"There is no more hope."

"As long as there is air in my lungs, there shall be hope in my heart."

"Isn't that sweet?" Boris's voice cuts like a fucking blade. Still clinging to each other, Allette and I turn our heads toward the king. "It almost makes me feel guilty for having to tell you that there won't be air in either of your lungs much longer."

I'm too afraid to ask, so I don't.

Boris crosses his arms, looking on expectantly. "What? No questions? No begging? No pleas?"

I love nothing more than to disappoint him.

His expression hardens, but his smile never falters. "We pushed forward the date for your trial. I hope you both enjoy your last night together. This ends tomorrow."

Forty-Nine

ALLETTE

THIS ENDS TOMORROW.

Those ominous words and the threat they pose hang in the air like a fog, chilling me to my marrow. Tomorrow, my prince and I will pay the price for our love with our lives. That is where this ends, with both of us passing beyond the veil to whatever lies on the other side of death.

This is our last night together, and as much as I don't want to waste it, my body is frozen in place, my lungs barely able to capture air, as if growing accustomed to the fact that soon, they won't be needed.

If only Iver were here to cut a hole in the marble slab beneath us.

But Iver isn't here.

It's just Senan and me, and from the devastation on my prince's face, it's clear he's feeling the same hopelessness as I am.

This can't be the end. I refuse to accept it.

Maybe I can move this cage with my magic.

That's it! I'll throw every last drop of power into commanding a great wind to blow the thing over. We'll have to fight off the new guards stationed at the servants' stairs, but between us, surely, we can manage.

I glance over at Senan, his eyes hollow, the skin beneath bruised by despair. From the way his gaunt cheeks cradle the shadows, it's clear that the king hasn't fed him more than stardust since his capture.

Senan is in no shape to fight anyone, so this responsibility must fall on my shoulders.

I push to my feet and stretch out my hand, calling a breeze to my palm. The time I spent in the sunlight this morning feels like forever ago. Closing my eyes, I reach deep within myself, begging my power to rouse.

"Allette?"

The sadness in Senan's tone, his resignation, crushes the shattered fragments of my heart.

Don't give up on us. On me.

The deeper I dig, the weaker I feel, as if I'm carving out my own insides for a foolish dream.

"Allette, stop."

If I stop, the king wins. If I stop, then I have to accept that this is the last night I'll ever spend in my prince's arms. We deserve centuries to love each other. Millenia.

"Allette, please." Senan's fingertips graze my ankle, nothing more than a wisp of a touch. "Save your magic in case there's a chance to escape tomorrow."

The anger and fear and sorrow pressing in on all sides cracks my fragile shell. Tears spill from my lashes, blurring the cage and my prince's vacant expression from where he remains on the floor, as if this world has knocked him down one too many times and he's no longer able to rise.

"*Tomorrow?*" I drag my palms down my face, wishing I could rip this cage—this bloody castle—in two. "Did you not hear the king? Tomorrow, we'll both be dead."

Senan's cold fingers curl around my ankle, his thumbs skimming up and down my shin. "I know."

How is he so bloody calm? "Don't you care?"

The barest hint of a smile curves his lips as he blinks up at me, his own eyes shimmering. "That I am to die? Not really." A single tear spills free, racing down his cheek to his sharp jaw, clinging to the stubble there. "I only wish I hadn't dragged you down with me."

Stepping out of his grasp, I sink to my knees and take his scarred hands in mine, pressing our matching bonds together. "You didn't drag me anywhere, Senan. I leapt into love with you with both feet and my whole heart. This—our love—has always been too good for this world." Perhaps that is why the stars have been so hellbent on cursing us, because they're jealous and want to be the only light we see on dark, moonless nights.

Senan's smile grows but so does the tremor in his voice when he whispers, "Then let us hope that it isn't too good for the next one."

I capture his final word with my lips, filling my lungs with his next breath. What starts as a slow exploration becomes an assault of crashing mouths and lashing tongues, a feast of desire that only leaves us panting and moaning for more.

More of my skin for his mouth as he drags down the front of my dress and devours my breasts with hot, needy kisses. More of my knees falling to either side of his hips. More of his stiffness pressing insistently against my core as I begin to rock, searching for friction to stoke the flames growing in my belly.

Our hips pulse, and I lose my hands in his hair, clutching him to my breast, seeking the only sort of release either of us will find this night.

"You are everything to me," he rasps.

"Until the sun implodes, and the stars no longer shine," I return. Forever and always.

His hair falls across his brow when he nods, whispering promises of love against my bare chest.

I rise off him to unlatch his belt, the leather slipping through the buckle with ease. The buttons on his trousers give me some trouble, but soon enough I've freed his stiff cock, my hand gripping him tightly, stroking slowly as I watch a lust-filled haze descend over his taut features.

His head falls back, exposing the strong column of his throat, and I lick at his bobbing Adam's apple as his hands braced on my thighs nudge my skirts higher, until only a scrap of lace separates us. With a groan, he hooks a finger around the wet fabric of my undergarments and tugs the lace aside, baring me to his fingers. His thumb slips through my folds to my clit, pressing and flicking in circles.

His eyes burn into mine as he strokes faster, both of us climbing together until I can take no more and knock his hand away. Positioning myself over him, I sink down until he's buried to the hilt.

His breath catches and throat works as he waits for my body to adjust. I brace my hands on his shoulders, capturing his lips once more as I start to move, riding him until my thighs are shaking, his hips punching up to meet mine.

"Touch me," I beg, the rigid peaks of my breasts brushing against the muscles of his chest, sending a tidal wave of desire crashing over me.

Even after all these years, after coming together more times than I can count, being with him is still so magical, so intimate.

One of Senan's large hands cups my backside, urging me to keep my pace as his other falls between us to work my clit with tight, frantic circles. "Harder." I want to feel the ache of him when I wake tomorrow. When I face the executioner.

"Harder."

With a curse, he nudges me off him and flips me onto my back, his body coming over mine, taking me with a devastating thrust, leaving me quivering and crying for more.

He hooks an arm around my thigh, bucking his hips with wild abandon, his pelvis grinding against my center each time he bottoms out, sending sparks of pleasure shooting through my core until I'm teetering on the edge of release.

"I'm almost there."

"Let go. I'll catch you."

He always catches me, unfailing, unwavering, undeniable. His devotion, his loyalty, his love. My body tenses, poised and ready as he rocks into me, grinding harder, filling every broken part of me with every broken part of himself until we are whole together, the way we were always meant to be.

Tension coils in my core, tighter and tighter, ripping through me like lightning, my body pulsing around Senan's as he drops forward on his elbows. His hips start to lose rhythm as he gives one final thrust and spills into me, both of us panting, fitting in as many breaths and heartbeats as we can, until it's too late.

I don't know how long we cling to each other, but eventually he pulls out, his palm flat against my stomach as he stares down at where I'm still bare.

"Best view in the world," he murmurs. With a heavy sigh, he pulls my undergarments back in place and fixes my skirts.

I sit up and fasten my buttons as he stuffs himself back into his trousers and puts himself to rights.

The haze of lust wanes with the darkening night, leaving room for fear to slither back in like a serpent, coiling around my heart. "I'm scared."

Senan's own fears grow in his eyes like the shadows on his handsome face. His hand laces with mine, his thumb skimming my knuckles. "Whatever happens, we will be together."

The door to the office swings open, and in strolls the king, trailed by six guards.

What are they doing here? He said the trial isn't until tomorrow. We still have a few hours left together, so why is he unlocking the door and telling me to come forward?

Senan pushes me behind him, as if that's going to stop his brother from getting what he wants. Boris waves his hand and steps aside. Two guards lunge, catching Senan's arms, dragging him out. His shouts fill my ears as the next pair of guards come for me, their hands like vises around my forearms, towing me from the cage.

"We have until tomorrow," I cry. "You promised us one more night!"

The king stalks toward his brother, withdrawing the dagger from his belt and dragging the tip across Senan's ribs, cutting through the beautiful blackbird in that cage.

Senan's howl of pain pierces my soul.

"Stop! Leave him alone! Please!" My cries fall on deaf ears, and I watch in horror as the king withdraws a glowing vial and dumps stardust on my love's wounds. The glass shatters when it falls to the ground, and the guards throw Senan back into the cage. My prince staggers, crumpling to his knees, his veins glowing brighter and brighter as he gasps, his wild eyes finding mine across the room.

I tug and wrench to no avail. "Let me go. I said, let me go!"

"Give her back to me," Senan slurs. "Please."

The king takes a knee at the edge of the cage, the sound of the guard turning the key in the lock like a death knell. "Sleep tight, brother. I'll see you at dawn."

Boris stands, his raven hair falling from its leather queue as he turns toward me, his lips curled in a sneer. "Bring her."

I won't go willingly. *I won't.* My feet drag on the smooth marble as they carry me away from my mate, his cries swallowed by the closing door. Silence fills the empty hallway, and I'm too turned around to figure out where they're taking me.

Boris comes to a halt in front of a door. When one of the guards drags it open, there is nothing inside the closet but more emptiness.

"Why do you hate him so much?" I need to know. To understand.

A blank mask settles over Boris's features. "Do you know what it's like to watch someone take and take, waste everything, and drag your family's good name through the mud, while you stand by and do nothing? There isn't a rule that coward hasn't broken, all for his own selfishness. You see him as your hero, but I see him for what he truly is." The king brushes back a few strands of hair, tucking them behind his pointed ear. Tugging his waistcoat, a harsh breath falls from his lips. "Sleep tight, Allette; your judgment comes at dawn."

Someone shoves my lower back, and I stumble forward. The door bangs closed, and I hear the key turning the lock. With nothing more than my tears and memories for company, I sink to the ground, holding my knees to my chest to keep myself from shattering, praying for an escape that never comes.

Fifty

ALLETTE

There's no need to wake me in the morning.

I didn't sleep.

Instead, I spent the night remembering.

Perhaps it's different when your life ends suddenly, but for me, knowing death would come for me in a few hours gave my memories time to run through my mind like a play on a stage.

Every time my eyes closed, I pictured a different scene from my life.

My mother and father teaching me to fly. How it felt to take that first leap from the balcony in our small tower, the prayer in my heart that my wings and the wind would catch me. The first damp kiss of the clouds on my cheeks.

Wynn, my friend and confidant. The way she would leave chocolates under my pillow when it was her turn to clean my room.

The day I met Senan in the market, his arrogance and the mischievous gleam in his starlit eyes.

The moment I realized I loved him.

The day he confessed his love for me.

All the times we met in secret, hiding from the world because they wouldn't understand our connection.

The fateful night we traversed realms.
The morning I woke up alone, surrounded by fire.
The agony of my wings being stripped from my back.
The grief of losing Senan...the joy of finding him again.

The pining, the pain, the triumph that has accompanied me through every step of this journey.

The love he has shown me, unwavering and all-consuming. The type of love people dream of finding, I have discovered not once, but twice in my life.

So unlike the man who claimed to love me only to keep me for himself.

As I ruminated over the depth of Eason's betrayal, I wanted to stab him all over again, only this time, I'd make sure he was dead.

As fate would have it, my former captor is the one who opens the door to the closet I've been locked in all night. The one who drags a pair of manacles from his belt and tightens them around my wrists, the sharp edges digging into my flesh as he leads me down a dawn-soaked hallway toward a set of arched double doors.

When the two men standing guard see us approaching, they haul the barriers aside, revealing a room thronged with faces I don't recognize. Women and men dressed in finery, wearing their wealth around their necks and on their cuffs. Their whispers are like tiny razors, nicking my skin as I walk past.

Whore...

His downfall...

Her fault...

The more I try to ignore them, the harder they are to drown out, because not all of them are lies.

A stretch of silver carpet cuts through the room, leading to a dais where a single throne waits. Boris Vale sits atop a silver cushion with a gleaming crown of gold like a halo on his dark hair. To his right, the littlest prince sits on a golden stool, a gilded dagger at his waist and his small face wearing the same fierce expression as his oldest brother. To his left sits the reclusive

Princess Consort, her face gaunt and eyes sunken like a living skeleton.

The most sinister of all is what waits on the balcony: A man wearing a black hood and mask, an axe resting on his thick shoulder.

The doors open once more, and two guards escort my prince into the room to a symphony of gasps and curses. The women flutter their fans and press tanned hands to their heaving chests. More than a few eyes swim with tears. The men seem to be wearing matching sneers.

Senan wears a clean shirt and a fresh pair of trousers, but when he walks, he does so with a limp. The chains on his wrists jangle as he continues forward, eyes scanning until they fall on me. His gaze sweeps down the same soiled uniform I wore to save him, his eyes narrowing into slits as they turn on the king.

Kyffin's lower lip quivers as he watches his brother being led to where I wait.

I long to hold my love once more, but Eason steps between us, blocking my view.

A portly man dressed in black robes moves from the front of the crowd, a thick tome open in his hands. Counsellor Windell. Philip's father. "My king, I present to you the accused, Lady Allette Rittey, and Prince Senan Vale."

The king inclines his head toward the older man, his expression almost bored, as if being woken at such an ungodly hour is an inconvenience instead of his own doing.

Counsellor Windell twists toward me, looking on through dull brown eyes. "Lady Allette Rittey, you stand charged with the murder of Darius Porter, a member of the king's royal guards. How do you plead?"

How do I plead? He cannot be serious. "Not guilty."

The murmuring begins anew, laced with snorts of derision and scoffing. You'd swear from the crowd's reactions that they had witnessed the bloody crime themselves.

Counsellor Windell shifts his weight from one foot to the

other, his thin lips pressing flat. "You're saying that you did not kill the man?"

"I'm saying it was not murder, but self-defense."

The way his lips twist makes my stomach sink lower. "So you *did* kill him?"

This isn't a trial; it's a charade.

No one in this room is interested in justice; they're here for a spectacle. For the bloody gossip.

I straighten my spine, standing to my full height and lifting my chin. They're going to execute me either way—the king will make sure of it—but I refuse to cower.

"Darius Porter punched me in the face, dragged me into the launderette, and threatened to rape me and slit my throat. So, to answer your question, yes. I killed him." And I'd do it again if I had to.

The crowd goes so silent, if I were to close my eyes, I could almost convince myself I was completely alone in this cavernous room.

Counsellor Windell twists toward the king. Even though I already know my fate, I still find myself holding my breath, hoping for a miracle.

The king sits up straighter, his bejeweled fingers tapping against the throne's gilded arm. "In this, the law is clear: An attack on one of the king's guards is considered an attack on the crown itself. You are hereby sentenced to death by beheading. May the gods have mercy on your soul."

A feral growl erupts from Senan's throat. He launches himself toward me, but Eason catches his chain, holding him still as he struggles. "You bastard," he bellows. "She was only defending herself!"

The king's knuckles go white where he grips his throne. "And was it self-defense when she stabbed Sergeant Bell?"

"He held her captive in the human realm for over four years—"

"I saved her," Bell snarls. "And she still tried to kill me."

He's right. I did the things they're accusing me of and am about to face the unjust consequences of my actions. But in fighting for me, Senan is only making this worse on himself.

I step forward. Eason's hand snaps out, catching my chains, but I've made it far enough to see the devastation painting Senan's crushed features. "It's all right. Everything is going to be all right."

His head shakes, his eyes glittering like a lake in the moonlight. "No..."

Counsellor Windell steps in front of Senan, keeping back far enough in case my prince fights again. "Prince Senan Vale, you are charged with orchestrating the kidnapping of Princess Leeri of Nimbiss, resulting in the abduction of your youngest brother, Prince Kyffin Vale. How do you plead?"

Kyffin sucks in a breath, his hands flying to his mouth, his eyes wide as saucers.

With tears streaming down his face, Senan raises his head, eyes narrowed on the king. "Not guilty."

"Do you have any evidence to prove your innocence?" the man asks.

"Sergeant Eason Bell and I met at the Nag's Head on the night in question, and afterward, the king exiled me to the human realm. Both of them can attest that I was not with the princess on either occasion."

The king chuckles, but there is nothing mirthful about the sound as he stretches a hand to pat his littlest brother's knee. "A fanciful story."

"Fanciful?" Senan tears open the front of his shirt; buttons fly across the room, landing with sharp *pings* on the marble. He shrugs out of the garment, and the crowd gasps when they see what remains of his beautiful wings. "Do you think I did this to myself?"

Counsellor Windell's eyes widen as he gawks at Senan's back. "Is this true, Sergeant Bell?"

Eason's jaw works, his gaze flicking toward the king. "I did meet with the prince that night."

The king sits forward, bracing his elbows on his knees, his hands flexing into fists. "That's not to say he didn't orchestrate Princess Leeri's kidnapping. My brother was the last person to see the princess before Carew abducted her. We have reached out to the princess, and she confirmed his involvement."

That's a lie.

Senan jabs a finger at the king, his chains swinging. "You're a fucking liar."

The crowd watches, mouths agape and whispers building to a crescendo.

"How about your kidnapping of a member of the Scathian nobility? Am I lying about that, Lord Windell?"

Windell steps from the crowd, bowing his head in deference to our terrible king. "No, sire. Prince Senan knocked me out and kept me in a cavern in the burrows for days."

Shit. Shit. Shit.

The king rises to his feet. "In light of the evidence, I have found Prince Senan Vale guilty. The punishment for such crimes is death."

Kyffin launches to his feet, the stool clattering to the ground. "No!" He races down the stairs toward Senan, dodging the guards who try to catch him. He throws his arms around Senan's legs, his small shoulders wracked with sobs. "You can't kill him!"

Dropping to his knees, Senan pushes the little boy's hair back from his tear-drenched cheeks. "It'll be all right, Kyff."

"No. No, it won't. Boris promised to keep you safe. He promised. You said he was a liar, but I didn't believe you." He hugs Senan's neck, burying his face in his brother's shoulder. "This is all my fault. I should've let her save you, but I didn't want her to take you away from me."

"This is not your fault."

"I won't let them hurt you. I won't."

Senan holds him close, his cheek pressed to his brother's hair, clutching Kyffin's head against him. "And I'll never forgive myself if something were to happen to you."

Senan raises his gaze to his former guard as his hands slowly fall.

Eason takes Kyffin by the elbow, gently prying him away.

"No, Sen. No!" The little boy kicks and scratches. Eason's grip does not falter as he leads Kyffin out of the room, his cries echoing through the stunned crowd.

Senan stands, his head hanging as he swipes at his eyes. When he finally finds my gaze, I fall into his arms, clinging to him one last time.

He presses a soft kiss to my temple, his lips trembling. "I am so sorry, Allette."

"Even knowing how this ends, I still would've fallen in love with you." My head falls against his chest, and I listen to his heart beating, strong and steady.

Beating for me.

"I love you, Senan Vale."

"Not as much as I love you."

"Guards," the king commands. "Bring them to the executioner."

I lace my fingers with Senan's, gripping tightly. "I'm frightened."

"There's no need to be afraid. I'll be waiting for you beyond the veil."

"What if you cannot find me?"

"I will. That much I can promise you. In this world or any other, I will always find you."

One of the guards pulls me away, his jaw set and eyes narrowed on Senan. I try to hold on, but there's no use. Two more guards have taken my prince, escorting him toward the executioner.

I scream until my voice breaks, unable to do anything but watch him drift away, his head held high, shoulders proud, and nothing but love in his quicksilver eyes.

Fifty-One

SENAN

I don't know if losing my head is going to hurt, but life is painful, so I imagine death will be as well.

There's no point in fighting the guards escorting me to where my executioner waits. So many people have come to watch the spectacle of our "trials" and executions, the gathered crowd of Scathian lords and ladies as large as any ball the king has thrown.

Refusing to let my brother see how thoroughly he has defeated me, I kneel on the marble without a word and place my neck on the wooden plank.

The memory of Kyffin's sobs fill my ears, as piercing as Allette's screams for mercy.

I know better than to beg the wretch who understands nothing of the concept.

If I am to die, I will do so with dignity.

Inhaling my final breath, I close my eyes and picture my girl, smiling, laughing, and buying lemons while I wait for the strike of the axe.

I love you.
I'll wait for you.
I'm so sorry I couldn't save you.

The balcony beneath my knees begins to vibrate, then shake

violently, rattling me to the bone. My eyes flash open, and I lift my head, glancing over my shoulder to where the executioner had been standing, only to find him careening backward toward the balustrade, the axe in his hand falling onto the marble.

A giant crack lances across the balcony between us and the entire ledge breaks away, tumbling into the clouds below, taking the executioner with it. Boris bellows for the guards, skirting backward into the castle even as the tower continues to shake. Large pieces of the ceiling crash down, splintering the empty throne and crushing the chair still holding his wife.

Blood oozes from her limp body, spreading around the rubble.

Screams slice through the mayhem and people start running, wings sprouting from backs as the Scathians take off for the sky.

I stagger to my feet, stumbling for the throne room.

Guards rip their swords and daggers from their scabbards and sheaths, some rushing toward where the king has been knocked flat on his arse, others surrounding a group of fae in cloaks holding their ground amidst the chaos.

A cloaked man kneels at the front, both hands pressed flat to the floor. When he raises his head, I catch a flash of silver hair beneath his hood.

Iver Nightingale.

A pair of forest-green wings appear over the broken balcony, and the executioner lands with a thump, fumbling for his axe. The moment his fingers wrap around the handle, thorns shoot from the smooth wood. The axe clatters to the ground once more, sliding right off the edge of the broken balcony. The whimpering man clutches his bloody hand to his chest before taking off with the rest of the lords and ladies.

"Senan!"

I whirl toward the sound of my girl's screams.

Eason Bell is dragging Allette toward the far balcony.

Shit. Shit. Shit.

"Allette!" My boots skate on the rubble as I sprint for her, running as fast as I can. But I'm too slow. He's going to reach the exit first, and then he's going to fly away with my girl.

"Iver! Help!" I shout.

In a flash, the archway collapses in on itself, blocking their escape.

Bell spins, his face twisted in fury and eyes slitted, promising death. When he sees me, he shoves Allette aside and reaches for his sword. My girl throws out her arms to catch herself, but the chains around her wrists get tangled around Kyff's broken chair and she goes down hard.

Bell stalks toward me, and I search the ground for any abandoned weapons.

One of the fae with Iver throws back her hood and grins—Regina. Low whispers fall from her lips as her hands move in sporadic circles. A bolt of water whizzes through the air, crashing into Eason.

Allette stumbles to her feet, running not for the hallway, but for me. I close the distance between us, and she melts into my embrace.

"Are you all right?" I ask, cradling her face.

"I'm fine," she says even as I trace a bruise on her cheekbone.

Chaos reigns as the tower shudders, but as long as my girl is with me, we will find a way through.

"You fool!" Boris hurtles toward us, his face twisted with rage. "What have you done?"

I can't help but smile as Iver and the rest of the Tuath sidle up next to us. One of them puts a hand to the manacles on my wrists, cutting straight through the bracelet. The chains fall away, clanging onto the ground at my feet.

He does the same to Allette's, leaving us free to access whatever power still burns in our hearts.

"Did I fail to mention my new friends?" I clap Iver on the shoulder, and he bares his teeth in a vicious smile. "They only wanted a bit of sunlight. And I gave it to them."

Two more Tuath drop to their knees. The tower shudders,

knocking Boris into the wall while his guards scramble to find purchase.

"Have you lost your fucking mind?" the king snarls. "They will destroy us all."

All of us? I don't think so. "They only want you." The fire deep within me burns with righteous indignation. The king is about to understand the meaning of wrath.

"Kill them!" Spittle sprays from Boris's pale lips as he clings to the quaking wall. "Kill them all!" He slips and stumbles for the hallway, demanding our deaths.

Guards surround us, but the Tuath don't appear the least bit worried even though we're outnumbered three to one with a sea of silver stretching all the way to what's left of the balconies.

A guttural howl echoes to my left, and one of the Tuath crumples to the ground, clutching his arm to his chest, blood spurting from where his hand should be. A guard raises his sword for the killing blow when a torrent of air whips through the room, sending the weapon flying to the far corner.

Allette's hands stretch toward the fallen Tuath, her expression fierce and dark waves lifting at her back.

We might be holding off the guards for now, but our magic will run out.

I must find a way to end this once and for all.

Stepping over the body of a fallen guard, I collect his sword and start for the hallway where the king disappeared.

My heart thunders as I sprint after him only to skid to a halt when I pass through the door and find Boris holding Kyffin by the hair, his blade pressed to our baby brother's throat.

The poor little lad's eyes are so wide and full of fear, they look as if they're about to pop out of his head.

"Take one more step and he dies," Boris growls, his face contorted and eyes wild.

No... Not Kyff. The blade in my hand wavers. "Let him go. He's only a child. He's innocent."

"He is a fucking traitor just like the rest of you."

What other choice do I have? Boris has proven he's capable of anything. I wouldn't put it past him to run the little lad through without batting an eye. Slowly, I bend down, abandoning the sword on the marble. "There. I'm unarmed. Let him go. I'm the one you want, remember?"

"This is why you will never be king. You are too fucking soft." He adjusts his grip on the dagger's handle.

I roar for him to stay his hand, but it's too late.

Boris drags the blade across Kyff's throat.

Kyff collapses onto the marble, blood gushing from the wound like a flood, painting the floor crimson. Boris sprints for the balcony at the end of the hall, his wings bursting from his back.

I fall to my knees next to my brother, barely able to make out his features through the tears in my eyes.

I press a hand to his throat to try to heal the wound, but there's too much fucking blood. I shed my shirt, wrapping Kyff's neck as tightly as I dare. His pale lips open, as if he's trying to speak, but the only sound he makes is a weak gurgle.

"Hold on, Kyff. It's going to be all right. You just have to hold on." His face grows paler as life leaves his body. Even as I call forth the dregs of my magic, I know in my broken heart that it won't be enough to heal him.

"Help! Someone! Please, help me!" *Anyone. Please.*

Allette falls down beside me, laying her hands on my brother's gaunt cheeks. Her palms begin to glow, but I dare not remove the shirt to check if the wound is still bleeding.

Kyff's lashes flutter shut, dark fans against milky white skin.

"We need more magic." He'll die without it. Hell, he might die *with* it. Allette nods and runs back to the throne room, returning with Harold. He sinks next to us and presses his hands to Kyffin's chest as Allette instructs him on how to heal.

I hold my baby brother's hand, praying it's enough, that he will live and laugh another day.

I should've gone straight to him, ensured his safety the moment all hell broke loose.

The slightest pressure brushes my fingers. One. Two. Three.

I love you.

He's still with us. Thank the gods. We're not out of the woods yet, but Kyff is strong and full of sunlight. Perhaps his magic will be enough to take over now.

One of the hallway doors opens, and a maid lurches into the room just as the tower sways. She throws off her mask. *Braith.*

Allette calls her over, asking for her to take Kyffin somewhere safe and find a healer. Before she can carry him away, a shadow passes over the balcony where Boris escaped, and a man with black wings lands with a thundering roar, dragging another by the throat.

A man I'd recognize in the dark.

"Aeron?"

My older brother tosses the king to the floor like the piece of garbage he is. I grab my sword and stalk toward where Boris gasps, his eye blackened and blood spilling from his split lip.

The cool hilt bites into my fingers.

A cough tightens in my chest, climbing my throat. A grim reminder of my fate. "Roll him over."

Aeron takes Boris's shirt in two hands, flipping him onto his stomach. Blood roars in my ears as I raise my boot and stomp the top of his spine. Boris's wings appear, the black feathers gleaming in the sunlight streaming through the windows.

Sunlight he and the rest of the Scathians have kept for themselves for far too long.

I bathe in the king's screams as I saw through bone and sinew, stripping him of his right wing.

His status.

His freedom.

When I finish, I hand Aeron the sword, letting him take the left.

For the woman he once loved and the life he lost because of the pathetic male whimpering on the marble.

Aeron's chest heaves, blood and sweat dripping down his brow as he scowls at our wingless king.

Hatred shadows my vision as I turn to Boris once more, his cries for mercy blocked by the memories of my own.

How I sobbed when he took Allette from me.

How I begged for one more night.

How he smiled through it all.

Blood pools toward my boots as I take the sword from my brother, raising the blade over my head, my heart beating a steady rhythm in my chest.

This isn't just for me.

It's for the woman I love and the years that were stolen from us.

For my baby brother who might not live to see nightfall.

For my guard Bilson who gave his life to save mine.

For the Tuath who've been locked in a cage beneath the clouds.

For all the lies we've been fed as truths.

My hands do not falter as I drive the blade into Boris Vale's black heart and watch the life fade from his eyes.

Before they close forever, I kneel beside the fallen king and whisper, "You once told me there was too much darkness in me. And you were right. But the difference between my darkness and yours, is that I will use mine to save this kingdom, not cast it into ruin."

Fifty-Two

ALLETTE

The king is dead.

As I stand here, searching for my next breath, I watch my prince slowly rise to his feet, his brother's blood on his hands as he turns toward me.

He did it.

Senan killed the monster responsible for our destruction, for the bleakness infecting our land.

Despite having won, this isn't the face of a man celebrating victory. Devastation paints his features as his eyes meet mine and a broken sob wrenches from his trembling form.

I want to tell him that everything will be all right, but we've been drowning in too many lies.

The king might be gone, but his influence is everywhere. There's no telling if the guards who continue to fight the Tuath in the throne room will heed Senan's orders or rebel against him.

Aeron presses a reassuring hand to Senan's shuddering shoulder. "There will be time for mourning, brother, but this is not it. The battle has been won but the war still rages. You must put an end to the fighting once and for all."

Senan's glittering eyes find mine, searching for a lifeline.

"I'm with you," I tell him. "No matter what happens, I will be by your side."

A breath trembles out of him as he faces the throne room and takes that first step toward his destiny, Aeron at his back, his wings wide and his sword painted crimson.

The marble beneath our feet rumbles, as if the castle itself is protesting the change in power.

Senan reaches for me, lacing our fingers together, our aching hearts beating as one as we walk toward the throne room. A handful of Tuath have fallen and more than a few guards lay lifeless amidst the rubble, blank eyes staring toward a hole in the gilded ceiling, the sky beyond a cerulean hue. Fire licks up the tapestries and wind rushes through the open balconies, coaxing them higher.

Senan's hand falls from mine, his dark brows slamming down over narrowed eyes. "Enough!" he bellows.

Heads swing toward him, and the whole room falls still, swords freezing mid-swing, jaws hanging open, and eyes bulging as they fall to something behind us.

Blood smears along the marble where Aeron drags in the king's body. "The king is dead," he announces. "This fight is over."

No one seems to know what to do. Even the Tuath are trading confused looks. Braith lingers in the doorway, her dark eyes hard as stone as she stares down the men attacking her people.

Not *her* people.

Ours.

Tuath or Scathian—it matters not what we are, but *who* we are. From this day forward, we shall be a people united.

Senan's voice rings with authority, deep and true. "The fight is over. Drop your weapons and tend to the wounded. Bring those who have fallen to Polaris temple so their bodies can be prepared for burial."

Swords lower and heads bow—even the groans of those who have been cut down seem to quiet as the king's men follow Senan's orders.

My prince turns, his eyes rounding as a cough climbs his throat. Blood spurts from between his lips, and he collapses onto his knees, his body ravaged by the poisoned dust.

I fall beside him, my knees slamming against the marble. "What do you need?"

He drags an arm across his lips, smearing more blood over his skin. "Tell me you still have the antidote."

As if I'd let those vials fall into the wrong hands. "It's safe and sound in Braith's parents' burrow."

With blood and smoke thick in the air around us, his forehead falls to mine.

What if it's not enough to save him?

No.

It *will* be enough. Soon, my prince will be healed, and all of this will be nothing more than a haunting nightmare.

A growl rises from my right, and I twist in time to see Eason's blood-splattered face charging forward, his sword aimed at me. I freeze, my body refusing to move even though I know what's about to happen. All I can do is gasp, waiting for the blade to pierce my heart.

Then someone leaps in front of me. *Braith.* The sword cuts straight through her uniform, the blood-soaked tip protruding from her back.

The sound of her screams forces my body into motion.

I throw what remains of my magic at Eason, stealing the air from his lungs.

Braith crumples and metal clatters. Aeron's sword falls to the ground, abandoned so that he can catch her before she hits the marble.

A feral roar rips from Iver's throat; his hands shoot out, cracking the stone beneath Eason's boots, sending him tumbling backward.

If he doesn't stop, the whole tower will collapse.

I scramble over rubble, diving for a dagger discarded between bits of wood and stone. Senan shouts but all I can hear is the sound of my own heart as I lunge for the man who stole me, swiping the blade in my fist across his throat.

Eason's eyes widen in surprise, and he dies with my name on his lips.

I hate him with every fiber of my being, loathe him with my entire heart, and yet my eyes burn as tears bleed from my lashes, tumbling down my cheeks to fall on Eason's still form.

I've been raked raw, torn open and thrown on hot coals.

He stole me, but he also saved me. Tried to love me at my most broken.

So much pain and death and loss...for what? For a throne that's been reduced to rubble? For a kingdom more broken than not? For power that can be stolen with one well-placed slice of a blade?

It's not worth it. None of these things matter at all.

"Allette." A hand falls to my shoulder.

Senan watches me, his eyes red-rimmed. The dagger still clenched in my fist tumbles to the ground, and I throw myself into his arms, letting my tears bathe his warm, smooth skin. "I'm s-sorry. I don't know why I'm crying." Eason tried to kill me twice now, so this shouldn't hurt so much.

My prince smooths a hand down my hair, his words a quiet whisper against my temple. "You cared for him, same as me."

Movement from the ground behind Senan catches my eye. "Braith..." Here I am, crying over an awful man who deserved his fate while my friend is fighting for her life. I run toward her, a fresh wave of worry washing over me.

Someone removed Eason's sword from her stomach and tore open her dress, but instead of a gash, there is only a mottled red scar and Aeron's hands glowing on her hips. He holds her in his lap, his eyes closed in concentration as he heals my friend.

Senan takes my elbow in his steady hand. "She'll be fine."

Braith might be healed, but as I take in the destruction in front of me, I can't help but wonder if there's any hope for the rest of us.

Fifty-Three

SENAN

As the dust settles, I look around at those who were lost, those who have fallen, including our king, and my heart breaks anew. Boris's lifeless body lies at my feet, the crown he loved so much askew on his head, still glinting in the sunlight.

Bloody rivulets trail like crimson rivers down my hands, dripping onto white marble as I bend down to pick up the crown.

So much death and destruction, all for this scrap of metal.

It seems so asinine, so pointless. Who in their right mind would want that sort of weight on their shoulders? How crippling. *How damning.*

Boris might have blamed me for what happened to the woman he claimed to love, but I blame this cursed relic for his madness.

Is it even possible to live a full, happy life knowing that one wrong move could cause your kingdom to fall? That one bad choice means good people pay the price?

It's all so overwhelming. *Suffocating.*

For as long as I can remember, this castle has felt like a cage, and this crown is like the manacles I no longer wear, tethering its owner to this world of gluttony and greed.

A world I long to forget.

Look at what this crown did to the people I love. Kyffin barely survived, and I have a sinking feeling that the scar across his throat isn't the only one he'll carry from these dark days. Allette was forced to take yet another life to save her own, and my own brother's blood still paints my hands.

I want nothing to do with any of it, and yet here I stand, still holding the damn crown, unable to pry my blood-soaked fingers from its golden facets.

Thanks to Aeron's magic, Braith is awake and able to sit on her own, but without him, she would have been another body added to the toll this coup has taken.

Allette sits beside her friend, the skirts of their uniforms as soiled and bloodstained as my soul.

Aeron's eyes widen on the crown, and he pushes to his feet, making his way through the wreckage to take the scrap from me. The gold gleams as he turns it over in his hands, swiping my bloody fingerprints from the gems. "A kingdom without a ruler is a sitting target."

I might not have been a very good student, but I remember the history lessons from before the Vale family took the throne. The horrors of the power struggle between the lords of this nation and the kings and queens on foreign thrones.

Kumulus has seen enough destruction.

Someone must wear this crown today and ascend to that broken throne, lest the cockroaches scuttle out from beneath the rubble to take both for themselves.

My original plan had been for Kyffin to become king, that we would find a trustworthy advisor to help him grow into his new leadership role.

When I think of my little brother, how can I possibly consider burdening him with this responsibility—and after he was so easily swayed by Boris?

He is far too trusting, too impressionable to be saddled with this kingdom upon his small shoulders.

What's more, Kyffin deserves to have a childhood—one where

he is free to make mistakes and grow into a man without this castle becoming *his* cage.

Rhainn has been shipped off to Allto, and by the time we bring him back, it might be too late.

Aeron has his own responsibilities, which leaves...

Gods help us.

That leaves me.

A duster. A murderer. An exile.

What if I'm not strong enough to fight the darkness that has plagued me for so many years? What if I give in and become a carbon copy of the man still lying on the marble?

Hell, if the antidote doesn't work, I might not even be here in a month.

What other choice do we have?

The law clearly states that a Vale prince must hold the throne of Kumulus. If one of us does not ascend, then the kingdom falls to the king's head advisor—Counsellor Windell.

In the burrows, Aeron told me that it was time I give back instead of continuing to take and take.

For a moment, I close my eyes and consider what that might look like, consider that I won't be as awful a king as my brother. That all these experiences I've endured might help me understand the people of Kumulus, make me more compassionate and understanding.

With the right people by my side to keep my selfishness in check, maybe I could do some good for this kingdom with whatever time I have left.

There's only one way to find out, isn't there?

When I open my eyes, I find Aeron staring back, a question in his eyes and a crown in his hands.

I nod down at the golden monstrosity, glad I'll only have to wear the thing on formal occasions. "We both know your head is too big for that thing, so I suppose I'll have to wear it."

A rare smile ghosts across Aeron's features as he raises the crown above my head and rests the circlet upon my brow. "Let those of you gathered here today bear witness to the crowning of your new king, Senan Vale."

The Tuath who have survived drop to their knees amidst the rubble. The guards are slower to bow, exchanging glances before they take a knee.

Allette stands by my side, beaming up at me with nothing but love and trust in her golden eyes. "I am so proud of you."

Her support means more than words can explain. That this woman is still by my side despite it all is the only reason I feel the same hope burning through my veins.

This world is still broken, but with time and love, we might find a way to mend the rifts caused by greed and power.

"I might fuck it all up." And if I do, it won't only be my own life and happiness at stake.

Her cheeks lift with her smile. "You won't. And if you do, then I will be there to help you fix it—for as long as you'll have me."

As long as I'll have her? I lace our fingers together and graze my lips along her knuckles. "I'll have you forever and beyond. Until the sun implodes, and the stars no longer shine."

She steps toward me—my life, my love, my world—and whispers, "Until the sun implodes, and the stars no longer shine."

Fifty-Four

SENAN

As soon as these pompous assholes vote, the first thing I'm changing are these chairs. The seats are hard as hell and don't get me started on the angle of the backs. I swear, they force you forward until you have no choice but to lean your elbows on the table.

That's what the seven other men sitting in the king's privy chamber are doing, hunching and glowering toward where I sit at the table's head. I refuse to do the same, so my arms are folded over my chest as I scowl right back. Of course, it's nothing compared to Aeron's scowl where he sits to my right, not at the table but close enough for everyone to know whose side he's on. That man could bring winter to June with his glacial looks.

"This is most irregular," Counsellor Windell says, his jowls swinging with each syllable.

"Most irregular?" another counsellor blusters, his face red as a beet. "That man murdered our king! He should be swinging from the gallows, not sitting at the head of this counsel, wearing the fucking crown."

The others scoot their chairs away from him like he's a bomb about to detonate. I can't help but like him a little more for his righteous indignation. At least he has the bollocks to stand up and fight for what he believes, unlike the rest of these sniveling weasels who would rather nod and acquiesce in here and then conspire to assassinate me the moment they step out of this chamber.

Aeron assured me that the law is on our side, so this meeting is a formality at best. Plus, Counsellor Windell and I have some unfinished business to attend to.

It's been a week since he led Boris's farce of a trial that sentenced the woman I love to death, and I'm afraid this is a grudge I cannot move past.

Windell shoots the man a dark look. "Calm down, Cormac. Prince Senan has a right to decline an official coronation."

"I believe you mean *King* Senan," Aeron corrects with a sneer, bracing his hands on his knees as he eases forward with menacing slowness.

Apparently, I don't need a coronation to be named King of Kumulus. Given all that's happened in this castle, I find it in bad taste to throw a big party for people I despise to come and pretend they're happy I've ascended. Maybe in a few months we'll organize an official event, but for now, I'd rather get started fixing all the shite that's broken.

There's more work to be done than I could have ever imagined. Not only did Boris collude with Cadoc Carew to distribute tainted dust, but also he filled the pit with fae who have publicly spoken out against him. There is no end to his dirty dealings and the seedy characters he was in bed with—and almost every single one of these bastards in front of me is on that list.

The color leaks from Windell's face as he nods. "Right. Of course. Forgive my slight, *King* Senan."

I lean back against the stiff chair, but the angle makes it impossible.

Enough is enough.

I push to my feet, my arse relieved to be free of that infernal board. "I don't think I will."

Windell glances at the rest of the counsellors, his eyes widening. "Excuse me?"

"As of this moment, you have been removed as a member of my counsel and are no longer welcome in this castle. It's customary to thank you for your service to the previous king, but I would prefer not to start my rule with such a blatant lie."

Windell shoves back from the table, his black robes shuddering. "You dare speak to me with such insolence?" He turns to the other men, who have all bowed their heads, refusing to meet his gaze. "I have been on this council for over a century."

Yet another reason to kick him out. No one should hold power for that long, and that includes kings and queens.

I don't even try to bite back my smile. "Then it sounds like this retirement is well deserved."

He does not like that comment one bit, and if this table weren't between us, I imagine he'd be doing more than seething. "I demand a vote."

"All right. All those in favor of Counsellor Windell's retirement, please raise your hands."

The men exchange glances, and one by one their hands lift into the air, all except the angry one who cursed at me, and I like him a little more.

"Oh, I'm sorry. You thought I was asking *you*. I was actually asking *my* council for *their* vote."

Aeron pushes from his chair, stalking over to the double doors and swinging them aside.

Allette steps in, her cerulean waves shimmering like a waterfall over the shoulders of her silver gown. She'd been hesitant to accept a position, but once I explained that I couldn't do this without her, she'd given in. She is full of brilliant plans to help the Tuath, not only those in the burrows, but also those in the factories and dens. I cannot wait for the kingdom to see the good she'll do.

Braith and Iver drift in next, followed by their father Harold Nightingale. Last to enter is a man I've had mostly negative interactions with. Not because of him, but because of me. Gerrard Tolken, the city's lead addiction counselor. When I showed up at his doorstep asking if he'd like to assist us in our venture to help those struggling with stardust addiction, he'd nearly choked on his tea.

Unlike the kings before me, I made the decision to diversify our table in order to better serve the people of Kumulus. How can we hope to make the laws fair if we do not have representatives from all walks of life?

"Well?" I ask. "Do any of you want Lord Windell on our council?"

Not one hand lifts.

Windell sputters as he takes in the new medallions around their necks. "The law states that any new council formed must include a sitting member of the previous council for at least a year."

I turn toward the angry man at the other end of the table and smile. "What do you say, Cormac? We have an opening if you're interested."

"Are you mad?" Windell throws a hand toward the man in question. "He hates you more than all of us combined."

I imagine he only hates me because he does not know me. Either way: "If this is to be a fair council, it's imperative to have opposing viewpoints represented; wouldn't you agree, Cormac?"

Slowly, the man nods, remaining in his seat while the others throw their medallions onto the table with grumbles and curses as they stalk out of the room to where guards wait to escort them from the castle.

They'll be followed until we're certain they are not a threat to me or those I love, and if they so much as set a toe out of line, there are plenty of free cells in the pit.

Allette takes the seat to my right, and the others drop into their chairs as well.

Aeron drags his chair closer, the legs screeching along the marble. "I really don't understand why you had to go through all that trouble when sending a letter would've been more efficient."

"Where's the fun in that?" Every man on Boris's council

agreed to damn me for my mistakes, and I wanted to look them in the eye when I told them to fuck off.

Vindictive?

Yes.

Worth it?

Absolutely.

Something moves in the doorway, and I turn to find my littlest brother waiting in the gap, his face solemn and eyes downcast. The poor lad has been at a loss since he woke. I wish I knew how to help him. "Come in, Kyff." The last thing I want is for him to feel unwelcome.

He drifts over to my side, casting a wary glance at the table of faces unfamiliar to him.

"What is it?"

"Boris—" Tears flood his eyes, but he quickly swipes them away with his fist. "*He* used to make me come to meetings, and I wasn't sure if I still had to."

Will there ever be a day when I stop cursing Boris Vale? I take both of his small hands in mine, squeezing his fingers three times. "From now on, your only job is to be a child."

"What does that mean?" he sniffs.

His quiet question breaks my heart in two. Excusing myself from the table, I keep Kyffin's hand until we're out in the hallway with only the breeze and the sunlight to overhear us. "It means I want you to go play."

His eyes glisten anew, round as saucers. "You don't want me with you?"

"I always want that, Kyff. Always. And if you want to join us in that stuffy room and sit on a chair that's going to make your arse hurt, then you are more than welcome. But if you want to do something else, then I encourage you to do that instead. Believe me, if I could be out playing, I would."

Sniffling, his lips turn down. "They do hurt your arse, don't they?"

I chuckle. "So much."

He straightens a little, and his head lifts. "When you're busy, I don't have anyone left to play with."

"What about Dahlia?"

I returned to the burrows a few days ago to visit those whose lives had been devastated by Boris's unprovoked attack. The little girl and her mother had no extended family, and her husband was the sole earner, working his whole life as a blacksmith. When I offered a room in the castle, Dahlia's mother initially refused, but yesterday they arrived to the gates with their bags in tow. They're now safely ensconced in the south tower along with another ten families who were displaced.

Kyff's nose wrinkles. "She's a girl."

"So?"

"So, she doesn't even know how to hold a sword."

"Then teach her."

His teeth drag over his lip as he considers. Suddenly, his wings appear at his back, and he nods. Without another word, he starts for the balcony. Once he's out of sight, I click my fingers at one of the guards further down the hall. He leaves his post to keep an eye on Kyff. After what happened with Nimbiss, I refuse to take any chances with my baby brother's safety.

Right.

Back to work.

Silence greets me when I return to the privy chamber. "Let's get this meeting started." I nod toward Iver. "What news from Dread Row?"

Braith's brother folds his hands atop the table. "Carew's offices are still empty, as are the mines beneath the Row. Our patrol at Serpents' says the place has been closed since you were crowned."

If that's the case, then I'll need to send someone out to find the men and women who were employed there to ensure they have means to earn a decent wage.

When I say as much, Cormac's gaze bounces between us, the wrinkles across his brow deepening. No doubt, he's wondering what sort of loon acquired the crown. I've had the misfortune of attending a handful of council meetings in the past and they always seemed such dreadfully boring, formal affairs. We don't have the time to waste on formality—and even if we did, that isn't how I want my council to operate. Formality creates distance, and with that distance, disconnect follows.

The meeting continues with Gerrard bringing his suggestions for rehabilitation centers in the abandoned homes across the city. His plans are all well and good, but as a man who has been forced to sit in those centers on more than one occasion, I have a few insights of my own. "You need to make them a place people *want* to come to. Sanctuaries with free meals. And for the love of all that is holy, do not make them smell like stale coffee."

This isn't a problem that can be solved in a day. It's a war we'll be fighting for years.

I swing toward my girl with a smile. "How is the initiative for those employed down at the dens?"

Allette sits forward, bracing her folded hands against the table's edge. "Not every person was interested in leaving, but we have about twelve who desire a different life."

At least that's something. And if we can show the others that there is a solid alternative, perhaps they will follow suit.

"Their biggest fears were housing and financial support. I thought perhaps we could use my aunt's tower, convert it to apartments for affordable housing alternatives."

I twist toward Iver. "How difficult would that be?"

The Tuath's grin is a flash of white. "As long as we have access to the sun, it shouldn't be hard at all."

Fifty-Five

ALLETTE

The bed I've been given is probably the most comfortable in the history of beds, and yet sleep eludes me. For a week, I've managed to keep the nightmares from what happened in the throne room at bay by exhausting myself and helping our new Tuath guests settle into their rooms here at the castle. There is so much to be done, and having no wings makes life in the tall towers exceedingly difficult, but we're doing the best with what we have.

They will need more practical homes as soon as we can manage them, which is something I plan to discuss with Senan when we get a moment alone.

Loving a man whose time is in such high demand is a bit like loving a ghost. Even when he's by my side, he's not really there, his mind drifting to the next day's tasks and ways to fix new problems that seem to arise each hour.

I thought we'd at least get to share our nights, but Kyffin has been glued to his side every chance he gets, going so far as to sleep in his bed. The poor boy is struggling and needs time to adjust, which means I will just have to get used to my new life on my own.

A soft knock interrupts my silent wallowing. A moment later, the door opens and Senan slips into the room. Instead of coming straight over to the bed, he leans against the wood, his head falling back with a sigh. "Good. You're awake."

I sit up a little straighter. "Why? Is there something wrong?"

He pushes off the barrier, coming to a halt at the side of my bed. "What's wrong is that I have not held you in over a week. I've seen you every single day and yet I've missed you all the same."

Fae light sparkles off the crown he wears. He looks positively irresistible, with the top buttons of his shirt left open, a scrolled "A" peeking through the gap. Hours spent in the sun have returned his skin to its healthy golden glow.

"I've missed you too."

He toes off his boots and falls down beside me with a groan.

"What about Kyff?"

"He's asleep. For now."

"Is he still having nightmares?"

A nod. "I don't know how to make them stop."

He cannot make the dreams stop, only be there for him until he works through all that has happened over the last few weeks. "Give him time and love." I'll still be here waiting when he can return to my bed.

Senan snuggles closer, burying his face in the crook of my neck. "Mmm... Is that a new perfume?"

"Yes." Braith and I went shopping on our way back to the castle from the burrows. She and her sister Regina have been helping set up classes for the Tuath to harness their magic. "Do you like it?"

"You smell good enough to eat." He nips at my ear as he plays with the thin strap of my shift. "Is this new as well?"

I smile. "Everything I'm wearing is new."

"*Everything?*" His fingers skim down my arm to the swell of my hip where he bunches the fabric of my shift, exposing my lace undergarments. "Oh, I like these. As a matter of fact, I like them so much, that it makes me feel bad knowing how ruined they're about to get. We should take them off so they don't get damaged."

"So chivalrous, always thinking of me."

"Always."

I lift my hips, allowing him to slide the lace down my thighs where they catch at my ankles. Apparently, Senan finds something more interesting to explore, nuzzling my neck as his fingers trace my folds. "Mmmm," he hums against the shell of my ear. "Drenched."

My legs part, falling open to allow him better access as he strokes against me, exploring, sinking deep and then twisting back out to toy with the sensitive nub at the juncture of my thighs. The tips of my breasts strain against the fabric of my shift, demanding attention. I writhe against him, whimpering when he captures the silk and draws it down to tease my nipple with his thumb.

"Allette?"

All I can manage is a hum in response, my hips working against his hand, desperate for friction.

His tone drops to the most delicious rumble. "Have you ever been fucked by a king?"

Heat climbs my jaw, this man and his wicked words driving me to the edge. "I have not."

His fingers curl inside me, stealing my sanity. "How would you like to remedy that?"

Stars... This man.

I capture his lips in a punishing kiss, our tongues clashing as he works me into a frenzy. Tension coils up my spine and low in my belly. As if he knows I'm on the brink, he comes over me with the wickedest of grins as I grapple with his belt. He grips the collar on his shirt, dragging the garment over his head and casting it aside.

I can't help but marvel at the glorious ridges and planes of his hard body, adorned with memories of us.

He draws back, the smile slipping from his face as he stares down at me, his brow furrowing. "Something isn't right."

My pounding heart grows quiet, the harshness of my panting breaths falling still. "What is it?" Tell me there isn't more trouble.

Heavens, it feels as if we've been plagued with nothing but problems for so long.

Sitting back on his haunches between my spread thighs, Senan reaches for the crown our frenzy has knocked askew, lifting it off his head.

I must admit, I'm sorry to see it go.

He is still a king, but part of me wanted him to wear it while we made love.

Instead of setting the crown aside, he places it on my head.

The corner of his lips quirk into a lazy smile. "That's much better."

"Senan..." When I sit up, the thing falls forward on my brow. "I cannot wear your crown."

He adjusts the front, nudging it back and tucking a lock of my hair behind my ear. "Because it's so ugly? I know. I'm commissioning a better one."

It is ugly, but that's not the reason I'm not allowed to wear it. "This crown isn't mine."

His head tilts, reminding me of the Senan I first met, a young, cocky, mischievous prince. "In Kumulus, the queen wears a crown as well."

"But I am not a—"

From his pocket he withdraws a black velvet box. Words fail me as he opens the top, revealing a gold band studded with glittering gemstones cut to resemble a moonflower. "I believe you were going to say queen, so let me remedy that as well." His throat bobs as he withdraws the stunning ring. "Allette Rittey, you have ruled my heart since the day I first heard you laugh. I have loved you from that day on and will continue to love you until I have turned to ash. Although you have been my wife since the night we exchanged vows in the human realm, I was hoping we could make our bond a little more official."

My lips tremble beneath my fingertips, and I have to blink through my tears so I can see his face properly. This man, this beautiful, broken man, wants me—*me*—to be his wife, his mate, his *queen*.

The tiniest wrinkle appears between his brows. "Well? Are you going to give me an answer or do I have to beg?"

"I'll give you an answer when you ask me a question."

His eyes flash. "Allette Vale, will you make me the happiest man in all the realms and officially take me as your husband?"

"I suppose I don't have much of a choice if I want to keep this." I tap my nail against one of the jewels at the front of the crown.

Senan clutches his chest with a dramatic groan. "I see how it is. You only want me for my crown."

"I want you for you, Senan Vale. I always have."

He slips the ring on my finger, the stones the same cerulean blue as the wings that were stolen from me all those years ago and the new ones inked upon my skin. The same color as the hair that falls down my back.

I give him a saucy smile and push him back onto the bed. He lands with a soft grunt, and I climb on top of him, straddling his hips. "Senan?"

"Hmmm?"

"Have you ever been fucked by a queen?"

His lips tug into the most devastating grin. "I have not."

"How would you like to remedy that?"

Epilogue

ALLETTE

My hands do not shake as they smooth down the cool silk of my silver gown. My heart remains steady, beating for the man waiting for me at the end of an aisle dripping in moonflowers. The cerulean feathers hanging from my ears sway in the light breeze, a reminder of who I once was and how far I've come.

Braith drifts down the stretch of silver carpet, the people stuffed into the pews watching her every step of the way, marveling at the way her skirts shimmer.

Golden light washes through the arched windows as the sun rises over Polaris Temple, gilding everything in its path. Music from the stringed quartet swirls through the air as my slipper meets the end of the carpet and I take that first step.

Toward my king.

Toward my love.

A man I never thought I'd be allowed to keep, a man who is wholly, irrevocably mine.

Senan's littlest brother stands at his side, clutching a pillow holding two rings tied with silver lace, the scar at his throat hidden by the cravat he reluctantly let me tie. Beside him stands Dahlia, clutching a wriggling bunny to her chest, her basket of petals abandoned at her feet.

Aeron waits behind him with a rare smile playing on his lips.

His younger brother Rhainn takes the final spot, his new wife somewhere in the crowd.

When I reach the end of the aisle, Senan steps down to take my hand, leading me up the steps to where the priest waits, robes of white reaching all the way to the petal-strewn ground.

Boris Vale has been gone for two months now, reduced to a terrifying memory.

Where mud and stone once ruled, green plants have taken over. Flowering vines climb the towers and window boxes burst with colorful flowers at every level.

And there are gardens. So many gardens.

Trees and plants grow between the cracks and in the crevices, healing and connecting, colorful scars in a land once drenched in gray.

Tuath who have been kept from their magic are taught to wield their power in schools established across the realm. Not everyone welcomed this change, but those who protested at first have returned to the shadows where they belong.

The priest begins the ceremony, his monotone voice growing faint as I stare into Senan's sparkling silver eyes. After waiting half a decade for this moment, here we are, together, holding hands and repeating vows once whispered in an abandoned shack in another realm.

To love and honor each other for the rest of our lives and beyond.

"I love you, Allette," Senan murmurs, stepping so close our chests brush, "until the sun implodes..."

My lips ghost across his in the faintest of kisses as I whisper back, "And the stars no longer shine."

Afterword

See. I told you it would be all right.

I hope the conclusion to Senan & Allette's love story has restored your broken heart and faith in true love.

I don't know about you, but I think these two earned their happily-ever-after.

If you're in the mood for some more star-crossed love, stay tuned for the next book in this series: BOUND BY STARDUST

Can anyone guess which couple I'm torturing next?

Acknowledgments

No matter how many books I write, I always get a little anxious when it comes time to thank everyone who has helped make my books reality. I really should start keeping better lists so I don't miss anyone.

Anyway, let's start with you, dear readers.

That's right. I want to thank those of you who were willing to take this journey alongside Senan and Allette. Who didn't hate me after leaving you on that cliff at the end of *Bound by Gravity*—especially the ones brave enough to face that cliff before *Freed* came out.

It's always a pleasure working with my cover designer, Saint Jupiter. Your talent knows no bounds, and I am in constant awe of how you can take my vision and make it reality.

To my map designer, the wonderful Andrés Aguirre Jurado (@aaguirreart), thank you for being such a delight to work with. You'll never be rid of me now!

I also want to bring your attention to the epic portraits of Senan & Allette by Anamaria Sandru (@gioviia). I loved working with you and appreciate the care you took creating these stunning pieces.

To my phenomenal editor Meg Dailey, thank you for working with my crazy schedule and for fitting me in when you could. I appreciate you more than words can express.

A special shout out to Rachel Hill who so kindly agreed to proof this book during the holidays. Thank you from the bottom of my heart for helping me out!

To my street team, thank you for shouting from the proverbial rooftops about my books and my characters, and for cheering me on in everything I do.

To my beta readers, Robin and Miriam, thank you so much for reading this one early!

And last, but not least, to my alpha reader Megs: Thank you from the bottom of my heart for your invaluable feedback and for braving my unedited drivel to help me shape this story.

About the Author

Jenny has been a fan of love stories ever since she picked up her first romance novel during summer vacation. She enjoys breaking readers' hearts and sewing them up by "the end." See that smile on her face? She's secretly plotting her next heartbreaking fantasy romance.

Also by Jenny

BOUND AND FREED

(Adult Fantasy Romance)

Bound by Gravity

Freed from Gravity

THE MYTHS OF AIRREN

(Adult Fantasy Romance)

A Cursed Kiss

A Cursed Heart

A Cursed Love

Prince of Seduction

Prince of Deception

THE PAN TRILOGY

(YA Sci-Fi Romance with a Peter Pan Twist)

The PAN

The HOOK

The CROC

CONTEMPORARY ROMANCE

(Co-written with Natalie Murray)

STILL SPRINGS

Hating the Best Man
Loving the Worst Man

INNER SHORES

Coming Soon